Journey Home

By: Virginia Scholl Hanson

Journey Home

Cover design by Erica Matagrano.

ISBN-13: 978-1539317531
ISBN-10: 1539317536

Acknowledgments

I am grateful to many family members and friends whose help made this book possible. I appreciate the time they spent to assist me and their efforts and contributions at various stages of the book's development.

First and foremost on this list is my granddaughter, Bess Donoghue. She is the reason Journey Home is a published book, not just an untitled manuscript on the floor of my closet. She took the reins and became the driving force behind getting this book to the final stage of being published.

For technical and textual assistance, I would like to thank Roxie Kaminski, Fran Wapole, and Mary Jane Grinstead. They had written or were in the process of writing books of their own; they were my mentors.

Thanks to my daughter and son-in-law, Meg and Dan Donoghue for the use of their summer home, in northern Wisconsin. Isolated, and free from all distractions, I was able to make great headway on my book. Dan read the first twelve chapters with a red marker in hand, and gave valuable feedback on each one.

Linda Grensing read the entire manuscript, chapter by chapter as I wrote it. Her enthusiasm for my story kept me motivated to finish.

I am deeply indebted to the following for editing assistance: Bess Donoghue, Liz Macias, Jim Scholl, Bob Hanson, Marilyn Zwick, Cassie Norton, Meg Donoghue, Therese Donoghue, Hannah Weinberg-Kinsey, Frank Matagrano, Krista Wodarz, Roxie Kaminski, Bob Scholl, Alice Wells and Roderick Wells. Nancy Hupp did the final edit.

Thank you to my daughter, Erica Matagrano, who created the artwork on the front cover.

To Bob, for his love and belief that I could actually write a novel, to my children and friends who encouraged me, to my grandchildren who are my inspiration, to the extended members of my family, all the Scholls, the Hansons, and the numerous descendants of William and Louise Burke (Burke-offs) for adding valuable strings of varied hues to the tapestry of my life.

PART ONE

Decisions

The Halvorson Family in 1848

Bestefar, grandfather

Far and Mor, father and mother

Halvor, age 25

Theo, age 23

Karine, age 20

Jorgen, age 17

Andrew, age 16

Christina, age 14

Niels, age 12

Edvard, age 9

Ole, age 8

Inger, age 6

One

Winter, 1848

"I'm leaving; Come with me." The hushed words scarcely penetrated Jorgen's consciousness. His eyes blinked open, but darkness prevented him from seeing the figure perched on the edge of the bed. "Come with me, Jorgen," Andrew whispered.

Jorgen didn't respond. He wasn't sure if he was dreaming or awake. If he closed his eyes would he wake in the morning to tell Andrew about the dream he was having?

"Please come! We won't get another chance like this for months. We're ready, Jorgen, we need to do it now. Come with me," Andrew pleaded.

This wasn't a dream; Andrew was leaving. While he slept, Jorgen hadn't been aware that his brother had left the bed that they shared, but now he sensed that Andrew was already dressed. If the whispered words hadn't awakened him, Jorgen wondered, would Andrew have roused him? Would he even have bothered to say good-bye? Jorgen wanted to shout at him, "you can't go!" Instead, anger welling within him, he rolled over and turned his back to his brother. Andrew had his answer.

Andrew leaned in closer. "Say goodbye to everyone for me...if you change your mind, I'll be with 'the big ones'...catch up with me, Jorgen...goodbye."

A floorboard creaked, and then he was gone.

Jaws clenched, eyes staring into the dark, Jorgen lay awake the rest of the night. His head throbbed with conversations that played over and over. The seventeen year old recalled the myriad discussions he and his brother had shared as, side by side, they performed their chores. Over the years, they plotted and planned their future: first, a temporary stay in Bergen where they would get jobs to earn enough money to emigrate. Someday, they agreed, they would leave Norway so that they could buy land, and own their own farm in America.

Questions and troubled thoughts nagged Jorgen, hour after hour. How had the plan gotten away from him? Since they were small boys, Andrew had always followed Jorgen's lead. At what point had Andrew taken the reins? Why had 'someday' come sooner for him? Was Andrew right? Were they ready to go off on their own to a strange country?

Jorgen recognized the truth in all of Andrew's recent arguments. He hadn't exaggerated the family's hardship, but would their departure really help all that much?

It was a fact that the farm barely supported their large family. The necessity of replacing the old barn after it collapsed had severely drained the family resources. To help with the family finances, the three oldest of the ten Halvorson children worked away from home.

Karine, Jorgen's older sister, had gone to live with and work for neighbors as a mother's helper. She was uniquely qualified as she had helped care for her seven younger siblings. Karine's meager earnings, along with the fact that there was one less mouth to feed, were a benefit to the family. The two 'big ones', the oldest children in the family, also supplemented the farm's income. During the late fall and winter months when they weren't needed on the farm, they lived on the coast in Bergen and were hired on as fishermen. After paying their rent and other living expenses, they, too, were able to contribute to the family income. Halvor, the older of the two, would one day inherit the family estate. He contributed more than his younger brother, Theo, who planned to marry in a few months and was saving some of his dalers for that eventuality.

Andrew's arguments from the previous day, in fact almost daily for weeks now, echoed anew in Jorgen's head. Like the tired refrains of childhood songs, Andrew's words played over and over, haunting Jorgen throughout the long night. "We're not needed...We're just extra mouths to feed...We should go."

Jorgen put his hands to his ears as if that could still Andrew's voice. He started counting, slowly, silently, back from one hundred, but the voice continued. "Land, Jorgen, we can have our own land...Let's go now, Jorgen, let's go now." He squeezed his eyes closed and counted faster until Andrew's voice faded. Jorgen stopped counting and felt cheered when a hopeful thought sprang to mind. He won't go through with our plans without me. He's stubborn and determined, but he's only sixteen. He'll be back before morning, Jorgen concluded.

Eventually the household began to stir. Someone left the house and returned a few minutes later, pausing on the porch to stomp off snow before reentering the kitchen. There was a soft thud when a bucket of water was set down on the floor. Jorgen's grandfather coughed, then coughed again. A shovel scraped up dying embers from last night's fire in the fireplace; the door of the old stove creaked when it was opened to receive the embers. Jorgen knew his mother was adding small pieces of wood, and he waited for the creaking sounds of the door when she closed it. He heard whispers and giggles from his two younger sisters in the next bedroom. The familiar sounds of morning, one by one, slowly extinguished all hope of Andrew's return.

Jorgen felt his anger building, but even more than that, he was hurt. He and Andrew always acted as one and now he felt sloughed off, like Andrew's unnecessary, second skin. Jorgen couldn't stop thinking about their plans. Actually, they were his plans! He had instigated the 'America' idea. That Andrew had acted on his idea, without him, caused indignation to rise from somewhere deep in Jorgen's gut and lodge in his throat.

"Andrew!" a child's voice called from across the room. When there was no answer, twelve-year-old Niels called out again. When there was still no answer, he called Jorgen's name.

Deaf to all but the angry rant that thundered in his head, Jorgen got out of bed, yanked a shirt over his head and pulled on his pants. Why is Andrew always so impatient? He seldom thinks things through and hardly ever considers the consequences before he jumps into the thick of it. Life is complicated; there is so much to consider. And what makes him think he can emigrate on his own? They were going to travel together, look out for each other.

"JORGEN!" his three younger brothers yelled, in unison.

"What is it?" He snapped, jarred back into the present,

"Where's Andrew?" said Niels, the oldest of the three.

"Gone to Helvete for all I care," Jorgen stormed. He jabbed his feet into his boots and stalked off to the kitchen.

He came to a halt just inside the doorway and took a deep breath. Jorgen combed his fingers through an unruly mass of light brown hair. His heart pounded in his chest, his head ached, and he felt slightly nauseous. He stood there observing the serenity of the early morning breakfast scene and began to feel calmer. A fire blazed and crackled in the fireplace across the room from where he stood. Tongues of red, orange, and yellow flames leapt brightly over a hefty pile of logs, that had already taken the early morning chill out of the kitchen by far the largest room in the house. Christina, Jorgen's fourteen-year-old sister, and Mor worked side-by-side at the ancient iron stove. Christina inclined her head toward her mother. She made a quick comment and they both laughed. Far and Bestefar sat at the long pine table engrossed in conversation, mugs of hot milk and a platter of flat bread in front of them. Inger, the youngest of the family, stood at Far's elbow, taking in the dialogue, content with the smiles her father and grandfather occasionally bestowed on her.

Jorgen searched for a way to break the unsettling news. His problem was solved when the three boys practically knocked him over as they tore into the kitchen, still in their

14

bedclothes.

"Mamma, Pappa," the youngest of the three yelled, shattering the calm, "Jorgen said Andrew went to Helvete!"

Mor spoke without turning from the stove. "You three, go back to your room, get dressed and return in a civilized manner. Ole, tattling is not allowed in this house."

When they had left the room, Mor turned to face Jorgen. "Cursing is a sin, Jorgen, you know that, and to do it in front of your younger brothers is doubly wrong."

Jorgen's face flushed; he hadn't been scolded like this since he was a child. In the months since his older siblings had left home, he had become used to being treated like an adult. This abrupt tug back to childhood was unnerving and it shattered what little calm had settled on him. He didn't feel what he had said to his brothers was cursing, but he knew Mor expected an apology. Far had turned in his chair and was giving him a stern look, so Jorgen said he was sorry for setting a bad example for his brothers.

"What's this all about, Jorgen?" said Far, "And where is Andrew? He's usually the first one to the table."

Jorgen took a step into the room then stopped. He opened his mouth as if to say something then closed it, his mouth too dry for speech.

"Jorgen," Mor said quietly, "I can't remember the last time you two had a disagreement. What has he done that has you so upset? You look like you're ready to fly to pieces."

Mor was right. This was the first serious disagreement they'd had in years. He and Andrew saw eye to eye on most things, and when they didn't, they handled their differences without involving the family. They hadn't physically fought since they were little boys.

"Where's Andrew?" said Far, repeating himself. "Why haven't we seen him this morning and what is this all about?"

After another long pause, Jorgen looked at his father and managed to blurt out three short statements. "Andrew's gone... to Bergen...and then to America."

Suddenly, everyone in the family had something to say. So many questions were fired at Jorgen he didn't know which to answer first. And then, just as quickly, there was silence as each family member struggled with the news, with the fact that their son, grandson, brother—Andrew—was gone.

Mor stopped stirring the pot on the stove and went to sit with the men at the table. The anguished expression on her face made her suddenly appear years older. Her father-in-law reached across the table and patted her hand. His wrinkled, leathery hand completely covered hers, and he left it there, a gesture of silent comfort. Christina stayed at the stove, picked up Mor's spoon, and stirred both pots. Her thin shoulders shook with noiseless sobs.

Jorgen shifted his weight from one foot to the other. His hands were sweaty and his face felt feverish.

Far looked at him expectantly, waiting for him to continue.

"You know how Andrew and I talked about going to America someday," Jorgen began, "Well, several weeks ago at church, Olav Gunderson told us that he and his father were planning a trip into Bergen. They would be there for a couple of days, Olav said, and if we wanted to go along, there would be room for Andrew and me in their sledge. We were waiting to see when they were going, and then we were going to ask if you could get along without us for a few days. We thought we could stay with 'the big ones,' and Andrew was going to sell his pelts so we'd have a bit of spending money. This past Sunday, Olav asked us again. He said that they planned to leave at first light today. Suddenly Andrew was talking about leaving home for good and emigrating as soon as possible. We argued about it all week. Yesterday, I thought I had finally convinced him that we should wait. I was wrong. I woke up sometime during the night just as he was getting dressed to go. He said he was leaving and told me to say goodbye to all of you."

"You didn't stop him!" thundered Far. He rose from the

16

table and went to stand in front of Jorgen, looming over him menacingly. "And you didn't come to us?"

Far had no qualms about striking a child, even one as old as Jorgen. Jorgen took a step back, out of arm's reach, and collided a second time with his younger brothers who were reentering the room. This time they apologized profusely, gave their angry-looking father a wide berth, and silently took their places at the table.

"Pappa," Jorgen said defensively," I tried to talk to him; I wanted him to wait, but he had made up his mind. Neither one of us could have stopped him, he was that determined to go."

"I would have talked him out of going. I would have forbidden it!"

Jorgen knew when to keep silent, but he also knew his brother. When he set his mind to something, he was unstoppable. Stubbornness was not in short supply in this family.

"Did Andrew go somewhere?" Ole loudly whispered to Inger.

"Yes," Inger answered smugly, pleased that she knew something that her brother didn't. "Jorgen told Pappa that Andrew ran away."

The children weren't concerned about Andrew and didn't understand why Far was so angry. They assumed that Andrew would come home. After all, Ole had run away just days ago after an argument with Edvard, and he had come home.

"Was Pappa this angry when I ran away?" Ole whispered.

"I don't think he knew you were gone. Shh!" she said, wanting her brother to hush up so she could hear what everyone was saying. This was exciting! But she was a little worried for Jorgen. He seemed to be in big trouble.

"I thought it was just fanciful talk. I didn't realize you boys were serious…he's so… young…" Mor said, her voice trailing off.

"Why didn't you go with him?" Christina stopped stirring the pots and turned to face Jorgen. She wiped her tear-streaked face on her sleeve and said accusingly, "He shouldn't go to America by himself."

She wasn't particularly close to either of these two brothers; their togetherness had not left much room for a younger sister, especially one whose idea of adventure was looking for blueberries on the hillside. "You should have gone with him, Jorgen," she said as she went to the table and slumped into her chair.

"This wasn't just a matter between the two of you," Far shook his finger in Jorgen's face. A vein on his neck bulged and he spoke through clenched teeth. "Mor and I should have had some say in this, at the very least an opportunity to talk him into waiting a while longer. You should have come to us. You should have told us."

"Gone with him!" "Come to us!" The family's accusations echoed in his head. Jorgen felt betrayed by his family. No one here hurt more than he did. Andrew was more than a brother; he had always been Jorgen's best friend. His departure had left him feeling crushed, no longer whole.

He took another step back from his father, stared for a moment into his blazing eyes, and then glanced around the room. Did all of them share Far and Christina's feelings? Why did they all seem so angry with him? Was he really to blame for Andrew's leaving home?

After a long, painful silence, Bestefar spoke. He was not one to dispute Far's words in front of his own children and would not have done so had it not been for Jorgen's stricken face. It was obvious to Bestefar that his grandson needed a little support. Bestefar would have preferred that this come from his son, but Far had said all that his anger would permit, and he had turned away from Jorgen.

"I think Andrew's actions were his own doing," said Bestefar. "He could have waited, like Jorgen wanted, as we all would have wished, but he felt the time was right for him to leave. Jorgen is no more responsible for Andrew leaving than Andrew is for Jorgen staying. We all have to make our own way in this world. Andrew is just starting a little earlier than most. He is clever and skilled at many things. I, for one, am confident that he can take care of himself. I will miss him more than he will ever know, but I'm certain that Gud will guide him."

Bestefar's Lutheran faith had always been a strong influence on the family. Jorgen wasn't completely sold on the whole Gud idea, especially the part about Him taking care of people. If He really loved everyone, why would He only take care of some? Reprimanded years ago for questioning faith, Jorgen had learned to keep quiet on the subject, but he didn't think that Gud would give them money to buy the land he and Andrew hungered for. Jorgen knew that preparation led to success, and he, for one, intended to be prepared for his move to America.

Bestefar left the table and limped to the stove. He dished out a bowl of grot that Christina had made, carried it back to the table, and placed it in front of her. He kissed the top of her head, gave one pigtail a playful little tug and said, "You are a good little cook; it's smooth and creamy, just the way I like it!"

Mor joined Bestefar at the stove and life slowly returned to the kitchen as they dished out bowls of porridge for the rest of the family.

Jorgen met his mother halfway to the table and took two steaming bowls out of her hands. As he set them down before Niels and Ole, Mor asked, "Does Andrew plan on staying with his brothers?"

"Ja, Mamma, he thinks they can get him a job on a fishing boat." Jorgen returned to the stove and filled a bowl for himself. His stomach was still churning and he hoped he would be able to eat something before going out to the barn for chores. He sat down at his spot at the table next to

Bestefar and directly across the table from Far who stared intently into his own bowl as he ate, anger slowly ebbing from his face. Andrew's empty chair next to Far screamed his absence into the now silent kitchen,

After several uncomfortably long minutes, Mor asked, "How long does he plan to stay in Bergen?" Her face was now composed, her tone, though questioning, was not the least accusatory. Her arm lightly brushed Far's shoulder and arm as she sat down. He looked at her, and they exchanged brief smiles. Bestefar, who like Jorgen was alert to Far's temperament, gave Jorgen a small jab in the ribs with his elbow. Perhaps the storm had passed.

"I don't know, now," Jorgen responded to his mother. "We had planned to stay in Bergen about six months. I figured it would take that long to earn enough money for our passage and expenses in America until we found jobs, but it seems that Andrew has his own travel plans."

"Maybe the 'big ones' will make Andrew come home with them," said Ole hopefully.

Mor smiled at her youngest son's optimism. "Maybe they will," she agreed. "Away can be good, but home is best."

Neither Far nor Jorgen said any more during breakfast. At this point, words were not going to bring Andrew back.

★ ★ ★

The Halvorson family—in truth, all of Norway—lacked a sense of cheerfulness. Granted, times were tough, but that only partially explained this national glumness. Perhaps it was the long, dark winters they were forced to endure, but Norwegians were prey to frequent bouts of melancholy. Some, like Andrew and Bestefar, seemed to have escaped this gloomy inheritance, but Jorgen and his father often were its victims.

The only thing that got Jorgen through that first morning was his sense of duty. He had been taught from an early age that chores were an expression of love to one's family. Now that his brother was gone, all his chores fell to Jorgen. He worked at a furious pace, barely pausing between jobs, for when he did, thoughts of Andrew flooded him with grief.

He started in the barn, milked the three cows and two goats, fed and watered those animals, as well as two horses, cleaned their stalls, and put down fresh straw.

Jorgen's next stop was the sheep shed, a small, squat building ten paces from the barn. It was divided into pens, that each held two or three sheep. It was there that Christina caught up with him. He felt the rush of cold air when she entered and looked up to see her tentatively approach him. Large snowflakes glistened in her hair and clung to her eyelashes. He leaned the shovel he was using against the rails that separated two of the pens then hopped up onto the top rung. He patted the spot next to him and extended a hand to help her climb up.

Christina shook her head, "I can't stay," she said, "I'm painting and I don't want my paints to dry out."

She looked down at the floor then up at Jorgen; her face bore a troubled expression. "I'm sorry for what I said this morning. When you said that Andrew had left home and was going to America by himself, I felt so scared for him. I can't believe he left without you. I can't believe he's gone and I'll likely never see him again." Christina paused, her tear-filled eyes threatening to spill over. She swallowed, wiped her eyes on the sleeve of her coat, and continued. "I know I would have said the same thing to Andrew if you had gone without him. I always think of you two together. I know you're feeling sad, and I didn't mean to make you feel worse, but I guess I did."

"Thanks," Jorgen said. He slid off the rail, went to his sister, and slipped an arm around her shoulder. "You're right,

I'm not happy about Andrew, but you've made me feel better." He gave her a small hug and released her.

Christina sighed, relieved that Jorgen had forgiven her, and returned his smile. As she turned to leave, Jorgen said, "I've been meaning to ask..." she turned back as he continued, "I was wondering if you'd paint something for me."

"Sure," she replied; her eyes sparkled with unshed tears. "What would you like?"

Christina had learned to paint, strangely enough, from a vagabond artist who had decorated their church with his colorful art in exchange for a place to stay and enough food to ward off starvation. When he finished that job, he worked as a custodian at the school, sleeping there nights and eating from the hampers of food which grateful parents shared with him. Throughout the years that he worked in Voss, Mr. Bergstrom, the school's lone teacher, gave him the opportunity to share with the children his special skill: rosemaling. His two most talented pupils were Christina and Olav Gunderson. They both seemed naturally gifted when it came to this form of Norwegian folk art. Christina's floral designs were particularly bright and colorful.

"I've been working on a chest for Karine's birthday, and..."

"I've seen it," Christina interjected, "It's beautiful; Karine will love it."

"Takk, but I've noticed your decorations on some of the tables and chairs that Far and Bestefar have made. The flowers and designs you paint are so cheerful. I'd like you to do some rosemaling on the chest."

"Are you sure?" she asked. "It's your present to Karine."

"Well, now it will be our present to her," said Jorgen. "It shouldn't take me long to finish the carving I am doing on it."

"Tell me when you're done, and I'll come to the shop

and paint it for you." She flashed him a huge grin, turned and walked out with a much lighter step, Jorgen noted, than when she had come in.

Jorgen stood gazing at the door for a few minutes savoring the camaraderie of Christina's visit. Then, spurred into action by bleating sheep, he went back to his chores. He worked steadily, not even stopping for lunch, and finished just as the winter sun was beginning to set.

A path from the sheep shed led away from the other buildings to a shanty that, in better times, housed pigs but was now used for storage. Andrew kept it in some semblance of order since his workspace was there. Jorgen hesitated, then trudged through the newly fallen snow, which had added several more inches to what winter had already heaped upon the landscape. He entered the shanty and with a few steps stood before a sturdy workbench that was positioned under a roughly framed window. Jorgen had made the bench for Andrew and together they had cut out the window so Andrew would have some natural light to work under when he skinned animals and prepared their pelts for sale. Jorgen saw that most of Andrew's tools were gone, along with the finished pelts. He stood in Andrew's place and ran his hand over the smooth surface of the bench as he stared out the window until the view was lost in darkness. Loneliness and sadness had crept back in to keep him company.

The effects of too little sleep and long hours of work had taken their toll on Jorgen, but the cold air energized him as he walked away from the shanty. The lamp was lit in the wood shop where Far and Bestafar spent most winter days. Jorgen usually stopped in once or twice a day. He helped with the larger pieces and usually had a project of his own to work on. Like his father and grandfather, he enjoyed woodworking. He appreciated exactness, the precise measurements, skillful sawing, careful chiseling, and the almost seamless way two well-planed pieces of wood could be joined together.

Far always insisted that Jorgen keep half the dalers he

earned when the items he made were sold at market. When the family continued to experience difficult times, Jorgen offered his life savings to help out, but Far was adamant that he keep it for starting his own woodworking business, someday. But who knew what the money was worth? So much currency had been issued during the war, and its value had risen and fallen so often since then that Jorgen had no idea if his savings had any value at all.

Since middag wouldn't be served for at least another hour, Jorgen considered going into the shop to work on Karine's present. The sooner he finished it, the more time Christina would have to do her painting. Karine would be coming home for her birthday the following week, and he didn't want Christina to feel rushed. As he drew near the shop, he saw that Far was alone. Bestefar must have gone back to the house, thought Jorgen. Not willing to risk another confrontation with his father, he too, headed for the house.

Jorgen didn't go into the house, however, but plodded along right past it. He wasn't in the mood to answer questions and, besides that, Andrew wasn't there. He crossed a pasture following the trampled path of deer that foraged daily for any morsel they could uncover in the snow. The path skirted deep snowdrifts and led into the forest.

As long as I'm headed this way, I guess I should check the traps Andrew set the other day, thought Jorgen. Although not fond of trapping, he occasionally tagged along with his brother to keep him company. *It's good that I went with him the last time*, he thought, *with all this new snow, we may not have found the traps until Spring.*

Andrew did not share his brother's love of carpentry. Most of the time that Jorgen spent in the shop, Andrew could be found in the forest setting his traps or in the shack, scraping and cleaning pelts of the animals he caught. The 'big ones' sold Andrew's furs when they went to Bergen and paid him when they returned home. He, like Jorgen, was allowed to keep this money for himself. Together, they kept their money in a small moneybox Jorgen had made, and stored it on a shelf above their bed. Jorgen hadn't checked, but he was sure that when Andrew left, he had taken his share of the dalers.

Jorgen could smell the forest long before he reached the tree line. The dampness of wet snow enhanced the pungent fragrance of acres of pine and spruce trees. He inhaled deeply and with each exhalation released some of the tension and sorrow that had gripped him all day. At the edge of the woods, Jorgen stopped in front of a tall stump the children referred to as "the throne." Sitting atop this vantage, one could view the entire estate like a king or queen overseeing a kingdom.

Jorgen sat down on the stump, as he had done so many times throughout his childhood, surveying what had been his world for seventeen years. A full moon had risen as he walked to the forest and now sat just above the kitchen chimney. It reflected off the snow and lit up the family estate. Their property consisted of thirty acres of arable land and more than one hundred acres of forest. Crops were planted in only ten acres because lack of fertilization and poor crop rotation had left one-third of the land unproductive. These acres were now pastures. Far rented additional pastureland from a neighboring estate. It was costly, but necessary.

The land had been in the Halvorson family for generations and had been passed down to Far's oldest brother when Bestefar was injured in an accident. Jorgen's father had inherited it when both of his older brothers died. Duty to family and not a small measure of guilt had reluctantly brought Jorgen's father back from Trondheim, where he had gone to live and work, to assist Bestefar with the farm.

Jorgen knew his father preferred the city life he had led in Trondheim. His talents had been put to good use in the carpentry and cabinet making business, and after a few years there he had established his own woodworking shop. Jorgen suspected that if given the chance all those years ago, Far would have sold the land and moved his father and mother to Trondheim.

It was a good thing that didn't happen, because shortly after Far moved back to the estate, he met Mor. "Once he met her," Bestefar told Jorgen, "the old farm didn't seem so bad. Your pappa began to smile again and whistled through all his chores." Jorgen had a hard time imagining that...he hardly ever saw Far smile, and he didn't even know his father knew how to whistle. "Your mama probably saved the estate for future generations of Halvorson's. Her, and of course, building the woodshop for your father to tinker in."

The snow stopped and through the moonlit night Jorgen could just make out the small shop. *Far is happiest when he's in there*, Jorgen speculated. *He doesn't understand that Andrew and I are happiest when we are working the land, making things grow, and caring for the animals.* As he continued to look down on it, the light within the shop was extinguished. Far was done for the day. Jorgen couldn't see him, but imagined him walking across the yard and into the brightly lit house.

Closer to where Jorgen sat, he saw that the deer had returned and he watched their spindly legs rake the snow packed ground. He closed his eyes but could still see clearly all that lay before him: the fields, house, barn, all the gard's small sheds, the wooded hills in the distance and the mountains beyond them. This was home, this was his life, and this was his weakness. Now that the time for pursuing his dream was at hand, it was difficult to think of leaving the people he loved, his country— this land of breathtaking beauty, and the safety of all that was familiar.

He knew Andrew loved all this as much as he did, and he envied Andrew's ability to just put it all aside. *I'll do it too,* Jorgen resolved. *When the 'big ones' return in a few weeks, if Andrew is not with them, I'll find a way to go to Bergen. And if Andrew hasn't left for America, maybe he'll wait until I've earned enough for my passage.* With this vague plan to console him, he got up and left the stump.

Jorgen sought out the places where he thought Andrew had set his traps and was puzzled when he couldn't locate them. He widened his search but still found nothing. Baffled, but too cold to continue looking, Jorgen finally gave up and went home. *The trolls must have taken them*, he thought. That was a family's response when someone inquired about a lost item. Every child in Norway knew that trolls who lived in the mountains and forests liked to hide things and play tricks on people.

★ ★ ★

The family was just sitting down to eat when Jorgen got home. The talking ceased when he entered the kitchen. Mor gave him a warm smile when he sat at the table. After a short, awkward silence, Far asked about his day, commenting that when he hadn't come home at the usual time, he sent Niels to help him finish the chores.

"You were already done," said Niels. "I looked all over for you. Where did you go?"

"I went out to get Andrew's traps. I thought I knew where he had set them, but I couldn't find any of them. They're not in his shanty, either. I wonder if he took them with him."

"He didn't," said Niels. "Yesterday, after your chores, when you went to work in the shop, Andrew took me out and showed me the best places to put the traps... and how to set them. He hadn't caught anything, but we brought the traps home because he said he thought it was going to snow and the traps would get all covered. Then he told me I could have them. He gave me all his traps, just…gave them to me. That's why I wanted to talk to him this morning. I wanted to ask him how to clean them. But he was already gone, so I took them to the shop to see if Far had something I could use. That's where the traps are, at the shop. And Jorgen, if you want, I'll help you with your chores from now on."

Niels said all this, barely pausing for a breath. It was the most Jorgen had ever heard him say. He looked at his younger brother and recognized in his face the eagerness he had felt years ago, wanting his older brothers to notice him. He realized with a sudden burst of insight that his exclusive relationship with Andrew had left little time in his life for all his younger siblings.

"Takk," said Jorgen. "I would really appreciate your help. And when you've caught something in your traps, I can show you how to kill and skin it." Although Jorgen did not look forward to this part of the bargain, he didn't want Niels cutting off his hand or for the animals to suffer needlessly.

"Did Andrew tell you why he was giving you his traps?" asked Far.

"I asked him, 'don't you like trapping anymore?' And he said he liked it fine but he was going to earn money some other way. I thought that maybe he was going to start working with all of you in the wood shop."

"He gave us these, last night, when we were getting ready for bed," said Edvard, as he and Ole dug wooden soldiers out of their pockets and lined them up on the table.

Jorgen recognized the little figures. "I have some just like those. The 'big ones' carved them for Andrew and me many years ago. I'll look for them; if the trolls haven't made off with them, you can have mine, too."

"Are you going away, like Andrew?" said Edvard.

When he didn't answer Edvard right away, Mor asked him the same question.

"Ja, Mor, I am. I hope that Andrew changes his mind and comes home with the Gundersons when they return in a day or two. If that doesn't happen, and if he doesn't come back with the 'big ones,' then I'll try to catch up with him in Bergen.

"Uff da!" exploded Far, "I can't for the life of me see why you two boys are so determined to leave Norway. There are plenty of jobs in Bergen. I've trained you in carpentry; you could get a good apprenticeship and even have your own business some day."

"Pappa, I enjoy making things and I wouldn't mind having my own shop someday, but I've been raised on a gard and I like the bonde way of life. I want my children to grow up on my own land and we both know that isn't possible here."

"If I'd known that you and Andrew were going to be taken in by all that damn emigration nonsense," Far spat the words out, "I never would have let you hang around the wharf in Bergen. I would have kept you here at home with the little ones. Your older brothers have heard all that talk, seen all the flyers posted about town, but they were smart enough not to be taken in by it."

Far took a deep breath and tried to continue in a calmer voice. "Jorgen, life isn't that easy in America. Those men in Bergen who are selling American dreams are paid by ship captains and shipping agents to do just that. They talk about how cheap the land is, but do they tell you if the land is any good? Do they ever talk about all the hardships you'll have to face? Do they mention the long and dangerous ocean voyage? The wild natives in America? The difficulty of clearing the land? Do they talk about loneliness and what it's like being without family? You and Andrew would do about as well if you tried to hold an eel by the tail."

He paused, but not long enough for Jorgen to reply. His voice had become louder, each word sounding angrier than the one before. His scalding tone and florid face were fraught with the frustration he felt over his sons' foolishness. "They need to fill the ships with emigrants going to America so they can fill the ships with cotton, tobacco and wheat for the trip back. Their livelihood, not yours, depends on convincing you to sail away to the 'Promised Land.' Honestly, Jorgen, I thought you were smart enough to see through all that."

Mor had shooed the children out of the room when Far had started his tirade. Bestefar had also disappeared. Jorgen could smell his pipe smoke coming from the great-room.

Jorgen, too, was angry. Far's repeated comment about being smart enough provoked him and emboldened him to respond. "My older brothers may or may not think it's smart to go to America, but they don't need to leave this country to have the kind of life they want. They have everything to gain by staying here. One will inherit this gard and the other can buy into his future father-in-law's fishing business when he gets married. Home is only best if it allows you to lead the life you want. I know life in America will be difficult, but Andrew and I will be successful there. I can feel it...and someday I hope my children will call it home."

"Oh, Jorgen, don't be a fool!" Far said, before storming out of the room.

★ ★ ★

A few mornings later, after he had done the milking, Jorgen hiked the two miles to the Gundersons. Olav met him at the door, he and his father having returned from Bergen the night before. The troubled look on Olav's face was enough. Jorgen knew in an instant that Andrew had made his departure permanent.

"My father said he never would have taken Andrew to Bergen if he had known what he was planning to do." Olav said. "I think he plans to ride over to talk with your father today. He wants him to know that he tried to talk Andrew into coming back with us, but Andrew said that he was on his way to America. My father argued with him, but Andrew wouldn't listen. We both feel we are to blame because we were the ones who took Andrew away."

"It's not your fault," said Jorgen. "Andrew had set his mind on leaving. If it hadn't been you, he would have found some other way to get to Bergen. No one blames you or your father."

The two boys stood side by side for several minutes, staring down the road, each lost in his own thoughts. Finally, Jorgen started for home. He walked a few steps, turned and gave a small wave, and then took off at a run. The rest of his chores were waiting.

Two

Weeks Later

Hunched down and shivering despite wool caps and their heaviest coats, Jorgen and Niels sat back to back on milking stools. Every head in the barn, boy and animal alike, was shrouded in the fog of its own breath, and steam rose from cold metal buckets of warm milk. Periodically, the boys paused, exhaled on their hands, and attempted to rub some warmth into them.

"Hey Jorgen, Do you think it's too cold to go skiing, today?"

"It's not just too cold, Niels, it's much too windy." Jorgen's whole body convulsed with shivers at the thought of skiing in these conditions. "We'll see," he said through chattering teeth. "If the wind dies down and the sun comes out later, it might get warm enough. There's a place I'd like to take you and the others. I don't think any of you have been there."

"Where is it?"

"You'll see."

"Is it across the river?"

"You'll see when we get there," Jorgen replied, laughing.

Niels accepted his brother's vague answer and said no more.

Somewhere in the barn, a horse nickered; the cow, still waiting to be milked, its udder bloated and heavy, shuffled her feet impatiently; and something rustled in the straw, over near the wall.

Jorgen listened as if hearing these sounds for the first time. He had not noticed them when he worked with Andrew because the barn was never quiet like this when Andrew was around. Andrew talked incessantly. He'd come into the barn first thing in the morning, and start talking to the cows. He wouldn't start the milking until he had chatted with each one. Jorgen accused him of wasting time, so that he, Jorgen, would have to do more of the work, but Andrew had an answer for everything and argued that his conversation with the cows relaxed them and they gave more milk. Throughout all their chores, Andrew continued his chatter, mostly with the animals, sometimes with Jorgen. Most of the time, Jorgen tuned him out as his brother droned on and on about nothing and everything, but occasionally Andrew would ask a question and he, Jorgen, would answer it, only to find out Andrew was talking to a cow or a horse.

Mor should interrogate the animals if she really wants to know Andrew's plans, they probably know more than I do, thought Jorgen. A sardonic grin briefly played at the corners of his mouth at the notion of his mother sitting down for a chat with Betsy. Jorgen suspected that Andrew carried on these conversations just to annoy him, so he did his best to ignore them. But, far too often, Jorgen had to admit, Andrew achieved his goal.

Niels started to say something, but it came out as a croak, and he had to stop to clear his throat. "I thought winter was over; this is the coldest day we've had all year." His comment punctuated the comfortable silence between them and was about as chatty as Niels ever got. Unless he asked a question, he wasn't expecting Jorgen to reply. Compared to Andrew's conversations with the animals and his constant harangue about leaving home, Niels's brief observations suited Jorgen just fine.

The rhythmic sound of milk spurting into the pail had a soothing, almost hypnotic effect on Jorgen. His hands, numb from the cold, performed their task as if detached from his body, and his mind, too, was elsewhere. It was hard to keep Andrew from creeping into his thoughts; their lives, their plans had been intertwined for as long as Jorgen could remember. Would they get back together again? Jorgen could see no way to get to Bergen in the foreseeable future. Would Andrew leave for America without him?

Thwack!

Startled by the unexpected sound, Jorgen jerked his head around to check out its source and almost toppled off the wobbly stool. He watched in open-mouthed amazement as a dazed rat staggered, then fell dead next to the boot that Niels had thrown at it.

"Mitt Gud! Niels, I nearly came out of my skin," said Jorgen, regaining his balance and composure. "But what a great shot! You really clobbered him."

"Takk, Jorgen." The look on his face showed that Jorgen's praise had hit its mark as well.

"I'll bet you couldn't do that again in a million years," said Jorgen. "I doubt if I could, either."

"See that dark knot hole?" Niels said, matter of factly. He indicated a spot on the wall plank, at least a dozen paces away, directly above where the dead rat lay. He slipped out of his other boot and hurled it, hitting the spot dead on. The boot fell to the floor, landing on top of the rat.

"Where did you learn to do that?"

"Oh, that's just part of a game I play with Ole and Edvard. We throw stones at trees. Edvard's aim is even better than mine; he can show you today if we go skiing." Then Niels quickly changed the subject. Jorgen figured it was because Niels was embarrassed to admit to playing the childish game, and yet, Jorgen and Andrew were the ones, many years before, who had taught Niels to play, 'Kill the Troll.'

"Well, your aim is better than mine. I don't think you need to use those old traps of Andrew's," observed Jorgen. "Just go out and throw your boots at rabbits. Or Andrew's boots, aren't those Andrew's boots?"

"Ja, he didn't take them. My boots are too small. These are a little too big," he said, walking over to retrieve the lethal boot and its mate, "but I'll grow into them."

Reveling in Jorgen's approval, Niels already felt inches taller.

That night the family gathered in the great room. This was everyone's favorite part of the day, the time for fiddles and dancing, and the time for story telling. But since Andrew's departure, though present as usual in the room, Jorgen had not joined in. Consequently, when he announced he had a story to tell, his news was greeted with smiles that said, 'welcome back,' and the younger children clapped with enthusiasm.

All eyes focused on his grave expression as he began. "I think you all should know that sitting here among you is a genuine hero," Jorgen paused; his somberness gave no indication of what was coming next. Everyone looked around the room to see who it might be.

"I think it's me," said Ole, "I played with Inger all morning, and Mor didn't even ask me."

"That's because you were mad at me," Edvard laughed, nudging his younger brother playfully.

"Nei," Jorgen said to Ole. "You are not the hero tonight, although it was nice of Inger to play with you." Inger giggled.

There were more guesses and more denials until Jorgen pointed to Niels. "The honor goes to Niels. Call him Niels the Warrior because he, my extremely brave and talented younger brother, saved both our lives this morning by slaying an evil fiend. It was the ugliest, most vicious looking thing you could ever imagine, with razor sharp teeth and breath so foul-smelling, it curdled the milk we had just collected."

"How big was it?" Inger wanted to know. She had sidled up to Niels and questioned him with awe in her voice. "Did it try to bite you?"

"It was this tall," continued Jorgen, extending his hand about two feet above the floor. "I doubt that any creature like it has ever existed in Norway. It must have slipped ashore from an English ship."

Making fun of the English was good sport, and everyone in the family laughed.

"Before the creature could even think about coming close enough to bite Niels...or me," Jorgen added with shock in his voice, as if that possibility had just occurred to him, "Niels had his boot off and hurled it the length of the barn, striking that beast right between its beady eyes. The blow was powerful enough to kill it outright, but then..." Jorgen paused, "It sprang back to life!" Jorgen leaped forward with both arms outstretched, a sudden move that surprised Ole and Inger, and they both shrieked.

"It sprang back to life," Jorgen continued in a calmer voice, "transformed into a drooling, cross-eyed troll that leered and growled at us, then jumped its slimy self into Niels's boot. What a sight it was to see that boot hop out of the barn and down to the forest. All the while it screeched and wailed; the noise was deafening. You must have heard it."

Jorgen looked expectantly around the room, but no one admitted to hearing a thing. Undeterred, Jorgen continued, "Well then, you may have noticed something different on Niels's feet. With one of his boots on its way to the forest, it was a good thing for Niels that we found Andrew's old boots in the barn."

Everyone laughed and applauded the story, and Niels, rarely the center of attention, glowed self-consciously but beamed with his unexpected attention.

★ ★ ★

It warmed up enough to ski a few days later so, after their chores, Jorgen and Niels went back to the house to get the others.

"I'm the only one going with you," said Christina. "Edvard and Ole have fevers and have to stay in bed. Mor thinks Inger might also be ill, so she has to stay home, too."

It was just as well, thought Jorgen. The place he had

in mind was a little further from home and more uphill than the trails where the younger ones usually skied. Jorgen had no doubt that they could do it, but their short legs slowed the group down, and today's jaunt would require some speed if they were to be home before it got too dark.

The three skiers traversed the pasture, avoiding the deep drifts as they skimmed over the trampled down snow on the deer path. Jorgen led them through a portion of the forest that extended down to the river, which due to the extremely cold winter was almost iced-over. This was the closest the river came to their home, and it narrowed there as it turned sharply away from their property. It was the children's favorite place to skate, and when the ice melted, they sat on the mossy bank and fished for the salmon and trout, which thrived in the crystal cold water.

They didn't cross the river but followed it until it curled away towards the valley. Jorgen led them into the woods on a winding path that gradually led uphill. The forest was thick on this side of the valley and spread up the mountain in long narrow strips. As they skied through the trees, the wind created a mini-blizzard of snow blown from the dark green branches that arched overhead. Finally, out of breath but exhilarated by the strenuous activity, they reached a small clearing.

"That was hard work," Christina said, taking in the panoramic view, "but I can see why you wanted to come up here." Her speech came in short bursts as she attempted to catch her breath, and her cheeks, glowing from the exertion, enhanced the paleness of soft blue eyes. The wind caught her black homespun skirt and partially unbuttoned coat, and they billowed about her like dark wings. "Niels and I came almost this far berry picking last fall, but I didn't know this glade existed. I don't think the little ones would have made it up here." Her breathing returned to normal as she spoke. "Did you and Andrew ski up here often?"

Jorgen nodded. He studied the landscape then closed

his eyes to commit it to memory; it was a sight he never wanted to forget. This was his second favorite spot, and he hoped that before he left Norway he would travel on the Hardangerfjord, and enjoy what he considered the most beautiful views of his country. He doubted that America or anywhere else on Earth had anything so breathtaking.

He turned to Christina. The afternoon sun glinted off slender tendrils of golden hair that had escaped the confinement of her small knitted cap. He discovered that he was enjoying her company and once again felt guilty that he and Andrew had been so exclusive.

"A few times, in the summer, we climbed higher than this, but the view is just as good right here." He had pointed vaguely toward the jagged mountain range that loomed behind her. Its craggy peaks sliced through small clouds that clung like veils over the topmost cliff faces.

Standing shoulder to shoulder, Jorgen and Christina looked down upon the long narrow valley that stretched for miles north and south: a white quilt, stitched together with fences and rows of shrubs, dotted with houses and barns. The river (black in some spots, ice covered in others) emptied, out in the distance, into a large, placid lake that reflected the deep blue sky.

To the east, the valley ended abruptly at the foot of the mountains directly opposite them. Clusters of trees clung to the mountainside, green and white spotted patches, but much of the terrain was too harsh for vegetation. Thin silver ribbons of ice clung to cliffs in places that would become cascading waterfalls with the spring snowmelt.

The sun crept lower and would soon slip behind the mountains. Excited to explore this new terrain, Niels had skied a short distance up the trail but had returned and now waited a short distance down trail for them to catch up. Jorgen lingered, his eyes slowly sweeping the scene from mountains to the top valley floor, gathering in every last detail.

When, after several minutes, he showed no signs of movement, Christina grabbed his hand. "We should go now. This will not change; it will still be here when you return, and I hope you do someday." She smiled at him and started to leave, tugging him with her as she skied toward the trail.

The way home was mostly downhill, and they covered the distance quickly. As they crossed the pasture, Jorgen saw Far standing on the porch, silhouetted against the last vestige of light in the sky. He paced in the confined area, head down almost to his chest. He stopped and looked up at them when he heard their approach.

"Jorgen, come to the shop as soon as your skis are off. Niels can put them away for you." He spoke gruffly, his expression bordered on a scowl.

Jorgen's heart began to beat a little faster and his hands fumbled with his skis, a reaction reminiscent of his childhood. He had never been good at reading his father's moods and while his father had not struck him in years, the stern command to 'meet him' at the shop elicited an old familiar dread.

Nothing came to mind as he attempted to recall what he might have done in the past few days to upset his father. They seemed to have settled on an unspoken truce, neither mentioning Andrew nor America. Jorgen had gone back to working in the shop and they were able to talk easily about carpentry and other safe subjects. Just yesterday, when Jorgen put the finishing touches on a new milking stool, Far admired his work saying that he could not have done a finer job himself.

Jorgen handed Niels his skis and, in return, got a weak smile of encouragement. He hurried to the shop, anxious to get whatever this was over with. *He hasn't lit the lamp, so it shouldn't take long*, he thought, grateful at least for that.

Far stood in the semi-darkness. His face had relaxed somewhat, and he now just looked very tired. He got right to the point. "Jorgen, I hate to do this, but I need to borrow your money."

This was certainly unexpected. Jorgen slowly let out the breath that he hadn't realized he was holding. His relief was short-lived as it dawned on him that something must be seriously wrong for Pappa to ask for his money.

"Of course, Pappa. I'll get it right away. Is there anything else I can do?"

"Takk, Jorgen, I knew I could count on you. Edvard and Ole are very sick. I'm going to get the doctor tomorrow, and I'll need your money to pay him. When the 'big ones' come home, I'll be able to pay you back.

"You don't need to do that, Pappa."

"It's your money, Jorgen, you'll need it for whatever life you choose." Far stiffly put his arm around his son and squeezed his shoulder, the unexpected gesture caught Jorgen off guard, and as they walked out of the shop together, he blinked back tears. *What is wrong with me*, he agonized, hating the tears that he had to blot with the back of his hand. *Grow up Jorgen*, he scolded himself, *don't be such a baby.*

Mor had devoted the entire afternoon to the care of her sick children and had not cooked anything for dinner. Niels and Christina, rosy-cheeked from their outing, were making quick preparations for smorbrods. They had set the table and were putting out cheese, pickled herring, smoked fish, and other toppings for the sandwiches when Jorgen and Far entered the kitchen.

"Pappa, I wish I had been here to help Mamma with the little ones," Christina said. "I wouldn't have gone skiing if I'd known how sick they were." She poured warm milk into the mugs that Niels had just placed on the table.

"It was good for you to be out in the fresh air, so don't feel guilty about not being here. Mor is afraid they may be contagious and wants you all to stay away from them. Your grandfather and I tried to help her, but she shooed us away, too." He shrugged his shoulders. "Made us go back to the shop."

Far turned to address Niels and Jorgen. "When you're through with middag, Niels, go out to the "big ones'" cottage and get the fireplace going. Jorgen, pack up whatever you two boys will need for a couple of days. We think it's necessary to quarantine the little ones, so you two will stay out there until Mor thinks it's safe for you to be around them. Inger's cot has been moved out of your room, Christina. She's showing signs of the same illness; we don't want you or Karine exposed to this either."

"Is Karine still coming home tomorrow?" asked Christina. She complained just about every day about how much she missed her sister and couldn't wait to see her.

"Ja, I will get her when I go to town for the doctor. Jorgen, you'll need to bring in more water when you've finished tonight's milking." Far paused for a moment to think if he had left out any instructions, then busied himself building up the fire in the kitchen's massive stone fireplace.

Built by a much younger Bestefar, the fireplace was the heart of the kitchen. It was the thing about the house that visitors always commented on and an accomplishment that Bestefar talked about with great pride. He and Jorgen's great grandfather had built it, stone by stone, and Bestefar liked to say that the fireplace was large enough to stable a horse. Andrew, always one to argue, said that he didn't think it was that big and would have brought a horse into the house to prove that Bestefar was exaggerating, had Jorgen not stopped him.

That night, despite its warmth and bright blaze, the kitchen fire did little to dispel the somberness around the table. Mor took a small bite and chewed absently. "Ole had a convulsion a few hours ago. I've got to keep his fever down," she said, obviously distressed. Worry lines framed her tired blue eyes and loose strands of hair stuck out at odd angles from the bun that she had quickly fashioned earlier in the day. Her hands were chapped and red from squeezing cold water out of washrags countless times to place on the feverish

42

foreheads of the sick children.

She moved to get up, but Far reached out gently to stay her in her seat. "You need to eat something, elskling," he told her, and then he left the table.

It was the first time Jorgen ever heard his father call his mother that. Endearing terms didn't normally spring from Far's lips. He sneaked a look at Christine and she arched her eyebrows at him. He looked away quickly to keep from laughing.

Far came back several minutes later carrying an empty bowl and reported that the boys were sleeping and he had replaced the cold cloths on their heads. "Inger is feeling better and wants to know if she can have some more soup."

After the meal, everyone scattered except for Christina and Bestefar who stayed in the kitchen to clean up. Niels went out to the cottage to light a fire and get the little room warmed up while Far went to the great room to rekindle that fire.

Meanwhile in the boys' bedroom, Mor attempted to get Ole and Edvard to take sips of cold water and sponged off their feverish bodies while Jorgen collected the things that he and Niels would need at the cottage during the next few days. Before leaving the room, he took down the moneybox, opened it, and stared in disbelief. It was empty.

Stunned, Jorgen replaced the box, gathered up the things piled on the bed, and went into the great room. He was relieved to see that Far was alone. He knew his father to be a proud man when it came to providing for his family and thought the loan request and missing money should remain between the two of them. He hesitated in the doorway and watched as his father placed a log on the fire and prodded it into place with a large poker. Jorgen walked to the fireplace and stood next to him.

"The money box is empty," he said. "All my money is gone."

Far replaced the poker then turned to face Jorgen. His

face looked more lined and tired than usual, and Jorgen was surprised to realize how much his father looked like Bestefar.

"What do you suppose happened to it?" Far asked.

Jorgen hated to say what he thought, but there was only one reasonable explanation. After a long pause, he said, "Andrew must have taken it."

"I can't believe that Andrew or any of my children would do such a thing," said Far. "This is a sad day. Even if Andrew didn't take it, someone in the family broke the trust that we have in each other. Why are you so sure that Andrew took it?"

"The shelf where we keep our money box is quite high, Niels might be tall enough to reach it, or Christina, but why would they? Neither of them have any need for money. I think the night he left, Andrew just reached in and took it all. Maybe he wasn't thinking or maybe he thought I'd come after him to get my money, and then we would travel together. It really doesn't matter why he took it. It's gone, it can't help you now."

Jorgen started to leave the room, then paused and turned back to Far. "What will you do tomorrow? How will you pay the doctor?"

"Don't worry about that. Dr. Larson and I will work something out. Go get set up in the cottage, and then you and Niels come back here. Bring your fiddles; a little music might make everyone feel better. I'll ask Bestefar to get out his hardingfele, too."

Jorgen doubted that music would make him feel any better, but he would come back later and play for the rest of the family, if only because Far had asked him.

★ ★ ★

Fiddles tucked under their arms, Niels and Jorgen were practically blown back to the little cottage when the improvised concert was over. They only played for a short while. No one was in the mood for storytelling, but Far said that Mor had enjoyed hearing the music. She had stayed in the room with the sick children and said that the music soothed them to sleep.

The wind snatched the cottage door from Niels as he opened it and banged it against the wall. As he struggled with the door, the gusts of frigid air chilled what little warmth the room had held. Jorgen hurried to add more wood to the fire then stood, warming his backside, as the fire roared to life.

"Will you teach me the last song you played with Bestefar? I like the middle part; it's so lively." Niels kicked off his boots and sat in the middle of the oversized bed. Covered with a thick down comforter (once white, now yellow with age) it dwarfed the other furniture in the room: a table, two chairs, washstand, and small wardrobe. Niels' head was bent over his fiddle as he attempted to play the melody.

"Here, let me show you how it goes," Jorgen offered. He picked up his fiddle and sat on the end of the bed to show Niels the correct fingering.

"You're really good, almost as good as Bestefar," said Niels. "I guess I need more practice."

"That and a new fiddle. That old thing you're playing is too small for you and doesn't have good sound." Jorgen handed his instrument to Niels. "Try mine."

Niels attempted to play the new song. He hit a wrong note, winced, and put the fiddle down.

"Nei, keep going," said Jorgen. "You were getting it."

Niels grinned, picked up the fiddle, and finished the song.

"See, I told you it was the fiddle. You need a new one."

"Bestefar said he would make a new one for me, but he can't get the right kind of wood until the weather clears. Have you ever played his hardingfele? He let me try it once when he was teaching me. It is so beautiful and sounds the best."

"Ja," Jorgen agreed, "It does have great sound, but Bestefar is also one of the best fiddlers in the valley. I've played it a few times, but I can't make it sound like he does."

★ ★ ★

When they finally crawled into bed, it didn't take Niels long to fall asleep. *Skiing must have tired him out*, thought Jorgen. He realized he was tired, too. The music had relaxed him, and the cottage, though still cool, was comfortable for sleeping. The fire crackled pleasantly in the fireplace and created dancing shadows on the rough wooden ceiling. Jorgen should have fallen asleep easily, but like the night that Andrew left, he was kept awake by troublesome thoughts.

Jorgen had never seen his parents as worried as they had been that day. Illness was not a frequent visitor to their home, and when it did come, it never stayed long. When he had been in his room earlier in the evening, he had seen his young brothers' lifeless forms tucked into their bed they shared. Mor sat beside them applying cold cloths to their feverish heads. It seemed so unnatural to see the active little boys lying so still.

Jorgen wondered how his father was going to pay Dr. Larson. With times being so tough, many folks didn't have cash, so often they paid the doctor 'in kind.' Far always paid cash because, he said, "The doctor can't buy medical supplies and drugs with chickens and pigs." Dr. Larson was a kind and generous man who didn't turn away those who couldn't pay. As a result, he and his wife were forced to lead frugal lives. Jorgen guessed that his father would end up, like so many others in these tough times, paying 'in kind,' perhaps with some chickens, cheese, and some of Mor's blueberry preserves or dried lingonberries.

What was Andrew thinking, Jorgen fretted anew, *taking all that I saved.* Although angry at his brother, Jorgen couldn't help feeling a bit disloyal. He knew if the situation were reversed and Andrew's money had gone missing, Andrew would not consider blaming him. He'd blame thieving trolls or his own forgetfulness before he'd accuse any member of the family. Jorgen didn't like thinking that Andrew took his money, but that really did seem to be the only plausible explanation. He hoped the mystery would be solved when the 'big ones' came home.

That thought led to other thoughts about Andrew. His absence had created a void that no other family member could fill. Although their personalities differed greatly, and Jorgen was often frustrated by what he felt was Andrew's haphazard way of doing things, he missed the excitement that Andrew generated, his optimism and his ability to see the humor in most situations. But mostly, he just missed his companionship.

Andrew loved to laugh and often laughed at himself, like the time he convinced Far to let him cut the grass roofs. With the exception of the barn and the house, all of the out buildings had sod roofs that were several years old. Tall weeds and even some trees had taken root and Far suggested that Andrew climb up and trim the overgrowth.

Andrew agreed to tackle this task but went on to suggest that as long as he was going to be up there, he could trim all the grass. Far wasn't sold on the idea. He thought it a waste of time, and furthermore feared that Andrew's actions might in some way damage the sod. Replacing a sod roof was not a huge expense; most of the materials needed for the job could be taken from their land and forest. It was, however, a time consuming project, time not spent in the fields or wood shop, time that would not generate income for the family.

The process began with several layers of birch bark laid on the roof boards. These were covered with two or four layers of sod. The first layer of sod was laid upside down on the birch bark then a second layer would be placed grass side up on top of the first. The layering continued with the last layer placed grass side up. Over time, roots grew through all the layers anchoring them in place. The thick sod was an effective means of insulation; it kept the blanket of snow from slipping off the roof in winter, and it let hot air escape the buildings in summer.

Andrew argued persistently that trimming the sod would make it grow thicker and thus it would become even better insulation. Jorgen suspected that Andrew had dreamed up this excuse and simply wanted to relieve the boredom of his regular chores by doing something risky and out of the ordinary. The matter was debated for days, but Andrew had a way of wearing down a person's resolve. Jorgen was surprised that his practical father relented and allowed Andrew to experiment on one building.

Scythe in hand, Andrew climbed to the roof of the small cottage, right above the bed where Jorgen now lay. He stood at the peak of the sloped roof and, ever the performer, bowed to the family members who had assembled to watch from below. Turning to his task, he gave a mighty swing of the scythe and lost his balance. He tumbled down the roof and onto the ground landing right at their feet. Before any of the stunned watchers could move, he jumped up, turned to his slack-jawed audience and announced, "Don't worry about me, I meant to do that, it was all part of the show."

He went on to trim all the roofs and would later insist, whenever the subject came up, that the sod had indeed grown much thicker. Most everyone else thought they looked about the same, just tidier.

Niels mumbled in his sleep. Jorgen turned his head to study his brother's face in the dim light of the fire. *He looks like Andrew but he acts more like me,* he thought. *He is so eager to please, just like I was at that age. He never questions, he works hard, and he's quiet. Doing chores with him isn't nearly as much fun as it was with Andrew, but it's also not as annoying and we're done in half the time.*

Jorgen next wondered what Ole and Edvard would

look like when they grew up. He couldn't help feeling sad when it dawned on him that if he moved to America he might never know. He got out of bed and went to the window to look across to the house. He saw that the kitchen lamp was still burning, so he dressed quickly and went to see how the little boys were doing.

When he entered the kitchen Far was pouring water from the bucket that Jorgen had brought in earlier into the small pan that Mor was using to keep the washrags cool. "Ole had another convulsion," Far said in reply to Jorgen's questioning look, "and Edvard's fever is also still too high. Go back to bed Jorgen, there's nothing you can do here. You may have to get the doctor in the morning, so get some sleep, son."

Before leaving the kitchen, Jorgen added more wood to the fire then returned to the cottage and threw in another log there. He lay in bed a long time before his body finally surrendered to sleep.

Far woke Jorgen and Niels early the next morning. "I am staying home to help Mor with the children; she was up all night and needs to get some rest. Jorgen, you'll go to Voss for Dr. Larson. Niels, Bestefar will help you with the chores."

"All right, Pappa," said Niels. "How are Edvard and Ole?"

"They're both very ill, but the doctor will make them better." Far put a reassuring hand on Niels's shoulder.

"Jorgen, Christina will go with you. Mor wants her out of the house, just to be safe. She also wants you to stop at the school to pick up some books. You can do that after you pick up Karine."

Jorgen wasn't surprised that his mother could think about schoolbooks during this crisis with Edvard and Ole. Educating her children was usually her first priority. In spite of near constant nursing care, Jorgen knew she would not fail to plan their next lesson.

It was still dark out when Far brought the sledge and

horse up to the house. Jorgen ate a hurried breakfast and Christina scurried about rounding up the books that needed to be returned.

Dr. Larson lived just outside Voss. It would take Jorgen and Christina more than three hours to reach his house. If he was home and able to leave right away, he could make it to the Halvorson's by early afternoon. If he was out seeing other patients, he might not get to see Edvard and Ole until tomorrow.

Niels stood in the courtyard waving them off. Christina waited until they were on their way before she related what she overheard.

"I heard Mamma and Pappa talking this morning. Jorgen, Mamma thinks that the boys have scarlet fever. She told Pappa that Ole has a rash all over his body and his fever is too high. She sounded scared."

"Listen Christina. Dr. Larson is the best doctor in all of Vestlandet. He'll know what to do. Ole and Edvard will be running around again in a few days, you wait and see."

Jorgen glanced at Christina and realized she was close to tears. He was frightened, too. They both knew that scarlet fever could be fatal. He tried to think of something else to talk about, then realized that they were passing the road to the Gunderson's house.

Unlike their family, the Gundersons did not own the estate on which they lived. They leased their house and land, a situation quite common in Norway. They were in a class of farmers known as Husmann; some people unkindly referred to them as cotters. Jorgen's family shared what little they could with them, a pail of milk, a dish of goat cheese, sometimes a few eggs, because they knew that the Gunderson's plight was far worse than their own.

"I know a secret," Jorgen teased. "It's about the Gundersons."

"Are they moving?" Christina asked. Olav had told her, without rights to the land, his family could be forced to move at any time.

"Nei," said Jorgen. "It's about Mrs. Gunderson. She's pregnant."

"Jorgen!" Christina protested. "We're not supposed to talk about those things, and Mamma said I shouldn't say that word. It's not polite." Then she started to giggle, which was precisely the response Jorgen had hoped for.

"Well, you didn't say it, I did. If you don't use the word 'pregnant' when someone is pregnant, what do you call it?"

"You don't...call...it anything," she gasped through fits of laughter. They both laughed. For the next several minutes, they'd look at each other then break into laughter. They talked and laughed about how silly grown-ups were about having babies, refusing to acknowledge a woman's condition even when her belly sticks out and looks like she's swallowed a pillow.

"I don't remember when Mamma was pregnant with Edvard, Ole, or even Inger. Do you?" Christina looked at Jorgen when she said 'the word' and they both grinned. "One day Ole was the baby, and the next day, Inger was the new baby," she continued.

"I remember when Inger was born," said Jorgen, "Mamma wore big dresses, but I knew she was pregnant. When I asked Far about it, he said she was 'with child.' I corrected him, and said, 'you mean she's pregnant.' Then Far told me I was impudent. I thought impudent meant something good, so I smiled at the compliment. He slapped my face and made me go to my room."

Christina was laughing again, "Oh Jorgen, it's not funny, but it is funny. Did you ever tell Pappa that you didn't know what the word impudent meant?"

"Nei, I don't think Far likes to be reminded about the times he's hit us. Sometimes it makes him angry all over again. Besides, even though I didn't know what the word meant, I was being impudent. I used the word pregnant just to see what Far would say. Just like I've used it now, to make you laugh."

★ ★ ★

They fell into a companionable silence, remarking occasionally about a tree cracked down the middle by the weight of the snow, or an animal darting out into the road. Stars were still visible in the early morning sky; it promised to be a beautiful day for a ride to town. The horse, long overdue for some real exercise, kept up a brisk pace. Andrew had named her Venn when he was younger because, he said, she was his best friend. Jorgen smiled when he remembered how hurt his feelings were that Andrew chose a horse as his best friend over him.

About an hour into their journey, the mountains to the east began to take on a golden hue and soon bands of pink and blue spread across the sky. When the sun finally rose over the mountains, long purple shadows gave way to blinding white snow. Jorgen pulled his cap down to shield his eyes from the glare. Christina put a hand up to protect her eyes, but eventually gave up and simply closed them. Before long she was leaning on Jorgen, fast asleep.

For part of the way, the river ran alongside the road to Voss, and both snaked down into the valley, cutting through estates and their fields and disappearing into the forests. Given the serious purpose of this trip to town, Jorgen wondered if he should feel guilty for enjoying it. He had felt restless ever since Andrew had gone, and it felt good to be going somewhere. He couldn't help thinking about his brother, the trip they had planned together, and his missing money. The more he thought about it, the more convinced he was that Andrew had taken the money to lure Jorgen into following him. He knew that Andrew would be in Bergen for a time, perhaps months. But, it was also true what Andrew said about the next opportunity to go to Bergen. That would also not be for several months. *I just have to be patient,* he thought. *When the 'big ones' come home, I'm sure they'll know what Andrew plans to do. At least they'll be able to tell me if he's still in this country.*

Venn slowed his pace as they started up a hill. The sledge moved easily on the icy hill, but the horse's hooves experienced some difficulty maintaining traction on the slippery road. Jorgen noted this; he would have to slow Venn down when they came over this hill on their way home. He guided the horse to the top of the hill and was relieved to see the slope going downhill was less severe and not as icy.

Jorgen relaxed his grip on the reins and sank back into the seat. The woods had thinned along this stretch of the road so more of the farmland was visible. He tried to picture his farm. Most of the barns he passed were old and rundown. He was proud of their modern barn and valued the experience of helping to build it. He knew that he and Andrew could build one just like it in America. He hoped that they would have enough money to buy a lot of land, acres and acres of it. He had heard that America had so much land they practically gave it away. *That's fine by me,* he thought, *land for pastures and land for planting. I would even like to have an orchard like the ones that grow on the sides of the Hardangerfjord. It would be nice to grow our own fruit. I'll have to ask Mor to show me how to make a pie.*

★ ★ ★

They were relieved to see Dr. Larson's sledge sitting outside his house, and even more relieved once he packed some things into his bag and set out for their home. Mrs. Larson insisted they stay for a while to warm up before starting back. She put some milk on the stove, and while it heated, Jorgen went outside to water the horse and give her a quick rub down. When he came back, Christina was telling Mrs. Larson about Andrew going to America.

"Christina tells me that you plan on joining Andrew in America." Jorgen was leery of confiding in her, but she seemed genuinely interested, so he admitted that was his plan. She smiled and said, "You'll have to look for my nephew's family. They left almost twenty-five years ago from Stavanger on a ship named the Restoration. I believe the ship was headed for New York City."

Other than Bestefar, Mrs. Larson was the first adult who had taken his plans seriously; she even asked where he wanted to settle. He appreciated her interest and her kindness.

"Andrew and I heard about a town named Kendall. It's a Norwegian settlement somewhere outside New York City. If I don't catch up with Andrew in Bergen, before he sails to America, I think we'll meet in that settlement."

"I don't know much about America. Is Kendall a good place for farming?"

"That's not our final destination," responded Jorgen. "That's just a place to meet; we plan to look for land further west, in Illinois or Wisconsin. Land is cheaper there."

"Goodness!" exclaimed Mrs. Larson. "I've never heard about those places. You sound just like my nephew, so full of adventure."

"How does your nephew like living in America?"

"Oh, we haven't heard from him in years," she said. "After my sister and her husband—his parents—died, he stopped writing letters home. That was about ten years ago. But from what he wrote, before then, he sounded happy and prosperous."

Mrs. Larson excused herself and left the room. While she was gone, Jorgen mulled over what she had just said. He wasn't much of a letter writer, but he couldn't see himself cutting off all communication with his family. And would they write to him? America suddenly seemed far away.

When she returned she was carrying a book with a piece of paper sticking out of it. She handed the book to Jorgen and told him that her nephew's name was written on the piece of paper. "The last I heard, he was living in New York. I hope he is still doing well.

"I bought this journal many years ago," she continued, "and put it away, waiting for something to happen that I could write about. It sounds like your life is about to become very eventful. I'd like you to have this, so that you can write about your exciting journey. When the book is full, send it back to your parents, and maybe when they've read it, they will share it with me. We're all family," she said, "are we not?"

"Ja," Jorgen said, "We are family. Takk," he said, taking the book. "I will use this, and I'll look for your nephew in New York."

He and Christina stood up to leave. Mrs. Larson stood up, too, and surprised Jorgen with a hug. "May Gud keep you safe," she said.

On the road, Jorgen was silent, his eyes fixed somewhere in the distance. His thoughts were of a young man in a distant city and a woman here who wondered about him.

Christina was also quiet, her gaze focused on Jorgen, her face wrapped in a smug smile. He finally turned to her.

"Now what?" he said.

"You turned red when Mrs. Larson hugged you."

"It was so hot in her house, it would turn a cabbage red. I wasn't blushing." He knew this wasn't entirely true. Although her home did seem uncomfortably warm, her unexpected hug had embarrassed him.

"Say what you want, cabbage head, but I'll bet she's the first girl, other than Mamma, to hug you. Or have you hugged that girl, whatshername, that you always want to sit next to when we go to school?"

Jorgen didn't need to look at Christina to know she was grinning at him and having a bit of fun at his expense. "I don't know if I'd call Mrs. Larson a girl. She's probably years older than Mor, and whatshername's family moved, so you'll never know if I hugged her."

"Didn't they move to Bergen?" Christina's tone

implied more than mere curiosity. "Why don't you look for her when you go there?"

"And then what, Christina?" He looked at her and explained, "I'm going to Bergen to earn money to pay for my passage to America. Marta—that's her name by the way—is history."

He knew what Christina was up to, with her not-so-veiled questions. She had discovered the idea of romance in the last year and was, Jorgen guessed, secretly in love with Olav. She would put on her Sunday dress and become all flustered whenever he was around. *She probably hopes that I will fall in love, marry Marta, and stay in Norway forever. Well, that isn't going to happen,* Jorgen thought, not that he didn't have misgivings about leaving home. Mrs. Larson's book had reopened a flood of feelings and the same questions that had nagged him before. *Go, or stay? Go, but when?* Hoping to end the conversation with Christina, Jorgen fell silent. It was all too much to think about.

The sun had reached its full height for the day and before long would begin its descent toward the mountains in the west. The wind had picked up, and the air felt damp. Clouds scuttled across the sky. Jorgen flicked the reins lightly, urging Venn to quicken her pace. If this wind continued, snow blown from the fields would drift across the road. Already, some fields showed the tell-tale effects of strong gusts of wind. Spikes of cut straw, like beard stubble, poked through the snow in the windswept areas.

Karine ran out and climbed into the sledge as soon as they got to the house where she was staying. Jorgen and Christina waved to a figure in the window, but Jorgen wasted no time in getting the horse moving again.

"I didn't know you were coming, I thought it would be Pappa and one of the boys," Karine said, giving Christine a brief hug. "And when the winds began to grow stronger, I thought you might not be coming. I'm so happy to see both of you. How is everything at home?"

They told Karine about the fevers and convulsions and ended by saying that they had to summon Dr. Larson before coming to pick her up.

When they had answered all her questions about the illness, Jorgen told her about Andrew's departure. He stopped short of saying anything about the missing money. It was upsetting to think about, and he just wasn't ready to talk about it.

"Oh Jorgen," Karine said, "I'm so sorry that your plans have not worked out the way you wanted. Andrew is too young. I wish he had waited for you. And I didn't get a chance to say goodbye...I can't believe he's gone. But, that's Andrew, isn't it? He gets an idea in his head and there's no stopping him."

Jorgen frowned. *Karine knows Andrew better than Far. I hope she makes that same comment at home when Far is around to hear it.*

"He did tell me to say goodbye to everyone."

"That's not the same as saying it himself and giving us the opportunity to say a proper goodbye. You don't just steal off in the dead of night." Karine said, still obviously disappointed in her younger brother.

There was quiet in the sledge while they all considered what Karine had said, but eventually the girls, anxious to get caught up with each other's news and gossip, broke the silence.

For a while, Jorgen continued to brood over his brother's actions, but it was difficult to ignore the girls' happy chatter. Their animated speech made it obvious they had missed each other. Despite the difference in age, their voices were so similar that at times, he wasn't sure which one was talking; Jorgen had never noticed that before. And when Karine had run out of the house, minutes ago, he had been struck with how much the two girls looked alike. They appeared now to be the same height, both had heart shaped faces, pale blue eyes with long lashes, a small gap between their front teeth, and light brown hair that was pulled back; Christina's was in braids, and Karine's long wavy hair cascaded down her back.

Last night it was Niels and Andrew, today, it was the girls. Strange, thought Jorgen, *it's like I've never really seen my brothers and sisters before now.*

Not long after picking up Karine, they arrived at the little schoolhouse, located across a wide yard from the Lutheran Church they attended. On Sundays, horses and carriages parked in the yard where the children played on schooldays. The one-room country school was too far away for regular attendance, especially in the winter months, but the Halvorson children attended as often as possible. Although they had always been country people, the Halvorsons valued education. When attending school was not possible, Mor tutored Jorgen and his brothers and sisters in reading and writing. Far helped them with mathematics and Bestefar was knowledgeable about Norwegian history and tried to keep up on world affairs. He passed his knowledge on to the children, engaging them in lively discussions about world events.

Bestefar loved music. He had learned to play the fiddle at an early age and was eager to share his passion for making music with his grandchildren. In time, they all learned to play, some better than others, because they loved having their grandfather's special attention.

Mr. Bergstrom, the teacher, was pleased with the unexpected arrivals and warmly greeted them. He spoke briefly to the students seated in the little classroom, gave them an assignment, and then turned to the visitors. He was dismayed to learn of their brothers' illness and said that three more of his students also had scarlet fever.

They hated to rush through their visit, but with a storm threatening the two-hour trek home, Jorgen was anxious to leave. So, the book and assignment exchange was made, along with hasty goodbyes.

In the valley where the Halvorsons lived, the weather was influenced by the flow of the North Atlantic current off the coast of Norway. The temperature rarely dropped below twenty degrees, but weather conditions could change rapidly. On this particular day, the weather had gone from sunny and calm, early in the morning, to overcast and windy. Now, as they neared home, a thick foggy snow blew over the mountains blotting out the horizon. Land and sky became one. The sledge glided past phantom trees and other landmarks, which had become all but lost in the squall. Venn, however, plodded along steadily, driven by instinct, to her next meal.

★ ★ ★

Karine's visit lasted several days longer than planned as the household was placed in quarantine. Mor insisted on being the sole caregiver for the sick children, so Karine and Christine took over other household chores, relieving their mother of fixing meals and doing the laundry. But there was no respite from worry; the whole family was consumed by it when they learned that two of Ole's classmates died from the fever. With his two youngest brothers gravely ill, Jorgen often found himself thinking about Andrew, sometimes with worry, sometimes with anger, but mostly with sadness.

Dr. Larson came back twice to check on Ole and Edvard and to bring different medications: lobelia, aconite, belladonna, and other strange sounding potions. Mor dutifully administered doses to her ailing sons praying that something would cure them. Perhaps it was these prayers, the doctor's drugs, or maybe it just wasn't their time to die; the boys' fevers finally broke, and they began to recover.

On Karine's last day home, Mor brought out the last of her precious sugar supply, and surprised everyone with a cake to celebrate Karine's birthday. Mor rationed sugar carefully always making sure there would be enough for a cake for each child's birthday and, in December, for a Julkake. Karine's other surprise was the beautiful chest that Jorgen and Christina had made for her. Her eyes lit up when Jorgen carried it into the room. Christina's beautiful rosemaling complimented the detailed carving that Jorgen had crafted on the chest.

"It's lovely," said Karine. She opened the chest, closed it, and ran her hand over the smooth surface. "It's very well made," she said to Jorgen. She traced her finger over the carvings and marveled at the workmanship. Then, turning to Christina she said, "It is truly a work of art. How well you paint! Takk, Christina. And takk, Jorgen, I appreciate your gift and look forward to using it for many years."

A few days later, the quarantine was lifted and days and evenings returned to normal. After middag, the children read and worked on the assignments either Mr. Bergstrom or Mor had prepared for them. When Jorgen and Niels finished their work, they usually went to the shop to spend time with Far and Bestefar. Mor and Christina baked bread, spun wool, or did some sewing in the great room. The little ones, freed from their sickbeds, played by the fireplace, either in the kitchen or the great room, wherever Mor and Christina happened to be working.

On one of these nights, Far and Niels left the shop early while Jorgen and Bestefar finished planning a table. They worked in silence, stopping every few strokes to run their hands over the smooth surface.

"You've been quiet for many days," Bestefar said, "Is something troubling you? Are you still angry with Andrew for leaving without you?" He started to say something else but was caught up in a fit of coughing.

Jorgen went to the old man, a stooped, gray-haired version of himself, and slapped him on the back until he stopped coughing and caught his breath. Jorgen helped him to a chair, and offered to get him some water.

"I'm fine now, Takk, I'll get some water when we get

back to the house. Do you want to talk about what's bothering you?" Bestefar lifted up his wrinkled face to smile at Jorgen, his eyes still watery from the coughing fit.

"It's just that everything's changed." Jorgen said, "I used to get so excited about the thought of leaving home, but now I realize how much I like things the way they are. I know I can't stay here forever, but I'm no longer sure about what I want."

"And then there's Andrew..." Jorgen paused. Although he thought about his brother all the time, talking about him, even saying his name, was difficult. "He and I were always so close; I thought I knew him, but now I'm not so sure. My money is missing and although Andrew probably took it, I just can't believe he would do that. I don't know if I'm angry with him, or even if I still want to go to America. I don't know if I want the bonde way of life or my own woodworking business. I don't know anything, anymore. I don't know what to do," Jorgen looked expectantly at his grandfather.

"The prospect of change is unsettling," Bestefar's speech was slow, and his breathing seemed labored. "Your future is full of possibilities; there is no harm in taking time to sort through them, try one or two out. No decision has to be final—" He paused for a moment to catch his breath. "No decision has to be final, Jorgen. As for Andrew, he may or may not have taken your money, perhaps you'll never know. What's important is what you believe about Andrew. If you believe that he could never do that, live with that belief until it is proven wrong."

The two sat quietly for a long moment until Bestefar's breathing returned to normal. Jorgen stood and went to help his grandfather to his feet. "Takk, Bestefar," he said. "You always give me something to think about."

Three

Mid-April, 1848

"I wonder if the 'big ones' will come home today."

"Niels," Jorgen chided, "You've said the same thing, several times a day, every day for days. Your impatience is getting on my nerves."

"I'm sorry, Jorgen, but the snow has practically disappeared, and anyway, I thought you wanted them to come home, too." Niels stopped milking Betsy and turned on the stool to speak to Jorgen's back. "I was going to ask you to help me with the traps today, but I don't suppose you want to." He turned back and resumed milking.

Jorgen knew he was not being fair to Niels. It wasn't the first time in recent weeks that he had lashed out at his younger brother. Jorgen recognized that he was the impatient one, too quick to snap at Niels.

In past years, he had been just as excited as Niels and the others for the 'big ones' to return home. But he faced this year's return with mixed feelings. *Yes, he would be happy to see his older brothers, but if Andrew was not with them, and they didn't have his money. What then?* As long as snow made the road impassable, he didn't have to think about his future. He was having some good times and was getting to know Niels, Christina, and the little ones. With the resumption of music and story telling at night, home was a good place to be – for now.

"How old was Pappa when Bestefar had his accident?" Niels posed the question from his perch atop the throne. Jorgen lay on the ground next to it, elbows out, hands cupping his head. He had come along on his brother's trapping expedition, after all, to make up for being short with Neils earlier that day, although his disposition had not improved all that much.

Neils had proved to be good at trapping. On the other

side of the stump, heaped in a brown sack, lay four freshly killed animals: a mink, a blue fox, and two hares.

"Around our age." Jorgen answered without opening his eyes. Today was one of those spring days, when the temperature spikes and layers of winter clothing are peeled off, exposing pale arms and faces to the sun's penetrating warmth. A large circle of grass was already turning green in the slightly elevated area surrounding the stump. Jorgen had thrown his coat on the damp ground and was lying upon it, basking in the sun, luxuriating in seldom-met idleness. That had been another reason to accompany Niels, it was too nice an afternoon to spend indoors.

"Yours or mine?"

"Huh?" Jorgen grunted.

"Your age or my age? Was Far your age or my age when the accident happened?"

In his semi-conscious state, Jorgen first thought Andrew had asked, as usual, interrupting his reverie with endless queries. Slowly, he came to realize that Niels had asked. "Your age." He finally responded. "Far was your age."

"And it was this tree?" Niels rapped the stump with his fist.

"Ja." Jorgen said, more loudly than necessary, then added in a tone that expressed his annoyance at being disturbed, "Too many questions!"

Jorgen heard Niels sigh and hoped that meant he had taken the hint. That was one thing about Niels, he could take a hint. And he already knew the answers. Jorgen suspected Niels of skirting the edges of a story, hoping to trap Jorgen into telling it. In a more sociable frame of mind, Jorgen might have obliged him, but for now, he just wanted to lie there and be a mute part of the earth.

Besides, the story wasn't Jorgen's to tell; it belonged to Far. It was a true story with a strong lesson about carelessness and disobedience, his own disobedience, which made it a favorite with his children. They always listened with rapt attention as he told about the first time, at age twelve, that he helped his father and brothers fell a tree. The children begged often for the story, but Far needed to be suitably disposed before he could tell how he nearly caused his father's death.

When in the proper frame of mind, Far would begin the tale by describing how careful Bestefar was when it came to felling trees, all the measures he would take to examine the area surrounding the target tree. This was to insure that when it came down, it would do so safely, not get hung up on other trees or crush saplings, and that it would land where the ground was most level.

The children would always nod their heads at this part of the story. They knew how their grandfather constantly stressed the need for good preparation. No matter the task, he frequently advised, "Measure twice, cut once."

The day in question, when Bestefar had figured out the path of descent, he instructed his two older sons where to cut the tree and watched as they got started. Then he specified the spot where Far should stand, well out of the way of danger. Far's role would be to saw off the branches and throw them into the wagon, once the tree was down.

Satisfied that his two older sons were handling the job properly, and his youngest was out of harm's way, Bestefar unhitched the horse from the wagon and led it a distance away where he tied it to a tree. This was to keep the animal from spooking when the tree crashed to the ground.

Absorbed in watching the felling process, Far edged away from the spot Bestefar had assigned to him. Inexperienced and ignorant of the unpredictability of falling trees, Far kept moving closer to the action. As Bestefar made his way back to the scene he saw that his youngest son had moved from his assigned spot and was now in danger from the falling tree. His shouts of warning could not be heard over the loud cracking of the fractured tree. Running full speed Bestefar reached Far, who stood immobilized, his eyes widening with terror as he realized the peril of his situation. Bestefar attempted to shove him to safety, still shouting at him to run. Far broke out of his trance, and they both scrambled to get out of the way.

The tree came down with a mighty thud and the ground trembled with the impact. Far was buried in a tangle of branches. Scratched and bruised but otherwise unhurt, he struggled to his feet. Panic set in, however, when Far couldn't see his father. He called for him and was relieved when Bestefar answered almost immediately, asking if Far was all right. Bestefar was only a few feet away, but he lay in a jumble of branches. He had been knocked to the ground and was pinned there by a heavy limb. It had crushed his leg.

The story always included the gory elements of blood and exposed bone, and how a stretcher had been improvised to carry Bestefar home. If their grandfather was present during the storytelling, the children would ask him to roll up his trousers so they could marvel at his scar, and listen as he told how Dr. Larson had patched up his smashed leg. As he got older, Jorgen noticed that at this point in the story his father found some reason to leave the room. He suspected that telling it made it real again and made Far sad.

Although Niels had stopped talking, all was not quiet. Clicking and scraping noises came from where he sat. Curious about this new distraction, Jorgen squinted into the sun's glare to observe Niels at work, whittling a chunk of wood. With his brother thus occupied, Jorgen closed his eyes and returned to his earlier daydreams.

He had been reliving another spring day, like this one, when he sat with his back against the gnarled trunk of an ancient apple tree that stood next to the schoolhouse. Crumbs of lunch flecked his dark shirt, the sleeves of which were rolled above his elbows. His eyes were closed; the sun was warm on his face and his long legs stuck straight out from the tree like two spindly roots. Marta, a friend he had known since his first day of school, sat beside him on his spread-out coat. He was her audience as she practiced the recitation, she planned to give after the lunch break. Jorgen loved the sound of her voice, and as he listened, he was suddenly aware of a new feeling stirring within him. The skin on his bare arm prickled where it lay on the ground just inches from hers, the blond hairs standing on end. He wondered if she could hear the thumping of his heart or if its wild gyrations were visible through his thin, washed-out shirt. At that moment, Jorgen knew he was experiencing his first feelings of love.

Months later, when she told him that her family was moving, he was heartbroken. He sulked for weeks after she left until the pain dulled, and finally, he tucked away all thoughts of her like the small wooden toys the 'big ones' had made for him. But in the weeks since Christina had mentioned her name, Marta had crept back into Jorgen's consciousness. It wasn't that he deliberately dredged up memories of her, she just popped into his thoughts at unexpected times. Christina's hair, down, but pulled back with a bright bit of ribbon, or Inger's infectious, bubbly laughter, were glimpses of Marta. A song that Bestefar played on his hardingfele brought back blissful memories of dancing with her at the church picnic. He found himself looking for her at church on Sundays, even though he knew she wouldn't be there. On most nights, her face was the last thing he saw before he fell asleep.

"Jorgen! Jorgen!" His daydreaming came to an abrupt end. Spurred by the excitement in Niels's voice Jorge bolted to a sitting position. Niels leapt off the stump and was pointing toward the house. "There's a wagon pulling up to the house. The 'big ones' are home." He jammed the piece of wood into his pocket, picked up the lumpy sack, threw the knife in with the dead animals and took off for home, tripping along as best he could with the stuffed sack banging into his legs with each step. Jorgen grabbed his coat and sprinted after Niels. He caught up with him, grabbed the sack, and they continued on, side-by-side.

"I saw three of them get out of the wagon," panted Niels. "I think Andrew is with them."

Jorgen had seen the same thing, and a smile of relief spread across his face. It was difficult to make out who was who because the whole family had come out and everyone was hugging and moving about. The group then moved out of sight, to the rear of the wagon. Jorgen guessed they were already beginning to unload it.

"They sure brought back a lot of stuff," Niels said, as they drew nearer. Jorgen saw, too, that the wagon was loaded with provisions, all most likely had been on the list that Jorgen's parents composed months earlier. When the wagon left for Bergen in the fall, it was crammed with things to sell at the market: wooden items constructed in the shop, yarn spun by Mor and Christina, bundles of wool, blueberry preserves, cheese, dried lingonberries. Anything the family could spare was sold. The profit went to buy essentials: flour, sugar, salt, fruits, and vegetables to be stored or preserved; fabric, shoes, and boots; hardware, tools and medicine. Sometimes, even with what the 'big ones' contributed, they didn't have enough money to purchase everything on the list. Other years some kroners were left to use for doctors or other emergencies.

"Hei," Jorgen and Niels called out simultaneously as they came within shouting distance.

"Hei, little brothers," A tall bearded man stepped around the side of the wagon. He picked up Niels in a bear hug, released him, and then cuffed Jorgen playfully on his shoulder. "You've grown up, Jorgen. When we left you weren't much taller than Niels."

"Takk, Theo," Jorgen said, reaching out to grasp his brother's hand, "And I'm not done growing yet. By the time you leave next fall, I intend to be even taller than you." Although Theodor wasn't the oldest child in the Halvorson family, he was the tallest. Jorgen's growth spurt had left him an inch or two shy of his brother's height. Theodor's years of fishing and working in the fields had shaped a tanned muscular physique, which, combined with his height and dark beard, gave a fearsome impression while concealing a gentle nature.

"Halvor!" Niels exclaimed as the other 'big one' approached. The four young men stood in a tight group, all talking at the same time, thumping each other on the back. Halvor ruffled Niels's hair, and they all poked fun at Theo's bushy beard. Jorgen was delighted when they all agreed that his height was exactly the same as his oldest brother's. Halvor was also very tan and muscular, but his clean-shaven, baby-faced good looks were in stark contrast to Theo's. He was also the wilder of the two, a risk-taker who had been rescued from some difficult situations by Theo, his cool-headed, younger brother.

In the excitement of greeting their older brothers, both Niels and Jorgen had temporarily forgotten about Andrew. Their boisterous reunion was quickly squelched, however, when the third, new arrival stepped out from behind the wagon. Jorgen was puzzled. *How and when did Olav Gunderson arrive?* As the truth sunk in, equal amounts of anger and sadness spread across Jorgen's face. Judging from Neil's shocked look, Olav could have been the devil himself.

"Well that's about the worst greeting I've ever received," said Olav. "Especially from friends."

"We thought you were Andrew," explained Niels as he walked to the back of the wagon and looked around, searching for a face not there.

"Ja," agreed Jorgen. He struggled to conceal his disappointment behind a tepid smile, then added flatly, "but it is good to see you, Olav."

Theo joined Niels, draped a huge arm around the boy's thin shoulders, pulling him close. "We had to let him go," he said. He lowered his head and spoke soothingly into the boy's hair, "And you do, too. He sailed for Christiania yesterday." Theo looked up to see Jorgen's hard stare fixed on him and nodded sympathetically. Jorgen willed his eyes to stay dry. He was a 'big one' now; there would be no tears. He just stood there feeling as lifeless as the animals in the sack at his feet.

"That's silly!" interjected Inger who walked up and stopped right in front of Theo. She craned her neck to look up at him. "He doesn't need to sail to her, she's right here." And she smugly pointed out Christina, just in case Theo had forgotten who she was.

Even Jorgen had to smile as Theo swept Inger off the ground saying, "Christiania is a city, little one, not just a sister." She squealed with delight as he propelled her high into the air, two or three times, before gently placing her back on the ground.

"Andrew sent some things with us for all of you," Halvor said brightly. "Let's get this wagon unloaded so you can see what's here." Far and Bestefar had been doing just that while the boys had greeted each other. Edvard and Ole, curious about all the new goods, scampered about underfoot, poking into everything. When Jorgen and Niels went to help at the rear of the wagon, Halvor and Theo went to the front and started removing items from that end. They set one cage-like crate a distance apart from the other barrels and containers. When the little boys happened upon it, Edvard decided to have a peek inside. Halvor turned in time to see his brother's hand on the latch, "Don't open that!" he yelled. But he was a second too late. Before Edvard could secure the latch, the crate was forced open from the inside and two pigs raced out between Edvard's legs.

The family was no match for two frightened pigs. A chorus of shouted directions filled the air as Inger, the boys, and all the men, except Bestefar, chased after the runaways. Mor, Christina, and Bestefar tried to stay out of the way and laughed until tears ran down their cheeks. After a time, Far stopped to catch his breath then held up a hand and yelled, "Stopp!" He was laughing so hard that he had to repeat it several times, "Stopp! Stopp! Stopp, now! Stopp chasing the pigs before you run them to death." The others finally heard the command and ended the pursuit, the little ones falling to the ground, laughing and gasping for air. Jorgen could not remember a time when he had seen the members of his family so helplessly giddy.

It took the pigs a moment to realize the game was over. They slowed to a walk and eventually one stopped right at Bestefar's feet. He quickly scooped it up and handed it off to Niels. The other casually ambled over to the open crate and lay down beside it. Jorgen grabbed that pig and together, he and Niels escorted the newcomers to their new lodging.

★ ★ ★

"So, Olav, what brings you here?" Jorgen asked, as the two boys carried tools, bags of seed, and other supplies into the barn.

"I'm looking for ways to earn some money and, now that Andrew is gone, I thought your father might need help, especially if Halvor and Theo didn't get back in time for shearing. I was on my way here when they caught up with me and gave me a ride."

"Have you had a chance to talk to Far, yet?"

"Nei, just as I was about to say something, your father asked Halvor about the pigs. He said they weren't on the list. Halvor told him the pigs were a gift from Andrew...that Andrew thought the family might enjoy something different to eat. Then your father said something strange. He said that if Andrew paid for the pigs, they were really a gift from you. He sounded really angry, his face turned red and he stomped off to the house carrying a large box. Even though he returned a few minutes later, I decided that this was not a good time to talk to him."

Olav paused, then asked, "Is your father angry at Andrew for leaving home?"

71

"Far thinks that Andrew was too young to leave home, especially by himself."

"And what about the pigs, what was that all about?"

"Just a family matter, a misunderstanding" said Jorgen. "It will pass. Why don't you stay for middag; that might be a good time to talk to Far."

The Gundersons must be going through tough times, Jorgen thought. He hoped his father would be able to find work for Olav, but with his brothers home now, he doubted it. Jorgen knew that cotters all over Norway were struggling to put food on the table, and that Olav's help was essential to his family. Olav had confirmed this, months before, when Jorgen and Andrew had asked him to emigrate with them. "Maybe later," he had said, "I'm really needed at home."

★ ★ ★

After everything from the wagon was put away, Jorgen and Niels went to the cottage to pack up their belongings. Theo came in before they had finished. "We'll be out of your way in a few minutes," said Jorgen, as he and Niels emptied the wardrobe and searched under the bed for wayward socks.

"No need to hurry," responded Theo. He sat down on the bed and continued, "I just came in to ask about your money. I understand it's missing and Far thinks that Andrew stole it."

"Nei," said Niels emphatically, before Jorgen had a chance to reply. "Andrew wouldn't do that!"

"Well, I don't think so either," said Theo, "but let's hear what Jorgen has to say."

"I didn't want to talk about this to anyone because I wasn't sure that Andrew had taken the money. I told Far about it because…" Jorgen paused, hesitant to give a reason.

"Far told me that he asked you for some money," said Theo, "Go on with your story."

"There really is no more to the story," said Jorgen. "I

went to get the money and it wasn't there. The only explanation I could come up with was that Andrew had taken it."

"That's not what happened," croaked Niels. His voice sounded strained, either from stress or puberty, or both. He got to his knees, then stood facing his brothers. He had been halfway under the bed rescuing a stray sock when Jorgen started to tell about the missing money. "I took it. But I put it back. I only had it a few days."

Theo sat there, shaking his head. He had guessed who the culprit was. Jorgen, on the other hand, was completely baffled. He had been pleased with the relationship he and Niels had forged and really enjoyed his company. He had not expected this.

"Why, Niels? Why did you take it?" Jorgen asked, anger creeping into his tone. "If there was something you wanted to buy, I would have lent you the money."

"I didn't need it," he said. "I just didn't want you to have it." Niels stood in the middle of the room looking so pathetic that Jorgen felt sorry for him, but he still wanted answers.

"That doesn't make sense," he said, "You took it because you didn't want me to have it, then you put it back?"

"Give him time," counseled Theo. He waited a minute while Niels fidgeted, then said, "Niels, tell Jorgen why you didn't want him to have the money."

After another very long minute, Niels turned to face Jorgen. "I didn't want you to go to America. After Andrew left, I was afraid that you would follow him, so he wouldn't be alone. I took your money because I didn't want you to go. We were having such a good time; I just wanted you to stay here. I hid the money in the shanty and checked to make sure it was still there every time I went to work on my pelts. Then I'd think about Andrew being alone in a new country and I'd feel sad for him. I didn't like feeling like a thief, even though I was going to give it back to you. I shouldn't have taken it."

Niels's face was red with shame when he finally paused for a breath. The sock he had found was now twisted and stretched to twice its original size. "I'm sorry Jorgen."

"When did you put it back?"

"It was the day you went to get the doctor. Mor was lying down and Far went to get water. I wanted to say hei to the boys, but they were asleep. I felt sad about them being sick, and that's when I put the money back. I didn't even know you thought it was gone, or I would have told you. I am really sorry, Jorgen."

"I know you are, Niels. I'm not angry. But Far thinks Andrew took the money. You need to tell him what you just told us."

"I'll go tell him now," said Niels. He picked up his things and walked slowly from the cottage looking contrite and more childlike than he had in weeks.

★ ★ ★

"Tell us about Andrew." Mor's request was made almost as soon as the family had gathered around the table for middag. She looked expectantly at her two oldest sons, "Is there any chance he'll come back to us?"

"Well mamma, there's good news and bad news about Andrew." Theo addressed his mother affectionately, as if he were still one of her little ones, perhaps, Jorgen thought, to soften the message he must deliver. "The bad news is, nei, he will not be coming home anytime soon."

"I never realized how thick headed that boy is," Halvor interrupted his brother. "We talked until we had no words left," he continued, "trying to convince him to come home and wait another year or two before emigrating. I told Theo we should hogtie him and put him in the wagon, but Theo wouldn't go along with my plan."

"Andrew said it was difficult enough to work up the courage to leave the first time, he didn't want to have to go

74

through it a second time. He has reasonable plans. He acted responsibly in Bergen. I thought there was nothing to be gained by insisting he come home."

Far cleared his throat to say something but didn't. His gaze fell from Theo down to his plate.

"He does hope that you will catch up with him, eventually." Theo said, addressing Jorgen.

"He wrote letters to everyone, I'll dig them out of my bag after middag," said Halvor between mouthfuls of food. "Mor, this is the best food we've had in months," and he took another large helping of lamb and cabbage stew.

Mor blushed happily at her son's compliment, then said laughing, "It's the best food we've had in months, too."

Jorgen knew his mother kept a few items in storage to celebrate a special occasion, but he was surprised that she had mutton available for a stew. She and Christina had spent the late afternoon preparing this feast, shooing family members out of their way when the mouth-watering aromas drew them into the kitchen. Between armloads of wood he carried in for the fire, he watched as Mor mixed and kneaded oats and water for flatbread. Christina divided the dough into small balls then rolled those into round sheets. Using a thin rolling pin, Mor rolled the sheets a second time, this time onto a very hot baking stone. When Jorgen set down the two buckets of water he had carried into the kitchen, he lingered long enough for Christina to take pity on his hungry, covetous stare. "Oh, here," she said with mock impatience, "take this and get on with your chores," and she thrust a piece of the hot, crispy bread into his eager hands.

Jorgen now held up a piece of flatbread and said in a voice guaranteed to capture everyone's attention, "To the bakers, Mor and Christina. We are in your debt."

"Ja! Ja!" Everyone agreed.

"And now for the good news," said Bestefar, addressing Theo. "Tell us the good news about Andrew?"

"As long as Dovre stands," began Theo, who like his

father, frequently used this expression, "I don't think I'll ever encounter another like Andrew who works so hard while talking so much." Jorgen burst into uncontrollable laughter. He could only shake his head wildly in agreement.

Olav, who Mor had insisted stay for middag, spoke up to say that when Andrew was in school, he generally did more talking than Mr. Bergstrom. "And," Olav continued, in obvious admiration of his friend, "he had lots of good ideas. He's real smart."

"Wilhelm Knudson thinks so too," said Halvor. "He and his sons were returning home to Christiania to fish the summer herring and offered Andrew a job."

"Well, I was impressed with my little brother," said Theo. "He had been fishing for less than a month when I heard him debating with the Knudson brothers the superiority of drift nets over scan nets. Wilhelm agreed with him and said he thought that Andrew had won the argument.

"Who is this Wilhelm Knudson?" questioned Mor, "And why is this good news?"

"Knudson is an educated man of many talents," said Theo. "He made a sizeable fortune from a variety of businesses; one had something to do with shipbuilding, another with architecture. But his love of the sea and fishing prompted him to sell everything, buy two large fishing boats and some land near Christiania, where his wife and daughters live. He was impressed with Andrew's adaptability to fishing and his knowledge of history."

Jorgen glanced at Bestefar, whose face lit up when he heard that Andrew had taken his history lessons to heart.

"Ja, Ja," prompted Bestefar. "What did he say?"

"He sounded a lot like you," Theo replied, "except when Christian Frederik's name was mentioned. Andrew got all red in the face; he called Frederik a traitor."

"Ja, we used to have some good arguments, Andrew and I," said Bestefar. "There's some merit in what he says about Frederik's poor judgment when it came to fighting with

Sweden, especially when he ordered the hasty retreat at Fredrikstad. But I don't think you can dismiss the leadership he showed in establishing our constitution. Christian Frederik wasn't a coward or a traitor. He was just too young and inexperienced to get the job done. I think that he sincerely hoped for an entirely independent Norway, but Andrew always argued that Frederik hoped to keep us tied to Denmark."

Bestefar took any opportunity to inject history into a conversation, but this short speech was enough to bring on a fit of coughing. He didn't like anyone mentioning these coughing spells, but lately, they seemed to occur more frequently.

Jorgen noticed his mother and father exchange glances. Far looked to the corner and nodded. Mor got up from the table, took a small glass from the cabinet, and then went to the corner shelf where some bottles of spirits were kept. The alcohol was kept for special occasions, holidays, or when neighbors visited, but Far also believed that it was a good remedy for stubborn coughs. Mor poured a small amount into the glass and wordlessly placed it in front of Bestefar.

"I think you should go see Dr. Larson," Halvor said gently to his grandfather.

Bestefar's coughing spasm had ended, and he downed the drink in one big gulp. "I'm fine, just need to shake this stubborn cough," he said, brushing off Halvor's suggestion, "Let's get back to Andrew and Mr. Knudson."

"Wilhelm is an honorable man," said Theo. He looked at his grandfather with concern, but continued with his account. "He treats Andrew like a son and will pay him good wages. Working with the Knudsons will give Andrew experience..."

"And who knows," interjected Halvor, "Maybe he'll marry one of the Knudson girls and stay in Norway."

"The good news," stated Theo, "is that Andrew will

be in Norway for several more months. He can gain some experience, and he's with good people."

Jorgen listened to all this and was happy for Andrew, but envy also stole into his heart. *Andrew has definitely started his own life,* Jorgen thought, *while I have yet to begin.*

★ ★ ★

Sheep had been sheared, field crops were planted, logging was underway, and Mor's vegetable garden was starting to produce lettuce and beans. As he labored in the fields and forest and worked in the shop, Jorgen grew restless with each passing day. He plied Halvor with countless questions about life in Bergen and the details of fishing. Would he be able to get a room in the house where his brothers stayed? How much did a room cost? A meal? Laundry? Which fishing vessels would they recommend for dependability, safety, and fair wages? If he watched his expenses, how much money could he save in six months? He wrote all this in the diary that Mrs. Larson had given him, planning his life, plotting his expenses, leaving as little to chance as possible. What surprised him was the more he prepared, the more unsettled he felt. He had difficulty sleeping, lost his appetite, and couldn't stay focused on his chores.

He also felt uneasy about Bestefar. Most days his grandfather slept right through breakfast. He worked in the wood shop each day, but tired easily. Then he'd pull a rocking chair over near Christina's worktable, where he seemed to enjoy watching her paint beautiful designs and flowers. Halvor had convinced Far that all the finished pieces should be decorated with rosemaling because they sold quickly and for the best prices in Bergen. Olav had been hired on to help Christina. After three months they had painted an impressive number of items, which were now ready for market. For now, Olav was paid in vegetables from the garden, but when the furniture was sold in Bergen at the summer market, he would be paid in dalers.

June seemed to last a lifetime. Theo was leaving at the end of the month, and Jorgen planned to leave with him. Andrew would be in Christiana for a few more months, but Jorgen knew he had to get a job. He would need a lot more money for his trip to America. The urge to get his journey underway had become a constant source of inner turmoil. If the family noticed his moodiness, they made no mention of it and the days passed with monotony that Jorgen found maddening. He found solace working the land, and therefore, the fields never looked better.

Late one afternoon, during the last week of June, Jorgen went to the wood shop as was his custom when he finished his fieldwork. Bestefar was not there, and when Jorgen asked about him, Far told him that a coughing fit had sent him back to the house for medicinal relief.

"Check on him, son, and see if he'd like you to finish the table he's been working on. I'd like to have Christina paint it so it will be dry enough for you and Theo to take to market."

Jorgen had been surprised at his father's reaction when he told him he was leaving with Theo. Far said that he would miss his son's help on the estate and in the wood shop, but he knew that Jorgen had to prepare for his future. Jorgen wondered if Bestefar or Theo had said something that had convinced Far to drop his opposition to Jorgen's leaving. Whatever had caused this change, life had suddenly been made easier for Jorgen.

He left the shop and waved to his mother and sisters who were behind the house hanging the laundry. His favorite shirt flapped in the breeze next to an assortment of aprons, blouses and underthings. Inger was meticulously hanging all the stockings on a low wooden frame.

The house was very still when Jorgen entered. Theo and Niels had taken the younger boys down to the river to fish for salmon. Halvor was still out in the fields. Bestefar sat at the kitchen table with a small glass of spirits in front of him. Jorgen went to sit across from him.

"Are you all right?" he asked.

Bestefar nodded and took a sip from his glass. His eyes were red-rimmed and watery, his breathing quick and shallow. He stared long and hard into Jorgen's eyes. Self-consciously, Jorgen looked away.

"You seem lost," Bestefar said, trying to hold back another fit of coughing. He sipped the liquor before continuing. "Maybe it's time for you to find your..." But he couldn't contain the cough. The hacking cough continued until the old man was struggling for breath. When he tried to stand, he collapsed to the floor. Jorgen raced to the other side of the table and knelt beside his grandfather. He slid one arm under the shaggy white-haired head raising it slightly from the floor.

"Bestefar!" Jorgen implored frantically, "Bestefar can you hear me?"

The old man's eyelids flickered. His eyes were fixed on Jorgen's face but were unresponsive. "Bestefar!" Jorgen said again, unable to keep the panic he felt out of his voice. "Say something! Breathe!"

He continued to look into the old man's eyes long after the light and life had gone out of them, and then he collapsed over the stricken figure, his tears dampening Bestefar's shirt.

★ ★ ★

"I'm leaving in the morning, are you coming with me?"

Jorgen was out in the barn, sitting on a milking stool. Although milking had been finished for more than an hour, Jorgen had been unable to summon the energy to walk back to the house.

The words brought Andrew to mind, but when Jorgen looked he was surprised to see Theo standing there.

It had been a week since Bestefar's death, and the shock of it still registered on Jorgen's face.

"I have to get back" Theo said gently. He knew the close bond that had existed between his grandfather and brother and sympathized with Jorgen's grief.

"I can't go," Jorgen responded. "I can't leave him yet."

Theo assumed that Jorgen was referring to his grandfather, whose freshly dug grave in the family cemetery Jorgen visited every day. But Jorgen actually meant he couldn't leave Far. The three of them had worked together in the wood shop for so long that the thought of his father in there, by himself, made Jorgen sad beyond words. As much as he wanted to go with Theo, he felt he could not abandon his father still suffering from the loss of his own father.

So Theo left, and Jorgen stayed. He threw himself into all the summer jobs that needed doing: repairing fences, felling trees to send downriver to the mill, chopping a winter's supply of firewood, enlarging Mor's garden, catching and drying fish. He even had Mor teach him to make a pie. But late in the afternoon, he could always be found in the wood shop. Often, Niels and Edvard were already there. Pappa was teaching them, just as he had taught Andrew and him, and Theo and Halvor many years before.

Nights were still given over to storytelling and music, but when the instruments came out, the sweet strains from Bestefar's fiddle were silent and missed. On some nights, Far and Halvor could be cajoled into playing, and Jorgen had to admit that Halvor was quite good. Nevertheless, when it came to instruction, the younger ones always turned to Jorgen.

These days, Jorgen didn't think far into the future. In fact, he tried not to think at all. Life, he decided, was easiest if one plugged away, filling each day with meaningful work. He thought he was making the best of what life had handed him and didn't realize how quiet and withdrawn he had become.

He was surprised, therefore, when Far turned to him in the shop one evening and said that he thought it was time for Jorgen to move on.

"I thought that's what I was doing," Jorgen said.

"Nei, you're standing still. You need to move on into your own life, not mine or Halvor's."

Four

Fall 1848

All hands were so engaged in stowing away a large catch that no one on the fishing boat noticed the gradual swell in the sea that preceded the rogue wave. When it struck, the wave seemed to come out of nowhere and it swamped the small vessel before the men realized what was happening. In the brief moment before the deluge thundered down on him, Jorgen made eye contact with Theo. His older brother looked at him with a calmness that failed to quell the panic paralyzing Jorgen's limbs. When Theo raised his arms and dove confidently into the towering sea, Jorgen's leaden arms refused to budge from his sides.

Jorgen awoke from the nightmare and sat up in bed, knowing that sleep would not come again that night just as it hadn't on previous nights. Since coming to Bergen and starting work as a fisherman, he had experienced this dream many times. Once again, he woke up gasping for breath and soaked in sweat. As on previous nights, the hot, airless room provided no relief; it also provoked feelings of self-pity.

If this is the start of my new life, he thought ruefully, *it's not an improvement. If Andrew were with me, we could afford a better room than this, maybe even the one that Theo and Halvor used to rent. Why did Andrew have to rush off in the middle of the night? Why did he abandon our plan?*

The more he thought about Andrew, the hotter he felt. Jorgen leaned against the wall and closed his eyes. *Think cool thoughts,* he told himself, but the sweat continued to trickle down his face. Recent weather in Bergen had been warmer than usual and the room's tiny, open window afforded little ventilation because the building next door was barely an arm's length away. Absent this morning was the nearly constant stench of fish in every stage of putrefaction. The fish market was a short distance down the street and its unpleasant odor, picked up by sea breezes, wafted throughout Jorgen's neighborhood on most days. *I'll never get used to that smell,* he thought. *Thank God the wind has shifted, maybe the weather will finally get cooler.*

After eight weeks in the cell-like room, Jorgen was familiar with its every detail. The papered walls, yellow with age and tobacco smoke, bore sooty streaks from a cheap and poorly functioning oil lamp. A distinct slant to the floor caused a gap under the door through which more than one mouse had gained entry.

The room's furnishings were meager: a cot, too short for Jorgen's six-foot frame, a scarred chair with two cracked slats, and a table barely large enough for a pitcher, basin, and the oil lamp. Two wall hooks provided the only means to hang a few things. There wasn't enough space for even a small dresser or wardrobe. A new pine chest that Jorgen had made for his travels looked out of place in shabby surroundings. Thanks to Christina's rosemaling, it was handsomely decorated with scrolling and flowers, large and small, in several shades of blue. When Jorgen looked at it, he saw not a painted wooden box, but his sister's tall, lean frame bent to her creative task and her happy smile when he said he would think of her every time he looked at her handiwork.

Following Theo's advice, Jorgen had installed a lock on the solidly built chest to protect his belongings. Woodworking saws and planes were on the bottom, then came extra pieces of clothing, and his moneybox hidden in one of Mor's quilts. On the top lay his most prized possession, the Hardanger fiddle that had belonged to his grandfather. Far had given it to him the night before he left home.

"Here," he had said, "take this."

Startled by his father's gruff voice, Jorgen turned abruptly to face him. Jorgen was packing and deep in thought trying to determine what he should take, what he would need most. Everything had to fit into one chest. He didn't want to be burdened with more than he could carry.

"Bestefar would want you to have this." Far continued. "One night, after you children went to bed, he told your mother and me that you were his best pupil and that he loved listening to you play his fiddle. I think it was the night I asked you to play when the boys were ill and we were all worried about them. As I remember, your music was very soothing to all of us."

His speech out of the way, Far stepped forward and thrust Bestefar's Hardanger fiddle into Jorgen's hands. Before Jorgen could react, his father had turned and was leaving the room.

"Takk, Pappa!" Jorgen called out to his father's retreating back.

Recalling what had just transpired, Jorgen's face flushed. He felt humbled by his grandfather's praise, yet honored to be the recipient of his Hardanger. He had been equally touched by his father's kind words.

As the blackness in his room faded to a dull gray, Jorgen began to hear the sounds of a city waking: the clip-clopping of horses' hooves, wagon wheels rattling over cobblestones, the tolling of a distant church bell. From somewhere, most likely the house next door, a baby cried out for its mother; a new day had begun.

Sunday. This was the only day of the week when Jorgen didn't work. He usually tried to make the most of it by rising early and spending the day walking around the city. It didn't make any difference where he went, as long as he got away from the wharf.

He swung his feet gingerly over the side of the bed and stood up causing the bed to creak ominously. He was afraid one of these days it would collapse and he would have to pay for its repair. Mrs. Steen, his landlady, had sternly warned him that he would be held responsible for any damage to the room or its contents. He was pleased that he had noticed the cracked slats in the chair that first day and had brought it to her attention. She, however, was not pleased, and as a result had been quite cool to him since. He wondered how many tenants before him she had tricked into paying for the damaged chair.

He stripped off the underwear he had worn to bed, splashed some water from the pitcher into the basin, and washed the night's sweat from his lanky body. Next, he washed the underwear along with three pairs of socks and a shirt, then wrung the soapy water from each item. In the process, he tore open a large blister on his hand, his most recent fishing souvenir. He dumped the dirty water out the window, refilled the basin, rinsed the clothing, and hung it to dry on rope he strung across the room.

Dressed in his Sunday clothes, he was soon out on the street and heading in the general direction of Theo's house. He was due there for middag, but that was hours away. In the meantime, he planned to wander past the shops and homes in the Floyfjell district. The shops would all be closed, but that didn't matter, he didn't want to spend money. He didn't really need anything, he merely enjoyed peering in the windows at the variety of merchandise on display.

First, he needed to make a stop at a shop that was always open. The old woman who ran the store barely eked out a living selling baked goods, small kakes and flatbread that she made in the hours just before dawn. Her loyal customers, (mostly single men, fishermen, and dockhands) visited every morning for their breakfasts. Mrs. Steen, the landlady, prepared two meals a day, breakfast and supper, six days a week for her "guests." She did not cook on Sundays, so it was fortunate for Jorgen that the old shopkeeper could not afford to close on Sunday mornings.

Jorgen greeted the small, hunched-over woman in the tiny shop.

"God morgen," she responded. Her broad smile of recognition revealed many missing teeth, and those that remained were discolored and quite crooked. Her smile was the dominant feature in a small, wrinkled face nearly lost in the shroud of a faded black scarf. In his younger years, Jorgen might have thought her features troll-like, but on these hungry Sunday mornings, Jorgen thought she looked quite pleasant. Her black jacket and scarf had a fine coating of flour, and Jorgen wasn't sure if her bushy eyebrows were white with age or the dusty remnants of baking.

"Everything looks delicious, I hardly know which to choose." A compliment always began their Sunday transaction. Jorgen stalled for a few minutes, looking at each item on display, and sniffed the air, taking in the doughy aroma while she fidgeted impatiently, her small, rheumy eyes never leaving his face. His mouth watered at the sight of tarts bursting with berries, but remembering his vow of frugality, he chose instead a small loaf of bread.

"Not this?" she inquired. She held up the tart that her watchful eyes had seen his gaze linger over. "Fresh lingonberries. Everyone says my tarts are the best." She offered the delicacy to Jorgen, challenging him to resist what she knew he really wanted.

"Nei takk," he responded. He quickly produced a coin to cover the cost of the bread before his resolve weakened. Every week the little drama ended the same way. Jorgen would feast his eyes on tasty looking treats, but he always chose inexpensive, but more substantial, grainy, loaves of bread.

She plucked the coin from his fingers, but instead of wrapping his purchase and sending him on his way as she usually did, she disappeared behind a curtain that shielded the small store from what Jorgen assumed was her living and baking quarters. He did not have long to consider her unusual action as she appeared almost as quickly as she had left.

"I can't sell this, it fell apart when I took it from the pan," she said. "You may as well have it." She placed the broken pieces of a tart next to the bread that Jorgen had selected, deftly wrapped them both in paper, and handed the package to Jorgen who stood in stunned silence. He hadn't expected generosity from one who seemed to have so little but was, however, already salivating at the thought of the unexpected treat.

Jorgen began to thank her, "That's very generous. I appreciate your…"

"Ja, ja," she interrupted, waving him off. "You go now. I know you have many things to do."

Jorgen left the bakeshop engulfed in a fresh wave of homesickness. The old woman and her shop brought back memories of baking day at home–the smell of freshly baked bread, berry pies, and flour smudges on Christina's face.

Although Jorgen had known he would miss his family when he left home, he had assumed the greater challenge would be moving from the quiet bonde life to a noisy city. But after a few weeks in Bergen, he realized his assumption had been wrong. He had easily assimilated into city life; he actually enjoyed looking at the colorful houses that lined the wharf. What he couldn't get used to was all the time to himself. How could he live in a city filled with people and yet feel so alone? He missed having someone to share all his new experiences. True, Theo was here, and Jorgen worked many days with him, but Theo's job kept him busy and often they were on different boats. And after work, Theo was anxious to get home to his new wife.

Jorgen missed being with Andrew, Niels, and Christina. Now, more than ever, he appreciated his mother's gentle ways and all the time spent in the shop with Far and Bestefar. He especially missed his grandfather's perceptiveness. What advice would Bestefar give to Jorgen about his total dislike of the fishing industry? Would he tell him to quit, to find… something he enjoyed doing?

Weeks before, when he had arrived in Bergen, Theo had taken him to meet his father-in-law, who also happened to be his employer. Jorgen knew he owed his job to his older brother. He was grateful for his help and tried hard to live up to Theo's expectations. Jorgen admired his older brother, his easy manner with the other fishermen, the way he handled disagreements and misunderstandings among the men, his insight into the vagaries of the sea, and his knowledge of the fish.

Unlike his older brother, however, the massive sea had the power to terrify Jorgen, especially when it boiled up in mountainous waves. Pressed to say why he disliked fishing, Jorgen would probably say that he feared drowning, but the grotesque sight of hundreds of fish dumped on board struggling to breathe, their gills pumping frantically, eyes glazed and protruding, mouths gaping; that was just too repulsive. Jargon shared this feeling only with Theo. His brother did not laugh at him or try to talk him out of how he felt; he merely pointed out to Jorgen that he did have a choice.

Jorgen knew that his father would say something like, you don't always like doing the things you have to do to survive in this world. Yes, Far definitely would encourage him to continue fishing. Jorgen discovered there were other jobs in Bergen he could do, but the pay was not nearly as much as he could make as a commercial fisherman, and so, he persevered.

At first, the job had been a real challenge. Compared to the fishermen he worked with, Jorgen knew his own performance those first weeks hadn't measured up. Gradually, he improved, sharpened his skills, and made fewer mistakes.

Theo's father-in-law had three sons who also worked with Theo, but it was obvious to Jorgen that Theo was in charge when his father-in-law was not present.

Hauk, the youngest of the sons, was Theo's age. He resented his brother-in-law's position in the family business and frequently muttered to one of his brothers, but loud enough for all to hear, "Why is Theo in charge? I could do a better job." Once or twice, Jorgen heard one of the older brothers silence Hauk, but for the most part, Hauk's brothers and Theo ignored these brash outbursts.

Hauk's brothers, both a few years older than Theo, worked alongside him, consulted him when problems arose, and seemed content to let Theo handle all the worries and difficult situations. *Theo's a natural,* thought Jorgen. *If we were soldiers, he'd be the general.*

Like Theo, the older brothers were married, each had children, and on most Sundays, the three men, their wives, and children met in the afternoon for middag. Theo and his wife, Anna, were hosting today's gathering and Jorgen looked forward to being there. He and Hauk had standing invitations for these get-togethers, and while Jorgen never missed them, Hauk seldom came.

Although Hauk made disparaging remarks about Theo, he never confronted him personally, perhaps fearing his father's wrath. But that didn't stop him from starting a fight with Jorgen's brother, Halvor. From one fisherman, Jorgen heard the story about the time Hauk sidled up to Halvor and punched him in the side of his head. He accused Halvor of stealing his pay. Halvor got in several good punches before Theo was able to break up the fight. Theo then handed Hauk the missing money and reminded him that he, Hauk, had given the money to a bartender a few nights before, when he was drunk and wanted to buy drinks for everyone. The bartender, a friend of Hauk's father, had kept the money and sent the drunken Hauk home.

Hauk tended to avoid Theo at work, but seemed to go out of his way to bump into Jorgen and make his job more difficult. He was sneaky enough to make sure no one witnessed the casual accidents and mean-spirited encounters, so Jorgen made it his practice to stay out of Hauk's way. It was obvious to Jorgen that Theo loved his job. He had the same passion for fishing that Jorgen had for farming. Although Jorgen acknowledged the beauty of the sea, he preferred to gaze at it with both feet planted on dry ground. He hoped that he would not have to spend too many more months on a fishing boat. But when he added up his expenses, rent, new boots (he hoped his feet were done growing), dental work (two teeth pulled) and medical bills (blood poisoning from a rusty hook), he had little savings to show for the months he had already put in. His pay should increase, however, now that he had gained some experience. Theo said that he was now pulling his own weight and had recommended him for full wages. Jorgen hoped that he could keep his expenses down by careful planning. If all went well, Jorgen thought, he would be able to book passage to America by the first of April.

Jorgen's observations of city life in Bergen, including the old baker and many other shop owners' struggles for survival, confirmed his desire to be a landowner. *I won't mind the difficulties and hard work,* he reasoned, *because I'll be doing what I love to do, on land that I own.*

Deeply absorbed in these reflections, Jorgen had paid little attention to the streets that he wandered or the shops that he passed and was barely aware of the fact that his route had lead him out of the city. He soon found himself on a broad path that led up Mount Floyen, one of the seven mountains that surround Bergen. As he climbed higher, the path narrowed and woods engulfed him. Although a stranger in these particular woods, he experienced a sense of home in the tall pines and felt energized by the fresh, clean scent. His spirits lifted as he ascended and breathed in the mountain air, identified birds by their calls, and caught sight of the familiar small animals that scampered in the underbrush.

Eventually, the path gave way to an open area, a large grassy plateau. Jorgen let out a surprised gasp when he turned and looked down on the panoramic view. It was breathtaking. He spied a large flat boulder a short distance away, climbed atop it and sat, like a Norse god surveying the kingdom. *Just like the stump at home,* Jorgen thought, *but here the view is much grander.*

Compelling as it was, however, the view was no match for the rumbling in Jorgen's stomach, so he focused his attention on unwrapping his breakfast. Gingerly, he peeled the paper from the bread and broken pieces of tart that had melded together while being carried in his large warm hand. He broke off a piece of the coarse, bland bread, now smeared with lingonberries from the tart, popped it into his mouth, and smiled in pleasure at the sweet, tangy flavor. He dabbed another piece of bread into the sticky tart, ate it, and then slowly ate the tart, savoring each bite. The taste brought back memories of lingonberries that he and Andrew had picked by the bucket during their childhood. He wrapped the last of the bread in the paper, still gooey with leftover red stickiness, and tucked it away. *When hunger strikes later, this will see me through to midday,* he thought, patting the slight bulge in his pocket.

Church bells tolled from below and Jorgen sought in vain to locate the church. The sound seemed to come from a distant stand of tall trees. It was easy, though, to pick out the Bryggen wharf where seagulls circled above boats, large and small. From where he sat, the wharf looked tidy and peaceful, not the center of chaotic activity he knew it to be. He wasn't up high enough to see them, but countless islands, patches of rich green, dotted the offshore landscape. Jorgen had sailed past these on fishing expeditions and had stepped ashore on two of them.

Fjords cut jaggedly into the coastline, their contents spilling out and mingling with the sea that stretched in varying shades of blue and gray into the horizon. The sun periodically broke through dense clouds and cast shafts of light over huge patches of water. And the waves, so fearsome up close, viewed from this height and distance were mere ripples.

Lulled by the peacefulness of his surroundings, Jorgen felt if he stayed where he was, he'd end up asleep on the rock. Before that could happen, he climbed down and made his way over to the trail that continued uphill.

"Hei," a voice called from behind him.

Jorgen paused. He hadn't seen anyone since town. Nevertheless, he assumed he was not the one being hailed and continued his climb.

"Hei, Stopp!"

Jorgen stopped, turned, and instantly recognized the figure that hurried toward him.

"Jorgen! It's you...saw you... pass our house...went to get... coat... you were too fast..."

Most of her speech, punctuated with short breaths, was conveyed as Marta sprinted across the ground that separated them. Now she stood in front of him and seemed to have run out of words and breath at the same time.

Jorgen's smile seemed destined to go clear around his head. At a loss for words, he stood there beaming at her until she regained her breath and could speak again.

"I hoped I would catch up with you, but wasn't sure you had come up this path. Was about to give up when I spotted you. I'm so happy to see you. When did you come to Bergen? How long are you staying?" Marta was so excited that the words and questions just tumbled out, one after another until she ran out of breath again.

Jorgen's spontaneous laughter effectively loosened his tongue. "Hei, Marta. It's good to see you, too." His heart raced wildly and he resisted the urge to draw her close and wrap his arms around her. Instead, he reached out and took her hands in his. They stood like this for several moments, then Jorgen led her back to the large rock where he had been sitting and helped her climb atop it.

"Sorry for gawking, Marta, but you really surprised me. It's a wonderful surprise, but I didn't expect to see anyone, least of all you. In fact I didn't even know I was coming up here; I started walking and it just sort of happened."

"Well, that's not like you," she said. "The Jorgen I remember always knew exactly where he was going."

"The Jorgen you knew wasn't miles from home." After a brief pause he continued, "I really wasn't paying much attention to the names of streets or the houses and shops that I passed. Where do you live?"

"Our house is on the last street before you turned and came down this path. I hope you have time today to stop and say hei to Mor and Far; they will be happy to see you and hear all the news from home."

"I have until middag. My plan for the next few hours was to discover places that I haven't seen, which is how I ended up on this mountain. I have plenty of time for a visit."

Jorgen studied her for a moment, "Your hair looks different. It suits you, but otherwise you haven't changed much. I'm glad."

"Takk, Jorgen, I feel the same way about you. But, your brother Andrew! I can't get over how much he has changed. He's no longer a boy."

"You've seen him? Here in Bergen?"

"Ja, several times. When he arrived here, he said he spent the first two Sundays looking for my family. After he found us, he stopped by nearly every Sunday to visit. My parents made a big fuss over him, and we enjoyed hearing him talk about you and your family. He told us about your plans and thought you'd join him soon after he got here. He seemed disappointed when you didn't come."

Jorgen shook his head. "Well, I was disappointed that he left home without me."

Marta waited for him to continue and when he didn't, she added, "He told us he was going to Christiania. Have you heard from him?"

"Nei, he said he'd write to my brother Theo, but he hasn't, so far. Do you know if he is coming back here, or does he plan on sailing to America from Christiana?"

"I asked him that, and he didn't give a definite

answer. He said there were too many 'ifs.' I'm not sure I remember them all. Your brother talked a lot and he kept coming up with different ideas for his trip. The one thing he was definite about, though, was earning money for the trip. He said he needed enough for travel and to buy good farmland in America."

"Well, at least he's sticking to one part of our plan," said Jorgen, "and he might come back here if he needs to earn more money. Theo says winter fishing is better here than in Christiania."

"So," Marta said. Her voice took on a serious tone and a small furrow appeared between her brows, "I find it puzzling that you've been here for some time and haven't looked for me." She made no attempt to fill in the awkward pause that followed her statement.

Jorgen admired her candor. It had, in fact, separated her from the other girls at school who seemed so afraid of their own opinions. *Did he want to admit to her that he had purposely avoided looking for her? Did he want to confront the feelings he had for her?* If a romance blossomed, he wouldn't ask her to leave her family to face a life of uncertainty in a foreign country. The truth was he hadn't looked for her because of his feelings for her. What they might lead to could complicate, even jeopardize, his plans for the future.

"You know why I've come to Bergen," Jorgen finally said. "I'm going to America in a few months."

"I know that," Marta responded, point-blank. "But in the meantime, is that a reason to avoid old friends?"

"You're right," he admitted. "I should have looked for you, and I'm awfully glad you're here."

They talked on for a couple of hours about all that had happened in the eighteen months since they had last seen each other. When Jorgen's stomach began to rumble he remembered the sticky chunk of bread buried in his pocket. He quickly retrieved the wrapped package and peeled back the paper, revealing a gooey mess. "It tastes better than it looks," he said, offering her the package.

Marta took it and broke off small pieces of bread for each of them. As they ate, Jorgen entertained her with his description of the baker and his weekly visits to her. Marta enjoyed his story and rewarded him with cheerful laughter, tilting her head back just enough to expose the lovely, smooth skin above her collar and the graceful curve of her neck.

★ ★ ★

Jorgen arrived at Theo's just before middag and was surprised to see Venn tied to a tree. The farm's wagon, loaded with an assortment of goods and supplies, sat alongside the house. He stopped a moment to pat the horse and heard the sounds of voices and laughter coming from inside the house. Eager to be part of the activity, he knocked at the door, which was opened by a small child. *Georg's oldest,* Jorgen remembered, but forgot the child's name. Georg and Henrik, (Theo's brothers-in-law) and their families had already arrived, and the two men were carrying on a lively conversation with Halvor.

The women all rushed about the kitchen making the final food preparations, setting dishes on the table, talking and laughing, bumping into each other, and dodging small children underfoot. Jorgen gave Anna, Theo's new wife, a quick hug and greeted the other women before joining the men.

"That's a full wagon. Looks like the family will eat well this winter," Jorgen said, addressing his brother. He grabbed Halvor's extended hand. "When did you come to town?"

"Got here Friday night, have to go back tomorrow after I get the last few things on the list."

Theo called out a greeting without turning around. He was in the process of cutting down one of two large herring that hung in the fireplace.

"Need some help? I'll get the other one." Jorgen offered.

"Nei, takk, I roasted it a short while ago and only just hung it." Theo responded, "It needs more smoking time."

Theo brought the fish to the table, placed it on a platter, and then looked at Jorgen. "You are smiling," he said, "I could hear it in your voice when you came in. I think it's the first time I've seen you smile since you arrived in Bergen."

Anna called everyone to the table and, after a brief blessing, Theo picked up the thread of his earlier observation. "So, tell us the secret of your good mood today? What happy event occurred? Did you dig up a buried treasure or find a new rooming house?"

"Or find a new job?" asked Georg.

"He's just happy to see his oldest, best-looking brother," said Halvor.

"Maybe he bought his ticket to America." added Henrik.

"Oh stop now, all of you," said Anna. "I don't know Jorgen all that well, but I recognize the grin he's wearing. It's the same one Theo wore the night he asked me to marry him. I think Jorgen's found himself a girl."

"I did run into an old friend, today," Jorgen said, hoping his casual attitude would end the discussion.

Fortunately, attention at the table was diverted to an upended glass of milk. Some at the table scrambled to avoid the sudden river headed for their laps, while others grabbed napkins and attempted to mop up the mess.

Just as order was reestablished at the table, the front door was thrown open and Hauk lurched in. "A knock would have been appropriate," chided Georg, "and," he added, as his younger brother staggered into the room, "you forgot to close the door."

"I don't need you to tell me what to do." He took a

few steps back and gave the door a shove with the side of his foot, closing it with a bang.

"Hauk!" Georg called out. His warning tone seemed to go unnoticed.

"I'm hungry Anna, you got any food left?"

Hauk's clothing had a rumpled, slept-in appearance and his shirt was improperly buttoned so that the shirttails hung unevenly. He was unshaven and, judging by his dirty hands, unwashed.

Theo was about to say something but Anna shook her head, her lips pursed in disgust, so he kept quiet. She got up from the table to get her brother a plate.

"You're late," Anna said. "We didn't think you were coming, so we didn't set a place for you. There's plenty of food, but I'm afraid the only empty chair is the rocker over in the corner. You can wash out back."

"Well, if that's the way it is, I won't come over any more."

Jorgen noted Hauk's slurred speech.

"But since I'm already here, I'll eat." He plopped down in Anna's chair and pushed her plate of food off to the side, upsetting the same glass that had just been refilled. It spilled into Anna's plate.

"You've been drinking, and I think it's time for you to leave," Theo said. He stood and walked around the table to stand beside Hauk's chair.

Hauk made no move to leave; he simply looked up at Theo.

"Now!" Theo said.

Hauk's two older brothers stood up at their places and stared at their younger brother.

The sneer on Hauk's face vanished for a second when he saw Halvor sitting across the table. He quickly looked away from Halvor and into Jorgen's startled eyes. "What's the matter, cotter, don't you want to help them throw me out?"

"No one is throwing you out," said Theo as he took a step back from Hauk's chair. "You're going to get up and leave quietly, this minute." Theo's eyes were blazing. He didn't raise his voice, but Jorgen had never seen him look so fearsome.

One of the little ones started to cry, and then another. "It's all right, children, Uncle Hauk is leaving now," said Georg, "and then we'll finish eating." Georg walked to the door and held it open while Hauk sauntered towards him. Those at the table comforted the frightened children and, once again, began to sop up spilled milk. Jorgen overheard Georg's whispered, "Go home and sleep this off. We don't want your company if you're going to be rude, disrespectful and frighten the children."

"I didn't frighten the children," Hauk hissed. He jerked his thumb toward Theo, "He's the scary one!"

★ ★ ★

When Jorgen arrived at work the following morning, hc was relieved to see that Hauk was not there.

"He's not coming," Theo said, noticing Jorgen's furtive glances. "His father was furious when he heard about his behavior last night. He told Hauk he was off the boats for two weeks and has to stop drinking if he wants to come back. In the meantime, he has to work in the warehouse, helping the women salt and pack herring into barrels."

"I'm not sure if that's a cure for drinking or a reason for drinking," said Jorgen. "I'm just happy he's not here."

The next few weeks were almost pleasant: no Hauk at work and Marta on Sundays. Jorgen's life had definitely taken a turn for the better. His new Sunday morning routine now took him to Marta's, following his customary stop at the baker's. The two young people attended church with Marta's parents, then went off on their own to explore the city or hike in the mountains. Marta's mother usually invited Jorgen to stay for middag, an invitation he accepted every other week.

Aware of Jorgen's friendship with Marta, Theo and Anna told him to bring her along on his visits to see them. Jorgen had yet to take advantage of their offer. To bring Marta to a family meal was to publicly acknowledge a relationship that both elated and perplexed him. He was comfortable with the relaxed atmosphere that surrounded him at Marta's house. She and her parents accepted the fact that he planned to emigrate and the four of them simply enjoyed their time together each Sunday.

But at Theo's house, his relationship with her was a constant cause for curiosity, innuendo, and good-natured banter.

"She's probably too good looking for Jorgen. He doesn't bring her here because he's afraid he'll look ugly compared to us."

Henrik's boast was countered by Georg's assertion, "Ja, and she's a teacher. She probably corrects his grammar."

"Or maybe she's the quiet sort, like my little brother. Maybe they don't say anything," Theo said, winking at Jorgen.

Jorgen laughed along with the others. He knew their teasing was just that, nothing more. Still, he wasn't eager to increase speculations by bringing her to meet them. He told himself and Marta that he was protecting her from the taunts and silliness of his inquisitive family, a justification that Marta tolerated for a few weeks.

★ ★ ★

Jorgen felt the chill in the air. He could feel winter closing in as he and Marta walked to Sunday service in early December. Her parents did not go with them; they were recovering from influenza, an epidemic that had felled many in recent weeks.

"What are your plans for middag? Are your brother

and his wife well?"

"Ja," Jorgen responded. "They're both fine. I think a couple of Anna's nieces and nephews were ill this week, but those who are still healthy will be at my brother's house. He invited us both, again."

"What did you tell him?"

"What I always tell him. Perhaps."

"You mean they never know if I'm coming or not? They must think I'm terribly rude." A frown bunched up her eyebrows, and she caught her lower lip between her teeth.

After a pause, she continued. "I really don't think your brother and his wife would be unkind. I'd like to go. I haven't seen Theo in years, and I'd like to meet his wife and the men you work with."

Jorgen was reluctant. "Shouldn't you stay home to fix middag for your parents?"

"I made a large pot of soup yesterday, that's all they feel up to eating and there's plenty left for today. But, if you don't want me to go..." she said, pretending to wipe away tears, " I suppose I could stay home and eat soup."

"Nei, that's not necessary," Jorgen grinned responding to her pantomime, "I'd love to spend the rest of the day with you. We'll go to Theo's for middag. But don't say I didn't warn you!"

After church, they walked up the mountain path returning to the rock they now claimed as their own. They sat for a while watching the antics of two puffins.

"They look well dressed," said Marta, "like they're wearing dark-hooded capes. But those feet and beaks kind of ruin the formal look." As if on cue, one of the puffins opened its large, colorful beak to protest her statement.

"And a voice that lacks dignity," added Jorgen. "It sounds like the buzz of a giant and crazed honeybee." He and Marta laughed when both puffins responded noisily.

"Most puffins have migrated for winter," said Jorgen. "I wonder why these two are still here."

Marta sighed. "Maybe they just can't bring themselves to leave such a lovely spot."

"I know how they feel," said Jorgen. "When I look at the mountains and valleys, the cliffs and fjords, this beautiful view, I ask myself, how can I leave Norway?"

"Then why are you going so far away from the land and people that you love?"

This was the same question Far had asked him, but unlike Far, Marta seemed to be interested in his feelings and really wished to understand his reasons for emigrating. He attempted to explain his passion for farming, how he loved the smell of damp soil, the sight of a field ripe for harvest, the sound of cows lowing in the early morning, the taste of eggs fresh from the nest. He explained how he hoped one day to raise his children, as he had been raised, but on land that he owned.

Jorgen finished by saying, "That's just not possible here in Norway. I want to own a lot of land, enough to give some to each of my children, not just the oldest."

"Well, I'm glad to hear that marriage is in your plans." Marta said when he had stopped talking.

"Um, ja, well, someday, I guess," he stammered then changed the subject.

"I have talked to men who have been to America. Although they were mostly sailors and ship captains, they have good stories to tell. They say there are jobs, good-paying jobs, and there is plenty of farmland for sale. I talked to a man who used to live here in Bergen. After settling in Pennsylvania, he came back here to convince his parents to return to America with him."

"Is that where you want to live?" In Pennsylvania?"

"I haven't figured that out yet. The man from Pennsylvania lived for a few years in Kendall, a small New York town, when he first arrived in America. Andrew and I heard about Kendall and talked about starting out there. A lot of our countrymen have settled there. The man said New

York has mountains, rivers, lakes, and a magnificent waterfall so beautiful it would take your breath away. But, the man said he missed his family and wanted them to join him in America.

"That will also be difficult for me," Jorgen continued. "I know I will miss my family and friends. I thought that I would have Andrew with me, but that may not happen now."

Marta turned to face him. "Maybe someone else will go with you."

"Well, I have thought about asking Theo and Anna, or perhaps I could wait a few more years until Niels is old enough. He enjoys farming and might want to own land somewhere in America. It is a lifetime commitment. It's not easy to ask others to change their dreams to help me follow mine."

Marta gave him a sidelong glance but said nothing.

One of the puffins attempted a landing nearby with comical, almost catastrophic results. "For such good flyers, they sure are clumsy when it comes to placing both feet on the ground," she observed.

"Well, look at those," said Jorgen, pointing to the bird's big red feet. " I'm sure they are useful for swimming but, you are right, not much help otherwise.

They both laughed as the puffin struggled to get airborne again. *I'm just like them,* thought Jorgen. *Leaving is difficult for me, too.*

★ ★ ★

Faced with six days of fishing before the next Sunday dawned, Jorgen was usually at his gloomiest on Monday mornings, but his mood was light on this Monday morning. His thoughts were diverted from the chilly December weather as he relived the previous day's events. He chided himself for his reluctance to bring Marta to the Sunday get-togethers. Yesterday couldn't have gone better. Within minutes of their arrival, it seemed like Marta had always been a part of the family.

Before going to Theo's for middag, they had returned home to see how Marta's parents were feeling. Assured of their comfort, Marta disappeared for several minutes. She reappeared, sweeping into the room like the breeze off the sea, wearing a dress that Jorgen had not seen before.

"My holiday dress," she said, responding to Jorgen's smile and raised eyebrows. "I was saving it to wear on Jul, but this occasion is special, too."

She looked stunning. Jorgen couldn't take his eyes off her. The dark blue dress complimented her pale ivory skin and grayish blue eyes. He was startled by the not unpleasant feelings of arousal that stirred within him. This wasn't supposed to happen, or rather he didn't want it to happen. His heart raced and he could feel the red creep into his face and enflame his cheeks. Attempting to regain his composure, he walked over to the window and looked out.

"Thought I'd check for more puffins," he said. "I think one just flew in."

"That's not exactly the look I was going for," Marta said, laughing. "I hope that I don't trip over my big red feet."

Remembering the ridiculous puffin comment, from the day before, Jorgen groaned. Why hadn't he just told her how pretty she looked?

"Marta." Jorgen said her name aloud and sighed. In the time it had taken to cover the distance from his rooming house to the wharf, his mood had vacillated from joy to anxiety. Perhaps he should stop seeing Marta. He was falling in love with her and felt that she was developing feelings for him. *I am definitely leaving Bergen,* he reminded himself, *and the last thing I want to do is hurt her.*

Jorgen arrived at work and all thoughts of Marta vanished when he saw that the seksring was being readied for use. Worse yet, there was Hauk, standing in the stern.

The large, six-oared boat meant that they would be

going out on the open sea, most likely for a two, possibly three-day fishing trip.

"Dress for the weather tomorrow," had been Theo's parting words the day before, when Jorgen escorted Marta out the door. Linked arm in arm and overcome with the nearness of her, Jorgen had given no thought to his brother's comment.

At least I remembered to wear my warmest clothes, Jorgen now thought. He hiked up his collar and yanked his hat even lower over his ears at the thought of how cold he was going to be in the hours to come.

He drew closer to the boat and two figures, who had not been visible before stood up in the boat. Jorgen was relieved to see Theo and Georg and waved at them. *They must have been checking the sails and nets,* Jorgen assumed, as the two men had been crouched in the fore section of the boat.

"I didn't want to say anything and ruin your day yesterday, but we decided that we need to fish farther out. The catch hasn't been good closer to shore. Also, Henrik has come down with influenza." Theo said, nodding grimly in Hauk's direction. Hauk was storing hampers of food that Jorgen assumed Anna and Georg's wife had prepared for the crew. Hauk looked up from his task, fixed his eyes on Jorgen, and his lips curled in an enigmatic smile. Jorgen felt a chill creep down his back and quickly looked away.

Three more men arrived, and when the final preparations were completed, the group shoved off. Theo was at the helm, Hauk and Georg manned oars directly in front of him, Jorgen was partnered with a friend of Theo's, and two men, the Brastad brothers, sat at oars in front of Jorgen. Jorgen had fished with all these men and, except for Hauk, liked their company. Although the boat had a small sail, the wind was not favorable for its use, so the men put their backs into rowing. Jorgen had great upper body strength and enjoyed the physical exertion. With Hauk sitting behind him out of sight, Jorgen's attention was drawn to the beauty that surrounded him as the boat made its way around the islands clustered along the coastline. The combined effort of the six men easily moved the 28-foot-boat through the water, and Bryggen wharf quickly disappeared from view. The hour was still early and conversation sparse, each man left to his own thoughts as they moved father away from shore. Jorgen's musing ranged from memories of home to wondering about Andrew's whereabouts, but his thoughts eventually returned to Marta and how she had made his time in Bergen bearable.

Coats were cast aside when exertion warmed the men, and the hours passed with mind-numbing monotony. To keep his crew focused, Theo periodically called out, "Watch for the oil, look for the shine!" These were reminders that oily areas on the surface or a phosphorescent shimmer below heralded the presence of herring. The tedium of this vigil was made more difficult by the glare of the bright sun that too frequently popped out from behind large cumulus clouds. The sun's brilliance reflected off the waves and caused the men to squint beneath the brims of their caps. Like rings that indicate the age of a tree, the squint lines on their faces bespoke the years these men had spent at sea. Jorgen's face, in comparison, was smooth as a baby's.

Towards midday the sky thickened, bringing blessed relief from the bright glare, but the wind picked up and rowing became more difficult. Fatigue and a dull ache was just beginning to settle between Jorgen's shoulder blades when one of the brothers sitting in front of him yelled and pointed to birds circling the water at a distance off his side of the boat. Theo turned the boat and it was soon in position near a broad oily patch. They had stumbled upon a substantial number of herring, probably enough to fill the shot room, the space near the back of the boat where the catch was stored. The men worked quickly to get the nets out. Jorgen's job was to attach buoys, at intervals, to the net, one end of which was attached to the boat and the rest was strung out in a straight line, falling curtain-like, into the sea. Rowing ceased, allowing the boat to drift as the fish below became trapped in the meshed net. The lull in activity once the nets were out gave the men an opportunity to feast on the two-day supply of food, knowing that a good catch ensured they would be going home in the morning.

Many hours passed, and darkness had fallen before the catch was entirely secured. Although they weren't that far from shore, the night was too dark and navigation too difficult to attempt the trip home. The exhausted fishermen wrapped themselves in blankets and settled in, as comfortably as the boat's confines would allow, for what they all knew would be a not-so-comfortable night's sleep.

The cool, stiff breeze rocked the boat, but the fishermen were quite used to that. One by one, the men drifted off to sleep, as evidenced by a chorus of snoring, until Jorgen was the only one still awake. He found he couldn't get comfortable. A headache that had begun in the late afternoon throbbed at his temples. His back hurt; in fact, his whole body ached. He twisted and turned, shifted his weight first one way then another, and stretched out his long legs. His boots made contact with something soft, and it moved.

"For God's sake Jorgen, if you don't stop flopping about I'll throw you in with the rest of the stinkin' fish," Hauk snarled.

"Sorry," Jorgen mumbled. He drew in his legs and pulled off his boots. He wrapped himself in a woolen blanket, but still he shivered uncontrollably. A few minutes later, just as suddenly as the chills had started, they ended, and Jorgen began to warm up. Before long he felt so warm, he no longer needed the blanket. He tried to lie still, but as the hours passed, this became impossible. The pain in his back and neck was no longer merely bothersome; it was severe.

Jorgen was ill. He came to this realization with the onset of nausea. At first just a vague uneasy feeling, it grew stronger, knotting his stomach and watering his mouth with bitter tasting saliva. The wind had intensified and more powerful waves buffeted the small boat. Whether it was the illness, seasickness, or a combination of both, Jorgen was finally forced to his feet. His sea legs were weak and wobbly. He hung on tightly as he leaned over the side of the boat and spewed the contents of his stomach into the sea. The feeling of relief was short lived, as the chills and fever returned. Nausea and vomiting continued throughout the night, as did Hauk's whispered curses.

The hours dragged cruelly. As dark, wretched minutes passed, Jorgen's feverish mind slipped in and out of despair responding to the message of the endless night: morning will never come. However, into the waning moonlight, morning did arrive, had to arrive. It crept over the turbulent water and outlined the boat, but its approach was lost to Jorgen. He dragged his weakened body to his feet once again, and slumped precariously over the side of the boat. He retched violently, his eyes shut tight against the salty sea spray whipped up by waves that slammed into the boat.

When hands clamped around his feet, Jorgen was grateful to whoever was holding him steady in the pitching, rolling boat. But the comfort did not last long. Before he knew what was happening, those helping hands had upset his balance and, to his horror, pitched him overboard. Instinctively, he attempted to call out but was only able to belch out a low, barely audible, guttural sound.

Jorgen 's body slid into the sea without a splash. He managed to right himself and bobbed to the top. Gasping for air, he took in a mouthful of seawater and choked. His limbs stiffened in the water and his mind, shocked into alertness, had lost control. As he sunk beneath the water's surface, he heard the muffled call, "Man overboard!" Then, nothing but icy cold blackness.

Five

December 1848

For days, Jorgen slipped in and out of consciousness. At times, he was vaguely aware of people coming and going, attending to him, asking him questions, and sitting by his bedside. He'd open his eyes, but he couldn't focus them. The effort exhausted him, and he would fall back asleep and into dreams, some frightening and some just strange.

Was he dreaming? Andrew seemed to be standing a short distance away and kept repeating the same thing over and over.

"I'm here, Jorgen, talk to me. I know you can hear me. Talk to me, Jorgen."

It was maddening! Jorgen answered over and over, but Andrew couldn't hear him.

"He's looking right at me, why can't he say something?" Andrew sounded concerned. Someone standing in shadow responded, but Jorgen couldn't hear what was said.

Andrew, I said I hear you, I'm glad you're back. Why don't you hear me?

Andrew gave Jorgen a long, sad look. He turned from the bed and said to the shadow, "I'll be back again tomorrow, maybe he'll be awake," and he walked from the room.

Jorgen stared at the spot where Andrew had stood. He was confused, but mostly he was exhausted; sleep overtook him again. When he awoke, Marta was sitting next to him, her head bowed over needlework. She glanced at him and when she saw that he was looking at her, she lowered the sewing into her lap. She reached over, picked up his hand and squeezed it.

"Mother is making you soup," she said. "Can you smell it?"

"Ja, I can," he replied, startled at the sound of his own

voice. It didn't sound like him.

Marta was startled, too. She jumped up, her sewing falling to the floor. "Theo," she called, "come quickly, Jorgen's awake!"

She sat and took up his hand again. "Oh, Jorgen," she said, tears springing into her eyes, "We've been so worried. You've been dreadfully ill and the doctor didn't know what else to do for you. He's been to see you every day."

Theo ran into the room and knelt at the other side of the bed. He picked up Jorgen's other hand. The gesture surprised Jorgen, and when he looked into Theo's face, his appearance surprised him even more. He looked ages older, tired and haggard with worry lines added to the creases in the rugged fisherman's face. His eyes, clouded with concern, lacked their usual merry sparkle. It alarmed Jorgen to see the stern, almost grim expression on his brother's normally pleasant face.

"Are you all right, Theo?" His voice cracked like it had when he was a young teen.

"I'm fine, now" said Theo drawing Jorgen's head closer until Jorgen could feel his brother's warm breath on his ear. "Thank God." he said. "This is the best Jul present ever." He patted Jorgen's forehead, stood, and continued, "You've been desperately sick for weeks. We weren't sure you if you would recover."

"I remember being sick on the boat." Jorgen said, his voice was hoarse and weak.

"Most likely you had influenza which developed into pneumonia as a result of nearly drowning. We'll talk more about that when you're feeling stronger."

Finally, Theo smiled. "Gud Jul, Jorgen."

"Today is Jul?" Jorgen said skeptically. He struggled to reset his mental calendar, his eyes sweeping the unfamiliar room. "Where am I?"

"You're with us." Marta's mother said as she entered the room. She was carrying a tray that contained a bowl of steaming soup. "I'm happy to see you're awake, Jorgen." She set the tray on a bedside table.

"After your accident, you stayed with Anna and me. But when Mrs. Aksdal heard what happened, she insisted we bring you here," said Theo.

"Ja," Mrs. Aksdal continued, "Theo and Anna were taking good care of you, Jorgen, but you were in their bed, and they had to sleep on the floor. We have plenty of room, so I convinced your brother to bring you here.

"Now, Marta," she said, taking the soup off the tray, "Why don't you help Jorgen with this. I'm sure he must be hungry."

Mrs. Aksdal left the room and Theo started to say goodbye but Jorge stopped him. "Wait Theo, before you go, tell me what happened. The last thing I remember is going down in the sea. How did I get out?"

"We pulled you and Georg out with a rope."

"Georg fell in, too?"

"Nei, Georg jumped in to save you. He had just awakened when he saw Hauk grab your feet and toss you overboard."

"Oh!" Jorgen was shocked at what he heard, but Theo continued.

"Georg grabbed one end of the rope and told the Brastad brothers to hold tight to the other end. I heard the commotion and got to my feet just as Georg yelled 'man overboard' and jumped into the sea. The brothers told me that Georg had gone in to rescue you. Lucky for you that you weren't wearing those heavy boots of yours or you would have sunk straight to the bottom."

"I remember," Jorgen said, "I couldn't sleep...I hurt all over and was sick. Hauk was angry at me...someone grabbed my legs...and then I was falling."

Talking had tired Jorgen; he closed his eyes momentarily, and then continued. "Is Georg all right? Did he get pneumonia, too?"

"Georg is fine. He's been here to see you a few times.

He'll probably stop by later tonight. Now eat your soup before you fall asleep. Anna is waiting for me. She sends her love and will be happy to hear that you're awake and feeling better. I'll be back tomorrow."

Theo started out of the room, then turned. "Andrew's back. He was here a while ago, but I'm sure he'll be back as soon as he hears the good news." Theo gave a small wave and left.

While Jorgen sipped his soup, Marta told him about the days that he had spent at her house, and what the doctor had said.

"He thinks it will be weeks before you are strong enough to go back to fishing. Mamma thinks you shouldn't. She says that Pappa needs help in the shop, and you can have a job when you are feeling up to it. You won't have to work outdoors, and Pappa has so much work that he needs to hire someone anyway. I know she is planning to ask you, so I thought I would give you time to think about it."

Jorgen nodded and smiled as she continued. "Mamma was so sure that you would get better, even when the doctor wasn't so certain. She told him, 'I knew his grandfather. He just about lost his leg in an accident and developed a terrible fever that should have killed him. But he survived, and Jorgen will, too.'"

She took the empty soup bowl from his hands and he fell back onto the pillow. "I'm sorry, Marta," he said, barely above a whisper, "I need to close my eyes for a minute." And with that, he was asleep.

★ ★ ★

Jorgen's eyes had not yet opened when he heard Marta's voice.

"I'll do no such thing," she said.

That was followed by a familiar laugh. "Raise one lid, just a little to make sure he's still in there. I used to do it to

112

him all the time," Andrew urged, still chuckling.

"And you almost poked my eye out!" said Jorgen. He opened his eyes and grinned at his brother. "I still owe you for that."

"You should have seen the little coward," Jorgen said, addressing Marta. "He ran from me like his hair was on fire."

"Well I was afraid it would be on fire if you caught me, but looking at you now, tucked in bed, I think I'm safe for a while."

"It's so good to see you two together," said Marta.

"And I think it's good to see you two together," said Andrew. His words caused both Marta and Jorgen to blush.

"You've seen all the togetherness you're going to see this morning," said Marta. She rose from her place next to the bed and pointed to the chair indicating that Andrew should take her place.

"I'll leave you two to suffer your own company. Mor and I are making lefse this morning. If you can keep from poking each other's eyes out, I might give you some."

She shook her finger at Andrew as they crossed paths, and Andrew came to sit in her vacated chair. The boys' laughter followed her out of the room.

The gaiety subsided and the room grew silent as the two boys studied each other. *Andrew looks fit*, Jorgen thought. *He's put on weight and he definitely looks older.* It was difficult to tell, lying down, but Jorgen suspected that Andrew had grown an inch or two.

Being together again, it almost seemed like Andrew had never left, and yet so much had happened in his absence. Looking at his brother now, it was impossible for Jorgen to dredge up even a shred of the anger that had consumed him on that night long ago when Andrew left home.

Andrew seemed to be lost in his own thoughts. Although he was looking in his direction, Jorgen knew Andrew no longer saw him.

"How did you like Christiania?" Jorgen said, at last,

breaking the silence.

Jorgen's question jolted Andrew back to the present.

"It's a busy place, too many people, but the fishing was good for a while. That's why I came back; it's better here in the winter." Once he got started, the old Andrew took over. One thing that hadn't changed was his ability to talk Jorgen's ear off. Jorgen had to admit, however, that Andrew's stories were still captivating, at times exciting or amusing, but always entertaining.

Andrew finally paused and Jorgen thought that he had, at last, run out of tales. The silence seemed to swell until it lay heavy in the room. It reminded Jorgen of what it is like outside after a big snowfall. The room even felt chilly.

The genial grin on Andrew's face slowly dissolved, his lips settling into a grim line. His eyes took on a hard, icy blue look and his nostrils flared like Mr. Gunderson's cranky old bull. The transformation was astounding. When Andrew finally spoke, his voice was strangely vicious.

"I've been thinking about how we make Hauk pay for what he did to you. We are not going to let him get away with this."

There was something more than anger in Andrew's voice. This was a side of Andrew that Jorgen had never seen. Andrew had always been the one to give others the benefit of the doubt. Vengeance was not a part of who he was.

This was not good. Jorgen's mind raced as he tried to think of what to say. He returned his brother's hard gaze and, when he answered, he imitated the harshness of his brother's speech.

"I suppose we could kill him."

The stare down continued as each assessed the other's will to do such a thing. Jorgen hadn't had much time to think about what Hauk had done to him, and what action, if any, he planned to take against him. It definitely would not include killing him and, given his present condition, there was nothing he would be able to do in the near future. For now, though, he was worried his brother might act rashly out of a sense of duty to family.

"I say," Jorgen continued, "we lay a trap for Hauk somewhere out of town, lure him there, and when we've snared him, skin him, chop up the rest, and sell the pieces for fish bait." He watched with relief as tension drained from Andrew's face. His eyes softened and the start of a smile formed on his lips.

Exhausted from the conversation, Jorgen fell back on the pillow, a wan smile creasing his face and disappearing into the hollows of his sunken cheeks.

"We'll do that!" Andrew said, and began to laugh. He stood and looked down at the still grinning Jorgen. "My brother, the big trapper who could never stand the sight of an injured animal. As long as the Dovre stands, I think Hauk is safe from you."

"And I hope he's safe from you. I'd hate to think of you going to jail over the sorry likes of Hauk."

The boys lapsed into silence. Jorgen assumed his brother was still contemplating Hauk's fate. As for himself, Jorgen couldn't help wondering if Hauk really intended to drown him or was too drunk to consider the consequences of his action. He knew Hauk had been drinking that day out of a flask he kept hidden inside his coat. He was sneaky enough to do it when Theo and Georg weren't looking but didn't seem to care if Jorgen observed the forbidden activity.

"Theo and I haven't had a chance to talk about this," said Jorgen, "It has to put him in a difficult spot with his wife and father-in-law."

"No," said Andrew. "As luck would have it, Hauk's father was at the wharf when you all returned that day, and he was alarmed that you had to be carried off the boat. Georg was wrapped in blankets and he, too, needed help getting off the boat. You know, he came close to drowning along with you."

Jorgen nodded his head, indicating that he knew that

Georg had saved his life.

"It's a good thing the old man heard the story firsthand from Georg because he had a hard time believing that a son of his could throw a shipmate to the sea. Hauk tried to deny the story, but one of the Brastad brothers backed up everything that Georg said. Hauk's father punched Hauk and knocked him flat to the ground. Then he took out some dalers and threw them down next to Hauk. He told him that he didn't deserve his wages, that the money was to ensure that he left town before he got thrown into jail. He told Hauk to go home and say goodbye to his mother, that Hauk wasn't welcome at home any more."

Andrew paced the room while he continued. "Hauk's been hanging around the wharf trying to find a ship that will hire him. But word of what he did to you spread, and no captain will take a chance on him."

Andrew stopped at the foot of Jorgen's bed and looked down at him.

"I think Hauk belongs in prison. Theo and Georg have decided not to have him arrested, but if you decide differently, they will support your decision. Theo's already talked to a lawyer."

"Theo told you that?"

"Not exactly."

"And what about Anna? Hauk is reckless and mean, but he's still her brother."

"Hold on, I'll get to her."

"I sailed into Bergen several days after the incident, the day you were moved here from Theo's. When I helped load you into Theo's wagon, he told me part of the story, but he became so upset that he couldn't finish. You were still unconscious, and I think Theo blamed himself for letting Hauk on board that day. When he couldn't go on with what had happened to you, Anna finished the story for him. She said she thought her father should have had her brother arrested. But since he didn't, she hoped that Hauk would leave town and never come back. She thinks that Hauk has become so dangerous that it's only a question of time before he kills someone.

"Yesterday, when you finally woke up, and Theo came back at middag to tell us the news, Georg said that if Hauk was still around and you decided to have him arrested, he would testify on your behalf. Theo was nodding so I guess he agrees with Georg."

"So, Jorgen, we're back to my question. What are we going to do about Hauk? If you want him arrested, I'll see to it tomorrow."

Jorgen was relieved to find out that Andrew wasn't planning to take matters into his own hands. Although he thought Hauk deserved to spend some time behind bars, he wasn't anxious to be the one to put his employer's son, not to mention Anna, Georg, and Henrik's brother, in jail.

"Thanks for the offer, little brother, but I can fight my own battles. I think being banished from his home and spurned by all the fishermen in town is punishment enough for now. I don't think our paths will cross again. If he's smart, he'll leave town and start over somewhere else. And speaking of leaving town, you have yet to say what your plans are."

"You're changing the subject."

"That subject is closed, for now."

Andrew considered this for a moment. He wasn't ready to move on.

"Your plans, Andrew?"

"I don't know," Andrew began, reluctantly. "With you and Hauk gone, Theo asked if I could help out for a while, at least until his father-in-law finishes the work he started on his house. Fishing is good money, and I haven't saved as much as I thought I would."

He paused and Jorgen thought he was getting ready to bring Hauk up again, but Andrew surprised him.

"Remember how we thought we could save enough

money in six months time? Well, its been nine months and I think I might just have enough. It wouldn't hurt to have a few extra dalers to invest in our land, and I don't wish to cross the Atlantic in winter, so," Andrew continued, "I guess the answer to your question is, I plan to help Theo until the weather breaks in the spring, then I'll go home to say goodbye. That was always in my plan. I'd like to leave for America on the first of June."

"You've got quite a head start on me," said Jorgen.

"And it will be a while before you can go back to fishing," Andrew said. "I'm not pushing you to join me, Jorgen. Theo told me how long you've been here in Bergen, so I have some idea about how much you've saved. I know it will take you months to save what you'll need. I have two friends from Christiania who will emigrate with me. They want to settle in Canada, and there's a ship we can take right out of Bergen that goes there. I'll keep in touch, and you can join me when you're able."

"That's quite a plan; I didn't know you had it in you," Jorgen said.

"I'll take that as a compliment."

"It was meant as one," Jorgen continued. "Bestefar's faith in you has proved true. When you left home, he said that he was confident that you could take care of yourself. I wasn't so sure, and I know Far thought you were too young to be on your own."

"That's not surprising. Far always talked to us like we were small boys."

Jorgen nodded his head. "As for my immediate plans," he said, "I'm not going back to fishing. Mrs. Aksdal has offered me a job here. I'm going to accept it as soon as I've talked to Theo."

"Mr. Aksdal offered me a job soon after I arrived here," said Andrew.

"Yes, I know, Marta told me that you turned him down because you enjoyed fishing."

"Well, that, and the fact that I enjoy being outdoors and working with Theo. He taught me so much. I was never good at cabinetmaking and carpentry; that was always your specialty. I know Theo will be happy for you. He knows that you never really cared for fishing. And don't worry, he won't have any trouble replacing you. Theo is respected by all the fishermen around here; there are always some good men wanting to sign on with him."

"Speaking of Theo, I promised to meet him at the wharf mid morning. He heard about a good spot for beach seining. Says the fish are practically jumping into the nets."

"Will you be on the beach or in the boat?"

"I'd rather be in the boat with Theo, but he may need me on shore."

"Well, at least it's warmer on shore." Jorgen was suddenly seized by a fit of coughing. Andrew tried to help by pounding on his brother's back. Gradually the coughing subsided and Jorgen lay back on the pillow, totally spent.

"I'll be back," Andrew said, rising from the chair. "Take care of yourself."

"I will, and thanks for coming."

The visit with Andrew had exhausted Jorgen to the extent that he could only manage to raise his hand slightly off the bed for a feeble goodbye wave.

★ ★ ★

On all those Sundays when Jorgen had spent time with the Aksdals, he had noticed that Mr. Aksdal seemed content to let his wife and daughter do the talking. Jorgen had assumed that when they started working together, Mr. Aksdal would be more conversant with him, but that was not the case. Very few words passed between them as they worked to fill the orders, which Mrs. Aksdal took from customers who called at their front door. She was thorough and her notes included measurements and all the details specified by the customer. Although he didn't talk much, Mr. Aksdal had a pleasant way about him. Often, when Jorgen chanced to look up from his work, he found the older man smiling at him. When this happened the first few times, Jorgen smiled back and tried to start conversation, but Mr. Aksdal simply smiled in reply and went back to his work. After a few attempts, Jorgen gave up and now returned the smile in silence.

The job was going extremely well and was more profitable than Jorgen had imagined. After a few half days, he felt well enough to put in a full day's work. He was exhausted by day's end and was grateful that Mrs. Aksdal had insisted that he continue living with them so she could put some 'meat on his bones' as she said to nosy neighbors who wondered at the propriety of his living under the same roof as Marta.

"I'll stay under two conditions," Jorgen had said. "First, Marta and I will trade rooms so she can be in her own bedroom, and second, I'll pay rent just like I did at Mrs. Steen's."

"It's too cold in the attic for someone recovering from pneumonia," Mrs. Aksdal fretted. When she saw that Jorgen was determined to stay up there, she deposited a huge pile of quilts on his cot.

When he learned that Jorgen intended to stay on at the Aksdal's, Andrew moved into Jorgen's room at Mrs. Steen's.

"The old crow wanted me to pay for a battered chair that she claims you broke."

It was an early Sunday morning and Andrew was up in Jorgen's attic room. "When I told her I would discuss it with you before I paid her anything, she got angry and said that she would rent to someone else. 'Go ahead,' I told her, 'but I have enough money to pay for two months in advance. I'm sure that I can find something else.'"

"Young man," Andrew continued, imitating Mrs. Steen's clipped speech and superior tone, "perhaps I've been a bit hasty. Your brother may have broken the chair, but I don't think it was in good repair when he moved in."

"In that case, I told her, perhaps you can replace it with a chair that I can actually sit on."

"Well, I wouldn't hold my breath," said Jorgen, "She's as stingy with a daler as Mor's hens are with their eggs."

"That could be," Andrew retorted, "but there was a new chair outside my door this morning."

"Well, it's good to see you have not lost your charm with the ladies. When Theo and Halvor returned home last spring and told us about your job with Mr. Knudson, they said he has daughters. Did you leave any broken hearts in Christiania?"

"Well, actually," Andrew confessed, "I was the one with the broken heart. Mr. Knudson's youngest daughter and I were attracted to each other from the first time we met. But when I told her my plans, she said that I was too adventurous for her, and that she could never emigrate. I thought that over time I would be able to persuade her, but she always changed the subject and refused to even talk about it with me. I still care for her, but finally realized that if I actually did convince her to go and she was unhappy once we were there, I would feel guilty, and probably end up bringing her back home. I want someone like your Marta. She would go to the ends of the earth with you."

"My Marta?" Jorgen raised an eyebrow.

"Don't act like you don't know what I'm talking about. You've been in love with Marta for years, and it's obvious she feels the same way about you. Surely you've asked her to marry you?"

Jorgen's mouth was open; he was about to say something.

"You have asked her, haven't you?"

"Nei," Jorgen finally responded, shaking his head and looking away.

Andrew waited for Jorgen to continue, but his brother

remained silent. "You'll never find another like her. I'd ask her myself, but I know she'd refuse me. She loves you Jorgen. I think she'd go anywhere with you."

"That's just it." Jorgen said. "I know she would. But if you could have seen the look on Mor's face when I told her that you had left...I'm not trying to make you feel guilty, Andrew. I just don't want to break up Marta's family. She is her mother's only daughter, and they are very close. Mrs. Aksdal has been very good to me. I can't repay her by taking away her only daughter."

"Marta has a brother back in Voss. The Aksdals could go back and live with him." Andrew countered. "You should at least ask Marta and not make the decision for her. After all she has done for you in the past weeks, I think you owe her that."

"Perhaps I do, but I'd feel terrible if the Aksdals had to go back to their farm. I don't think Mrs. Aksdals likes farm life. I've heard her say many times how much better life is here in Bergen, and Marta says that her father and brother don't get along."

All the talk about the Aksdal's and their problems made Jorgen feel uncomfortable and somewhat disloyal. He purposely changed the subject. "Speaking of not getting along, any news on Hauk's whereabouts? Marta thinks he left town."

"What does Marta say?" Marta's sudden appearance in the room startled both boys.

Jorgen was glad he had changed the subject. "I was about to tell Andrew that on your trips down to the market you've heard no news about Hauk."

"I haven't," she confirmed. "Have you heard anything, Andrew?"

"Some down at the wharf say that they've seen him. They think he's taken refuge on board one of those ships in the harbor that hauls any kind of cargo for a price. Knowing what kind of seamen those ships take on, he'll get his throat slit when he crosses one of them."

Marta winced at Andrew's comment, and said to him, "Theo's waiting for you in the wagon." Andrew and Theo had delivered Jorgen's chest and some other belongings that Theo had taken to his house for safekeeping, shortly after the accident. After they had carried it up to the attic, Theo had gone down to place an order with the Aksdal's for a clothespress.

Jorgen's blue chest, now situated along the far wall of his attic room, caught Marta's eye. "Oh, Jorgen, what a beautiful chest!" She rushed over to get a closer look.

With Marta's attention temporarily diverted, Andrew began a little pantomime for Jorgen's benefit. He pointed to Marta, then to Jorgen, back to Marta and again to Jorgen. "Ask her," he mouthed silently.

"Goodbye, Andrew," Jorgen said, pointing to the door. "Theo's waiting."

"Goodbye Marta," Andrew said over his shoulder nearly colliding with Mrs. Aksdal as he left the room. "Sorry, Mrs. Aksdal, goodbye," he said, then clamored noisily down the stairs.

"I didn't realize he was still here," she said.

"Oh Mama!" exclaimed Marta. "Look at this!"

Mrs. Aksdal went to her daughter and said quietly, "Now that Jorgen is well, it is not proper for you to be in his room."

"I understand," said Marta. "I only came up to tell Andrew that his brother was waiting for him, and then I saw this. Isn't it lovely?"

"It is," agreed Mrs. Aksdal. "Did you make this Jorgen?"

"Yes," he said, joining the women. "I made it, but my sister Christina did the rosemaling."

"She is very talented," said Marta's mother. "Is she your older sister? I never could keep all you Halvorson children straight."

"I know," laughed Jorgen. "Most people can't. We're a very large family."

Mrs. Aksdal sighed; she sounded sad when she said, quietly, "Your mother is very fortunate." She looked at Marta and said apologetically, "I really wanted you to have brothers and sisters."

"I have a brother. The rest just wasn't meant to be, and anyway, I like getting all the attention." Marta flashed her mother an impish grin, then turned to Jorgen. "I'm amazed that Christina did this painting. She's just a little girl."

"Don't let her hear you say that," said Jorgen. "She's fifteen, and no longer thinks of herself as a child. She's always been very grown up for her age and she does have a real talent for rosemaling."

The three stood for a moment staring at the chest.

"Mrs. Aksdal, I think you have Christina confused with Katrine, my older sister. She went to school with your son, but I think he's a few years older."

Jorgen fished a key out of his pocket and knelt beside the chest. "There's something inside I'd like you to see." He lifted the lid and there, on top, was his moneybox.

"What a precious little box," Marta exclaimed.

"Takk," said Jorgen as he rummaged through clothing, taking out chisels and saws as he came to them.

"You have an interesting method of packing," Marta said, stifling a laugh.

"Things seem to have gotten jumbled during all the moves this chest has made. I'll have to complain to the haulers," Jorgen looked up at the women. "Knowing Andrew, he probably shook it up on purpose."

The three of them laughed as Jorgen continued to unpack, amused at the wild assortment that he pulled from the chest.

"Whatever you're searching for," said Mrs. Aksdal, "I hope it isn't fragile." Jorgen had just placed two rather heavy planes on the floor. "You have an impressive assortment of tools," she added.

"These belonged to Bestefar. He taught me woodworking and always let me use his tools. When he died, Far told me to take the tools that I wanted. I think he's hoping I'll stay here in Bergen and open my own woodworking shop."

Jorgen picked out a small chisel from the set he had placed on the floor and ran his thumb over its beveled edge. "This is the one I use for carving," he said, and demonstrated by fitting it into the carving on the chest.

"Pappa should see this," said Marta. "Remember how he used to do work like this all the time, Mama? He makes beautiful things, but it just occurred to me that they're much plainer than they used to be. He doesn't seem to enjoy carving anymore. Why do you suppose that is?"

Both Marta and Jorgen looked at Mrs. Aksdal for an answer. After a moment's reflection she replied, "I think he likes the simple things. Now what else were you going to show us, Jorgen?"

He took out some books, including the journal that the doctor's wife had given him to record his adventures, and was then able to pull out the fiddle case. "This also belonged to Bestefar," Jorgen said opening the case.

"Oh Jorgen, it's beautiful," said Marta. "I remember when your grandfather played it at the summer fair, but I never saw it up close. What a treasure!"

"Ja," Mrs. Aksdal agreed, "It is a lovely Hardanger. Your grandfather could make it sing the sweetest songs. You must be able to play, or I doubt he would have left it to you."

"Actually, all my brothers and sisters were taught to play, but I guess I was Bestefar's most serious student."

"Well, feel free to play up here any time you want, you won't disturb us," said Mrs. Aksdal. "And we'd welcome a little music any night you care to play for us."

"How about tonight?" Marta chimed in. "Will you play for us tonight?"

Jorgen considered the request for a moment. "I haven't played since I left home and need to practice if I'm going to give a concert tonight. So, if you lovely ladies will excuse me…"

"Oh Jorgen, your flattery sounds just like Andrew's. Let's go, Mama, I think we've been asked to leave this room, a room in the house that you own."

"It is Jorgen's room now. He's renting it,' said Mrs. Aksdal, as she ushered Marta out and closed the door behind them. Jorgen could hear the echo of their laughter and the clatter of their shoes as they descended the stairs. The door at the bottom squeaked noisily as it closed; then all was quiet.

He sat on the cot for a long while. The bow, limp in his right hand, touched the floor. The fiddle rested lightly on his knees. When, at last, he began to play, he felt strangely like a student again. He closed his eyes and memories of his teacher guiding his hands.

★ ★ ★

Jorgen played for the family that night. Although he was a bit rusty, he didn't think his playing merited the shocked look on Mrs. Aksdal's face when he glanced her way during his liveliest tune. Her eyes widened, and when she pointed to the window, Jorgen turned to see what had her so distracted.

All he saw from where he sat was a narrow section of polished glass that was visible through the partially closed curtains. Reds and yellows of the firelight reflected back into the room.

"Someone's out there; I saw a face in the window."

Jorgen reached the door with a few quick strides and threw it open. He ran out, fiddle in hand, and the Aksdals followed closely behind. Cold air and a steady light rain greeted them, but the peeping stranger was nowhere in sight.

"I'll get my coat and have a look around," said Jorgen.

"Has this ever happened before?"

"Nei!" the two women responded in unison.

"Our neighbors would never do that," said Mrs. Aksdal. "Whoever it was, he's gone now. Let's get out of the rain. No need for you to get pneumonia again chasing shadows; maybe I was just seeing things."

They went back into the house. Marta closed the curtains and Jorgen played another song, but they all thought about the face in the window.

Six

Spring 1849

Jorgen found it difficult to stay focused on the job at hand. He had been working feverishly for days trying to complete an order and was fatigued. His shoulders ached. For now, Mr. Aksdal was engrossed in his part of the work, but Jorgen wondered if he would stay at it long enough to finish the job. It was already apparent to Jorgen that he would have to come back to the shop after middag. How long he would need to stay depended on how much Mr. Aksdal was able to accomplish this afternoon.

Jorgen paused for a moment and slowly shrugged his shoulders; he rotated them backward and forward. He repeated this exercise a few times, then went back to work. Mr. Aksdal looked up from his work and smiled. "Looks like you'll finish that table today." Jorgen said hopefully. He attempted a smile but knew he hadn't succeeded. It really didn't matter, Mr. Aksdal hadn't noticed the slight; he simply smiled again and went back to his work.

Losing his mind. Those three words played over and over again in Jorgen's head. Mrs. Aksdal had come to the shop several days before and asked him to come to the house to discuss an important matter. When he arrived, Marta was with her mother. Jorgen wondered if they were going to get a lecture about how much time they spent together, or worse yet, she would ask him to leave. He looked closely at Marta. She sat with downcast eyes, hands tightly clasped in her lap. When she looked up at him, her eyes were red and teary.

"I've already talked to Marta about this, and we both feel that since you are a part of this household and you work with my husband, you need to know what we think is happening."

Mrs. Aksdal's normally strong, confident voice was

shaky and her hand trembled slightly as she brushed a wisp of hair from her face.

This must be terrible news, he thought.

"Each time the doctor came to see you these past weeks, he also took time to examine and observe Mr. Aksdal. I'm sure that you've noticed his behavior has changed since you first started to visit us last fall. Yesterday the doctor confirmed what I have suspected and feared for several months." Mrs. Aksdal glanced at Marta, then reached out and placed a hand on her daughter's knee. Marta blinked back tears and nodded for her mother to continue.

"Jorgen," Mrs. Aksdal continued, "My husband's mental state is deteriorating." This time when she paused, it was Jorgen who nodded.

Now it all made sense. The strange smiles, the long periods of silence, the forgetfulness. How awful for him, for all of them.

"His condition will only get worse with time." Mrs. Aksdal continued. "The doctor can only speculate on how much time he has until he can no longer work or take care of himself. It could be years…or months."

"What can I do to help him?" Jorgen asked.

" If you would stay on to help us complete the orders we have now, I will be truly grateful. I will not take any more. Also, the doctor thinks that Mr. Aksdal should have someone accompany him wherever he goes. He's gotten lost twice in the last month when he's gone for his evening walk."

"I didn't know that," said Jorgen.

"Neither did I," said Marta. "Mamma just told me." She paused for a minute and Jorgen could tell she was thinking of something. "Remember the night when he was gone a long time? We all wondered where he was?"

Jorgen nodded, as he recalled the night.

"Yes, that was the second time," said Mrs. Aksdal. "After you two went to bed that night, Mr. Aksdal confided to me how frightening it was when he became lost. He was fortunate to come upon our neighbors and was able to follow them home. The first time he forgot how to get home, you were both out for the evening. He managed to find his own way back. There may have been other instances, but twice is scary enough. I've told him that I will walk with him, and have asked him not to go out by himself. I'm worried that he'll forget. So, I need both of you to watch out for him. It's not safe for him to go for walks by himself."

"I'll keep an eye on him," said Jorgen, "and make sure that when he leaves the shop, he goes into the house. But if you don't take any more orders, how will you live?"

Marta's blank expression told Jorgen that she hadn't had time to consider this eventuality. They both looked expectantly at Mrs. Aksdal. Jorgen knew what was coming and was amazed at the optimism Mrs. Aksdal was able to show.

"Oh, we'll be fine," she said breezily. "As soon as we sell this house and the shop, we'll move in with our son. It's beautiful at the farm in summer. And Jorgen," she continued, changing the subject, "since you will be taking on added responsibility, we'll no longer expect you to pay rent."

Jorgen studied her briefly before speaking. He found it difficult to believe that she was as unconcerned as she sounded.

"And you," he said, addressing Marta. "What about your teaching job? Will you stay here or move back to live with your brother?"

"I'd like to stay here in Bergen, but it will depend on whether I can find a respectable rooming house."

"Maybe a widow who is looking for a companion," offered Mrs. Aksdal. "This situation is so new to both of us," she continued, "but I'm confident that we'll get it worked out in the end."

And work it out was just what Mrs. Aksdal did. She talked to the pastor after Sunday service to ask his advice. He came up with several suggestions, parishioners who might be willing to rent a room to Marta.

★ ★ ★

"Poor Mr. Aksdal," said Andrew. "Do you think he knows what's happening to him?"

"It's hard to know anything about him. He says very little to me when we're working and doesn't join in conversations when we're all together. Marta says that he remembers things from long ago but can't remember what he did or who he saw yesterday. Thank God he still remembers how to use a chisel and saw. I have to remind him what needs to be done, but once he gets started, things seem to come back to him. Somehow, we're keeping up with the business. How about you?"

"The spring herring has kept us working like ants. Theo, the Brastads, and I spent days on the Sognefjord, and we could hardly keep up with the catch. Theo says he's never seen a run like we've been having. We haven't even needed a watcher to point out the fish. The water has been so calm that the shoals are easy to spot."

Jorgen could picture the activity, having participated in it the previous fall. At one end of the ground, seine would be anchored on the shore with the other end attached to the boat out in the water. Rowers would take the boat in a large circle around the shoal and end up at the shore where the net would be anchored. Both ends of the net would be pulled and gathered in until the fish spilled into a pouch-like section of the net, which in turn was emptied into the boat. Jorgen had preferred this method of fishing to the one that nearly got him drowned, but even fishing in the fjords was not without risks and the Sognefjord was the longest and deepest.

Jorgen's thoughts turned from fishing back to the table and chairs that he and Mr. Aksdal would finish in the coming week. He was proud of his work and grateful that he didn't have to depend on fishing as a means to earn money.

As was their weekly custom, Jorgen and Andrew met early in the morning to spend a few hours together. It was a sunny Sunday in early spring. Usually, Marta went with them, but on this morning, she and her mother had decided to do some baking. As usual, Mrs. Aksdal had invited Andrew to have middag with the family and Jorgen.

Jorgen and Andrew walked up Mount Floyen and sat on the large rock where Marta and Jorgen had sat, months before, renewing their friendship. It was a favorite spot for all three young people, and they came here often.

"Is everything all right?" Jorgen asked after several minutes of silence. "I can't remember a time when you've been this quiet. Don't tell me you've finally run out of things to say."

"Just thinking," said Andrew. "I'm trying to work out when would be the best time to go home. If I go now, I could help Halvor with the planting. But then, Theo really needs me now, and extra money will be useful. My friends and I thought we would leave for America on the first of June. If we put it off until July, would you be able to go with us?"

"I do believe your brain may explode," laughed Jorgen. "I'm not used to all this planning. First things first, I doubt that Halvor needs your help. Neils is a big strong boy. Even Edvard is old enough to help with the planting. Pappa and Christina can help, and some years, Olaf comes over to lend a hand. If Theo needs your help, stay here in Bergen a while longer. The shop is going to be closed the last two weeks of June. I'm going home then, and I'd like for you to be there with me."

"And then we leave for America," said Andrew.

"Not so fast, little brother. Mr. Aksdal's illness has complicated things. They are planning on selling their house and business and moving back to the farm with their son."

"That solves your problem," said Andrew, not waiting for Jorgen to finish. "Now you can marry Marta, and she can come to America with us. She won't have to worry about her parents. We're only a marriage and a trip home to say goodbye to the family away from our departure." He gave Jorgen his best, 'it's all settled' smile.

"Nei," said Jorgen. "I can't do that. I promised Mrs. Aksdal that I'd stay until all the orders are completed, and then I plan to help them sell everything and move."

"And how long do you think that will be?" Andrew's voice sounded deflated, his smile had vanished.

"There's no way of knowing, weeks, a few months…"

"Years?" Andrew inquired. He jumped off the rock, then turned to face his brother. "I'm beginning to think you have no intention of ever leaving Norway."

"That's not true," Jorgen retorted, matching Andrew's tone, decibel for decibel. "I'm emigrating just as soon as I've done what I can to help out here."

Andrew sighed and turned to look out over the sprawling city and the ocean that separated them from their dream.

"Besides, I've asked Marta to marry me," said Jorgen, "She's excited about going to America, but we can't leave…"

Andrew did an about-face. "Whoa, back up," he said. "Did you just say…" A huge smile spread across his face. "We've been together for over an hour, and you're just getting around to telling me that you asked Marta to marry you?"

"We planned to tell you at middag."

"That's great news!" Andrew reached out with his forefinger and jabbed Jorgen in the shoulder. "You asked her, and she said yes?"

Now it was Jorgen's turn to grin. "Did you think she would say no?"

★ ★ ★

Jorgen's earnest promise to keep an eye on Mr. Aksdal was not easy to keep. Often, absorbed in his work,

Jorgen would suddenly become aware that his silent and elusive charge was nowhere to be seen. Fortunately, when that happened, Mr. Aksdal was quickly located. He enjoyed wandering in the garden and sometimes could be found sound asleep on his bed. But then came a morning when the poor man could not be found. He was working next to Jorgen one minute, gone the next.

Mrs. Aksdal and Jorgen searched the Aksdal property, the house, the garden, and two small outbuildings used for storage. All the while Jorgen apologized profusely to Mrs. Aksdal for losing sight of her husband.

Finally, in exasperation and frustrated with the situation, Mrs. Aksdal turned to Jorgen and said, quite sternly, "Enough of this talk. My husband is not your responsibility. I know you've done your best to watch him, but you were hired to work in the wood shop. No one can do two jobs at once without one of those jobs suffering."

"Would you like me to look up on Mount Floyen? Marta and I have taken him with us on walks up there. It's such a beautiful day, maybe he just wanted some fresh air?"

"Nei. You go back to work. He may have followed Marta. She'll be back within the hour. If he's not with her, she can help me look for him."

Jorgen had an uneasy feeling, but he went back to work on the three remaining chairs that were part of an order for the largest law firm in Bergen. The job had come to the Aksdal's shop on the recommendation of Mr. Lande, Theo's father-in-law.

"Now don't go thinking I suggested the shop where you work because of what my son did to you," Mr. Lande said after he introduced Jorgen to Mr. Een. "I saw a chest you made, at my daughter's house, and I think you are a very talented young man. Aksdal did work for me years ago, and I was more than satisfied with his craftsmanship.

The three men had stood in the dining room of Mr. Een's house. It was the largest, grandest home that Jorgen had ever been in. He tried not to gawk as he took the measure of the room for a new table and chairs.

"You do a good job for Een, and I know you'll be well compensated." Mr. Lande winked at Jorgen as he clapped Een on the back. "Jorgen is saving up to go to America."

"Come back and see me before you go," said Mr. Een. "I know many fine men who have emigrated. Their names might be useful to you."

That meeting had taken place shortly before Mr. Aksdal's condition had been diagnosed, and Jorgen thought that he and Mr. Aksdal had made good progress on the order. He hoped Mr. Aksdal would turn up soon so that he would not have to interrupt his day's work to look for him. He could also use his help with the sanding and the carving.

Jorgen was so focused on the swirls that he carved into a table leg that he wasn't aware of the commotion coming from the house. Marta's scream, when it came, pierced his concentration and he ran to the house, chisel in hand.

Mr. Aksdal was lying across the kitchen table surrounded by Mrs. Aksdal, Marta, and three men. Jorgen recognized only one of the men, the tailor, whose shop was down the street from the Aksdal's. He came to the house frequently to have coffee with Mr. Aksdal.

As Jorgen hurried across the kitchen floor one of the men turned from the table and brushed past him on his way to the door. "I'll get the doctor," he said.

Jorgen stood next to Marta and looked down at Mr. Aksdal. Mrs. Aksdal called her husband's name but got no response. Although his eyes were closed, his chest moved slightly with each breath. Blood coursed from his nose and from a split in his lower lip. The hair behind his left ear was matted with dirt and blood. A small pool of blood had started to form on the table under his head. Mrs. Aksdal gingerly pushed the hair aside to find the source of the bleeding.

"Marta," she said, "Get me a pan of water and some clean cloth."

Her calm, controlled voice had its effect; Marta stopped wringing her hands and sprang into action. Jorgen jammed the chisel into his pocket and looked for some way to help.

Mr. Aksdal's legs hung awkwardly off the end of the table. The tailor and the other man each raised and supported a leg, while Jorgen began removing Mr. Aksdal's wet, muddy shoes. "Do you know what happened to him?" Jorgen asked the tailor.

"This man," the tailor nodded in the direction of the stranger, "had no sooner come into my shop when we heard shouting. We went outside, and the gentleman who just left was running and shouting at two people who were down between my barn and the woods. I recognized Mr. Aksdal but the other man had his back to us. He held on to Mr. Aksdal with one hand and was hitting him with the other. I think he heard us shout to him, but before we could reach them, he hit Mr. Aksdal once more and then took off running into the woods. Mr. Aksdal fell backwards and hit his head on a rock."

Mr. Aksdal began to make gurgling and choking noises. His face was turning red and his whole body stiffened. It was like watching Bestefar's last moments and Jorgen could barely hide his fear of impending death.

"Help me turn him on his side," Mrs. Aksdal said, "He's choking on blood"

Jorgen dropped the shoe he had managed to pull off and rushed to help her. They got him turned and Mrs. Aksdal struck him several times on the back. After a few tense moments, the choking ceased. Mr. Aksdal's body relaxed, his hand opened slightly, and something small fell to the floor. It went unnoticed by most of those attending the injured man, but when it fell at Marta's feet, she instinctively picked it up and stuck it in the pocket of her apron.

★ ★ ★

Hours later, after the doctor had gone and Mr. Aksdal had been carried to his bed, Jorgen and Marta sat at the table trying to understand the violent attack.

"It just doesn't make sense," Marta said. "Far treated his customers like friends. I don't think I ever heard him say a cross word to anyone. He's not wealthy and wasn't dressed like a rich man, so I can't imagine that someone was trying to rob him."

"Maybe that's it," said Jorgen. "Maybe he was being robbed, and the thief was angry because your father couldn't give him anything."

"The trouble is," Marta continued, "Far's memory has been so bad lately that we may never know what happened." As she spoke, she smoothed her apron and, feeling a lump in her pocket, withdrew what she had picked up from the floor. She turned it over a couple of times, examining it. Eyebrows bunched, she looked up at Jorgen. Dark circles of fatigue did not conceal the intensity of her gaze.

"What do you suppose this is?" she asked. "It looks like a small, broken piece of carved wood." She handed the item to Jorgen.

Jorgen was dumbfounded by what Marta placed in his hand. "Wh…where did you get this?" He stammered. His face took on a puzzled look and he could feel the red as it crept up his neck and spread into his cheeks. He turned the object over and over in his hand. "I don't understand…"

"What is it, Jorgen? Is it something you've seen before?" She paused, and when he didn't respond, continued. "It fell out of my father's hand shortly after he was placed on the table."

"I don't understand how your father could have this?" Jorgen's voice had become almost a whisper. It was as if he could not bear to hear his own words.

"Maybe my father picked it up when he was walking," Marta suggested.

"Picked what up?" her mother asked as she joined them in the kitchen.

"This," Jorgen said. He opened his hand and showed her the piece of wood. "It's part of a button and it fell out of Mr. Aksdal's hand when he was lying on the table."

"Maybe he pulled the button off the coat of the man who attacked him." Mrs. Askdal said. "I had to cut threads off his fingernails just now, when I cleaned his hands. Perhaps he reached out when he was falling and grabbed at the other man's coat."

"That's not possible," Marta said quietly. Her eyes were trained on Jorgen.

"And why is that?" her mother asked.

"Because," Jorgen answered for Marta, "I carved that button myself, and it was on my brother's coat."

★ ★ ★

Theo shook his head in sympathy as Jorgen described the assault on Mr. Aksdal. His thumb slowly traced the distinctive design on the half button that Jorgen handed him. He had been pleasantly surprised, moments before, to see both Jorgen and Andrew standing at the front door, but he now knew that this was not just a social call. He passed the broken button to Andrew who turned it over and over in his hand before passing it back to Theo.

"I just can't imagine how Mr. Aksdal came to have this," Theo said, studying the object in his hand as if it could tell its secret.

Anna sat quietly at the table with the three brothers. As she listened, her face reflected first the horror of the attack, then concern for Mr. Aksdal, and finally the anger they all felt.

"You've met him, Theo," Jorgen continued. "He's not a

big man and he's not well, either. Most of the time, he can't even tell you the day of the week." Tears had formed in the corners of his eyes and threatened to spill over. "What kind of coward attacks someone so defenseless?" He quickly wiped away the tears before they could slide down his face.

"Growing up as we did, we were sheltered from this kind of violence," Theo said. "I'm not sure anyone knows why some people take out their anger and frustration on those who are weaker. You call it cowardice, and you're absolutely correct. That sort of person usually doesn't prey on anyone who can properly defend himself."

Theo's words were no match for the voice of disapproval that sounded in Jorgen's head. *Tears, Jorgen, you're worse than a woman. Marta and her mother got through the day without a tear...show some toughness, Jorgen! Don't be so weak!*

"Money is tight and has been for some time." Theo's voice broke through to Jorgen. "Farming has not been good; work is scarce for those who have come to the city to find jobs. Some men only know how to wage war or how to farm. They are angry when they drift into Bergen thinking they'll become fishermen and become even angrier when they discover it's not the life for them."

"And I know that for a fact," Jorgen said, forcing a smile in spite of his own gloom.

They all laughed at Jorgen's admission, grateful for a little levity in the conversation.

"It may not be the life for you," said Theo, "but you did it anyway and didn't take your frustration out on others."

Anna finally spoke up. "How are Mrs. Aksdal and Marta? This had to be horrifying for them."

"Marta..." Jorgen paused for a few moments, willing his eyes to stay dry. "Marta was frightened by her father's injuries, but Mrs. Aksdal took complete charge and probably saved his life. She is an amazing woman; nothing seems to faze her. She kept everyone calm."

"We saw that in her when she took you into their home," said Theo. "Mor could not have done any more for you than she did. If anyone can nurse Mr. Aksdal back to health, she can.

"What concerns me now is the button and how it came to be in Mr. Aksdal's hand. Halvor treasured that coat and those buttons that you carved for him. He always said that it was the warmest coat he ever had. I'm sure it's back at the farm with him."

"He borrowed a needle and thread from me last year," said Anna. "He told me the buttons on his coat were loose, and he didn't want to lose any of them. I offered to help him, and when the thread kept getting snagged I realized that one of the buttons had a crack in it."

"Well that's good to know, Anna," said Andrew, and he pointed to a loose button on his coat.

"I'll lend you my sewing box." she replied with a chuckle.

"Maybe it broke off somewhere and Mr. Aksdal just happened to pick it up" Andrew continued, ignoring his brothers' laughter.

"I don't think so," said Theo. "There's no dirt on it; it doesn't look like it has been lying around on the ground."

"Well, then" said Jorgen, "the only explanation I see is that for whatever reason, Halvor did not take the coat home with him.

"That night, after she got him cleaned up, Mrs. Aksdal said there were threads caught on her husband's broken fingernails. I think that during the struggle, Mr. Aksdal reached out and grabbed the front of the other man's coat, Halvor's coat, and the button broke off in his hand. The man who attacked Mr. Aksdal must have Halvor's coat."

"The magistrate will want to see this," said Theo, and he gave the button back to Jorgen. "I assume that you'll accompany Mrs. Aksdal when she goes to see him tomorrow."

"Ja, I told her that I would," said Jorgen.

"And if it's alright with you," Andrew said to Theo, "I'd rather not go out on the boat tomorrow. I'd like to poke around town, go into some shops and taverns to see if I can find whoever is wearing Halvor's coat. Can you find someone to replace me for one day?"

Theo nodded. "Good idea. If the assailant did get some money off Mr. Aksdal, he may be looking to spend it. As soon as you two leave, tonight, I'll write to Halvor and ask about his coat."

★ ★ ★

Mr. Aksdal clung to life for ten days, never regaining consciousness. The doctor said brain injury caused by hitting his head on a rock had killed Mr. Aksdal, but Jorgen felt that the person who hit Mr. Aksdal was responsible for his death. He and Andrew spent countless evenings searching for the murderer. The local magistrate was doing all he could to find the perpetrator, but his identity remained unknown, the crime unsolved.

One Sunday, a few weeks after Mr. Aksdal died, Theo came to visit Jorgen at the Aksdals. Jorgen ordinarily did not work on Sundays, but he was not feeling particularly friendly towards God these days, so he was catching up on work while Marta and her mother were at church.

"I thought you'd like to know that I heard from Halvor." Theo handed Jorgen the letter. There were two pages addressed to Marta and her mother. Jorgen recognized Mor's writing. He refolded and stuck those pages in his pocket. The rest of the letter was from Halvor.

After expressing his shock over what had happened to Mr. Aksdal, Halvor went on to say that he was dismayed to hear about the coat button. Jorgen began to read the letter aloud.

"Although it was old and frayed at the sleeves, I wore

it last fall because it was a warm coat, perfect for the long, cold ride to town. When I arrived, Bergen was warmer than the country, so I took off the coat and put it under the wagon seat. I didn't think about it again until I was halfway home and felt the chilly mountain air. That's when I discovered my coat was missing."

Jorgen stopped reading. A thought had just occurred to him. "Halvor's wagon was just outside the door the day you ordered Hauk out of your house."

Theo shook his head. "Anna said the same thing, but I don't think we can jump to any conclusions based on that. We don't know who took Halvor's coat, and we can't accuse Hauk just because he happened to be at the house. Halvor made many stops that weekend, and the coat could have been taken at any time."

★ ★ ★

After Mr. Aksdal's death, Jorgen's days fell into an exhausting routine. He rose in the early hours, worked by lamplight until the sun came up, had a light breakfast, and then worked until middag. By sticking to that rigid schedule, he finished Mr. Een's order. True to her word, Mrs. Aksdal had stopped taking orders as soon as she realized the permanence of her husband's illness, but several orders remained that had been promised. If he worked steadily, Jorgen thought he would have those finished by summer's end. Then, Mrs. Aksdal planned to close the business. To that end, she was currently making inquiries around Bergen to see if she could find a buyer for it.

On most days, Jorgen walked to Andrew's after middag, and if he wasn't on a fishing trip, they made the rounds of drinking establishments. At those places, they described what happened to Mr. Aksdal, showed the broken button, and described Halvor's coat to anyone who would listen. A few men thought they had seen the coat, one man even described the person who wore it as, "a tall man with arms too long for the sleeves," but he could provide no other useful information.

The long workdays and late night searches were taking their toll on Jorgen. Mrs. Aksdal stopped him at the door early one evening as he prepared to go out.

"Jorgen, I appreciate your loyalty to my husband and your desire to find who attacked him. I would like to see justice done, but not at your expense. You work hard all day, walk around town half the night, and have dark circles under your eyes that show how tired you must be. I want you to stop these nightly searches."

Jorgen looked at Marta and she nodded.

"You're both sure?" Jorgen asked. He felt both relief and disappointment.

"We're sure," Mrs. Aksdal said. "I went into town, today, and spoke with the magistrate. He assured me that his investigation will continue. I also talked to Mr. Een. He, too, is making inquiries on my husband's behalf and promised his case will not be forgotten. I am prepared to move on with my life and realize that I may never know who did this terrible thing. If it's meant to be, the law will catch up with whoever did this."

Although disappointed that he had been unable to find Mr. Aksdal's assailant, Jorgen was relieved to have his evenings back. Andrew was still expecting him that night, so Jorgen invited Marta to go with him to tell his brother they were ending the search for the man with Halvor's coat.

The walk to Andrew's was quick and purposeful, but returning home the couple slowed their pace. Marta described her day at school and told Jorgen about the lessons she had planned for the next day. Jorgen realized that he had been so preoccupied with his work and her father's death that they had barely spoken in days.

He took her hand in his and gave it a gentle squeeze then raised it and pressed his lips to her fingers. "I seemed to have lost sight of the good things in life," he said. "I promise I'll do better."

"Please don't apologize!" Marta said. "Mor and I are grateful for all that you've done, for completing Far's work, and for trying to locate who killed him. You've been a good and kind friend to him and to us."

Jorgen stopped walking. He drew Marta close and wrapped his arms around her. "And someday soon I hope to be a good and kind husband." He lowered his head and their lips met. He wondered if she could feel his body trembling. His desire for her was intense.

Although the hour was not yet late, the moonlit road was deserted. Marta rested her head on Jorgen's shoulder, Jorgen's cheek pressed into her hair and he whispered, "I love you, Marta Aksdal. You are all that I need in this world, and I will love you til the end of our days."

They kissed again, a gentle touch that lingered and ignited their passion. Jorgen raised his hand to support the back of Marta's head as the kiss deepened, exposing their stirred emotions and the raw need they had for each other.

Reluctantly, their lips parted. "Oh Jorgen," Marta said breathlessly. "Let's get married right away. I can't stand living in the same house with you without being a part of you. I want to be your wife and have your children. I love you so much I sometimes think my heart will burst."

Jorgen drew back and looked into her face. Moonlight glistened in her moist eyes and her face had never looked lovelier. *What did I do to deserve her,* he thought, *I must be the luckiest and happiest man alive.*

Jorgen took her hand again as they continued their walk home. "Would Midsummer's Eve be soon enough for you? That's when I planned to go home to say goodbye to my family. We could get married in Voss."

"That's a marvelous idea. Having our wedding on the longest day of the year...the celebration will go on all night. What fun that will be."

"All night, that's what I'm looking forward to," he said. The look on his face was such an exaggerated leer that Marta couldn't help herself; she blushed and laughed shamelessly. Jorgen joined her in laughter and their eyes met, communicating something deeper. Silently they came together, embraced again, and shared another kiss.

The approach of a horse and rider separated them, and they continued the walk home.

"Mor and I can stay with my brother," Marta said, picking up on their previous conversation. "We even have an extra room for Andrew, or Theo and Anna. I can't wait to tell Mor, she will be so happy for us."

Marta stopped talking and Jorgen could tell that something was bothering her.

"What is it?" he said. "Are you worried about your mother?"

"I just wonder what she'll do after we are married. Do you think she'll want to stay at the farm after we leave? She likes it well enough here in Bergen, but I think life here would be lonely for her. Too many memories."

"It needn't be…I mean it doesn't have to be a lonely life for her. We've lived together as a family for several months, and it has been good. Do you think that she would come to America with us? I know it would make you happier and less lonely if your mother came with us."

"You'd do that?" said Marta. She ceased walking and stared at Jorgen, wide-eyed. "You'd ask her to live with us?"

"I've given it a lot of thought since your father died, and I think the three of us could make it work."

Marta's face lit up in a huge smile. She threw her arms around Jorgen's neck. "You are the kindest person I have ever met. That would make everything just perfect. Do you think she'll come with us?"

"Why don't we ask her?" Jorgen said. "I think it's time to make some plans."

★ ★ ★

The lamp stayed lit well into the night as Jorgen, Marta, and Mrs. Aksdal talked about their future as a family. Mrs. Askdal had, at first, turned down their offer.

"Jorgen, you must get over the feeling that you are somehow responsible for me," she declared. "Whatever debt you thought you owed us for helping you after your accident you've more than paid. You and Marta deserve to live your own life."

"And we shall," said Jorgen. "We just want you to be with us in America. We want our children to have at least one grandparent who is not an ocean away."

Jorgen could see that Mrs. Aksdal was considering the possibility, so he continued. "You and I have worked very well together and our evenings are always pleasant. I'm not sure where our adventure will take us, but I will always see to your comfort and privacy."

Unable to sit still, Marta paced the room while Jorgen spoke to her mother.

"Marta, please sit down," her mother said, "You're wearing holes in the floor."

Marta plopped down next to her mother. "Say you'll come with us, Mamma, we really do want you."

"This is quite a surprise," said Mrs. Aksdal. She shifted her gaze from Marta to a quick sweep of the room. "I thought I would live in this house until I died. Now that your father is gone...I don't know...maybe I do need a change."

"America will be a fresh start for all of us, Mor. You came to Bergen because you thought country life was dull. Our new life probably will be hard work, but I think it will be exciting. Think of all the new places we'll see and interesting people we'll meet. Say you'll come. At least, say you'll think about it. You don't have to decide this minute."

"Actually, Marta, that's not why your father and I left the farm, but that makes no difference now. I promise to think about your offer. You've taken me by surprise, and I love you both for it. No matter what I decide, I am deeply grateful and honored that you've asked me."

"Now, let's hear the rest of your plans. Have you made any decisions about your wedding?"

"We have," Marta said. "If Pastor Dahl can marry us, the wedding will be on Midsummer's Eve."

Even though she was happy and excited for the young couple, Elen only half listened as Marta talked about the wedding plans. Their offer to have her join them had caught her by surprise, and her thoughts slipped back in time to her dear husband's proposal.

History has a strange way of repeating itself, she thought as she mechanically filled the kettle and placed cups on the table. Back then, she had been in another vulnerable situation. Both her parents died shortly before her eighteenth birthday, victims of the influenza outbreak of 1829. Elen's father had been a cooper, his shop and their home was in Bergen. He bought the wood he needed to make his barrels and tubs from Mr. Aksdal.

Mr. Aksdal had inherited his land near Voss. He did some farming but made his living off the forest he owned, milling the lumber and selling it in Bergen. At that time in his life, woodworking was a hobby and he gave away most of what he made. His wife had died in childbirth along with his second child, a daughter, leaving Mr. Aksdal with an eight-year-old son to raise by himself. Fredrik had been devastated by his mother's death, and three years passage had not lessened the boy's grief.

Elen's father was one of Mr. Aksdal's best customers. He rented their attic room for himself and Fredrik when they were in Bergen. He had known Elen since she was a child.

Unaware of her parents' deaths, Mr. Aksdal came to town and was shocked by the news. Mr. Aksdal saw the same look of abandonment in Elen's eyes that was ever present in his son's expression. He stayed in town for several days to help Elen settle her parent's affairs. He was a gentle man who patiently explained how her father had run his business and tried to get a sense of whether she was capable of running it by herself. Of course, she would have to hire a cooper to make the barrels and buckets her father's business produced.

Elen was grateful for his help and for the picnics he planned for her and his son. The two young people were able to talk to each other about their losses, something that Fredrik had not been able to with his father. As the days passed and the friendship developed, Mr. Aksdal began to realize the depth of his feelings for Elen.

The time came when he knew he had to get back to his own life and business. He had hired a man to look after things for him, but he needed to be back on the scene to make decisions.

"I have business to attend to," he told her. "Fredrik and I will have to leave soon."

Elen attempted a brave face when she told him that she would manage on her own, but Mr. Aksdal wasn't fooled. The way her shoulders sagged, the brief look of panic on her face at the mention of his leaving gave him the courage to give the speech he had rehearsed in his mind.

"My dear friend, these past days have made me realize how much Fredrik and I have missed having a woman in our lives. I am fond of you, Elen, and I know that you and Fredrik have enjoyed each other's company. He is smiling again, the first time since his mother died. I am thirty-five years old, in good health and I own some property and a business. I know you don't love me, but perhaps in time..."

There, he had said it; he had asked her to marry him...or had he? He wasn't sure. He couldn't remember what he had just said.

"Do you know what I am saying?" He tried again, wondering if he knew what he was saying. His tone was calm and quiet; the question hung in the air like a caress.

"I think so," she answered. She had been staring at the

ground as he had spoken to her, but now she looked into his eyes. Her own were glassy with tears.

"Oh, Elen, I'm so sorry! I didn't mean to upset you. It's too soon after your parents' death to think of marrying me. I'm so clumsy at this. Do forgive me."

Elen dabbed at her eyes with her sleeve. "There is no need for forgiveness; my tears are those of happiness. I, too, am fond of you and Fredrik. I think my parents would be happy for me. I accept your offer of marriage."

They would talk about it years later, the unexpectedness of his question, her hasty decision, and unequivocal answer, and they would marvel that it had turned out so well. Their trust in each other had paid off in a loving marriage. The dissimilarity in their ages had made no difference, until Mr. Aksdal began to show signs of early onset dementia.

Elen never had reason to regret her quick, sensible decision. Love did blossom between her and Mr. Aksdal. If it was not a passionate love, it was, to be sure, marked by tenderness and respect. He was a good husband and loving father to Marta, and Elen had been happy in her marriage to him.

Dare she tempt fate again with another hurried decision that could immensely affect the rest of her life? Should she follow her heart, her love for her daughter, or stay with what was known and safe, her life in Bergen? The kettle's insistent whistle finally got her attention.

"Mor," Marta said, "you've not heard a word we've said. Your mind's been a million miles away." She went to the stove and brought the kettle back to the table.

"More like a million years away," Elen laughed. "Asking me to go with you..." She looked up at her daughter and knew she didn't have to finish what she wanted to say.

"I know we surprised you, and there is a lot to think about," Marta said as she prepared their tea, "but you know you don't have to give us an answer right away."

"I know," her mother answered, "This time I'll have to give it more thought."

Jorgen gave Marta a puzzled look that said, 'this time?' Marta shrugged. It was late, they were all tired, and no more was said. The three drank their tea, buried in their own thoughts.

★ ★ ★

Preparations were well under way when Jorgen and Andrew arrived home, two days before the wedding. The aroma of fresh bread and other baked treats hung in the air, and the house had been given a thorough cleaning.

Jorgen, Andrew, and Niels carried armloads of freshly cut pine boughs into every room and used them to decorate the doorways. The girls gathered wild flowers. Some were woven into the pine boughs while others were fashioned into bright bouquets for the table and mantels.

On the day before the wedding, all seven brothers gathered after middag to participate in their favorite holiday preparation. After choosing a hilltop site, they foraged for brush, branches, and logs and amassed a huge pile, which would be lit on Midsummer's Eve. Although Jorgen and Marta's wedding would be the main event, this traditional bonfire was equally anticipated by the whole family. Besides being fun and festive, according to folklore, the fire would protect them all from bad luck and illness in the coming year.

That evening, when the others had gone to bed, Halvor drew Theo, Jorgen, and Andrew into a conversation about what had happened to Mr. Aksdal.

"I've had time to think about it," Halvor said and he looked at Theo, "and I think my coat disappeared the day I was at your house. I know it was there when I arrived because I removed the letter Mor wrote to you from one of the pockets. I folded the coat and placed it under the seat. When I was getting ready to leave, you gave me a large package of dried fish to take home."

"I remember," said Theo.

"I had to rearrange what was under the wagon seat, to make room for the fish, and though I didn't realize it at the time, now that I think about it, I'm sure my coat was not there."

"Hauk," said Andrew. "It had to be Hauk."

"It was," Theo said, "I only found out the day before we left to come here. Anna's mother told her about a visit she had from Hauk, a few days ago. He sneaked home one morning to beg money off his mother. He said he had been staying aboard a boat that was getting ready to sail, and he needed money. He was leaving and never coming back, he said, so he wanted his inheritance now, not after his father died. Those were his exact words, and they shocked his mother. She told Anna that she was ashamed of her son. He looked like a beggar in an old coat and dirty pants. Anna's mother didn't recognize the coat. She knew it did not belong to Hauk and so she asked him where he had gotten it. He swore and told her it was none of her business where he got his clothes."

"He swore at his own mother," Jorgen said in amazement.

"Anna asked her mother to describe the coat," Theo continued, "and the first thing her mother said was that it had carved buttons. Anna didn't tell her mother about the coat and Mr. Aksdal. Her mother was already upset about Hauk, and Anna didn't want to make her feel worse. But, she did want me to tell all of you, because she thought you had a right to know."

"Murderer," Andrew said under his breath.

Jorgen felt terrible. He remembered his conversation with Andrew after his near drowning. Andrew was right, they should have done something about Hauk then. Mr. Aksdal would still be alive if he had acted.

"I'll leave it to you to tell Marta and her mother," said

Theo.

"Yes, I'll tell them," said Jorgen, "but not tomorrow."

★ ★ ★

The wedding day, June 23, 1849, dawned cloudy. Rain poured during the night and throughout the early morning. After much scurrying around to locate oilskins to protect everyone from the weather, the rain had stopped. And now, chores having been completed and the carriages made ready, it was nearing time for the family to leave for the church.

One by one, the family gathered in the kitchen, all dressed in their finest.

Inger twirled excitedly, showing off the dress her mother had finished the night before. "This is the most wonderful day ever," she said, her cheeks feverishly red from her many bursts of energy.

Normally, Mor would have admonished her youngest to calm down, but she, too, was caught up in the excitement and the pleasure of having all her children reunited. Earlier that morning, she had enlisted Karine's help in fashioning her hair, and the results had made her feel younger than she had in years. She beamed with pride while she surveyed her offspring: Halvor, her first born, tan and muscular from working the farm; Theo and Anna, arms linked, still looking like newlyweds themselves; and Karine who confided, earlier, that she wished her friendship with Mr. Bergstrom would develop into something more serious.

"Your day will come; I'm sure of it," Mor said as the two had walked into the kitchen.

The bittersweet feelings Mor harbored for her emigrating middle boys, were all but forgotten as she listened to Jorgen's and Andrew's stories and joined in their laughter. She took comfort in the children still at home: Christina, beautiful and serene; dependable Niels, who had spent the last two days following his four older brothers, adopting their every mannerism; Edvard, still frail from his bouts with illness, so anxious to please Far in the workshop; and finally Inger and Ole. *My last two little ones,* she thought, *in no time they'll be as big as the others.*

Edvard had taken sick again the previous fall, preventing the family from attending Theo and Anna's wedding. Mor was acutely aware that today's wedding would most likely be the only wedding where the whole family would be present. *Bless Jorgen and Marta for coming home to get married,* she thought.

★ ★ ★

By the time the Halvorsons arrived at the church, the sky remained cloudy, and rain could be seen advancing over the mountains that hugged the western edge of town. Pastor Dahl, handsomely attired in a long black robe and frilly white collar, rushed out of the church to greet Jorgen and his family.

"Everyone is inside. I thought it best to cancel the bridal procession," he said, pointing to dark, billowing clouds that were rapidly advancing in their direction. "I hope this isn't too great a disappointment."

Jorge assured him that a little rain wouldn't dampen his spirits and asked if Marta and her mother had arrived yet.

The pastor smiled. "Your bride is waiting," he said.

Jorgen's family entered the church and took their places to the sweet strains of hardingfele music. A few minutes later, Jorgen and Pastor Dahl walked down the aisle together and stood in front of those assembled.

Jorgen was stunned and suddenly self-conscious. It looked like the whole town, everyone he had ever known, was seated in front of him. The little church was full, people stood along the sides and the back of the church.

Mrs. Aksdal was seated on the aisle in the second row,

next to Jorgen's parents. Seeing her there, without her husband, triggered a feeling of loss and sadness for her in Jorgen. She smiled at him and nodded, as if to say, she was all right. He nodded in return.

Jorgen's brothers and sisters were still arranging themselves in the seats behind their parents. Andrew sat between Karine and Christina, having traded places with Christina so that she could be on the aisle. He was in high spirits. He was the one, after all who had encouraged Jorgen to marry Marta. His sisters, however, had very mixed feelings. Karine was pleased for Jorgen and Marta but felt, as the older sister, she had missed her turn. She wondered if her relationship with Mr. Bergstrom was going anywhere. She wasn't desperate, but she also knew she wasn't getting any younger. And, she was tired of the thoughtlessness of people asking why she wasn't married. Christina, on the other hand, had concerns other than marriage. Although she was happy for Jorgen and Marta, she was uncomfortable with change. She had no desire to ever leave home and mourned the fact that neither Jorgen nor Andrew would ever live at home again.

Sitting next to Karine were Theo, Anna, and Halvor. They were quietly discussing details of the picnic lunch and what to do if it should rain.

Ole made a face at Jorgen trying to get him to laugh aloud. He, Edvard, and Niels were seated between their parents. Jorgen winked at Ole but managed to keep a straight face.

A stirring at the back of the church signaled Marta's arrival. Jorgen looked up in time to see Inger walk quickly but solemnly down the aisle. She carried a bouquet of purple heather that she and Ole had picked the day before. Behind her, Marta, her arm looped through her brother's arm, advanced more slowly. She looked regal; her head was held high. Light from the tall east windows glinted off the ornate crown that adorned her lustrous hair.

Like many families, Jorgen's family did not own a wedding crown nor did Mrs. Aksdal. Although the church owned one that Marta could have used, the bridal crown she was wearing belonged to Dr. Larson's wife who had graciously loaned it to Marta.

"I can't think of anyone I'd rather see wearing it," Mrs. Larson said when she had presented it to Marta the night before.

The bridal costume Marta wore had been her mother's, but it fit Marta perfectly, as if it had been made for her. The simplicity of the new, white linen blouse offered stark contrast to the brightly colored embroidered vest. The bottom of the long, black, wool skirt had a wide band of embroidery, which complemented the stitching on the vest. Resting in Marta's hands, her prayer book sat atop a small red purse, which matched the predominant color of the embroidery.

This was the easiest decision I've ever made, Jorgen thought and in truth, it was. When he had finally acknowledged to himself the deep feelings he had for her, the way forward had been quite clear. What was difficult was the nagging worry about emigrating with her, that she would not be happy in America. He wanted to fulfill his dream of owning land, but when he looked at her coming down the aisle to be with him, to go with him wherever he took her, the enormity of responsibility, his obligation to ensure her safety and provide means for her happiness, suddenly seemed overwhelming.

A small cough in the front row diverted his attention, for just a moment, to his father. But what he saw in the eyes was his grandfather – kind, wise Bestefar.

One step at a time, he told himself. *I'll do all that I need to do, one step at a time, and I'll have Marta by my side to help me do it.* Jorgen smiled at Far, then turned to face Marta with a feeling of renewed confidence. As the wedding ceremony commenced, Jorgen dropped his gaze attempting to stay focused on Pastor Dahl's words. He spied an ant carrying a load, almost as big as it, across the floor. Jorgen watched the ant labor over the rough boards; it paused when it reached Pastor Dahl's shoe. If the minister shifted his weight, the ant was doomed.

A sudden quietness in the church interrupted Jorgen's inattentiveness; Pastor Dahl's eyes were on Marta and him. Jorgen stole a look at Marta, and she mouthed the words, "I do."

"I do." Jorgen said with such enthusiasm that many in the church had to stifle a chuckle. After their vows were completed, Jorgen slipped a slim, gold band on Marta's finger. Her father had given the ring to her mother. Remembering him brought tears to her eyes. She blinked them away as quickly as they appeared and smiled at Jorgen. Today was a day for happy thoughts; her father would not have wanted her to be sad.

Pastor Dahl led the congregation in prayer and delivered a short sermon. During the latter, Jorgen took the opportunity to check on the ant's progress. At first, when he didn't see it, he feared it had come to an unhappy end at the bottom of a shoe. But then he saw it, still struggling with its heavy burden, as it approached, and then disappeared into a crack in the floor.

After the ceremony, Jorgen and Marta led a procession from the church across the large square into the center of town where Jonsoksdag, the Midsummer's Eve festival, was held each year. There, the women gathered in small groups talking, mostly about the wedding they had just witnessed, while the men saw to the horses and wagons. The men returned with baskets of food their wives had prepared earlier that morning.

As if on cue, the sun popped out from behind the thinning clouds and soon quilts were spread over the nearby hillside that overlooked the lake. Mrs. Aksdal's quilt adjoined the ones spread by the Halvorsons, and together, the two families—now united by marriage—combined the contents of their baskets for a wedding feast.

Eager to participate in the festival contests, games, and races, Edvard, Inger, and Ole barely took time out to eat. Inger joined all the other young girls as they grabbed boys to be their husbands for mock weddings. This was an old Jonsok custom, and, along with the bonfire that evening, was a highlight of the children's day. No girl could catch Ole, a fast, elusive runner, but Edvard, an easygoing lad, was effortless prey and eagerly joined the charade. Meanwhile, Inger, having chased down a boy her age, was finding him a most uncooperative spouse. Their make-believe play entertained the adults, who in turn reminisced about their own childhood and relived memories of long ago Midsummer's Eve holidays.

When food hampers were empty and bellies full, the celebration moved back to the square. Fiddles were produced, and when the music began, all the children gathered around Jorgen and Marta and danced and sang to the bride and groom.

Well-wishers and the curious offered congratulations and inquired about Jorgen and Marta's plans to emigrate to America. Some of their old school friends confessed that they, too, were also considering emigration and had dozens of questions. Many in the older generation gave cautionary advice; for them, America sounded too strange and distant.

For Jorgen and Marta, it was both a homecoming and a farewell to their former lives. If they'd had more time to reflect on it, both would have felt some degree of sadness, but the day had not been designed for contemplation and the afternoon's celebration proved too entertaining and passed too quickly for much reflection.

In the late afternoon, Jorgen and Marta joined the rest of the family as they packed up their carriages to leave. Daylight would stretch long into the night, but now, many of the revelers, especially those with farms and animals to tend, needed to return to their homes. Some would return much later for the lighting of the town bonfire.

Jorgen's family, like others who lived at greater distance from town, would light their own bonfire, as custom dictated, on the highest point of their estate. There, with flames licking at the low hanging stars, the family would give thanks, hope for a good harvest, and speculate about the coming year.

The longest day was far from over. With so many extra helping hands, the chores were done quickly, and the Halvorsons found themselves together again for one last meal. Later, when dusk finally settled in, they would delight in the bonfire, but in the meantime, once dishes had been cleared from the table, the room echoed with laughter as family stories were told and relived.

Marta was thrilled to be part of this large, boisterous group. "Aren't you going to miss all this?" she said to Jorgen when there was a slight lull in the conversation. "You have such a beautiful family, and you all have such fun together."

Jorgen squeezed her hand. "I'm sure Mor would agree with you, but someday we'll have our own family, and they'll be even more handsome than this lot." He reached across the table and gave Ole's hair a quick mussing.

"Only if they look like Marta," Halvor shot back.

"Which reminds me of a story," said Andrew and he launched into the first of many stories the family would tell on that Midsummer's Eve.

★ ★ ★

"A hunter whistled as he made his way down the path that led into the marsh," Andrew started, using his best story-telling voice. "The noise attracted a snipe who approached him cautiously."

The family responded with smiles of recognition. The older children all knew the story, even Inger and Ole had heard it before, but that did not diminish everyone's enjoyment of Andrew's recitation.

"'The woods are full of animals,' said the snipe, as he pointed in the opposite direction. 'You might have better luck there.'"

"Takk for the advice,' replied the hunter, 'but I might as well have a look around, as long as I'm here.'"

"'In that case,' said the snipe, 'take care that you don't shoot my children.'"

"The hunter liked the spunky snipe and was willing to oblige him. 'How will I know they are your children?'" he asked.

"'That's simple,' said the snipe."

Andrew paused and pointed to Mor to add the next sentence.

"Mine are the loveliest children in the marsh," Mor said, and Inger giggled with delight.

Andrew continued, "'Ah,' said the hunter, 'I'll remember that. Your beautiful children are safe with me.'"

"A while later they met on the same path, both returning to their respective homes. The hunter had a brace of snipes slung over his shoulder.

"'Oh no.' howled the snipe, 'my dear children!'"

"'How can these be yours?' said the bewildered hunter. 'I only shot the homeliest ones I could find.'"

"'Don't you know,' mourned the snipe, 'that each mother thinks her own children are the prettiest?'"

PART TWO

Journey

Seven

July 1850

Jorgen and Marta were up early the morning of their departure and were surprised to find Marta's mother already in the kitchen sorting out the food they would take on their journey. They all commented on what a poor night's sleep they had endured the night before. Jorgen felt compelled to ask Marta and her mother if they were having second thoughts about the voyage. Both women vehemently denied having any such feelings.

"No," Mrs. Aksdal said, "I think it was just the excitement that kept me awake. That, and trying to remember where everything is packed. I can't remember where we packed the bedding that we'll need tonight. I wish I had made a list."

"Jorgen and I made a list of everything that went into each chest," said Marta. He left to retrieve the list while Marta continued her explanation. "The bedding is packed in the same chest as the clothing we will use on the trip. That chest and the one there at your feet will stay with us in our cabin. The rest will be sealed and stored in the ship's hold."

Mrs. Aksdal peered into the chest and nodded at the assortment of pots, pans, and cooking utensils. "I've gathered the food, and it looks like it should all just fit," she said.

Jorgen returned and handed Mrs. Aksdal a piece of paper. As she studied it, a big smile spread across her face. She handed it back to Jorgen and said, "I should have known you would have everything organized."

When Theo arrived mid-morning to take them to the ship, a steady rain was falling. He and Jorgen loaded the baggage into Theo's wagon, and the four of them set off for the harbor. They huddled under oilcloth attempting to stay dry, but the wind whipped at their protective covering, exposing them to the driving rain.

In spite of their best efforts to be organized and to stay within the limits of the ship's baggage allotment, an unforeseen problem arose when they reached the dock. Theo's horse had just come to a stop when the ship's supercargo charged up to the wagon to tell them that he had changed the baggage limit.

"Unexpected cargo," he said, curtly. "We need to make room for it." He lifted the oilskin covering their baggage, counted their trunks, and asked how many were in their travel group. He recounted the baggage and told them they were over the new limit; they had one trunk too many. Jorgen started to protest, but the man raised his hand to silence him.

"No exceptions!" he bellowed, and hurried on to the next wagon.

Without hesitation, Mrs. Aksdal volunteered one of her trunks; the one that contained her china, flat wear, and many items that had been in her family for years.

"But Mama, those things belonged to your mother…"

"And are not essential," said Mrs. Aksdal.

"If it helps any," said Theo, "when your home is built, I'll send the trunk to you."

"You see? It's all settled," said Mrs. Aksdal. She gave Theo an appreciative smile. "Takk, it is good of you to go to that trouble."

A small group of well-wishers stood on the dock. Jorgen was surprised to see Mr. Aksdal's friend the tailor was there as was Mr. Een, the lawyer. They stood next to Theo's father-in-law, Mr. Lande. Anna arrived with Georg and Henrik, and they huddled with the others. Each one smiled, and they were all effusive in their wishes for a safe journey, but their eyes expressed traces of doubt that belied their cheerfulness. The unrelenting rain discouraged long goodbyes and all too soon, the three travelers found themselves aboard the ship.

The excitement leading up to this day—the anticipation that had driven Jorgen from bed earlier than usual that morning—had ebbed with each parting hug and handshake. The reality and finality of their leaving hung on him like a heavy mantle. Nothing could have prepared him for the intense feeling of sadness he felt when he shook Theo's hand for the last time and promised to write. Raising his hand in a final salute to his brother and the others who had braved the miserable weather to say good-bye, he stood at the rail, memorizing each face, grateful for the rain that hid his tears.

★ ★ ★

Jorgen left the cabin and climbed the stairs to the deck. He looked forward to spending some quiet time by himself. He pushed aside a large crate, revealing a dry spot on the rough plank floor and sat down. He leaned against the crate, opened a small pot of ink, dipped his pen into it, and began to write in his journal.

"Monday, 1 July, 1850, we set sail from Bergen." He paused and laid the pen down so he could rub his hands together to stop them from shaking. He had dreamed of writing that for so long, and often thought this day would never come. He wiped his sweaty palms on his pants, picked up the pen, and continued.

"I am traveling with my wife, Marta, and her mother, Mrs. Aksdal. We are going to Hull, England, a journey of three or four days. We will travel by rail from Hull to Liverpool where we will book our passage to America."

That's as good a start as any, thought Jorgen. He was a slow writer and having to contend with the motion of the boat had made the task even more difficult. It had taken him the better part of an hour to compose and legibly write those four sentences, and he was pleased with his effort. He reread the short entry then looked around him while he thought of what he would write next.

Small groups of passengers gathered here and there along the rail, their conversations muted by the wind and the harsh slap of waves on the boat's hull. Sailors went about their jobs in silent concentration.

Jorgen picked up his pen again and added, "I am thankful that Marta's mother chose to come with us and am looking forward to seeing Andrew." He found it difficult to believe that Andrew had sailed almost a year ago and that more than a year had gone by since he had married Marta. The time had passed so quickly.

Helping Mrs. Aksdal sell her home and Mr. Aksdal's shop and business had proven time-consuming and made Jorgen realize how little he knew about how the world operated. Worried that potential buyers might try to cheat Mrs. Aksdal, Jorgen sought advice from Mr. Een and was relieved when the lawyer offered to represent her.

Winter was fast approaching; it was too late to sail to America when Mr. Een announced he had a buyer for both the house and business. The price the buyer was willing to pay was more than Mrs. Aksdal had hoped for, but the best part of the negotiation was the buyer didn't want to move into the house until the following summer. They could rent from him until they were ready to emigrate. The buyer also asked Jorgen to keep the business going, which Jorgen readily agreed to do. It would provide income until they left the country and would enable him to keep his savings intact.

Mr. Een's friendship proved helpful in another way. He had contacts in many foreign cities and was able to provide Jorgen with letters of introduction to the proprietors of boarding houses in Liverpool and New York City. Jorgen suspected they would have to spend a few days in those two large cities and it was a relief to know the location of safe, inexpensive lodging.

Selling Mrs. Aksdal's property was only the first of three complications that had slowed Jorgen's timetable for emigration. The second involved sorting through possessions and weeding out items that would not make the journey with them. All that Jorgen owned could be fit into the chest he had made before leaving home, but Marta and Mrs. Aksdal had a houseful of items to consider and a future American home to furnish. The shipping lines placed limits on the amount of baggage passengers were allowed to take, so aside from personal articles, everything chosen to make the trip had to be scrutinized and agreed upon by all of them or it wasn't packed. This had proven time-consuming; in some cases, deliberations had gone on for days.

To the extent that the women found this sorting-out process vexing, Jorgen was equally burdened with the final complication: the voyage itself. He now had women to consider. Knowing how uncomfortable and frightening life at sea could be, Jorgen was determined to make the journey as pleasant as possible for Marta and her mother.

He also had to confront his own discomfort with the sea. Nightmares about giant waves engulfing him still bedeviled his sleep, even though he hadn't been on water in more than a year.

Newspaper stories about disasters at sea fueled his consternation. Shortly after coming to Bergen, Jorgen read about the barque, Ocean Monarch. It caught fire soon after leaving Liverpool and more than 170 emigrants had perished. The same fate had befallen the Caleb Grimshaw the previous November, resulting in 90 deaths. Although these tragedies were rare, the fact that they could and did occur made Jorgen cautious, almost to a fault.

He made inquiries into every shipping line that had an office in Bergen, plying them with endless questions. He sought advice from anyone whose family members had already emigrated. In the end, he chose the Wilson Line to sail from Bergen to Hull, England. Its safety record was the deciding factor, but Jorgen also liked that it had a reputation for treating its passengers fairly and with respect.

Although he could have done so from Bergen, he decided to wait until he was in Liverpool to choose a transatlantic line so that he could gather information and compare the shipping lines that embarked from there. Jorgen considered it crucial that he be able to look over the ships before selecting one.

He had picked Liverpool as his embarkation site both because that port offered the greatest number of ships from which to choose and because competition among Liverpool's numerous lines resulted in the lowest rates of all European routes.

Tobacco, lumber, cotton, and wheat were a few of the goods that arrived in Liverpool, shipped from America. These items were off-loaded and replaced with America-bound manufactured goods like finished textiles, dishes, and tools. With most shipping lines, ships that were unable to fill their cargo area sold space to passengers at an average rate of 25 dalers per passenger. Jorgen hoped to book passage on a ship that had transported clean, dry materials; perhaps one that had carried cotton. If that didn't work, he thought he might be able to trade his service as a sailor for a cabin that Marta and her mother could share. Cabins for such a long voyage could cost as much as five or six times the steerage rate. Unsure of his ability as a sailor, Jorgen hoped it would not come to that, and he tried to put it out of his mind. That was one worry that would have to wait until he reached Liverpool.

The Wilson Line ran more than one ship to Hull, so Jorgen made inquiries about the individual ships. In that regard, Mr. Lande, Theo's father-in-law was quite helpful. He knew most captains and ships that traveled in and out of Bergen. On his recommendation, Jorgen booked passage on the Lykke Til. Mr. Lande surprised him by purchasing a cabin for him and Marta. "Consider it a belated wedding gift," he had said. Jorgen suspected Mr. Lande's largesse was in response to his son Hauk's callous acts. However, Mr. Lande seemed sincere in his offer and would not take no for an answer.

So, with the knowledge that he and Marta would enjoy the comfort of a cabin, Jorgen insisted that Mrs. Aksdal upgrade her ticket to a shared cabin, thus insuring they would all have a pleasant start to their long journey.

★ ★ ★

"I am probably the only Norwegian who hates the sea," Jorgen thought as he contemplated what to add to the journal before rejoining Marta in the cabin. When they sailed out of port, he had noticed birds flying over Bryggen Wharf, despite the rain. *It would be wonderful to be a bird,* he thought, *to fly to America far above the sea, perhaps even above the rain and the clouds.*

The sun finally poked through the clouds, and Jorgen adjusted his hat to shield his eyes from its glare. He dipped his pen into the ink and continued writing. "The captain says the weather and ocean should stay calm for the next day or two. That should give Marta and her mother a chance to get used to sailing."

And finally, he added, "This is what our ship, looks like."

He sketched the Norwegian ship and smiled as he wrote its name, 'Lykke Til.' *I hope it's an omen,* he thought. He whispered the name as if it were a prayer, "Lykke Til, Lykke Til, Good Luck."

He blotted the page, closed the book, and secured the stopper on the ink bottle, then stood, stretched, and deeply inhaled the damp salt air. *I must bring the women up here for some fresh air while there's still daylight left,* he thought, and left to do so.

The smell of wet wool, like the odor of the sheep shed, assailed Jorgen's nostrils when he opened the door to his cabin. The damp clothing they had worn earlier in the day was hanging from rope that crisscrossed the cabin.

Marta's voice greeted him from the other side of the clothing. "I hope you don't mind, but I had to hang Mor's dress in here; her cabin is so much smaller than ours, there was no room to hang anything."

"I shared a bedroom with four of my brothers," said Jorgen. "As long as this wool doesn't bleat during the night, it won't bother me." Jorgen parted the clothing and approached Marta who was lying on the bed.

"I think the excitement of the day got to me; I felt I had to rest for a few minutes."

Jorgen lay down next to her and enfolded her in his arms.

"I know these last few months have been difficult for both you and your mother. Selling the house and your father's business, saying goodbye to your friends, packing, putting up with your husband..." He paused, waited, and was rewarded with her sweet laughter.

"Now that's the one thing that hasn't been too difficult," she said, and kissed him tenderly, gently at first, and then with a passion that surprised him by its sudden intensity.

Jorgen needed little more from her than a flicker of desire, so strong was his overwhelming love. They responded eagerly to each other's needs with touches and caresses that climaxed in the ultimate intimacy, then lay together for a time in each other's arms.

Marta looked up at her mother's dress hanging over their bed and began to giggle. "I feel like a child caught in the act of doing something," she said, "but it was glorious, wasn't it?"

"Ja," replied Jorgen with a satisfied grin on his face. "I almost wish we could stay at sea forever; no cares, no worries, just lots of time for making love."

"You don't like the sea," Marta laughed, "but it will be nice to have these next few weeks together."

Jorgen propped himself up with an elbow and leaned

down over Marta. He kissed her eyes, first one, then the other, kissed the tip of her nose, then his lips found hers. He knew she understood what was in his heart, the indescribable love that he felt for her, because he could feel her joy, the intensity of her own love for him.

A crash outside their cabin, followed by a rant of obscenities, ended their lovemaking. Pulling on his shirt and pants, Jorgen dodged the hanging clothes and tripped over his shoes as he made his way to the door. He yanked it open and came face-to-face with an angry looking man who berated a young girl. She scrambled about the narrow, dimly lit corridor picking up potatoes and onions and putting them into a large pot.

Although the girl's face was lost in shadow, her size and the way she moved reminded Jorgen of his sister.

"Inger?" The name tumbled from his lips before he had time to think.

"Her name's not Inger!" The man shouted at Jorgen then directed his wrath at the child.

"Clumsy, stupid girl! I knew you'd be trouble, I should have left you at home!" He kicked a kettle at his feet, which missed hitting her as it clattered down the passageway spewing water in its wake. "If you don't hurry, we'll be eating raw vegetables tonight."

Jorgen had to take a step back. The smell of whiskey and the man's unwashed body was overpowering.

"What's going on out there?" asked Marta. Jorgen filled the small doorway blocking her view.

"Nothing that concerns you," the man snarled. "Mind your own business." He stalked down the passageway and when he reached the end, where stairs led to the deck, he turned back, swore at the girl, and ordered her to get the food to the cookhouse immediately.

The girl frantically threw two errant potatoes and a small cabbage into one pot, a jug of water and the teakettle in another, and attempted to juggle the lot.

Marta had maneuvered herself in front of Jorgen and spoke up before the child left. "That's a heavy load. Would you like some help?"

"Nei, nei!" The girl said without turning around. "Pappa wouldn't like that."

Jorgen and Marta watched as she stumbled after her father. They could still hear the clatter of pots long after she disappeared from their view.

Back inside their cabin, Marta said, "Poor thing, she looked so frightened."

"I know," said Jorgen. "The man's a bully. It was good of you to offer help, but the child is probably right. Her father wouldn't like our interference. I'll speak to the captain about the way he treated the girl, but I don't think there is much that can be done."

He drew Marta close, encircling her waist with his arms. "I think, my sweet, thoughtful wife, we'd better do something about our middag, too."

Despite the intimacy of their relationship, even now, standing with his arms around Marta, Jorgen was oblivious to subtle physical changes in his wife. Changes that had taken place gradually over the past few weeks: her weight gain, thickened waistline, and the rounder, fuller shape of her breasts. He saw what he had always seen in Marta, a woman so lovely, so perfect, that had her hair turned green, he would not have noticed. In his eyes, she would always look like the girl who sat under the tree with him in the schoolyard.

★ ★ ★

Earlier that afternoon, after they weighed anchor, the captain had assembled all the passengers on deck for a roll call while the sailors searched the boat for stowaways. When they were satisfied that all onboard had paid for the journey, each passenger was issued the first day's three-quart allotment of water and were told that the cookhouse, a galley located on deck, would be open until 8:00 p.m. that night.

Their ticket price included two meals a day starting on day two and ending the day they reached port. Although the trip would only take three or four days, Marta and her mother had planned enough food to last the trio a week. Their food chest was stocked with ample amounts of cheese, dried fish, potatoes, onions, cabbage, oatmeal, rice, bread, and some staples such as sugar, molasses, and flour. They packed a kettle and a sufficient supply of tea, as that would be the easiest beverage to prepare on board the boat.

The shipping line had informed Jorgen that they would need this food once they got to Hull because that town had a strict policy regarding immigrants. Because of the possibility of spreading illness, passengers were not permitted to leave the ship until the weekly train to Liverpool was in the station. And that could mean several days in port.

★ ★ ★

Jorgen, Marta, and Mrs. Aksdal heard the commotion in the cookhouse as soon as they arrived on deck. When they got closer, Jorgen recognized the man who had been outside their cabin. This time, he was directing his anger at several women who were preparing food and tending pots on the stove. Forgotten for the moment was the little girl. She stood just outside the galley doorway, barely visible behind the pots, which she still clutched.

The man demanded that the women make room at the stove for the girl.

Most of the women ignored him, although one did say to him that he should have come sooner. This enraged the man even further. He grabbed her by the arm and attempted to pull her away from the stove.

An internal debate raged within Jorgen. *Should I intervene or mind my own business?* If he didn't do something, he was afraid the man would injure someone. He could see that Marta was agitated and decided if he didn't act soon, either she or her mother would say something and the man might turn his fury on them.

"Marta," he said quietly, "I'd like you and you mother to go back to her cabin."

Once they turned to leave, Jorgen approached the group in the cookhouse.

"Excuse me," he said loudly, getting everyone's attention. "How much longer before someone is finished?"

"The woman standing nearest Jorgen told him fifteen minutes, another said, "I'll be done in less than an hour." Others agreed that they would also be done in times varying from one-half to an hour's time.

"Takk," he said to the women. Then he turned to the angry man. "Since you were here before me, you can take this woman's spot in fifteen minutes. I'll wait for the next open spot."

Jorgen stared at the other man until he released the woman's arm.

"This man's right!" Jorgen flinched at the suddenness of words bellowed from behind him.

"Everyone must wait their turn!"

Jorgen turned toward the voice and looked into the face of the captain.

"Stay right here until I get back!" the angry man commanded the girl. He glared at Jorgen and hurried away.

When the man was out of sight, Jorgen approached the girl, took the pots from her, and set them on the floor. "Perhaps you'd like to sit down while you wait for your father." She looked tired and was definitely in need of a bath. Her eyes looked so fearful that Jorgen knew as soon as he turned his back, she'd pick up the heavy load and stand in place as she had been told.

"May I have a word with you?" Jorgen asked the captain. When they had walked far enough from the girl so as not to be overheard, Jorgen told the captain what he knew of the young girl and her father.

"I'm sorry for the girl and fear for her safety." Jorgen said as the two men parted. When he reached the stairs to go below, Jorgen turned and saw that the captain was speaking to her. Two of the women from the cookhouse had joined him, and the girl, now surrounded, was lost from view.

★ ★ ★

"An hour! I don't think I can wait an hour." complained Marta. "We haven't had anything to eat since early morning, and I'm beginning to feel nauseous."

They were back in her mother's cabin and Jorgen had just explained the situation in the cookhouse.

Marta sat on her mother's bed and Jorgen noticed, when she resumed speaking, that she still looked tired. "If we have to wait an hour before we can begin to cook anything, that won't give us enough time. The steward said the cook house would close at 8:00 p.m. sharp."

"I guess our naps were a bit too long," said Mrs. Aksdal. She opened the food chest.

Jorgen stole a quick look at Marta. Her head was bent, but he could see her mother's comment about their 'nap' had forced a smile to form on her lips.

"But we have plenty here that needs no cooking. We can have smorbord," said Mrs. Aksdal. She took out cheese, fish, and bread for the sandwiches, and returned the vegetables she had taken out earlier. "Perhaps later we can boil water for tea."

Although he was hungry, Jorgen didn't eat much. He feared consuming too much of their supply lest they run out of food before reaching Liverpool. His years back home, when, more times than not, he left the table still hungry, made this light meal seem normal. When he finished eating, he rummaged in the food chest until he located the teakettle. "I'll fill this and go wait for a spot at the stove," he said, before

175

leaving the cabin.

Mrs. Aksdal and Marta had not put much on their plates either, but unlike Jorgen they ate slowly. Marta especially savored each bite.

"My stomach is slightly upset," said Mrs. Aksdal. "Can you finish this for me?" She placed half her smorbord on Marta's plate.

Marta started to object. "Really, I've had enough," her mother said, "I think my stomach needs to adjust to sailing, and you need this more than I do."

★ ★ ★

"Look who I found on deck," said Jorgen when he returned. He held a steaming kettle of water in one hand and his fiddle was tucked under the other arm.

"Did you have a nice nap, Mrs. Aksdal?" her cabin mate asked. She had preceded Jorgen into the cabin and was now sitting on her cot facing Mrs. Aksdal. Their knees touched in the cramped space.

Marta had been sitting next to her mother but rose when Jorgen entered and took the kettle from him.

"We're all feeling rested," replied Mrs. Aksdal. "We practically slept through middag. How was your afternoon?"

"I found a sheltered seat, out of the wind, and enjoyed watching the activity on deck," the woman replied. "This is my first time on a ship and I find the sailors a fascinating lot. They seem to come from all over the world and speak so many different languages. I don't see how they understand one another."

While the two older women chatted, Marta prepared tea on top of her mother's trunk of clothing and linens, and Jorgen adjusted the strings on his fiddle.

"I didn't know that I would be treated to a concert," said the roommate. She was a short, cheerful woman who appeared to be a few years older than Mrs. Aksdal. Her name was Mrs. Klark, and Jorgen marveled at her lighthearted spirit despite the sad tale that she had told them earlier that day.

She was on her way to Liverpool to bring her daughter and granddaughter back home to Norway. They, along with Mrs. Klark's son-in-law, had been forced to stay in Liverpool for several months because the money for their trip to America had been stolen. Her son-in-law had been able to find a job, but then cholera struck all three, killing the son-in-law and leaving Mrs. Klark's daughter too weak to travel alone.

Marta handed each woman a cup of tea, took one for herself, and sat down next to her mother. Jorgen raised the fiddle to his chin and began to play an old folk song. The women hummed along with him. When he finished, there was a knock at the door.

"Uh oh," said Marta, "Perhaps we've disturbed the other cabins."

When Jorgen opened the door, the captain stepped inside the cabin and smiled at the cozy group. "I wonder if you'd mind keeping your door open," he said. "Some of the other passengers would like to listen to your music."

The captain stepped aside and Jorgen could see several people standing in the passageway.

"Also," the captain continued, "if you could play on deck tomorrow, I think the passengers and crew would welcome the diversion."

★ ★ ★

The trip to Hull could not have gone better. The ship made good time despite weak easterly winds and sailed into port on Wednesday morning, their fourth day at sea. The Captain had insisted that all passengers walk on deck as often as possible. He claimed that breathing sea air was good for one's health and warded off seasickness. Whether it was the exercise, the fresh air, or the fact the sea had been unusually calm, illness had been kept at bay, even in steerage. Jorgen was pleased and relieved that Marta and her mother had enjoyed a pleasant voyage.

The ship's food had been fresh, due to the shortness of the trip. Aside from the angry man who kept to himself the rest of the trip, the other passengers were friendly and most knew Jorgen by name because of his daily fiddle sessions on deck.

When daily water rations were passed out, they had seen the young girl, and Mrs. Aksdal had attempted to talk to her, but the girl's father warned the child with an angry look and the poor thing seemed too frightened to answer.

The day they entered the port, everyone gathered on deck to catch their first glimpse of England.

"Look," whispered Mrs. Aksdal. She inclined her head left to indicate the angry man and his daughter. They approached the rail a slight distance from where she, Marta, and Jorgen stood. The child walked with head cast down but glanced up briefly when Mrs. Aksdal made a show of clearing her throat. A smile flickered then the child nervously returned her gaze to the deck.

"She's such a pretty little thing," Mrs. Aksdal said, her voice barely audible over the sound of waves and the excited chatter of passengers. "I'd love to give her a bath and fix her hair. I have some blue ribbon that would look lovely in her long hair."

Marta linked her arm with her mother's. "I wonder what happened to her mother?"

"And I wonder why a man, blessed with a lovely child, doesn't have the good sense to take proper care of her?" Mrs. Aksdal's peevish speculation was drowned out by the shouted commands of the sailors and the noise of the anchor being lowered.

"It doesn't look like I thought it would."

Jorgen wasn't aware he had said the words aloud. He had been standing at the rail ever since Hull had come into view, transfixed by the sight of this country, long loathed by his family and all Norwegians. He didn't know what he had expected to see. Everything looked so ordinary. This was the country that had descended on the Norwegian fleet in 1807 sweeping it into its war against France. When the Napoleonic Wars ended, seven years later, Norway was bankrupt. The passage of time had not brought better conditions, and as a result, Jorgen grew up in a country where nothing good was ever said about England.

The River Humber, Jorgen noted, spilled into the sea, just like the fjords in Bergen. As in Bergen, fishing boats were everywhere and large sailing ships crowded the harbor.

It's no different here than home, thought Jorgen. *Everyone's just going about his or her business.*

Shortly after they dropped anchor, passengers whose final destination was Hull were told to prepare to disembark. Boats were lowered that would row them to shore because the Lykke Til would not be given a place at the wharf until the train to Liverpool arrived.

The captain announced that there was room in one boat for a few passengers whose final destination was not Hull, but might have a need to go ashore. They would be allowed two hours to take care of business while sailors ran errands for the captain, then they would be rowed back to the ship. "Only healthy ones can go," the captain said. "All those taken ashore will be examined by a doctor, and anyone sick will find themselves in a hospital, perhaps for weeks."

The captain asked for a show of hands and several were raised including one belonging to the angry man.

"That's too many," the captain said. "You'll all have to meet with the bosun. He will make the decision."

While all this was taking place, Marta and Mrs. Aksdal collected their water rations, and went to the cook shop to prepare the morning meal.

Jorgen lingered on deck to watch the awkward process of disembarkation. He assisted passengers who struggled with cumbersome baggage and listened to the English that was spoken by many of them.

"Thank you," he was told by those grateful for his help. "Takk." At least he understood that. He had heard English spoken on the Bryggen wharf and in taverns where fishermen hung out, but had never paid much attention to it or the men who spoke it. Jorgen had been taught to distrust and dislike all things English. But, after the first day on this ship sharing close quarters with English passengers, he realized that they were not his enemy. In fact, they seemed a lot like him. But their language sounded strange and complicated; they spoke rapidly, making it difficult to tell where one word stopped and the next word began. Jorgen and the others, especially Andrew and Marta, had talked about the need to learn English, and all had agreed that once they were in America, they would learn to speak as Americans. It had sounded so easy. However, as Marta had acknowledged just the day before, "We'll have to find someone to teach us this language; I'll never learn it on my own." Jorgen was inclined to agree with her.

"Thank you," he repeated over and over to himself. He practiced the only English words he knew as he went back to his cabin for breakfast.

★ ★ ★

Jorgen and Marta spent the rest of the morning in their cabin. As had become a daily habit on this trip, Jorgen made an entry in his diary. He also wrote a letter to his parents and one to Theo and Anna.

Marta sat beside him on their cot and knit feverishly. The steady click of her needles countered the scratch of Jorgen's pen on paper. Her conscience troubled her and as more time passed, her agitation increased.

I have to tell him, she scolded herself. She knew she should have confided in him as soon as she was sure. He should have been the first to know. Nevertheless, she knew his thoughtfulness, had witnessed how he put other's needs before his own dream. She suspected he would have delayed their plans if he knew her secret.

Reluctance to leave his family and then his grandfather's death had stalled his plans initially, then his accident and recovery, her father's death, their wedding and farewell visit with family, and finally, the time it took to settle her mother's affairs kept pushing his plans further into the future.

Then, just as things were coming together for their journey, she discovered she was pregnant. She had not wanted to shake his confidence with news of his impending fatherhood, did not want him delaying their departure out of concern for her or the baby. Had she been wrong? Anxiety and guilt had settled over her, weighing on her every thought. She feared he would be angry with her, at her deceit, and she knew he had every right to be. She loved him so much that she couldn't stand the thought of his anger at her, no matter how justified.

"I need some fresh air," she said abruptly. She set her knitting aside and rose from the cot.

"Almost finished," said Jorgen. "As soon as I address these letters and put my things away, I'll join you."

★ ★ ★

Jorgen dashed up to the deck, eager for fresh air and a walk with Marta, but a thick fog had settled on the ship, and it was difficult to see anything beyond five or six paces. He walked the length of the ship, but with so many of his fellow passengers also out for exercise, he was unable to locate her. He walked the deck a while longer and was about to go back to the cabin to see if she had returned when he heard a familiar voice.

"When is the baby due?"

181

Jorgen recognized Mrs. Klark's voice before he could actually see her. *I'll ask her if she's seen Marta,* thought Jorgen.

"Four, maybe five months."

Jorgen froze. *That's Marta! What is she saying?* Shocked by what he had heard, he turned and hurriedly walked in the opposite direction.

A baby... Marta's pregnant. Why didn't she tell me?

Wave after wave of emotion washed over Jorgen as he tried to come to grips with what he had overheard.

Fear, for the baby, who would be born God-only-knows-where, for Marta, giving birth under what circumstances.

Anger. *She was telling a complete stranger, telling her before he knew their personal news. Weren't married couples supposed to confide in each other?*

Doubt. *Why didn't she trust him? Maybe she didn't love him. He quickly dismissed that last thought. But why hadn't she told him? She had obviously known for weeks, if not months.*

Jorgen skulked through the farthest reaches of the ship, places that he knew the women would not include in their walk, attempting to understand why Marta had excluded him from this huge, exciting news. *It was exciting, wasn't it? Maybe she thought he didn't want children, or wasn't ready for a child. Was he ready? Was this good news or bad news?*

Jorgen's emotions raged on and on, anger, supposition, doubt, until a light went on...and an explanation emerged. Jorgen could see Marta telling him, weeks ago, and the dilemma it would have caused. And at last, he understood, or at least he thought he did, and he went to find Marta.

"Did you have a nice walk?"

Marta didn't look up from her knitting. The needles darted in and out of the pale green yarn like small silver fish in sea weed.

"I went looking for you." He paused, then continued.

"It's very foggy isn't it?"

There was a long silence.

"I heard you," he said softly. He came and sat beside her on the cot.

"I thought maybe you had. That was you standing by the rail." She put her knitting down and looked at him.

The last time Jorgen had seen that expression on her face was when they stood across the table from each other looking down on her father's battered face.

"I am so sorry, Jorgen. I should have told you. You should have been the first to know."

Whatever anger still remained in him, whatever doubt he had felt, was instantly extinguished by the remorseful tone of her words and the look of misery on his wife's face.

"I'm sure you had your reasons, but I hope that in the future you will trust me to handle all news, good or bad."

"I don't blame you for being angry with me, I do trust you. It's just..." she paused. "You always think of others first, and I didn't want to be the reason for postponing your trip, again."

Jorgen placed his finger gently over her lips. "Shhh...I'm not angry. I admit I was at first, but I think I understand why you didn't tell me."

He lowered his hand and placed it on her abdomen. A look of surprise registered on his face as he slowly rubbed the bump that was there.

"How did I not notice this?" he said, genuinely amazed at his own ignorance. "What kind of father will I make if I can't even recognize when my own wife is pregnant?"

"You'll be a very good farmer and a very good pappa, and your wife's job will be to tell you when she pregnant."

They laughed and hugged and talked some more. "A father... we're going to be parents, that's wonderful news," said Jorgen as he came to terms with the idea. They were happy in the moment, in love, and Marta felt relieved that the burden of her secret had been lifted.

"We have plenty of time," she said, "at least four months, maybe a little longer."

"A new country, a new home, a new baby," said Jorgen. "And I'm not going to worry about any of it." He looked at Marta and they both started to laugh. He would worry, they both knew he would worry, to think otherwise was laughable. And so they laughed again until tears of relief and worry streamed down their faces.

★ ★ ★

Later that evening, the fog lifted. The glow from hundreds of lamps in Hull made a beautiful display. Most of the lights radiated from fixed places, store windows, street corners, parlor windows, but some moved about Hull like large fireflies. They came from lanterns attached to wagons moving about the city. Jorgen had observed similar occurrences upon returning to Bergen from a fishing trip, just after nightfall.

A large group gathered on deck, anxious to take in some final breaths of fresh air before retiring to their stuffy quarters for the night. Although the cabins that Jorgen, Marta, and Mrs. Aksdal had were cramped and airless, the passengers in steerage were subject to conditions that could only be described as sickening. Even the departure, earlier that day, of those going to Hull did not improve the situation. With little or no privacy, people in steerage slept in their clothes, and fearful of losing their shoes, most wore them to bed. Due to the limited quantity of water, bathing placed a distant third after drinking and cooking. The fresh air that did make it down there was insufficient to remove the stale stench that passengers were forced to breathe all night.

Jorgen played a few songs on his fiddle, then sat down next to Marta, and they listened to an old man who entertained the group with folktales about the Askeladden.

Jorgen knew all these stories by heart, having heard Bestefar or Far tell them on long winter nights. The tales had appealed to him as a child because the hero of the stories, the Ash Lad, was like Jorgen, the youngest of three boys.

The group on deck laughed and clapped in appreciation when the old man told how Askeladden outwitted the troll when they competed in an eating match. It was as though Jorgen had been transported back to his childhood. He sat transfixed while the old man brought the characters to life. Some children giggled, others cast furtive glances into dark corners, fearing trolls that might lurk there.

The old man had just launched into his next tale, The Ash Lad and the Good Helpers, when someone tapped Jorgen on the shoulder.

"Come with me!"

It was a command, not a question. Jorgen looked up into the grave expression that creased the captain's face.

"Be back in a minute," he whispered to Marta, and he followed the Captain to the far end of the ship. The sailors who had gone to Hull earlier that day had returned and were unloading provisions from the boats they had used. The passengers who had been allowed to go with them were standing off to one side. The captain stopped in front of the frightened-looking group and motioned Jorgen to his side. Jorgen recognized the men—they were Norwegian, good men, family men. Their expressions on this night were grim.

The captain pointed to one of them and told him to tell what happened on shore.

The tall, thin man began to talk. "After the English doctor examined us, he said we could go into town. The bosun told us to be back at the boat at five o'clock, and then we went our separate ways. When Mr. Bjorn wasn't there at five, the bosun asked us where he was. I told him that I had overheard Mr. Bjorn say that he needed to buy medicine for his daughter. The bosun laughed at that and told us to go look for him in all the places near the wharf that serve drink."

The tall man paused, looked out to sea, and shook his head. He seemed too shocked by what he had seen to continue.

"We found him in a narrow passageway between two taverns," another man continued. "A crowd had gathered around his body. There was a lot of blood...his throat had been slashed...he was dead. A man in a uniform was asking questions, but we couldn't understand what was being said. We were afraid to admit we knew Mr. Bjorn, so we left."

"None of you were with him? No one saw what happened?" asked the captain.

The men responded with head shakes. They denied knowing anything else about the murder of their fellow passenger.

The captain dismissed them, then turned to Jorgen.

"I'm sure you're wondering why I brought you here." He didn't wait for Jorgen's response. "I know your brother Theo to be an honorable person and have judged you the same. You showed concern for Vidar Bjorn's child the first day we were at sea."

"I didn't know his name," said Jorgen. "And I didn't like him, but he didn't deserve to die like that. What will happen to the child?"

"I have to go into Hull tomorrow to make arrangements for the body. We'll sort out the child's situation when I return. I know it is a lot to ask, but I am hoping that your family will look after her until I can determine what should be done. The child is too young to be in steerage by herself. Your wife and her mother are fine ladies. I know the child will be safe with you. Please talk to your wife while I go fetch the child."

"Will you tell her about her father?" asked Jorgen.

"Yes," he replied. "I will tell her what happened."

Jorgen left to talk to Marta. He felt they really didn't have a choice in the matter; the captain seemed to expect that they would take on this responsibility.

The old man was finished telling stories, and the passengers were shuffling back to steerage for the night when Jorgen returned to the women. All three looked at him expectantly. Marta's mother and Mrs. Klark were like old friends now.

Although the women detested the angry man, they were horrified by the murder, and the pity they felt for the young girl turned to a united resolve to help her. Jorgen was speechless as he listened to the women. They had no further questions and didn't consider the possible consequences of helping the child. Indeed, they never even considered not helping her.

"She's a tiny thing, she won't take up much room," said Mrs. Klark. "She can share my cot."

"Or mine," said Mrs. Aksdal. "We'll have to clean her up, first. We certainly don't want to share our bed with vermin." Just the thought caused her a momentary shiver.

"Well, Mother, looks like you'll be using that blue ribbon, after all," said Marta.

"A man's life should be worth more than a bit of blue ribbon," Mrs. Aksdal said. "That child was his greatest treasure. I know I shouldn't judge, but it appears that he squandered it on drink. Now, what's to become of his treasure?"

Mrs. Klark reached over and patted her hand. "We can offer her comfort tonight. That's what she needs now."

"I'll find the Captain and ask him about getting us an extra ration of water, and see if there is some place to bathe her," said Jorgen. *At last*, he thought, *something I can do.*

★ ★ ★

The women sprang into action when Jorgen and the captain arrived with the stranded child in tow. She was a pathetic sight: tearful, frightened, shy, and filthy.

"Her name is Mary," the captain said. "I'll leave you

to get acquainted and will go instruct the cook to heat some pots of water and to place a tub for bathing in the cookhouse."

The girl barely acknowledged the long locks of lice-infested hair that Mrs. Aksdal clipped and Marta hastily swept up and threw into the fire of the cook stove.

"I'm sorry that I have to cut it so short, Mary," inch-long stubble stuck out on the girl's head, " but there's no other way to get rid of these pests," said Mrs. Aksdal.

"You can have this," Marta pulled a cap from her pocket. " It might be big for you, but it ties, so it won't fall off. You can wear it until your hair grows back."

Tears trickled down Mary's face while she submitted to the haircut and the vigorous scrubbing that followed. Marta's mother continued to murmur words of encouragement, a continuous stream of quiet conversation attempting to calm the child. Mary nodded once or twice responding to questions, but she said nothing.

She has reason to weep, Marta thought as she watched her mother and Mrs. Klark leave the cookhouse, each clutching one of Mary's hands. The child wore one of Mrs. Klark's nightdresses, cinched at the waist with the blue ribbon. Marta's cap concealed not only the ugly hair stubble but most of Mary's small head. She reminded Marta of a doll that she had seen in a Bergen shop window.

Marta went back into the cookhouse and dumped the meager contents of Mary's cardboard suitcase into the tub of water. If bugs had taken up residence in the girl's clothing, Marta surely didn't want to bring them into their cabin. Also, judging by the soiled dress that Mary had been wearing, Marta assumed all the child's things probably needed a good washing.

Marta strung Mary's clothing in the cabin to dry and collapsed, an exhausted heap, into bed. She was sound asleep before Jorgen extinguished the lamp in their cabin. He lay beside her, aware of the pungent scent of soap that permeated the air.

The news of a baby on the way had taken him completely by surprise and while still coming to terms with that development, another child had been thrust into their lives. For someone who planned every inch of his life, these events presented a challenge.

Jorgen lay on his back, positioned for thought, not sleep. His hands cupped the back of his head, his arms and elbows stuck out on either side of his head. His eyes stared straight up at the ceiling he knew was there but couldn't see in the dark cabin.

Mary will be gone in a day or two, he speculated, *but in four months, maybe five...we'll have a baby. Where will we be? Will we have time to get settled before it comes? It would have been safer to have the baby in Norway...Marta should have told me she was pregnant before we left Bergen.*

Jorgen heaped one concern and worry on top another. *How expensive is a baby? Do we have enough money? I don't want the baby born in New York City or, worse yet, aboard some crowded ship. How soon can an infant travel? What if it gets sick...and dies?* Jorgen didn't like the thoughts he was having. He rolled over onto his side and closed his eyes. *Sleep,* he told himself, *I need to sleep.* He imagined looking into a deep, dark well. He slowed his breathing to match Marta's and finally fell asleep.

Eight

Two Days Later

Dawn was still hours away, yet carriages and wagons already formed a line on the wharf, waiting their turn to transport passengers to the train station. Because of the weekly immigrant train, Monday was the most profitable day of the week for wagon drivers. Some weeks, more than one ship waited offshore for the train, and by days end, the drivers' pockets bulged with cash. Today, there was just one. Unscrupulous drivers would be looking for ways to cheat unsuspecting passengers to make up for fewer fares.

The Lykke Til was moored at the pier, and an orderly procession of passengers filed off the boat onto the Humber Dock. The captain ran a highly organized ship and, until Jorgen and his party set foot on shore, disembarking was uneventful. On the wharf, however, all was chaos. Shipping agents, whom the captain refused to allow on his ship because he said he couldn't tell the thieves from the honest ones, brazened it out on the wharf attempting to distribute tickets to passengers who held vouchers for subsequent travel, and to peddle transoceanic tickets to those who, like Jorgen, planned to purchase tickets in Liverpool.

Knowing what scoundrels the agents were, Jorgen had hoped to avoid them at least until he got to Liverpool. This was not to be, however, as events over the previous twenty-four hours had left Mary under his protection. More precisely, she was in the temporary care of Mrs. Aksdal and Mrs. Klark. No final decision had been made, but Mrs. Klark had offered to take custody of the child.

The Captain had found vouchers for two transatlantic tickets in the dead man's baggage. Jorgen needed to locate the agent from the Whitley Shipping Company to exchange the vouchers for tickets. The tickets represented all that

Mary's father had left her, as no money had been found on his body or among his possessions. Once in Liverpool, Jorgen would seek a refund for both the father and daughter's ticket to America and give the money to Mrs. Klark. She would purchase Mary's ticket, along with her own, when she was ready to return to Norway with her daughter and granddaughter.

If finding the agent hadn't been difficult enough, convincing him to give Jorgen the tickets was maddening.

"How do I know your story is true? What happens if Mr. Vidar Bjorn shows up after you leave to claim these tickets?" The agent's eyes darted here and there as if he expected the dead man to appear. His tone was hostile. "You have nothing to prove what you say."

In the end, Jorgen had to take the agent onboard to talk to the captain before the agent would relinquish the tickets.

In the time it took to deal with this problem, the temperature dropped and a cold heavy mist had stolen in from the sea, enveloping all the confusion on the wharf. When he returned to where he thought he had left the women and baggage, they had vanished, their whereabouts hidden in the fog. Jorgen called out to Marta and, despite the commotion that surrounded him, he was able to follow her voice to a carriage the women occupied. The baggage was stowed in a wagon directly in front of them.

"Well done," Jorgen said to Marta and her mother.

"I think the driver thought we were unescorted; he was eager to help us. He summoned the wagon and loaded our baggage into it," Marta said. She blew on her hands to warm them.

Jorgen tipped his hat to the driver "Thank you," he said, trying out his newly learned English words. Judging by the scowl he received in return, Jorgen suspected the driver was not happy that he had arrived on the scene.

Jorgen whistled to the wagon driver and when he had his attention he gestured that he wanted the driver to stay close to their carriage. He had heard that stolen baggage had become a profitable industry in English port cities. The driver said something that sounded like a curse and flicked the reins, impatient with the delay. Jorgen scrambled aboard the carriage but kept his eyes on the wagon as it led the way to the station.

"It's not far." Jorgen said, "We should be on the train in no time at all."

"Unusual weather for summer," observed Mrs. Aksdal. Although used to Norway's cold weather, Hull's cool, misty air chilled them all to their bones. "Then again," she sniffed, "maybe this is normal for England." She placed an arm around Mary and the shivering girl allowed herself to be drawn closer for warmth.

When they arrived at the station, Jorgen haggled with the coach driver who attempted to charge him double the fare. And the wagon driver refused to carry the baggage to the train until Jorgen paid him twice the worth of his service.

"Those two rogues," Jorgen complained to Marta, "I hope we don't run into anymore like them. I think they'd cheat their own mother if they had the chance."

Having dispensed with the baggage and the drivers, Jorgen was now able to look around the train station. "Would you look at that!" he exclaimed. He stepped back and peered down the length of the train. A dozen cars down from where he stood, steam hissed from the engine.

"We have time, let's go see it up close." He put his arm through Marta's, and they started for the engine. The others trailed behind. He walked quickly, his excitement growing at the thought of his first train trip. "Isn't it beautiful, Marta?"

She laughed. "You men and your machines. That sounds like something my father would say. I'm not sure I'd call it beautiful, but it is impressive. It's hard to believe one engine can pull this many cars."

They were almost adjacent to the engine when it emitted a blast of steam and the whistle sounded. Mary unloosed a frightened scream and pulled away from Mrs. Aksdal. The terrified child took off at a run, and when Jorgen realized what was happening, he ran after her. He had no difficulty catching up to her, but it took some coaxing and the promise of buying her a sweet to get her to return and board the train. Her anxiety eased once the journey began and the train sped smoothly on its rails. She sat with her nose glued to the window for the first hour.

Although captivated by the train, Jorgen found the four-hour trip to Liverpool disappointing. He had looked forward to seeing the English countryside, but rain and fog obscured most of what lay on the other side of miles and miles of stone walls and hedgerows. Occasional breaks in the weather revealed glimpses of pastures dotted with sheep, and fields of what appeared to be wheat.

The fog lifted when they approached some of the towns, but that didn't seem to improve their atmosphere. Smoke belched from factory smokestacks in Leeds and Stalybridge, creating its own smoggy dreariness.

Jorgen closed his eyes; he had seen enough. In his judgment, based on what he glimpsed through the fog, England did not come close to matching the beauty of Norway. He wondered if any country could compare favorably with his homeland.

He relaxed into the seat, feeling his body becoming one with the rhythm of the train. Its movement was gentle, a steady rocking motion like a ship on calm water. Jorgen's mind wandered as though it, too, rolled on rails that stretched from his home in Norway to the conjured image of land— land that would be *his* somewhere in America.

His love for the land and his flair for growing and nurturing plants had produced bountiful results in his mother's garden. When he was young, perhaps seven or eight, Bestefar admired his work in the garden and told him that he had been born with green fingers. At the time, this had puzzled him and, much to the amusement of the older members of the family, Jorgen had scrupulously examined his hands for signs of greenness.

The satisfaction he received from using his hands to grow and craft things most likely affected his choice of a favorite Bible story. Words from that story came to mind as the English countryside hurtled past the train window. 'And God called the dry land Earth...and God saw that it was good.' *If He thought it was good,* Jorgen reasoned, *it had to be good all over, not just in Norway. America must have its share of beautiful places, and England probably does, too...somewhere.* He smiled with the confidence of one who has just unraveled some great mystery.

As frequently happened, Jorgen's thoughts turned to Andrew. The last he had heard, Andrew had arrived in Kendall, New York, but that had been several months ago. He said he planned to stay there until Jorgen arrived, and that he should write when he was on his way. "And I hope that day comes soon," Andrew cajoled. If there were any changes to his plans, Andrew said he would write to Jorgen care of the New York City post office.

At the sound of Marta's voice, Jorgen's attention returned to the present.

"I'd like for us to be friends, Mary. Would you like that?" Jorgen opened one eye in time to see the girl nod her head. Marta continued. "Is there anything you'd like to say, or a question you'd like to ask me?" They were seated in the seat directly in front of Jorgen. Mrs. Aksdal and Mrs. Klark appeared to be asleep in the seat in front of them.

Other than yes and no answers, the child had not really spoken to any of them. After three days of Mary's silence, Jorgen had asked Mrs. Aksdal if she thought there was something wrong with the girl. "Give her time," Mrs. Aksdal had replied. "She's had a big shock and now she's with strangers. She's probably more than a little bit afraid of what will happen next."

Jorgen. too, wondered what was next for Mary. Again, he

thought of Inger, so carefree, happy, and loved. *Life is so unfair,* he thought. *This poor girl has nothing.* Jorgen hated to consider the unfavorable options open to an orphan. Institutions were notoriously bleak. He hoped that Mrs. Klark would be able to take her back to Norway.

Mary shook her head at Marta's inquiry. She did not have anything to say.

"Well then," Marta persisted, "I'd like to hear about you. That's what friends do. They share stories about themselves."

"I don't know any stories," Mary said.

Marta felt encouraged. The child had finally said something. Maybe she should try a more direct approach. "I'm twenty," Marta said. "How old are you?"

"Twelve or thirteen," Mary answered, barely above a whisper. "That's what Pappa said the last time I asked, but he doesn't..." she paused, corrected herself and continued, "didn't... know my birthday."

Jorgen was stunned by Mary's answer. *She's almost as old as Niels!* Because of her small size, he had thought she was much younger. And what kind of father didn't know when his child was born? Jorgen's dislike of the dead man only intensified.

"My father died last year," said Marta, "and you know my mother. But I also have a brother, an aunt, an uncle, and some cousins. What can you tell me about your family?"

Jorgen sat forward in his seat, anxious to hear Mary's answer.

Mary shrugged. There was a long pause. Jorgen thought that perhaps Mary had no family or for some reason did not want to talk about them

"That's all right," said Marta. She patted the girl's hand. "You don't have to tell me if you don't want to.

After a few minutes, Jorgen relaxed back into his seat. Nothing more was said for several minutes. When she began to speak again, Mary's voice sounded different. It was flat, devoid of any feeling, like she was repeating something she had heard many times.

"My mother died when I was born. I'm bad luck, I killed her."

Marta started to put her arm around Mary's shoulders but stopped when Mary tensed and drew away from her.

"Did your father tell you that?"

Mary didn't answer. She turned her head to look out the window.

Marta leaned over so that her mouth was inches from the girl's head.

"Whoever told you that was wrong, Mary! A baby isn't responsible for its birth; it has no choice. You did not kill your mother any more than the sun shining that day killed her, or the flowers blooming, or your father drawing a breath of air. Those things happen according to nature, just like your birth."

Marta placed a hand on Mary's shoulder, and Jorgen was surprised when the girl didn't pull away. "And had your mother lived, you would have been the most important thing in her life. It would make her very sad to know that you blame yourself for her death."

Though her words to Mary had been supportive and kind, the intensity in her voice revealed an anger that Jorgen had never seen in his wife. When Marta finished, she sat back in her seat and looked straight ahead. Jorgen could not see her eyes close to stem the flow of tears, nor the tears that trickled down Mary's face.

The thought of a mother dying during childbirth was too horrible to contemplate, but Jorgen did wonder about the callous nature of someone who would blame it on the child.

★ ★ ★

There was a crowd at the Liverpool train station eager for the arrival of the immigrants. Some stayed in the background waiting to render honest service. Others hovered over the passengers who had gathered around the baggage cars. As each passenger attempted to gather his belongings, a bold individual from the crowd would snatch up one of the immigrant's boxes or chests and motion for the bewildered immigrant to follow him. Jorgen had been warned about these "runners." They collected fees for taking unsuspecting newcomers to the worst rooming houses in the city, ones that charged exorbitant rates and, in some cases, outright stole from the immigrants.

Prior to the train entering the station, Jorgen had formed a plan. Upon detraining, Mrs. Aksdal and Mrs. Clark would position themselves as close to the baggage cars as possible. Jorgen would locate the baggage and bring it to them, piece by piece, until it was all collected. "You'll have to be on your guard," he warned, "Runners will try to grab anything they can right from under your nose."

"Not if they know what's good for them," said Mrs. Aksdal. Her tone was threatening and Mrs. Klark shook her head vigorously in agreement. Jorgen pitied any poor devil who tried to get too close to their baggage.

Marta and Mary's job was to find a wagon for hire. Marta had proved adept at that in Hull, and Jorgen thought it best to remove Mary from the crowded station as soon as possible.

Jorgen's strategy worked. The baggage made it from the train to the wagon without any interference. Jorgen assisted Mrs. Klark and Mrs. Aksdal into the wagon. Mrs. Klark would be dropped off at the address where her daughter was staying, and then the wagon would take Mrs. Aksdal to a rooming house that Mr. Een had recommended. It was within walking distance of the train station, so Marta, Mary, and Jorgen chose to walk.

Such a mass of people and wagons crowded the vicinity of the station that Jorgen was confident that the walkers would beat the wagon to the rooming house. Mary clung to Marta's arm who in turn, locked her arm in Jorgen's as they traversed the rubbish-strewn streets near the dock. Agents followed after them attempting to impede their progress. They waved contracts and called out the names of ships in the harbor that were in need of additional passengers.

"Nei, nei," Jorgen said again and again, and tried to wave them off. The agents persisted until one audacious man grabbed Mary's arm to stop them. Mary reacted like a threatened animal. She clamped her teeth over his hand and bit down, hard. He let out a howl, but Mary didn't release him until Jorgen called her name. He had the young man by the collar and walked him a few feet away then gave him a shove toward his companions. The young man stumbled, and then fell into the street. "Stop bothering us," Jorgen yelled. "Next time I'll let her bite your hand off." The agents didn't need to understand a word of Jorgen's outburst; anger requires no translation. Like frightened rats, they scurried away from the enraged Norwegian.

A small group of passers-by, mostly beggars attracted to the commotion, shuffled away once the excitement was over.

Jorgen and Marta tried to engage Mary's interest in the sights they passed, like St John's Church and St. George's Hall, a grand piece of architecture under construction. But she would not be distracted. The agents and beggars along with the noise and confusion of the city kept her wary and silent until they reached their destination, a large house on Standish Street.

What he had assumed would be a boarding house appeared to be a family home. He knocked on the recently painted front door and when it was opened by a pleasant looking woman, he presented her with the letter from Mr. Een.

Just then the wagon pulled up to the house and Marta waved to her mother.

The woman studied the group and gave Jorgen a puzzled look. "Four persons, not three?" she inquired in Norwegian.

Jorgen was surprised. He thought Mr. Een said she was

English. "We are four," Jorgen replied. "I hope you can help us."

The woman nodded and motioned them into the house.

An hour later, the driver had been paid and the newcomers were establishing themselves in a good-sized, spotlessly clean room. It contained a bed, a wardrobe, and a small table with two chairs. A pitcher and basin sat neatly on the table along with an English bible. One wall had a long shelf and a row of at least a dozen hooks under it. Mrs. Aksdal and Mary would share the bed while Jorgen and Marta's bed was in a small alcove opposite the wardrobe.

Down the stairway and outside the back door was a small shed that contained a toilet and sink.

"We are so fortunate to be staying in a nice residence," said Mrs. Aksdal. "Mrs. Klark's daughter is staying in a dreadful looking rooming house in a very poor neighborhood. How did Mr. Een know about this place?"

"He comes to Liverpool every six months on business; he found this place on one of his first trips several years ago. It was owned by a Norwegian gentleman. This lady was his housekeeper."

"I guess that's why she can speak Norwegian," said Marta.

Jorgen nodded, then continued. "He left her the house when he died. Mr. Een said she only rents to those she knows or have been recommended by an acquaintance. As you've already noticed, there are some rough characters in this city. Mr. Een told me to warn you about going out unescorted. I'm afraid you will not have the freedom here that you had in Bergen. The streets are not safe here, especially for foreigners. You should stay together when you go out, if I'm not here to go with you."

Jorgen looked solemnly at each individual, even though he knew Mary would never venture out by herself. Marta and Mrs. Aksdal nodded in agreement with him.

★ ★ ★

Jorgen traversed Waterloo Road and walked around the Goree Piazza observing the agents who plied their trade among the immigrants. He could have gone to a shipping office in Liverpool, but Jorgen knew the agents had the best bargains on transatlantic travel. "The difficulty," Mr. Een had explained, "is finding an agent who is honest." To that end, Jorgen watched and listened to many transactions and saw first hand the results of dealing with unscrupulous agents.

"Today, I met a family from Christiania," Jorgen said one night, "Father, mother and four children. They were sent away from the dock even though they had tickets for the boat in the harbor. The agent had booked too many passengers, so the family stood there and watched as the boat left without them. The agent told them he could book them on another ship in three weeks. He called a runner to take their baggage to a boarding house, but the man said they would find their own place to stay. They've been here two weeks and are worried about their children. The last place the agent sent them, near the Waterloo Dock, was a damp cellar. The children are sickly looking and all have bad coughs."

"Those poor people," said Marta.

She, her mother, and Mary sat three abreast on the edge of the bed listening to Jorgen and watching as he paced the tiny room.

Mrs. Aksdal shook her head saying, "What a nightmare for them."

"Well that's one agent we don't want to deal with," said Marta.

"That's the problem," said Jorgen. "'There are dozens like him who seem to take pleasure in cheating people like us...but there is one agent that I've been watching. He's not like the others."

All this talk about agents had made Mary anxious. Her dainty hands trembled in her lap.

"What makes him so different?" said Marta jumping to her feet to stand before Mary. "Is he tall, or short, or fat? Or does he walk with a limp?" She imitated these characteristics in an exaggerated fashion, a silly act, but it had the desired effect on Mary, who giggled.

It was the first time Jorge heard the girl laugh, and he and Mrs. Aksdal were also forced to laugh at Marta's antics.

"No limp," said Jorgen," but he does carry a fancy, carved walking stick, and he's very well dressed. He appears to be a gentleman. That makes him different, but also, he seems to treat people fairly. I haven't seen anyone yell at him or walk away angry or unhappy. I intend to talk to him tomorrow. I thought I'd try to sell him Mary's tickets. I've checked, and her ship doesn't sail for another two weeks, so he should be able to resell them.

Jorgen saw Marta look at her mother and frown at the mention of Mary's name. Something must have happened when they went to visit Mrs. Klark. He turned, looked out the window, and said, "Why don't we all go for a walk before middag?"

★ ★ ★

Jorgen and Marta dropped back a distance from her mother and Mary so they could talk privately.

"We went to see Mrs. Klark today. She looked old, like she hasn't slept in days. We had a short visit outside; she didn't want us exposed to her granddaughter's illness."

"I thought it was her daughter who was ill."

"She was. She's better, but still very weak and needs care. Mrs. Klark's granddaughter has relapsed and is now quite ill."

"Wouldn't Mary be able to help?"

"I'm sure Mary would be a huge help, but not if she got sick. There's a good chance that could happen if she lived with them. Mrs. Klark says cholera is contagious; she's

202

worried about getting it herself. And Jorgen, you should see where they're living, filth and garbage all over the courtyard...It's a horrible situation."

Jorgen agreed. He felt sorry for Mrs. Klark. He liked the short, feisty lady and hoped her daughter and granddaughter would soon be well enough to leave Liverpool.

"Mrs. Klark said she would like to help Mary, but can't handle the responsibility of another child. And she has no idea when they'll be able to return to Norway," Marta continued.

The understanding had been that Mary would stay with them until Mrs. Klark sorted out her daughter's situation. They hadn't counted on a lingering illness or a relapse.

"So where does that leave us?" Jorgen feared he already knew the answer to that question.

"We need to talk about that," Marta replied. "Mor would like to take her to America with us. She says that she will pay all her expenses."

Jorgen sucked in his breath and was quiet for a moment.

"It's not just the cost," he said, finally, "although she will need shoes, clothing...whatever else a girl needs. It's the responsibility."

He looked at Marta and knew his excuse sounded flimsy. "Besides," he continued, "we can't just take a child without knowing anything about her. Maybe she has family."

"According to Mary, the only family she knows about is an uncle who lives in America. That's where she and her father were going. Please think about it for a day or two, and then talk to Mor. She loves you Jorgen; you've been like a son to her. I know she'll accept whatever decision you make."

They continued their walk in silence. Jorgen couldn't help wondering at the speed with which his life and plans kept being altered.

He loved Marta and could not imagine his life without her, and he was getting used to the idea of being a father. Mrs. Aksdal was a good person; he thought of her first as a friend and then as a mother-in-law. And Mary was a quiet little girl, uncomplaining, agreeable, quite easy to be around. But, in spite of his feelings for all of them, he felt overwhelmed, outnumbered and maybe even a little bit manipulated.

On his last trip home, his brothers, especially Halvor, teased him about living with his mother-in-law. "They'll stick together, women always stick together. You'll never win an argument," he joked.

"And you know this," Theo had retorted, "because of your vast experience with women?" The boys had all laughed because it was well known in the family that Halvor had yet to master the art of love and romance. "Besides," said Theo, who could always be counted on to defend the victim of the moment, "when you finally do find someone who is willing to put up with you, she'll live here and will have to contend with your whole family, not just your mother." Jorgen had laughed along with the others.

"You're miles away," said Marta. "Are you concerned about Mary?"

"About her and other things." Jorgen paused, then continued. "Does it seem to you that our lives keep getting more and more complicated?"

"It does," she agreed.

Marta sensed that Jorgen was troubled. She knew she had to give him time to think about the situation, so she remained quiet. They walked for an hour, and it was not until they approached the house on their return that he finally broke the silence.

"I wish I could give you and your mother my answer right away, but I need more time to think about it. I'm going to talk to that agent tomorrow morning. When I return, the three of us should talk about what's best for Mary—and for us."

★ ★ ★

The next day, Jorgen was so deep in thought as he strode down Water Street that he passed by the Town Hall without stopping as he had on previous days to gawk at the friezes around the outside of the building. They had reminded him of his woodcarving days and he admired the skill of the person who had carved the lions, crocodiles, and elephants that were depicted there.

But this day, his thoughts were on more practical matters. If they took Mary with them, in a short span of time they would be a family of five. Could he provide for that many? How large a home would he have to build? Maybe they could get by with two bedrooms for a while. He and Mrs. Aksdal needed to talk about expenses. They had not counted on having a baby so soon or taking in an orphaned child.

The noise and bustle of the waterfront interrupted Jorgen's reflections. He had arrived at Waterloo Road too early and the agent was not yet in his usual spot. Jorgen continued down the road for some distance and as the crowd thinned, he drifted back into his thoughts. Distracted, he turned down a narrow lane mistaking it for the street with all the import and export dealers. He had been down that street before and had enjoyed looking in their windows at the displays of interesting objects from around the world. But, on this morning, he had made a wrong turn.

Jorgen didn't hear the quick, stealthy steps behind him. He did hear a loud crack, and when he felt a searing pain slice through his head, knew that the crack was the sound of something solid hitting his skull. Dazed, he fell to his hands and knees but was violently jerked to his feet. A gag was stuffed into his mouth and his eyes were covered. He was led, stumbling and confused, a short distance, then he heard a door open and he was shoved into a building.

The pain in his head was so severe that Jorgen began to retch and would have vomited except for the rag in his mouth. He thought he might choke to death and was on the verge of panicking when the rag was jerked from his mouth. Jorgen coughed and swallowed hard, forcing his stomach to stay in place. He was suddenly and roughly pushed into a chair, and when he stopped coughing, the rag was stuffed back into his mouth. His hands and feet were tied to the chair and then he heard the footsteps of his assailants as they went out the door, closed and locked it. All this had happened in the space of a few minutes and not a word had been spoken.

Jorgen wondered what this was all about. If they had wanted him dead, that could have been accomplished when they attacked him out on the street or here in this room. And it didn't seem to be a robbery, they hadn't even checked his pockets. He was thankful that his money was safely hidden back in the room with Marta although they could have taken Mary's tickets.

There didn't seem to be any motive for what had happened. Then a thought suddenly occurred to him. Maybe those agents he had yelled at when they first came to town were getting even with him or trying to show him that they were in charge here in Liverpool.

The nausea subsided and Jorgen felt calmer. He knew he needed to make an escape plan. He needed to think. If only his head would stop hurting. If only he didn't feel so drowsy. His eyes closed and he lost consciousness.

He awoke when he heard the door open and the scuffle of footsteps. A chair was dragged a short distance, a thump, rustling noises, footsteps to the door, and the door clicked shut.

Jorgen heard something that sounded like a moan and suspected someone had joined him. He made the only sound he could with a gag jammed half way down his throat, and his suspicions were confirmed when he heard a muffled echo. It was oddly comforting to know that he was not alone in this predicament.

The assault and kidnapping had taken place early in the morning. Jorgen's head throbbed steadily like the tick of a clock but gave no clue to the passage of time. He dozed for minutes—or was it hours? At some point, he became aware of the need to urinate, and at first, was able to put it out of his mind. The urge only grew stronger until Jorgen was sure that he would have to wet himself. And then, the door opened. *Please,* Jorgen thought, *let this be over.* He heard a match strike and smelled a burning lamp. Its dim light nearly blinded Jorgen when the cloth was snatched from his eyes, but he saw clearly the gun pointed at his head. The gag was removed from his mouth and Jorgen was unticd by a second man. Both men wore hoods. Two more hooded figures worked to release the other prisoner and they began to curse the man and strike him about the head when they saw that he had soaked his pants.

The man with the revolver beckoned Jorgen to follow him. He rose gingerly from the chair. His whole body ached except for his hands; they were numb. He tried to rub some life into them as he was led from the windowless shack. Outside, the man stopped, pointed to the wall, and with a gun pointed at his head, Jorgen was finally able to relieve himself. The sun had recently set; Jorgen judged the time to be around nine o'clock. He had been missing for more than twelve hours and knew that Marta would be terribly worried.

A horse and wagon stood nearby with a driver who faced away from them to conceal his identity. The gunman motioned for Jorgen to climb into the back and indicated that he should lie facedown on the floor of the wagon. When the other prisoner had joined Jorgen on the floor, the gunman clambered aboard and covered them both with what Jorgen recognized as an old sail. The wagon started up and although it moved slowly, it bounced in and over every rut and bump in the road. Jorgen tried to rest his head on his arm, but that brought little relief to the buffeting his body took. Each turn of the axle brought more pain to his still aching head and stiff muscles. When the man next to him groaned, the gunman kicked him and hissed at him to shut up. To make matters worse, the other man smelled so badly that Jorgen had to bury his nose in the crook of his arm to keep from feeling sick. The man hadn't had a drink in hours, yet he still smelled of cheap ale and vomit, and his pants reeked of piss.

They hadn't gone far when the wagon slowed, turned, and lurched to a stop. Jorgen heard water lapping at the shore. He and his unwilling companion were dragged out of the wagon and hustled into a skiff that took them out to a large clipper ship. On board, they were examined by a man who appeared to Jorgen to be slightly inebriated, presumably a doctor of sorts. The captives were ordered to open their mouths and stick out their tongues. The man nodded his approval to the captain. When the doctor made his unsteady departure, two sailors approached with buckets of water and doused Jorgen's foul-smelling counterpart.

"Captain," protested Jorgen, "you have no right to hold me. I am a Norwegian." The English captain most likely couldn't understand his words, but Jorgen's furious state of mind hadn't stopped to consider this or the fact that the captain didn't really care where his captives came from.

The captain gave Jorgen a cruel look, barked an order, and then stormed away. For a moment, Jorgen feared his outburst would result in a beating. Instead, he and the other captive were thrown to the deck and tied to each other, back to back. The breeze was cool and the other man shivered in his wet clothing. Jorgen felt the gradual spread of cold dampness as his own clothing absorbed the wetness.

The sailors were a rough-looking bunch of men. Some were white, the rest were Chinese and African. For the most part, they ignored the two men and attended to their duties, except for one old Chinese man. He stood for a while staring at Jorgen. The intensity of the old man's gaze unnerved Jorgen and he looked away. Eventually the old man left, but he returned later with some hard biscuits and water. He untied the men and sat next to them while they ate. When the old man started to talk, Jorgen was surprised that he spoke English instead of Chinese. Jorgen didn't understand what the man said until he used the word 'family' and pointed to shore.

"Ja, familie" Jorgen replied, and pointed to shore. "Familie!"

The Chinese man gave Jorgen a pitying look and shook his head. He picked up the empty cups and bowls, and left.

Later, the captives were taken below deck for the night where they were placed in irons. Mental anguish gradually replaced Jorgen's physical discomfort as he recognized the hopelessness of his situation. He was going to be forced labor on this ship...for how long, he didn't know.

The ship sat in the harbor for a week as more captive laborers were brought on board. Like the man who came aboard with Jorgen, many of these were young Irish lads who had the misfortune of trading one bad situation for another. Some had come to Liverpool to escape the potato famine and find a job; others had planned to emigrate to America. Jorgen speculated about their experience as seamen. He grasped the gravity of their situation, his too, and knew that the more experienced among them would survive. As for the rest, their fate, most likely, would be a watery grave. Almost all had arrived on board in various stages of drunkenness. As they sobered up, they cursed the crew who had bought them drinks and lured them out of the taverns and into captivity.

Jorgen remained vigilant for any means of escape, but no opportunity presented itself. When he was unshackled, he was closely guarded by men with pistols. One captive who did attempt escape was shot.

Jorgen was distressed about his own situation, but mostly he worried about Marta. He hated that she was forced to spend all this time in Liverpool. With him gone, Marta, Mrs. Aksdal, and Mary would have to go down to Waterloo Street and deal with the agents. He hoped that they would not stumble into the high-risk areas of the city, and worried that even their visits to Mrs. Klark might have dangerous consequences.

During the long hours of captivity, he agonized over his

decision to come to Liverpool. They could have taken the same route as Andrew and sailed from Bergen to Canada, but he heard that the ocean could be much rougher which would cause the voyage to be longer so he had opted for the southern route. He looked back over the time he had wasted in Liverpool and regretted that he had not acted more quickly, purchased their tickets, and left the city as soon as possible. *This is all my own fault,* he chided himself and slipped into despondency.

The old Chinese man continued to favor Jorgen with his company and conversation that Jorgen couldn't understand. The man seemed lonely. For his part, Jorgen tried to explain with words and gestures that he was from Norway and that he and his wife wanted to go to America. During each exchange, the old man would look at Jorgen with sad eyes, and then pad away in his worn slippers.

The captives were unshackled during much of the day and forced to work. The mates gave the instructions and stood over the captives as they performed their assigned tasks. Jorgen spent most days suspended over the side of ship scraping off barnacles and encrusted salt. Those who performed their job poorly or were disposed to laziness paid the price of a lashing. Jorgen was on the receiving end of a lashing one time. His duty that day as cook's assistant brought him under the whip of the first mate who, displeased with the poor quality of the meat, chose to take it out on Jorgen.

But that incident aside, Jorgen preferred to work because it kept him from thoughts that nearly drove him mad. When sleep eluded him, questions pursued him deep into the night. *What was Marta doing now? Was she in danger...frightened...sad? Where was he going and when would he return? Would he be there when his child was born?*

He was grateful beyond words that Marta's mother was with her and wished that he had agreed immediately when

Marta said her mother wanted to keep Mary. It now seemed like such an easy decision and the right thing to do. He assumed that with him gone, the three of them would return to Norway. How much longer would they wait for him in Liverpool?

On his eighth night in captivity, the old Chinese man was not the one who brought dinner. In fact, Jorgen had not seen him all day. He sat and picked at the food in silence and desperation. Judging by the day's activities, it was evident that they would set sail tomorrow, and their destination, Jorgen surmised from the bits of conversation he was able to understand, was China. That knowledge lodged in his gut like a hot boulder.

Although he missed him at dinner, Jorgen was thankful when the old man did not show up later to take him below deck for the night. It had been a warm day, so sleeping conditions down there would be suffocating. The deck would be far more comfortable. He lay awake for a long while, staring into the sky. Eventually, fog descended on the ship, damping down starlight and moonlight until there was nothing left but vapor. Jorgen closed his eyes and the tears that had pooled in the corners trickled down the side of his face.

★ ★ ★

He awoke when a hand clamped on his arm and another one over his mouth.

"Shhh!" The command hissed in his ear.

Jorgen nodded and hands moved to untie him. He was helped him to his feet by the old man who picked up a large sack and led the way, noiselessly, to the far end of the boat. With the sack slung over his back, the old Chinese man nimbly climbed over the side of the boat and disappeared into the dark below. Without any hesitation, Jorgen followed him down the rope ladder. His foot hit something solid and to his relief, it was a boat.

They untied the skiff, pushed off from the ship and drifted until they were concealed in the fog. The old man took up the oars and rowed through the fog toward what Jorgen prayed was shore. *He's escaping, too,* marveled Jorgen. He was overcome with joy at this turn of events, but too fearful of being detected and recaptured to say a word. Both men knew the consequences of being caught.

The trip to shore seemed to take forever and at one point the old man stopped rowing and put his hand to his ear. They could hear men's voices and Jorgen's heart began to pound in his chest as they realized the voices were growing louder. The old man put his finger to his lips and Jorgen nodded back, too terrified to make a sound even if he'd wanted to. The boat passed only a few yards to Jorgen's left, but miraculously far enough away that they were not seen.

When they reached shore, Jorgen lifted the sack out of the boat and handed it to the Chinese man. "Thank you," said Jorgen. He repeated it several times as they shook hands.

"Goodbye, Jorgen," his rescuer said, then he turned and hastened away.

Although the hour was late, a few people were still out. Trusting no one, Jorgen kept to the center of the road and was keenly alert to those who looked even slightly suspicious. He relaxed a bit when he reached the Town Hall, feeling the elephants and lions watching over him as he passed by.

How did he know my name? The question suddenly popped into Jorgen's head. He had refused to give his name, even to the Chinese man. It was his act of defiance. They may have captured his body, but not his identity. The crew had made up names for him but the one they settled on was Lummox. Jorgen had no idea what it meant and didn't care to know...he knew who he was.

He ran the last few streets to the house and had to restrain himself when he knocked on the door to keep from beating it down. He bounded up the steps trailed by a beaming landlord and burst into the room where Marta, her mother, and Mary all huddled in one bed.

The lamp had burned low, but by the dim light it cast, the three startled women gaped at the unexpected sight of Jorgen. Then, one by one, they began to cry. Marta bolted from the bed and flew into his outstretched arms. Mary and Mrs. Aksdal hugged each other, crying and laughing at the same time. The landlady watched from the doorway with hands clasped to her breast and tears in her eyes, as well.

Jorgen pulled away from Marta after a brief kiss. "I must smell awful, and I'm sure I'm covered with lice," he said. "I'll just sit here," he indicated one of the wooden chairs, "until morning."

"You'll do no such thing," said Mrs. Aksdal. As usual, she jumped at the opportunity to take care of someone. "Marta, get Jorgen some clean clothes. Mary, there's soap and towels in that chest." And before either of them could act, she had Jorgen by the arm, propelling him down the stairs and into the kitchen. A bewildered landlady followed them.

While water heated on the stove, Jorgen was served a late meal of cold meat and boiled potatoes. The women peppered him with questions and, in turn, filled in the details of what had transpired in his absence.

"When you didn't come home for middag that first afternoon, I knew something had happened to you," said Marta. "Mor and I went down to Waterloo Street, then to the police, and finally we went to the hospital."

"That was quite a walk," said Jorgen.

"We never would have made it without the help of a friendly carriage driver."

"I don't know how friendly he was," said Mrs. Aksdal. "I think he just liked the looks of our money."

"Perhaps so," said Marta, "but at least he was polite, and he waited for us at the hospital."

"I'm glad you came home."

Jorgen looked at Mary and smiled. These were her first

words to him, ever.

"Thank you, Mary, I'm glad you're here to welcome me home."

Mary blushed and looked down at her small bare feet.

Marta continued her recitation. "The next day we went back to Waterloo Street. We were about to give up when Mor spotted the man with the cane. When we drew near, we heard him speak our language. He was just as you described him. But when we asked if he had talked to you the day before, and he replied, nei, I began to cry." Recalling the distressing scene caused Marta to choke up.

Mrs. Aksdal continued for her. "He took us to a quiet courtyard off Waterloo Street where we could talk. He said that some men have second thoughts about emigrating, they panic, and run out on their families. I told him that you were not like that," said Mrs. Aksdal.

"Thank you," said Jorgen.

"Then he told us something even worse," said Marta. "He said that there is an underground in Liverpool that deals in kidnapped men and boys. They are sold to corrupt merchant and fishing vessels that always seem to need extra crew. The captives are gone weeks or months at a time, sometimes they're never seen again."

"The agent asked us to describe you and said he would ask questions around the docks to see if anyone remembered seeing you. He said if you were on a ship, you could be going as far away as America or Australia. Do you know where that ship was going?"

"I didn't have the words or heart to ask, but I think it may have been China."

The color drained from Marta's face. "Oh, no," she said. Then added, "Goodness!"

Mrs. Aksdal continued the story for Marta who sat with a stunned looked on her face.

"We went back each day, but he never had good news for us. Yesterday, he said he had talked to a Chinese man who thought he may have seen you on a ship, but he wouldn't say which one. The agent thought he was just looking for a reward. I told the agent to find out what the man wanted, that we would reward him if he could tell us where you were."

"I think the ship was sailing today," said Jorgen, "and that the Chinese man decided that it was time for him to leave that life behind. He was not seeking a reward, but took me with him because he felt sorry for me; I could see it in his eyes. Perhaps he had seen enough brutality...he was the only crew member who ever showed any kindness. He seemed as frightened as I was during our escape. The captain is a cruel man, I'm sure he will kill the Chinese man if he ever catches him."

★ ★ ★

The next morning, Mary giggled when she saw Jorgen. To rid himself of lice, he had shaved his head clean, as well as all other parts of his body.

"Marta, are you going to give Jorgen one of your hats to wear?" she asked.

The others were not sure if the girl was serious and didn't want to laugh at her if she was. But when she was unable to suppress a smile, they all laughed with her.

"Mary," said Jorgen, his voice took on a serious tone. "Would you like to go to America with us?"

Mary nodded solemnly.

"Well, I think we would all like to have you travel with us, and when we get to New York City, we can look for your uncle. He is your kin, and perhaps you would choose to stay with him. The choice will be yours, if we can find him."

Mary nodded again, but this time a smile lit up her face.

★ ★ ★

After breakfast Jorgen suggested they all go down to talk with the agent and look over the ships in the harbor. "I think I need all of you to protect me," he said.

"You do and we will," agreed Marta.

The agent seemed pleased to see the group reunited. "So you're the one who belongs to these lovely ladies," he said. "Your absence had them most distressed."

"My wandering got me into trouble," said Jorgen, "I was trying to watch my dalers and I almost lost my life. Thank you for helping us."

"I only asked questions," the agent replied.

"My wife said that you talked to an old Chinese man. I'd like to find him and offer him a reward."

"So, he did know where you were," said the agent. "I didn't believe him."

Jorgen told him about how the old man had helped him. "I think he deserted the ship."

"He won't come around here any more; it would be too dangerous for him," said the agent. "The kidnappers most likely live in town. If they find out that he helped you, they'll surely kill him. He's probably hiding among his own people. Liverpool has a large Chinese population.

"It's probably not safe for you, either," the agent said to Jorgen. "The kidnappers might be afraid that you can identify them."

"They wore hoods and didn't talk. I wouldn't recognize them...but I could probably find the shed where they kept me before taking me to the ship. I think I should talk to the police."

"That's not a good idea," said the agent. "Some officers, I fear, are bribed to turn a blind eye to certain crimes. I think your life is in jeopardy if you stay here. My advice would be to sail as quickly as possible. I have tickets for three ships that sail in the next day or two. The trouble is, I wouldn't want my family to travel on any of them; the conditions on board are deplorable and the food isn't fit to eat."

"We plan to bring our own food," said Marta.

"Mrs.," he said patiently, "the trip is a minimum of thirty-five days, that's a lot of food to take on board. And there are other reasons that cannot be discussed in front of the child. I'm sure your husband has heard all the stories, which is why he's been wary about buying tickets."

Jorgen nodded, then pulled Mary's tickets out of his pocket. "I have two tickets on the Newark. What do you know about that ship, and could you get us two more?"

"The Newark will be a few days late...Too much bad weather, I guess...But it has a good reputation. I've met the captain and he seems decent enough. The criticisms I've heard are the typical complaints, crowded steerage, bad food. As for tickets, they'll be expensive, it's a Whitley Line ship and they usually sell out fast. I don't have any, but I'll ask around."

"We just need two," said Marta.

"If it makes any difference," Jorgen said. "I know my way around a ship; I was a fisherman and I am a fair carpenter. If the Captain needs an extra hand, perhaps he would hire me. Then we would need only one more ticket."

"There is always that possibility. Crew members get sick or quit. I'll get word to the Captain when the Newark docks. Meanwhile, Jorgen, you should stay out of sight. The ship should arrive early next week. Come back to see me then; I hope I'll have good news for you."

It was a glum group that walked back up Water Street. Even the stop at the Town Hall to admire the friezes did little to raise their spirits.

"I'll go crazy cooped up in that tiny room," said Jorgen.

"You can catch up on your journal," suggested Marta.

"Mrs. Aksdal is teaching me to knit," said Mary. "It's so easy, I bet you could learn."

Marta began to laugh.

"For your information, Mrs. Halvorson, I know how to knit, so the joke is on you."

"I will be happy to join you," he said to Mary. "What are we making?"

"Mrs. Aksdal's making a blanket for Marta's baby and I'm making little stockings for its feet. You can make one and I can make the other."

"That sounds like a good plan," said Mrs. Aksdal. "Now I have a plan. Let's stop at the confectionary shop. I think we all need something sweet."

Nine

Mid-August 1850

Marta craned her neck to see the top of the mast, her mouth agape at the imposing size of the Newark.

"It's so big," she said to the back of Jorgen's head. She and her mother shadowed him through the crowd as they approached the ship.

He nodded in agreement. Even though he had been on board once before, he, like Marta, was in awe of the ship's great size.

Jorgen buffered the women from the disorderly mob jostling to get on board. The crowd's eagerness was fueled in part by the fact that steerage berths were not assigned, so passengers raced to get the most desirable location. There were even those who foolishly thought that by pushing to board quickly, they could speed up the ship's departure, a departure which was already one week behind schedule. The ship's mast and hull had sustained damage during her last voyage, which had necessitated the delay for repairs.

With his cap pulled low to his eyes, Jorgen was keen to get on board for a much different reason: apprehension. News accounts in recent days showed kidnappings had increased threefold over the past month. Reason told him he was safe in daylight and in the company of others, but just being down on the dock made him nervous. He had felt the same unease the previous week when he had come down with the agent to meet the Captain and apply for the job of carpenter's assistant.

Jorgen was not the only one with a case of the jitters. Sandwiched between the two women, Mary inched her way forward, her eyes focused on the hem of Marta's cloak. Every few seconds she reached behind her to make sure Mrs. Aksdal was still there. Fearful of all these strangers who babbled and shouted in a mishmash of foreign languages and afraid that somehow she might get left behind, Mary had reverted to the shy, terrified child they had encountered on the Lykke Til.

It hadn't helped that they had just been subjected to a cursory medical inspection conducted by a rude, short-tempered doctor.

"Open," he demanded as soon as Mary stepped before him. She had watched Marta and Mrs. Aksdal take their turns, so she understood and complied with the command.

"Wider," the doctor shrieked, as though she were deaf. When she failed to understand and comply with the strange English word, the doctor took her head between his large hands and roughly pulled on her chin. Instinctively, Mary opened wider to scream, but was too terrified to utter a sound. It was the opportunity the doctor needed to peer down her throat.

"Next," he yelled stamping her medical form and pushing her away in one fluid move.

Just as Jorgen stepped before the doctor, the man in line behind him cleared his throat and coughed nervously. This caught the doctor's attention. With barely a glance at him, he snatched the paper out of Jorgen's hands, stamped it "approved," and turned to the next man.

"You coughed," the doctor accused.

The man did not appear ill to Jorgen; nonetheless, because of that cough, he and his family were denied approval to board the ship. Jorgen wondered how many truly ill people were allowed to board simply because they were able to stifle a cough or a sneeze.

The Newark, a three masts and square rigging, sailed regularly between New York and Liverpool. American built, it was one of the largest of its fleet and designed to carry four hundred sixty passengers and a crew of twenty-six, roughly three times the size of the Lykke Til. Jorgen was unofficially the twenty-seventh member of the crew, hired on as a carpenter's assistant thanks to the helpful agent.

After the kidnapping incident, the agent had befriended Jorgen and his family. He came frequently to visit them at the house on Standish Street so that Jorgen would not have to endanger himself on Waterloo Street. His first two visits were strictly business, but when the agent continued to drop by after they had purchased their tickets, Marta's mother said she suspected the agent had a romantic interest in the owner of the house. Whatever his motive, he was good company and a source of news. Besides getting Jorgen the job on board the ship he had also secured an extra ticket and a cabin berth. Although Jorgen's pay would be meager, it would offset the additional cost of the berth that Marta, her mother and Mary would share on the voyage.

"It's a large cabin," the agent reported, "with four double berths meant for eight passengers, but families manage to crowd in children, like your Mary, raising the occupancy to almost twice that."

Regardless of how many would share their cabin, Marta and Mrs. Aksdal knew they were extremely fortunate to have one. Initially, Marta had been opposed to the idea of a cabin because of the expense involved and because she wanted to be with Jorgen.

But the agent had been adamant in his advice to Jorgen. "Your women and young Mary will be far safer in a cabin. I don't wish to alarm you, Jorgen, but disease can be epidemic on these trips. Also, I have heard that the stench in steerage from so many cases of seasickness and overflowing slop buckets is unimaginable."

Jorgen nodded. "I've heard that it is unpleasant," he began...

"Unpleasant doesn't even begin to cover the situation. In far too many cases it's deadly," the agent cautioned. "I know you are concerned about the expense, but what price do you put on your loved ones' health?"

Jorgen told the agent of Marta's desire that the group stay together.

"You all wouldn't be together. You and your wife would be with couples and families. The other two would be in the section designated for single women. You know, Jorgen," he had continued, "if some of your work has to be done at night, your wife will be by herself. If I were you, I'd talk to your wife's mother. She'll agree that her daughter is better off in a cabin. Let her convince Marta, mothers are good at that."

In the end, Marta did agree that for the safety of her unborn child, her mother, and Mary, the cabin was a wise decision. Nevertheless, she was not happy that she and Jorgen were going to be separated, and that he would have to spend the duration of the voyage by himself in the single men's section of steerage.

★ ★ ★

When they had settled in their cabin and made up one of the berths, Jorgen picked up his small bag and some bedding and started for the door. "I'm going to find my cot, then I need to report to the carpenter to see if he needs me today," he said.

"Can we see where you will be staying?" asked Marta. She sounded anxious. He turned and looked into her troubled eyes.

"I'll only be there at night," he said, "but if you'd all like to see it…"

Mary vigorously nodded her head.

"Yes," Mrs. Aksdal said, "I think we'd like to know where you'll be."

"It's most likely a madhouse down there, but today is probably the best time for you to see the steerage deck," said Jorgen. Although he would have preferred to keep the women from going down into steerage, Jorgen appreciated their concern and understood their curiosity. *At least it should still be clean down there,* he thought.

They descended the stairs to steerage and caught up with a family of five headed in the same direction. The father carried a large chest; the mother had a bundle tied to her back and a crying infant in her arms. A young boy, perhaps three or four years old, trailed his mother, holding on to her skirt, and behind him a girl smaller than Mary struggled with a heavy basket.

"Per, stop that," the girl said when the little boy let go of his mother's skirt and began darting in circles around his sister. A few seconds later, she stumbled over him and dropped the basket.

"May I carry that for you," said Mrs. Aksdal. She had been walking directly behind the child and stooped to pick up the basket while the child got to her feet and brushed off her knees. "Here, let me," said Jorgen, squeezing past Marta and Mary in the narrow passageway. He placed his bedding on top and picked up the basket.

The mother turned her head to see who had volunteered to help. "Thank you," she said to Jorgen. To the young boy she commanded, "Per, take your sister's hand." When the toddler complied, the group continued on its way.

In steerage, two levels of berths stretched in long lines down both sides of the ship. The group edged around those who, having claimed berths, were attempting to settle baggage and spread quilts over their cots. Marta noted that the berths, intended for couples, were the same size as the one she, her mother, and Mary would share in the cabin.

The family they were following stopped in front of two vacant berths. The father set down the chest and stepping to his wife's side, untied the bundle on her back, easing it onto the lower berth. He finally turned his attention to Jorgen and took the basket from him.

"Thank you for your kindness," he said.

Marta looked around steerage and sadness welled inside her, not only for this family, but for all who would be living down here during the long journey. She suddenly realized how dismissive she had been about the unpleasant aspects of the voyage and the discomforts and perils they would face in the weeks ahead. Her main focus during the past weeks had been on preparation and packing. She had shrugged off any thoughts of the journey itself.

Passengers seeking open berths streamed by them, and the level of noise increased with each new arrival. Marta knew it would only get worse as the berths filled up. Surrounded by so many people, how could one sleep? It was obvious to her that privacy would be non-existent. She looked at the weary mother who had sunk down onto her cot and was discretely nursing the infant. The baby made small sounds of contentment while the mother eyed Per who, testing his boundaries, wandered further and further from their berth.

When a man and his wife walked past Marta to claim the next vacant berth, Marta detected an unpleasant odor. Since the start of her pregnancy, her sense of smell seemed overly sensitive and, at times, made her gag. Feeling one of those bouts coming on, she tugged gently on Jorgen sleeve and began to move away from the smell.

"Sorry, Jorgen," she said, a few steps later.

She didn't need to say any more. He squeezed her hand, the smell had reached his nostrils too.

A seemingly endless row of tables, placed end to end, extended down the middle of steerage between the rows of berths. Walking single file alongside the tables, Jorgen's group managed to stay out of the way of the activity surrounding each berth.

Eventually they came to the bow end of the ship and the area designated for single men. The berths here were narrow, intended for one, and there were no tables. There was a similar area in the stern for single women. Jorgen placed his bag under one of the berths and spread a blanket over the cot to indicate that it was taken.

Jorgen decided the tour was over. He did not take the women to view the area where the poorest of the travelers would spend their days and nights. That was known as lower steerage, a large hold below steerage that was also used for cargo. On its most recent crossing to Liverpool, the Newark had carried lumber in the hold, but it had not been successful in filling that space with cargo for the return trip to America. Dozens of immigrants would sleep down in that dismal, airless space. Lumber was not clean cargo, so chances were good that lower steerage was probably very dirty. Jorgen hoped that his duties would not take him down there.

"Now that you've seen steerage," Jorgen said as they started back to the cabin, "there is no reason for you to come back. Other than to sleep, I don't plan to be down here. I'll come to your cabin any time I am not working."

"I'm still sorry we can't be together," Marta whispered. She and Jorgen had slowed their pace allowing her mother and Mary to get ahead of them. They were savoring this last bit of time alone, knowing the coming weeks would afford them few such moments. "And I hate the thought of you trying to sleep in that wretched place."

"I can sleep anywhere," Jorgen whispered back. "I'll miss you, too, but it's just for a few weeks."

Returning to the women's cabin, they found it consumed in a flurry of activity. A group of German immigrants with an assortment of crates and trunks spilled into the passageway. Jorgen pointed to his companions and then to the quilts covering the berth they had chosen. One of the men pointed to the berth and then to Jorgen, Jorgen shook his head.

"Nei, ikke meg, I won't be here," he said, shaking his head for emphasis.

The German man considered this for a moment, then spoke to his companions.

"Ja," the women answered in unison. It seemed a decision had been made. The four men stowed some of the crates in the cabin and took the rest to another cabin a short distance down the passageway. The four women who stayed behind immediately began to pull out bedding and make up the three remaining berths in the cabin. Three children climbed up to sit on the baggage and the oldest spoke to Mary.

"Wie ist ihr name?"

Marta was relieved to see Mary let down her guard and smile at the other children.

"I think she wants to know your name," Marta said.

"Mitt navn er Mary." Mary replied quietly.

"Mitt navn er Mary, mitt navn er Mary," the children sang out until one of the women shushed them. "Her name is Mary," she explained to the children in German, "now tell her your names."

"Mila," said the girl who had asked Mary her name. She was almost as big as Mary, but Marta judged her to be younger, perhaps nine or ten.

"Oscar," replied the boy.

Marta thought he was probably the same age as Mila. Maybe a twin or a cousin, it was difficult to tell. *The youngest one is definitely Mila's sister,* thought Marta, *they look so much alike.*

"Ich bin Petra," the little one said.

"Ich bin Marta," Marta said, introducing herself to the other women.

Jorgen remained in the passageway. He watched the introductions and listened to the friendly chatter, and it struck him how quickly and effortlessly the women and children adjusted to this new situation. He admired their ease in admitting strangers into their lives. He wondered if all women were like that. He thought of Mrs. Aksdal and Mrs. Klark. They had become friends almost as soon as they laid eyes on each other. And Mary had taken to Mrs. Aksdal, Mrs. Klark, and Marta long before she had accepted him as a friend. Although Jorgen had helped the German men carry their crates into the cabin, neither he nor they thought to introduce themselves. They could and probably would go the whole trip without knowing each other's names. Jorgen doubted he would learn the names of any of the men in steerage.

Jorgen had a job that he knew would keep him busy and make the days go faster. He was happy that Marta, Mary, and Mrs. Aksdal would share genial company on the long voyage. He hoped that would make the time pass more quickly for them.

He was suddenly aware that the cabin had grown quiet and realized that all eyes were on him. He looked at Marta, and she was smiling at him. "I think they would like to know your name."

"Oh," he said. He felt self-conscious, like an outsider being admitted to a secret society.

"Mitt navn er Jorgen."

"Jorgen," the German children repeated.

He smiled at them, then said to Marta, "I'll return as soon as I'm able."

He turned to leave, but Mrs. Aksdal called to him. She rummaged in the food chest and pulled out a large biscuit and some cheese.

"Take this," she said, offering him the food. "You can't work on an empty stomach."

★ ★ ★

Assuming that the carpenter on an American ship would speak English, Jorgen went to find an interpreter. Grateful to Mrs. Aksdal for thinking of it, he wolfed down the snack hoping he wouldn't run into any crew members before he finished. It was probably against ship rules to eat outside of designated dining areas, and he didn't want to be the one passenger they made an example of to the rest.

"I don't think you'll be needing my services with old Fykerud," the interpreter told Jorgen when he caught up with him. "He's from Trondheim, as Norwegian as you, although he does speak English. Everyone calls him Fyke. He's getting too old for the job, but the captain likes him. Must be why he hired you to help...I think he'd hate to lose Fyke."

Jorgen wondered if all interpreters were this talkative.

"And did you know" he continued, "Fyke's son is the helmsman? He's not much on conversation, but he is the best wheelman in the North Atlantic. Both are good men. Old Fyke's been working on the Newark since her first voyage, his son," he stopped to think, "two maybe three years."

Eventually, he got around to telling Jorgen where he could find the carpenter.

★ ★ ★

Later that afternoon, after the last passengers had boarded, the Newark left the dock and dropped anchor in the River Mersey. No one seemed to know how long they would stay in the harbor. The captain would decide that based on how quickly the agents on shore could find passengers willing to travel in lower steerage. Those poor passengers added to the ship's profit, which also meant more money in the captain's pockets. But the captain had to be cautious; too many passengers down there increased the risk of illness on board. He also had to figure out how many additional mouths the ship's store could feed. A successful captain was one who achieved the best balance between his profit and risks to the passengers. If there were too many deaths, the shipping line would fire him.

"Go back to your family," Fyke told Jorgen shortly after they anchored in the river. "We're done for the day. Rations will be distributed now that we've left the dock, and you don't want to miss that."

They had spent the afternoon making a few repairs, but mostly Fyke walked Jorgen through the ship explaining, as they went, the kinds of problems that usually occurred.

"What about you," Jorgen asked. "Don't you need to get your rations?"

"No, I usually eat with the crew except when the captain is looking for a game of chess. Then I take middag with him."

Jorgen started to walk away, then turned and asked, "Who usually wins?"

Fyke scratched his head and thought for a minute. "Usually the captain," he replied with a wink.

★ ★ ★

The shipping company estimated the voyage would take thirty-seven to forty days. For that amount of time each adult passenger was allotted four pounds pork, two pounds dried beef, five and one-half pounds flour, ten pounds rice, twenty-five pounds oatmeal, ten ounces tea, a jar of vinegar, two and one-half pounds sugar and three pounds molasses. Each week, one sixth of that would be distributed with lesser amounts going to children, depending on their ages.

"I've seen worse," said Mrs. Aksdal, looking over her portion of pork. "But I think we should eat this before the beef."

Marta opened her portions of oatmeal and rice and poked through them half expecting to find something lurking among the grains. After listening to the agent's stories about the poor quality of food on the ships, she seemed pleasantly surprised with the contents of the bags.

"It looks like we'll eat well this week," said Jorgen, "but we had to repair the door to one of the storerooms today, and I didn't like the smell coming from it. Fyke told me that the first week's ration is usually the best. I think we'll be grateful for all the extra food we've brought with us."

As they had on the short trip from Norway, Marta and her mother had packed food for this voyage, only much more of it. They had canisters full of rice, flour, and oatmeal as well as cheese and dried fish. They would be able to supplement the ship's provisions with several pounds of potatoes, onions, cabbage and carrots that Jorgen had paid a runner to carry on board. Those items had been bought just before boarding the ship. The last purchase had been a bag of limes being sold to passengers as they stood in line on the dock. Mary carried them on board and when she was safely in their cabin said, "They smell like a summer day, I hope we don't eat them right away, they'll make the cabin smell so nice."

"We'll try to make them last as long as we can, but we have to eat some every week," said Mrs. Aksdal, "Otherwise, we'll get sick."

"I've never eaten limes and I'm hardly ever sick," said Mary. "Can I just keep mine?"

"You've never been on such a long voyage," said Mrs. Aksdal, "where you will have to go without fresh fruits and vegetables."

"That's why the ship supplies vinegar and we bought the limes. They'll keep us from getting scurvy. And if you get scurvy, your teeth fall out and you have to talk like this," said Jorgen. He spoke the last half dozen words with his lips stretched over his teeth, making it appear that he had no teeth. The effect sounded funny, in fact he was all around a comical sight. His hair had grown back just enough to stick out all over his head, and for the first time in his life, he had a full beard.

Mary laughed heartily at this bit of nonsense from Jorgen. It amused her so much that for the rest of the day, she talked as if she had no teeth. The other children in the cabin imitated her, not knowing why she did it, but because it was fun and because children didn't need a reason to act silly.

The Newark stayed in the harbor for three days taking on more and more passengers until finally Mrs. Aksdal remarked, "How can they put so many people into steerage. I would have thought it filled up on the second day."

In fact it had. They were now filling the hold, the lower steerage compartment that the women had not seen. Jorgen had passed through it just that morning and felt an overwhelming sense of pity for those whose impoverished circumstances led them to such grim accommodations. It dismayed him to see so many women and children housed down there.

On the fourth day, it appeared that they were finally getting underway. A tug pulled the Newark down river, but headwinds associated with an approaching storm became too strong as they approached the sea, and they had to drop anchor in the river again. Blustery weather was relentless for two days. For hours at a time, rain pummeled the ship and any passengers who ventured out to the cookhouse or for exercise. During brief lulls, passengers hurried on deck. They walked in the fog and drizzle to get relief from their stuffy quarters.

It was mid-afternoon of the third day at anchor. Despite the light rain, Mrs. Aksdal and Sophia, one of the German women, continued to walk on deck after their cabin mates returned below. The two women stopped when they reached the bow and looked upriver to where it joined the sea. *Was it her imagination,* Mrs. Aksdal wondered, *or did the sky look a bit brighter?* She pointed to the sky and the other woman nodded. Heartened by this observation, the two women turned to continue their exercise. As they approached mid-ship they heard the first mate call out, summoning all those present on deck. He looked right at the two women and waved his hands in a beckoning motion. Sailors assisted him by gathering the passengers and blocking the stairs so none could leave. One sailor, taller and more muscular looking than the others, stood with his hands behind his back, to one side of the first mate.

When everyone on deck was assembled, the first mate began a lengthy explanation that the non-English speaking in the group could not understand. Most seemed to comprehend that it had something to do with the thin, disheveled looking man who was flanked by the second and third mates. Each had a firm grip on one of the man's arms. The first mate ranted on for several minutes. He pointed repeatedly to the crowd and jabbed his finger into the captive's chest, a gesture Mrs. Aksdal understood to be an accusation. She overheard someone near her whisper in Norwegian that the man had been caught smoking below deck. This, she knew, was strictly forbidden. At first, the accused man looked desperately around him, perhaps hoping for some means of escape, but as the tirade continued, the man's gaze fell to the deck. Mrs. Aksdal almost hoped the floor would open up and swallow him. Not that the man didn't deserve some sort of punishment. She knew he did; she just had a bad feeling about what was to come.

In due course, the first mate issued an order; the captive was led to the mast where he was tied and his shirt was ripped from his back. The tall sailor stepped forward. Brandishing a cat o' nine tails in one hand, he approached the offender.

Mrs. Aksdal stared at the First Mate, willing him not to go through with this flogging. But as she watched, he nodded to the sailor to begin, rubbing his hands together as if anticipating a fine performance.

Mrs. Aksdal turned away as the whip came down on the man's back. The whoosh and cracking sound sent shivers down her spine. She heard several in the crowd gasp. She also heard the victim whimper. By the time the whip cut into the man's flesh for the fourth time, the crowd had grown silent and the man's anguished screams pierced the air. Then there was quiet. Thinking it was over, Mrs. Aksdal looked up in time to see the sailor put down his whip. He picked up a piece of the torn shirt and stuffed it into the man's mouth to muffle his cries for mercy. Blood trickled down the man's back, and all three mates, huddled nearby, were laughing and yelling things that Mrs. Aksdal understood to be taunts to the victim and encouragement to his tormentor.

When the sailor picked up the whip and raised his arm to deliver another lashing, Mrs. Aksdal impulsively turned and pushed her way through the crowd. She could not be a witness to this cruelty any longer. The sailors had left their post at the stairs and were now nowhere to be seen. She darted down the steps and was halfway to her cabin when she heard footsteps rushing up behind her. She was too angry to be frightened, but was relieved, none the less, when she turned and discovered her German companion whom she had forgotten in her haste to get away.

"Bad, bad," the woman said using one of her newly learned English words. Her look of distress added to the guilt Mrs. Aksdal felt about abandoning her. She reached out and took the other woman's hand.

"Ja, bad," she replied.

★ ★ ★

All on board were impatient to get underway, but none so much as Jorgen. It was now more than a month since he had learned of Marta's pregnancy, and although she tried to assure him that she still had months before the baby came, he worried nonetheless.

He decided to discuss this with Marta's mother and found the opportunity when she left to take a walk after their evening meal.

"I'm concerned about Mor," Marta said to Jorgen. The cabin door had just closed behind her mother. "She's been quiet and seems troubled ever since her walk this afternoon. When I asked her if anything was wrong, she made light of it. Perhaps it's nothing. We're all weary of the rain and disappointed that we've been on this ship for a week and haven't even left England. Mor says she's fine, but I'd feel better if you talked to her."

Jorgen found his mother-in-law standing at the rail. When she heard him approach, she turned, and the frown she wore turned to a smile when she saw it was him.

"Jorgen, just look at what a beautiful evening it is turning out to be."

She was right. The clouds were moving out, giving way to what promised to be a beautiful sunset.

"Perhaps we'll have favorable sailing conditions tomorrow," she added.

"That seems to be true," Jorgen said, "which makes me wonder about the sad look on your face when you turned around."

"Did Marta send you?" Mrs. Aksdal smiled.

"Actually, she did," Jorgen admitted, "But I also have a reason of my own."

"Well then, we're in for a long chat," said Mrs. Aksdal, "because there's something I've had on my mind, a request I have for you."

"I'm intrigued," said Jorgen. "What would you like from me?"

Mrs. Aksdal paused to gather her thoughts. "Well," she began, "Mary came to me yesterday and wanted to know if she could call me something besides Mrs. Aksdal. When I asked her what she had in mind, she asked what my first name is. When I told her, Elen, she said, 'I'd like to call you Aunt Elen.'"

"She is fond of you," said Jorgen. "I assume your answer was yes."

"It was," Mrs. Aksdal replied, "I'm pleased that she wants to call me that. Which brings me to my request. I realize that I am breaking with custom, but Mrs. Aksdal does sounds so formal. Since we are now a family, I am hoping that you will call me Elen."

"It will take time to get used to calling you by your first name, but I will try," said Jorgen. "I appreciate the friendship behind your gesture. We have become a family, haven't we?"

Elen nodded.

"Is there something else on your mind?" said Jorgen. "Are you worried about Marta?"

"Worried about Marta?" she repeated. "Is there a reason I should be worried about Marta?"

"Well, that's what I wanted to talk to you about. I'm worried about her. I'm afraid she will have the baby...that she will have to go through childbirth on this ship," said Jorgen. "Each day her belly grows larger and larger. She's told me that she still has lots of time left, but when I look at her, I'm not so sure she's right. You know more about these things than I do. Do you think there's a chance she'll have the baby while we're at sea?"

Elen patted her son-in-law on the arm. "You're a good husband, Jorgen, and I do understand your concern. From what Marta has told me, I would estimate that she has almost three months before the baby comes. We should definitely be on dry land by then." She hesitated, and then continued. "But, babies don't know about calendars, and they arrive when they see fit. If that should happen while we're still on board this ship, we'll manage. Marta's a strong, healthy woman and you've done everything that you can to see to her comfort. And don't forget, I've had some experience. Besides having one of my own, this won't be the first childbirth I've witnessed. Before moving to Bergen, I assisted a few women on neighboring estates."

She patted his arm again. "Now you've got to stop fretting about what may happen and take care of yourself in the here and now. I think this trip holds more danger for you than Marta. I do not like the first mate or the other mates, for that matter. They are cruel men who seem to care nothing for the lives of the crew that serve under them. You will need to be very careful around them."

"They are a rough lot," agreed Jorgen. "but I report directly to the ship's carpenter."

"I never met that man Hauk," said Elen. She looked out to sea and swallowed. "But when I see the first mate, Hauk comes to mind." Elen's face was flushed and her voice rose with anger. "The first mate ordered a beating today that was vicious and cruel."

"You saw that?" said Jorgen.

"Ja, I saw it," Elen responded. She put both hands to her face and shook her head. Her fingertips briefly massaged her forehead.

"Fyke's son was also caught in the crowd. He came to tell us about it when it was over. Is that what has you so troubled?"

Elen nodded. She still seemed distracted by the memory.

Jorgen gave her time to collect her thoughts.

"I didn't mention it when we were all together at middag because I didn't want to alarm the others. It was so savage. How can we spend weeks on board with mates like that? I know that man shouldn't have been smoking below deck, but I hardly think he deserved such a severe thrashing. I was caught in the crowd and couldn't get to the stairs. I saw the first mate grin as the first lashes fell. He enjoyed it, even goaded the man with the whip and laughed when their victim cried out in pain. They gagged him so they wouldn't have to hear his pleas for mercy, and then continued the beating."

Now it was Jorgen's turn to pat his mother-in-law's arm. "I'm sorry you had to see that, but it was a good thing that Marta and Mary were not with you."

"Ja," said Elen. "Mary would have been terrorized by the sight. It was upsetting for most of those forced to watch. The captain seems like a good man, I can't understand why he tolerates that behavior," she added.

"I think," said Jorgen, "he chooses not to know all that they do. Fyke says that it is difficult to find good men willing to serve on these ships. If we follow the ship's rules, the mates will have no cause to harm us. But you're right, Hauk would fit right in with the mates. Believe me, Elen," Jorgen hesitated when he spoke her name, it sounded strange. "I will be careful."

Ten

Later That Month

Jorgen was awakened in the morning by the noise of the anchor being hauled in. He joined the cheering crowd on deck and walked across the deck to watch the sails billow out as they caught the gentle breeze. His step was lighter than it had been in days, and the muscles in his face fell into a relaxed smile. He looked out over the sea. *This is it,* he mused, *this is the final obstacle. Somewhere on the other side of this ocean is the land that we will call home, where Andrew and I will plant and harvest crops and Marta and I will raise our family.* He took it as a good omen that the sea was calm. *We're off to a good start,* he thought as the ship moved effortlessly through the water.

Thinking of Marta, he turned from the rail to go to her cabin, but advanced only a few steps when he saw her coming toward him. It amazed him how often it happened that he would think about her, look up, and there she'd be. Or an idea would pop into his head and before he could share it with her, she would say it first.

"I was just coming to get you," he said when she arrived at his side. He took her hand and they strolled on deck until they reached the stern where they stopped to watch the English coastline recede in the distance.

"I suppose England is much the same as any other place, no better, no worse, " said Marta, "but Liverpool is like no place I've ever seen or hope to see again. I wonder how Mrs. Klark and her daughter are coping."

"Mrs. Klark strikes me as a woman who can handle any situation. And don't forget, your mother gave her the agent's name. I know he'll do what he can to help her..."

"You're right. He is a good man," said Marta. "And as long as Mrs. Klark doesn't become ill herself, they should all be able to go home soon."

"Let's get my mother and Mary. We need to get our rations for the week and have our breakfast before you go to work."

They paused in the dimly lit corridor outside the cabin and embraced. Finding time alone this last week had not been easy. Jorgen could feel his wife's pregnancy between them.

"I love you," said Jorgen. He pulled away just enough to meet her eyes. "I hope this trip will not be too hard on you and the baby."

"I'll be fine, and so will this baby; its father is a seaman," she said with the hint of a smile.

Jorgen laughed. "That's what scares me."

She reached for his hand and placed it over her abdomen. "The baby's moving," she said, "Can you feel it?"

"The baby stirred under Jorgen's hand. "I think he knows I'm here. He can feel my hand," Jorgen said.

"Or she," corrected Marta.

They grinned at each other and Jorgen pulled her close again.

"He, she, I don't really care," he said, as he caressed her hair. "I just want you both to be safe and healthy... and I miss you."

Her face was nestled against his cheek. "I miss waking up in your arms and seeing your face first thing in the morning." She reached up and stroked the side of his face. It now sported a full month's growth of beard. "Your beard's become so smooth," she said, sounding surprised. "You're not prickly anymore."

Jorgen laughed, gave her a quick kiss, and they went in to get the others.

★ ★ ★

The deck was crowded when they returned with Elen and Mary. Everyone seemed to be in a celebratory mood, milling about on deck, smiling at one another, laughing.

Strangers talked to strangers. It was so good to be underway, at last.

But as time passed with no sign of rations, the mood shifted: first to impatience and then to anger. Some of the late arrivals on board, mostly lower steerage passengers, had gone without food for a day or more. They had neither the foresight nor the money to bring on board an adequate supply of food before leaving shore. At their sides, small children cried that they were hungry.

Minutes turned into an hour, then two hours, with no sign of the mates or the passenger's rations. Jorgen finally had to leave for work, but Fyke sent him back upon his arrival. "Work can wait, you can't miss your rations," he told Jorgen.

At last, the first and second mate showed up and threw open the door to one of the storerooms. They had a few sailors to help them, but not enough to get the job done in a timely fashion and also control the angry and unruly passengers. Many of whom, driven by hunger and impatient with slow moving food lines, surged to the front of the line and began to shout threats, obscenities, and insults. Whether out of fear or anger, the mates closed and locked the storeroom and tried to walk away.

Jorgen saw the captain make his way into the midst of the passengers whereupon he drew his pistol and fired it into the air. The crowd was startled into silence. In spite of the ringing in his ears, Jorgen heard the captain summon the two mates, and all watched and listened as the captain upbraided his officers for their tardiness and lack of organization. Although the diatribe was in English, all within earshot had no difficulty understanding the captain's meaning. Then he turned his attention to the unruly passengers demanding order. Quickly and quietly the large group formed two lines and waited for the mates to resume the distribution.

Having restored order, the captain left the deck and the chastised mates returned to their task with a new sense of purpose. The passengers would pay for causing them trouble. Although several dozen people were in line ahead of Jorgen, he was surprised to reach the front of the line so quickly. He discovered the reason for the speedy progress when he opened his sack to receive his ration. The first mate pitched a few items into his sack, but Jorgen knew that he had not received his full allotment.

"Next!" yelled the mate, roughly shoving Jorgen out of the way.

Marta was next in line. Her allotment lacked even more than Jorgen's.

"Next," yelled the Mate, and Marta, too, was given a rough push. Fortunately, Jorgen was close by and steadied her when she started to stumble.

Receiving a partial ration was enough to raise his hackles, but when the first mate laid hands on Jorgen's wife and nearly causing her to fall, Jorgen erupted.

"You don't touch her!" he shouted. Totally forgotten in his angry outburst was his vow to steer clear of this wretched man.

Like a wild animal roused by the sound of his prey, the first mate slowly turned to face Jorgen.

"Not good," Jorgen shouted, using two English words that he had recently learned. He took Marta's sack of food, and holding it up with his own, took a couple of steps toward the mate. Reckless with fury, he yelled again and again, "Not good! Not good!"

The first mate threw the ration intended for Mary's bag onto the deck and advanced on Jorgen. His eyes were hard and hateful, his mouth twisted in an ugly grimace. Jorgen stood his ground until the mate slammed his fist into his face. He staggered a step or two back but did not fall. The first mate took a menacing step toward Jorgen and raised his fist.

"Nei," screamed Marta rushing to Jorgen. A tall, rough-looking man stepped out of line, walked over, and stood beside Jorgen. He said nothing, just stared at the first mate silently, daring him to make a move. The mate lowered his hand, glared at the two men, then turned and went back to the food line, rubbing his fist as he went.

While the mate had been occupied with Jorgen, Mary had scrambled about picking up the items he had thrown to the deck. When he returned to his task, Mary innocently opened her bag and received a second helping. She scooted away before the distracted man realized his mistake. The timid, shy little girl had learned two valuable lessons in her short life: anger blinds a man, and hunger is worse than a beating.

Elen received her partial ration and joined the others who waited for her. Instead of taking them to their cabin, Jorgen searched out the interpreter and asked him to accompany them to the captain's quarters.

To his dismay, the interpreter advised him that the Captain did not meet with the passengers. Complaints were to be made to the mates who were supposed to take them to the captain.

"But the mates are the problem," argued Jorgen. "Look at what they are giving as a week's ration. This is barely half what the shipping line promised. It won't last the week. Everyone will run out of food before the week is up. Passengers will go hungry on these short rations."

"When my husband complained, he was struck in the face by the first mate," added Marta. "The mates are not going to take our complaints to the captain."

"Perhaps if you were to prepare a petition," offered the interpreter, "and get it signed by as many passengers as possible, I could see that the Captain gets it."

Addressing Jorgen, he continued. "It is unfortunate that you tangled with the first mate. He could make your life extremely unpleasant for the rest of this voyage. You'd do well to avoid him in the future."

★ ★ ★

Elen wrote up a petition on paper that Jorgen removed from the back of his journal. The women in her cabin and their husbands were only too happy to sign once they understood what it said. They had not brought much food on board with them, and they were angry about the inadequate allotments they had received that day.

Meanwhile, Jorgen shaved his beard and in so doing took ten years off his age.

"You've become a real troublemaker," laughed Marta as she trimmed his hair. "What happened to the quiet boy who used to read poetry to me in the school yard?"

"You were the one reading poems," Jorgen retorted, "I was the one who didn't understand what they meant."

When she finished the haircut, Marta rummaged in one of the chests until she found one of Jorgen's old caps.

"There," she said, plopping it on his head. "You look like a new man. I doubt that anyone will know that you are you." The makeover had been successful. Their hope was that the more youthful looking Jorgen would be able to go unnoticed by the first mate.

The next morning Jorgen was relieved when Fyke didn't even recognize him. Although he still intended to stay far away from the first mate, he was not going to worry if their paths happened to cross.

In just three days Elen collected so many signatures on her petition that she had to borrow two more pages from the journal, and true to his promise, the interpreter presented it to the captain. Before the week was out, the captain had ordered another food distribution and this time he stayed to oversee the process. Rumor had it that the captain threatened to put the two mates in irons if there were any more problems.

For the second time that week passengers waited patiently for rations. Dark clouds billowed up over the horizon and what had been a mild breeze grew into a strong wind. Fearing a storm was imminent, the captain had ordered all mates to assist in and hurry the distribution process.

Jorgen, wisely avoiding the first mate's line, stood between Marta and Elen, lending them each an arm for support. Mary, adept at maintaining her balance on the rocking ship, seemed to enjoy the challenge.

"She's more of an adventurer than I gave her credit for," Jorgen commented to the women. "I was afraid that rough seas would frighten her."

Mary received her ration and waited while the others got theirs.

"I'll carry yours, Aunt Elen," she offered, "and Jorgen, you can take Marta's. That way they can hang onto you with both hands."

"Isn't she something?" said Elen as they watched the young girl stagger across the rolling deck under the weight of double rations.

They struggled to make it back to the cabin, and Jorgen was relieved when Marta and her mother were finally able to sink down onto their berth. He and Mary stumbled and bumped their way about the cabin getting the rations stored away.

"I have some work to finish, but afterwards, I will prepare middag. It's too hazardous for you two on deck," Jorgen said to Marta and her mother.

Marta nodded. The ship's movement was making her feel ill.

"You're pretty steady on your feet," Jorgen said to Mary. "Would you like to help me later with middag?"

Mary gave him a big grin. "Sure," she said, "I can do that."

Although the sea remained rough, and the sky had looked threatening for hours, when Jorgen returned to the cabin later that afternoon rain had not yet fallen. He and Mary set off for the cookhouse hoping they wouldn't have to wait long for a place at the stove. He was dismayed, however, to see so many passengers grouped along the rail, just outside the galley. With that many people waiting to prepare their food, it would be hours before he and Mary would be able to cook anything. But as they drew near, he realized the passengers' hands were empty, there were no cooking pots or sacks of food. They stood instead, somber faced, assembled around the captain. With a sudden jolt of comprehension, Jorgen knew what was taking place.

The captain began to speak.

"Someone has died," Jorgen whispered to Mary. He removed his hat and bowed his head at the sound of the captain's deep baritone voice. When he heard the interpreter translate the words of Psalm 30 into Norwegian, Jorgen realized the fatality was one of his countrymen.

"Sing the praises of the Lord, you his faithful people, praise his holy name.

For his anger lasts only a moment, but his favor lasts a lifetime;

Weeping may stay for the night, but rejoicing comes in the morning."

Because she was so short, Mary was unable to see the four sailors raise a wooden slab over the ship's railing. Nor did she see the small bundle that slid off into the ocean when the slab was tipped.

Jorgen was concerned. Already a child was dead, and they had been at sea less than two weeks.

During the moments of silence that followed the burial, Jorgen could feel Mary's questioning eyes boring into him. He was about to whisper an explanation to her when those nearest the captain turned, and the crowd parted to let them pass through. Jorgen watched, stunned and horrified, as the family they had met on their first day aboard the Newark teetered across the swaying deck and started down the stairs to steerage. The father cradled the infant in the crook of one arm and he steadied his wife with the other. The young girl whose basket Jorgen had carried held tightly to her mother's other hand. The lively youngster, the lad who had darted about, was not with his family.

Jorgen heard Mary's startled gasp. She clapped her hand over her mouth as they watched the family leave the deck. "Where is their little boy?" she whispered frantically. "Per, his name is Per. Is he the one who died, Jorgen?"

Not able to trust his voice, Jorgen simply nodded.

Mary didn't flinch when Jorgen placed a hand on her shoulder. Neither moved for a few seconds, and then Jorgen picked up the kettle and pot at their feet. He handed Mary the kettle and led the way into the galley.

"How did he die?" Mary asked, her voice barely above a whisper.

"Perhaps he took ill," Jorgen responded. "Some in steerage are not well.

"What's wrong with them...Aren't they eating enough limes?"

"Perhaps not," Jorgen replied. He knew the illness had nothing to do with limes, but he said no more. No sense worrying the child. He had heard there were many cases of dysentery in lower steerage, but nothing about serious illness in the area where the little boy's family was berthed. He would have to ask Fyke; he would know.

God help us all, Jorgen thought, *if it is something like cholera.* He did not place much faith in the ship's doctor to handle such an epidemic.

No more was said as the two prepared their meal. It required all their concentration and agility to maintain their balance and keep the pot and kettle on the stove. The weather had gradually grown worse and wind whistled outside the galley door. They worked quickly and finished just as the first mate poked his head into the galley. He issued a gruff command then stepped aside to allow an interpreter to enter the crowded cooking space. "The galley is closed now," he said, "due to rough seas."

The first mate's tone had been such that Jorgen hadn't even waited to hear the translation. Anxious that he would be recognized, he pulled his hat low to his eyes, "Let's go," he said to Mary. She snatched the kettle of hot water from the stove and started for the door. He grabbed the pot of stew and was close behind.

Jorgen needn't have been worried. The mate's attention was fixed on those who did not respond immediately to his orders. He latched on to the nearest dawdler and pushed her out of the galley. She stumbled and fell at Jorgen's heels. One by one, the first mate turned on the others, roughly dispatching them all without their food or their pots. Jorgen knew those unfortunate passengers were not only going hungry tonight, but if they didn't get their cooking pots back, they would have difficulty preparing future meals. It angered him because he knew the mate was filching an extra ration of food for himself at the expense of passengers who most likely had little to spare.

"I think Per's in heaven," said Mary. She had not said a word since returning to the cabin. Jorgen had told Marta and Elen about their traumatic afternoon. His account of Per's on board burial and the outrageous actions of the First Mate left them all in low spirits.

The first two weeks aboard the Newark had passed at an agonizingly slow pace. Seasickness was an everyday occurrence for many of the passengers including two of the German women and two of their children. Elen, like Jorgen, experienced queasiness when waters were rough, but never actually became ill. They both worried about Marta. Of the four of them, she was having the most difficulty. Unlike Mary, whose sea legs failed her only once, during the first storm, Marta had difficulty keeping food down in all but the calmest weather.

Elen's purpose in life during those weeks was to coax and cajole the ill members of her cabin to eat small amounts of food and drink frequent sips of water. She did not trust the ship's water and insisted that every drop consumed had to be boiled first.

"I don't know what we would do without you," Jorgen

said one morning after a particularly rough night. He had just returned from the galley with two kettles of boiled water and he set about making tea for everyone in the cabin. Elen, meanwhile, helped Marta into clean clothes so that she would be ready to take in some exercise and fresh air. Anytime walkers were permitted on deck, Elen encouraged her ill cabin mates to leave their sickbeds and the stale air of the cabin. She did not accept queasiness as an excuse.

Indeed, those with seasickness did feel better after breathing in the fresh air. Most times, Marta reached the deck by clinging to her mother and Mary for support, but the more she walked the stronger she felt, and gradually she was able to return to the cabin unassisted.

Whether young Per died from dysentery or something else Fyke didn't know, but he did tell Jorgen that the ship's doctor suspected two cases of cholera in lower steerage.

Jorgen relayed this to Elen and Marta and suggested that Mary avoid the other children on the ship as much as possible. The German women also kept their children isolated.

A daily routine gradually evolved that began with early morning time on deck before too many other passengers were up and about. After their morning walk and breakfast, the children had lessons in the cabin. They took long naps in the afternoon, which enabled them to stay up late at night to exercise on deck while most in steerage slept.

On one of their last days in Liverpool, Marta had prevailed upon the landlady of the boarding house to help her find an English language book. This finally was put to use. In between bouts of nausea and seasickness she studied the book, intent on learning this new language. She began to teach the children, but soon found that Elen and the German women were intent on learning English too. For the most part, Marta's daily lessons were unscheduled, depending on the state of her health. However, she proved to be no layabout and insisted on most days that she was well enough to conduct a lesson. Late at night, when they all took exercise on deck, they practiced the new words they had learned that day. It became a game that the children excelled at and a challenge for the adults to keep pace with them. At these nightly sessions, Jorgen was able to contribute the English words he picked up from Fyke. With such constant reinforcement, each individual's English vocabulary grew daily.

"We're off to a good start," said Marta, "and it will be helpful when we do get to America."

Elen continued to teach Mary to read, write, and do sums. The German women did similar work with their children. There were also knitting and drawing sessions. With so much to do, the children seldom got bored, and for all in the crowded cabin, it made time pass more quickly.

When Jorgen was around, he'd play his Hardanger. He would have liked to play on deck, under the stars like he had on the Lykke Til, but because of the first mate, Jorgen did not want to call attention to himself. On many evenings, the German men crowded into the room to visit their wives and children and enjoy Jorgen's music.

The first Mate continued to harass and intimidate passengers and the sailors under his command. It was rumored that he had raped a female passenger who had the misfortune to be caught alone in one of the many isolated passages on the ship. Her young husband sought retribution, but after confronting the First Mate, came away with a broken nose and eyes that were bruised and nearly swollen shut.

The first mate was especially brutal with the black sailors on board. He found a reason to lash every one of them for minor infractions, some multiple times. Jorgen began to wonder if the captain knew about his first mate's cruelty. If he did know, why did he allow it? Was he afraid of his own Mates?

Jorgen brought these questions to Fyke and was disappointed when the old man said that the only reason he had lasted so long aboard ships was that he minded his own business.

★ ★ ★

Jorgen's earlier prediction about the quality of the rations proved all too accurate. By the fourth week, the meat doled out was rancid and the flour was bug infested. Jorgen boiled the meat until it was almost gray and no longer foul smelling. The women sifted through the flour, culling out the unsavory elements. They made the most of what they were given and never went to bed hungry. Every three days, Elen carefully divided a lime into quarters. Four mouths watered in anticipation of the mouth-puckering treat. On the other days, they all had a spoonful of vinegar. The limes were much preferred.

At the end of the fourth week they were down to their last three limes. Elen divided one of those into quarters and gave each one a share. "I think we need to space out these last two," she said, "perhaps have one in five days and the last five days after that. We should be in New York by then. We have plenty of vinegar left, should the trip take longer than expected."

Mary made a face, and they all laughed.

"I share your opinion," laughed Elen. "That vinegar has a nasty taste."

"I think next week we can begin to supplement our rations with some of that," said Jorgen indicating the food chest. "We've come most of the way, winds have been favorable and as you said, we should be in New York harbor within a week or two. Of course we need to be careful with our supply. We may get held up in the harbor for a few days because of all the sickness on board, and the ship's rations may have run out by then."

"No more rations," said Marta. "How will people survive? Some of them have no extra provisions, or will have used all they brought on board."

"According to Fyke," said Jorgen, "if we get stranded in the harbor for more than a few days, food will be ferried out to us. But Fyke said it's barely enough to feed everyone, so we really have to save enough, just in case."

★ ★ ★

Jorgen and Fyke worked steadily one morning replacing buckled planks in a passageway. An elderly passenger had tripped on them and suffered a broken leg. He was a man of some means and created such a ruckus about the dangerous conditions on board that the captain himself ordered Fyke to make the necessary repairs.

They were nearing the end of the job when Fyke abruptly stood up and cocked his head.

"We're not moving," he said.

Bang! Bang! The sound of Jorgen's hammer echoed, as it had all morning, down the passageway.

"That should do it," he said, rising to stand next to Fyke. "How long do you think we've been motionless? I didn't realize that we had stopped?"

Fyke rubbed his hand across his grizzled beard. "It just happened...wind must have quit." The morning's work had left him winded. "Hope it doesn't last long...captain's not gonna like this."

They packed up their tools and Fyke said, "We're done here, go back to your family. I know where to find you if I need you."

Jorgen was happy to have the afternoon off. They had worked many extra hours the last several days. After weeks at sea, the weather and passengers had taken their toll on the ship. The two men had worked the long hours to keep it in good order. Jorgen hoped there would not be too much to do before they reached New York, and that that day was not far off—perhaps as soon as four or five days.

But five days later they were still stranded, becalmed in

water eerily unruffled by waves. The limp sails had been hauled in, and the flags, though they teased with an occasional flutter, remained lifeless day after day.

Passengers flocked to the decks to stroll in the sunshine. Seasickness had abated and those who had suffered the most, their bodies emaciated from lack of food, crowded the galley, cooking all that they had been unable to eat for weeks.

With cases of cholera still cropping up, Jorgen insisted that Marta and Mary continue to avoid the deck during its most crowded periods. He and Elen did all the cooking. Mary grew bored within the cabin and Marta found it challenging to keep her occupied. Both eagerly looked forward to time on deck, their early morning and late night strolls and those odd times, usually when passengers were taking their meals, when Jorgen felt the danger was not so great.

So it was that they were out enjoying the stars on that fifth night when the wind began. The sailors cheerily called to one another as they hoisted the sails that filled and billowed like enormous wings propelling the ship forward. Jorgen fell asleep that night smiling as he imagined the land that was so close to being his.

When he awoke it was still dark and the ship was, again, not moving. Rations were distributed shortly after sunrise, but were of the poorest quality yet. The slivers of beef they were given would hardly feed a child. A man from lower steerage smashed the door to one of the storerooms intent on stealing food, but it was empty. The poor man, who was placed in irons and beaten for destroying property, had nothing to show for his crime. For the next three days, tempers were short in steerage and flared at the slightest provocation. A fight broke out and the result was two broken tables.

Fyke told Jorgen to repair the tables, and he went to work on the broken storeroom door. No sooner had Jorgen begun on the first table than he could feel the movement of the boat. He hoped this time would not be a false alarm.

"Keep on blowing, wind," he muttered. It was more a prayer than a command.

But now, his efforts to repair the tables were thwarted by the movement of the ship as it pitched and yawed in the waves. *This is next to impossible,* he thought and was about to give up when large hands steadied the pieces he was attempting to join.

"Takk," he said, looking up at the man who smiled in return.

"It looks like you could use a little help," said Per's father.

Jorgen, Marta, and Elen had expressed their condolences to this man and his wife a few days after the burial, and Mary had generously gifted her pretty blue ribbon to their daughter. Since then, Jorgen had seen the man several times. Jorgen always smiled and nodded but they had not spoken. Anything he thought to say sounded hollow; the right words wouldn't come to mind.

In spite of winds growing ever stronger, with four hands instead of two both tables were quickly rebuilt. The two men walked together along the rows of berths talking easily about the job they had just completed. When they reached the other man's family, the mother was reading to the girl while the baby slept next to them on the cot. Jorgen noticed the blue ribbon in the girl's hair and thought, *I'll have to tell Mary.*

The family seemed to be weathering the rough weather while, all around them, many were overcome with seasickness. After greeting the mother and daughter, Jorgen thanked the man again for his assistance and left to see if Fyke needed help with the door.

"I'm almost finished here," said Fyke, "but the captain was looking for you. Injuries and illness among the crew have left them shorthanded. The captain thinks we're in for a stormy night and would like you to fill in on deck. You are to report to the first mate and he'll assign you to the crew you'll be working with tonight. If you have rain gear, you'd best put it on."

Jorgen started to leave.

"Be careful, Jorgen, the deck is a dangerous place in this kind of weather."

"Ja," said Jorgen. "And that mate is dangerous in any kind of weather."

"Be careful," Fyke repeated.

Where had he put his oilskins? As he hurried back to the cabin, Jorgen tried to picture which chest he had packed them in.

Nightfall was still a couple hours away and yet, as he made his way across the deck, Jorgen saw that the darkened sky had become one with the black water. He grabbed one of the lines that had been strung across the deck to assist the sailors and keep them from being swept overboard. *And to think that just this morning there wasn't enough of a breeze to fill the sails,* Jorgen thought as he hung on while the ship rode high on the crest of one wave, then plunged into the valley before the next.

The sails had been trimmed and the helmsman struggled to keep the boat from being hit broadside by waves. In this weather, no one but crew would be allowed on deck, and Jorgen was not looking forward to being a member of that crew. He wasn't worried about the first mate. Covered in oilskin with the hood shrouding his face, Jorgen knew he'd be unrecognizable. He was worried that if the storm got really bad, his fear of the raging sea would keep him from performing his duties. He hoped he wasn't walking into his old nightmare. The dream had resurfaced again in the weeks aboard this ship, especially in windy weather.

Jorgen shrugged off thoughts of his nightmare. *I need to stay calm, like Theo,* he told himself. *I can do it,* he vowed.

He knocked when he reached the cabin, and Mary let him in. Jorgen was surprised to see Marta lying on the berth she shared with her mother and Mary. Elen was leaning over her and had just placed a cloth on Marta's forehead.

Seasickness he thought as he walked to the bedside. The small basin next to her head confirmed his suspicions.

"I have been summoned to work on deck," Jorgen said. "Is there anything I can do for you before I leave? How about if I help you walk a short distance in the passageway?"

Marta forced a smile to her pale lips and replied that her mother could help her, if she felt up to it later. "It's a little rough for that now. I must have eaten something that doesn't agree with me. I just want to lie quietly for a while."

Jorgen stood at the bedside not quite sure what to do. He knew he could not ignore orders to appear on deck, yet he felt a compelling need to stay with Marta.

"Mary and I can take care of Marta," said Elen. "She's just a little seasick. You go and do what you have to do. We'll be fine here."

Jorgen wasn't so sure. Marta looked very uncomfortable. He picked up her hand and was surprised by its coolness.

"Really, Jorgen, I'll be fine. I'll get up and walk a bit later, and there's a full kettle of hot water left from middag, Mor can make me some tea as soon as my stomach settles. Go!" She dropped his hand and pointed to the door.

He found his oilskins and put them on. "I'll be back as soon as I can to see how you're feeling," he said, and he left the cabin.

Eleven

Late September 1850

Marta was annoyed with herself. She hated being the sickly one of the group and was uncomfortable when people hovered over her like she was some sort of invalid. She had always been healthy and, like her mother, was more at ease giving comfort to others than being the recipient of it.

Over the course of the voyage, her bouts with seasickness had become less frequent. She attributed this to her determination to feel well. When she felt the usual feelings of queasiness setting in, she forced herself to stay active, to not give in to sickness. "Do something for someone else," she told herself. "Stop thinking about yourself!"

For the most part, this change in attitude had helped; she had felt better. Until today, she had woken early in the morning with bothersome abdominal cramps, and as the day progressed, the old familiar feeling of nausea had returned. She blamed these nuisances on something she had eaten. Stomachaches had grown more common among all of the passengers due to the spoiled or rancid nature of the ship's rapidly dwindling and aging rations.

In spite of her discomfort, Marta had participated in the routine activities of cabin life. But by late afternoon, forced to give up the pretense of wellness, she took to her berth, felled by the unknown. Bad food? Or was it seasickness? *Probably a combination of both,* she thought.

When Jorgen had returned to retrieve his oilskins, he affirmed what all in the cabin had suspected, that they were in for a stormy night. Though Marta had been pleased to see him, her illness and the accompanying feeling of disappointment she felt for not being able to shake it off, had combined to make her too miserable, too distracted to contemplate his plight.

Fortunately, she was lying down when a cramp, more powerful than what she had thus far experienced, took her breath away.

Alarmed, she considered for the first time a different possibility. The baby. But by her own reckoning, the baby was not due for another six weeks.

She looked around the rough, crowded cabin. It couldn't be happening now. She didn't want to give birth on this ship.

Marta closed her eyes and tried to remain calm. After several minutes passed, she felt another strong cramp. This wasn't how she had pictured giving birth. She vowed to herself that she was not going to have her baby on this disease-infested ship. And then, a third, attention-commanding cramp.

"Mor," she said urgently, "I'm having contractions. I think the baby is coming."

"I doubt that," said Elen. "It's too soon, you still have weeks to go. Rest for a while, the contractions will pass. False labor is very common with first births."

Marta watched her mother attempt to make their evening tea. It was difficult enough for her to maintain her balance, let alone pour water. "I think we're going to have to wait for our tea," Elen said.

After a while, the storm seemed to subside. More light came through the small porthole and the ship's motion was smoother so Elen decided to try again. "Before we have our tea," said Marta, "I'd like to get up and move about a little."

"I'm glad you're feeling better," said Elen. "Some exercise and then a cup of tea; sounds like a recipe for recovery."

Marta stood, leaned on her mother for support, and stretched. It felt good and eased the unusual ache she felt in her lower back. She relieved herself in the chamber pot and with her mother's help walked halfway down the passageway. Returning to the cabin, Marta halted. "I can't stop it," she said. Her voice was a mixture of astonishment and shame. "I'm wetting myself!"

"Let's get you back," said Elen. "This happens in most pregnancies. It's nothing to be ashamed of." She suspected the baby was putting pressure on Marta's bladder and thought if Marta could lie down, the problem would solve itself.

No sooner had Marta settled in bed when she felt the next contraction. It started with the ache, growing deep in her lower back, and spread around to the front. Her abdomen tensed and was hard for many seconds, perhaps a minute, and then the muscles relaxed.

Five minutes later it happened again. "I don't think this is false labor," said Marta.

Elen came and sat beside her. Perspiration beaded Marta's face and her hands fluttered nervously over her swollen abdomen. "I think I've wet myself again," she whispered, her face colored with embarrassment. Within minutes there was another contraction. Elen feared Marta was right; this no longer looked like a false alarm.

"I need to see what is going on," said Elen. "Your waters may have broken."

A quick examination confirmed this and heightened Elen's anxiety. She knew a premature birth under the best of circumstances could be perilous, if not fatal, to both mother and infant. Obviously, these were not the best of circumstances.

Elen fought to contain her apprehension. Marta needed her and Elen knew she had to remain calm and confident if she wanted to do her best.

Mary came to stand at the bedside. She took hold of Elen's shoulder to steady herself when the ship lurched. The storm seemed to be intensifying. Elen could feel the child's fear in her tight grip.

"Is Marta going to be all right?" Mary's voice was small and trembled.

Elen put every bit of conviction she could muster into

her words. "Marta will be fine," she said, then lightened her tone, "but it looks like this baby wants to meet us, and I'm going to need your help." She smiled at the child who nodded, but remained somber.

"All right then," said Elen. She handed Mary the cloth she had used earlier to wipe off Marta's face. "Put some fresh water on this and cool off Marta's forehead."

The German women approached the bed and indicated their desire to help. Elen dispatched them to collect as much water as possible from neighboring cabins.

Mary was eager to do something. She wiped off Marta's face then carefully folded the cloth and placed it on her forehead.

"That's helpful," said Elen. "Now I need you to search in the chests for a small piece of string, soap, wash cloths, clean bedding and something to wrap the baby in."

For the next two hours, the cabin was charged with quiet, purposeful activity that swirled around Marta. And then...the contractions stopped and Marta dozed off.

"This is good," Elen said to Mary, "if her labor starts up again, she'll be rested and feel stronger."

The German women made room for Elen and Mary to sit on one of their berths. Knitting bags were opened and soon the women were hunched over their needles in the semi-darkness. Mary and the other children played one of their made up games. The scene gave an air of domestic tranquility, but further scrutiny would reveal Elen's bunched up eyebrows, her nervous glances at her daughter; Mary's sweaty hands and racing heartbeat when she'd look briefly at Marta; and the German women, their needles going faster and faster as they, too, worried about their young cabin mate.

Gradually, the storm intensified and the ship rocked back and forth. This prompted additional stress as Elen began to worry about Jorgen. *He's not an experienced sailor,* she thought, *it must be very dangerous on deck. And what if the first mate recognizes him.* Her hands started to shake, so she put her knitting away. *I can't think about those possibilities,* she told herself. *I need a clear head for what will take place in this cabin.*

She didn't have long to wait. Within the hour, Marta was roused from her nap by the resumption of contractions.

"Mor," she called out.

Fearing she would topple over if she tried to stand, Elen crawled to Marta's bedside. She beckoned Sophia to join her. She hoped the presence of the other woman would bolster her own confidence. Also, another pair of hands would be useful, especially in the unsteady circumstance of this storm-tossed situation.

Mary withdrew from the children's game and watched the proceedings, hardly daring to draw a breath. She thought about her own birth and wondered who had been there to help her mother. Maybe there had been no one. Maybe that's why her mother had died. She hoped that Marta would not die.

"Bear down, Marta, push!" Elen encouraged her daughter.

Marta cried out in pain, but did as she was instructed.

A few seconds passed, and there was another command to push.

Mary could see the pain contorting Marta's face, and it frightened her.

"Aunt Elen," Mary said. Hearing her own voice added to Mary's panic.

"Come here, child," was all that Elen managed to say. The baby was presenting itself, and Elen's involvement was both physical and emotional.

The German woman and Mary traded places. Mary knelt next to Elen and watched her turn the baby's face to the side and swab its mouth with the corner of a clean towel.

The newborn's first gasp for air followed by a brief, small cry was drowned out by the sounds of the storm. Despite the stuffy confinement of the cabin, Marta shivered violently, her body in shock, her emotions charged with excitement, fear, and the wonder of birth.

Mary longed to touch the baby, but instead placed a hand on Elen's arm. This time fear and tension were absent in her grasp.

"It's so small," she said. Her tone was reverential. She looked at Marta, "I've never seen a just-born baby. Did it hurt a lot?"

"Some," said Marta, "but not too much."

Elen's attention was intensely focused on the fragile-looking infant that lay very still and pale between Marta's legs. She was still on her knees, leaning on the berth to steady herself against the boat's rollicking movements. Elen gently massaged the infant to stimulate its circulation and watched its thin chest rise and fall ever more steadily with each small breath. Her relief was palpable when she observed the infant's lips and skin begin to take on a healthy pink color. Assured of its well-being Elen stopped rubbing the baby's arms and legs, tied the cord, and cut it. She wrapped the baby in soft, white cloth Mary had found in the chest and placing the infant on Marta's chest, buttoned Marta's chemise around baby and mother.

Elen's worried frown softened to a smile as she attended to her daughter's needs. She delivered the afterbirth and cleaned Marta as best she could under the circumstances, grateful for the ample amount of water the German women had been able to gather. The ship bounced around continually, and several times Elen lost her balance and nearly fell on top of the new mother and infant. When she felt she had done all she could to make Marta comfortable, she kissed her daughter's forehead, and said, "Rest now, I'll go find the new father."

Elen hurried off, bumping against the walls of the dark passageways, not sure how she would accomplish this task. If she had been thinking clearly, she would have knocked on the cabin door belonging to the German men and asked one of them to go for Jorgen. But the euphoria of delivering her grandchild had left her in an uncharacteristically giddy state and less cautious than her normally sensible self. Although women and children had been strictly ordered to stay below deck, she felt circumstances rendered her immune to that command.

★ ★ ★

Marta's eyes fluttered open when Jorgen knelt beside the cot and took her hand. He moved as if to cradle her in a hug but stopped short when he saw the tiny head peaking out of the bedclothes. Marta pulled him in close and whispered in his ear.

"Jorgen, we have a daughter." She unbuttoned the top buttons of the chemise exposing the infant's pink shoulders and one thin arm.

"How did this happen? When did..." Jorgen was confused. "Are you...is she...are you both all right? I'll get the doctor."

He started to rise but Marta grabbed his arm.

"We're doing fine, Jorgen. We don't need the doctor. Mor, Mary, the others here, they all took care of everything. It happened so fast, we didn't have time to look for you. I'm so glad that Mor found you."

Jorgen's mind was so muddled that Marta's words did not immediately sink in. Less than an hour had passed since his battle with the storm. He was still thinking about the cocky young sailor who he had helped rescue. Strong winds and a slippery deck had made it nearly impossible to maintain footing on deck, but the foolish lad hadn't used the safety ropes. Meanwhile, Marta was...here.

The baby moved her head and arm, then stuck a tiny finger in her mouth and started to suck. Jorgen bent down, kissed her downy head, then kissed Marta.

He glanced over at the dark outlines of the other

women seated on their berths, looking for Elen, and realized she was missing.

"Did you say that your mother went to find me?" Marta's words finally registered with him. "How long has she been gone?"

"I'm not sure," said Marta. "I closed my eyes and may have dozed off."

"She left just before you came back, didn't you see her?" Mary asked. She jumped down from the chest where she had been sitting.

Jorgen tried to hide his concern. "I'll go look for her," he said, and rushed out of the cabin.

Because of the storm and rough seas, all the hatches but one were battened. The only access to the deck was the way Jorgen had come moments before, so he headed back in that direction.

Where could she be? Jorgen wondered. *Could she have passed by when he was in Fyke's cabin?* He had stayed only long enough to deliver a message from his son, the helmsman.

Fueled by an uneasy feeling that grew with each step, Jorgen hurried, bumping off the walls of passageways with each roll of the ship. He passed Fyke's cabin, rounded the final turn, and was about to dash up the stairs to the deck when he heard scuffling sounds and a muffled cry coming from somewhere close by.

Jorgen squinted into the darkness and located a closed door behind the staircase. He crept over and listened; the sounds were definitely coming from within. He grabbed the handle and yanked open the door.

The muffled cry was louder and although Jorgen couldn't see her, he knew it was Elen. What he could see were the soles of two big feet. Enraged, Jorgen moved into the room and tried to pull the man off Elen. He was successful partly because the man sprang to his feet. Jorgen moved in closer as Elen scrabbled out of the way, and he began to throw punches, some of which actually hit the assailant. The man started for the door, but Jorgen, following close behind, tripped him and sent him sprawling to the floor. Jorgen jumped on him and the two wrestled on the floor until Jorgen, the larger of the two, finally had the man pinned down. Jorgen straddled him and beat him savagely about the head. He could now see who the man was and wasn't surprised to discover that it was the first mate.

Jorgen pummeled the mate, oblivious to the man's threats to kill him. He had no thought other than the hate he was experiencing and the need to revenge the attack on Elen. Jorgen continued to strike the mate until suddenly two pairs of hands clamped on his arms and lifted him off the subdued man. Terror replaced anger as Jorgen looked up, expecting to come face to face with the other mates. Instead, he was shocked to see the faces of two black sailors. As they hauled up Jorgen, each sailor planted a large bare foot on the mate keeping him pinioned to the floor.

At that moment, Elen emerged from the shadows. She held the bodice of her dress together with one hand and a bit of cloth to her mouth with the other.

The men released Jorgen and he rushed to her side.

"You're hurt!" he exclaimed, and he gently removed her hand to see the extent of the injury. Blood sprang from a split in Elen's lip, and Jorgen quickly placed her hand back to staunch the flow.

"This will heal soon enough," she said with some difficulty, "You saved me from real harm." Jorgen saw frightened tears spring into her eyes.

He turned, eyes blazing, to look down at the first mate. The man did not look so menacing now. In fact, he looked terrified. Jorgen looked at the men who had pulled him off the mate and saw what was so frightening. One of the sailors standing guard over the mate held a long knife.

"Go," the man with the knife said.

Jorgen did not need to be told twice. He put his arm

through Elen's and led her away from the men. After a couple of steps Jorgen stole a quick look over his shoulder. The man with the knife was on top of the first mate.

★ ★ ★

Fortunately, Marta had dozed off, and the others in the cabin had gone to bed. Only Mary was awake to witness Elen's return.

"Ohh!" she gasped, when she saw Elen was injured.

Elen shushed her. "It's not serious; let's not disturb the others."

"Do you have any water left?" whispered Jorgen.

When Mary nodded, Jorgen told her to help Elen wash the blood off her face and change her clothes.

Marta woke briefly when her mother lay down next to her. The baby stirred, and Marta put her to her breast. The infant nursed for a while, then she and the new mother fell back asleep.

Elen finally fell into troubled slumber, and when she sobbed in her sleep, it was Mary who comforted her and held her hand until she fell asleep again.

Tired and emotionally drained as he was, Jorgen had to return to his duty on deck, but towards morning, the storm ended and he was finally dismissed. On his way to his berth to catch a couple hours of sleep, he ran into one of the black sailors, the one who had wielded the knife. As they passed each other, the sailor averted his eyes as he and all the black sailors were required to do when they passed a white person. Jorgen could only speculate on what had happened the night before. He fell asleep, too exhausted to be worried about what the new day would reveal.

He was roused from a sound sleep by Fyke. "Captain wants to see you, immediately," the older man said. He waited while Jorgen put on his boots, and the two started off for the captain's quarters.

When they reached a spot where they were alone, Fyke stopped and turned to face Jorgen. His expression was grave. "I was with the captain this morning when the second and third mates showed up. They reported that the first mate has been missing since some time last night, and there is a trail of blood starting near the stairs and leading up to the deck."

"Why does that concern me?" A knot had formed in Jorgen's stomach. How had the captain found out? It had been just the two black sailors, Elen, and him. He felt confident that no one else had seen them.

"The second mate told the captain that he saw the first mate talking with the old woman who is with your wife. Lucky break for you that the captain didn't send one of the mates to get you. They are convinced of your guilt and want you thrown in irons."

"And what would they charge me with?" said Jorgen, sounding bolder than he felt. "It could be someone else's blood. The first mate could be somewhere on the ship sleeping off a drunk."

"That could be," said Fyke, "but the mates are in a rage. They are convinced the first mate has been murdered, and I think they are afraid they could be next. They are demanding that the captain find whoever is responsible for the first mate's disappearance, and so far you are the only suspect. Your wife's mother is with the captain. He sent me to get her at first light, and he has already questioned her. She told him about your wife giving birth and how she ran into the first and second mates when she went to find you. She said the first mate dismissed the second mate. Then the first mate started yelling at her and pointing in the direction of the cabins. Your wife's mother said she thought the first mate was telling her to go back to her cabin, so she left. She said that was the last time she saw the first mate. When the captain asked how she got her injuries, she said that she lost her balance when the ship suddenly pitched and she fell, hitting her face on a wall. She also said that when she returned to her cabin, she was surprised to see you were there."

Jorgen winced when he walked into the captain's quarters and saw the dark bruise and swelling that covered half of Elen's face. In spite of her injuries, Elen sat and sipped a cup of tea in the midst of the three men. The two mates turned their scowling faces from her to Jorgen when he entered.

"Good morning, Jorgen," the captain said.

"Good morning, captain." Jorgen replied in English. He smiled innocently at the two mates. They responded with cold, silent glares.

Jorgen turned to Elen, "How are you feeling this morning? Your face looks very painful."

"I fear it looks worse than it feels," she said. "It will heal quickly."

"Well," continued Jorgen. "I hope you didn't do any lasting damage to the wall." Although he smiled briefly, his eyes sent a different message to Elen.

"Enough of his talking," thundered the second mate, "he's telling her what to say."

The captain raised his hand to silence the mate, and asked Fyke to translate what Jorgen had said.

"So," the captain said, "you believe this woman's injuries resulted from a collusion with a wall?"

"You have reason to believe otherwise?" said Jorgen. "What is this all about? My wife gave birth last night, and because of the storm, I've barely had time to see to her and my new daughter. You have taken both her mother and me from her side and left her in the care of a young child."

Jorgen didn't need to feign indignation. The thought of Marta and what her needs might be at this very moment with neither him, nor her mother at her side infuriated him.

One of the mates started to speak, but Jorgen raised his voice to speak over him.

"What are they doing here? They were not there when

she fell into the wall."

The captain raised his hand to silence Jorgen. He asked Fyke to translate all that Jorgen had said, and then asked, "When did you go to your wife's cabin?"

"When the eleventh hour bell sounded," said Jorgen. He sensed the captain's impatience with this confrontation. He also seemed suspicious of his second and third mates. At least they appeared to be on not so friendly terms.

Jorgen's tone was now calm and reasonable as he described the previous night's events. "The bosun told me and the sailors in my group to take a rest and instructed us to be back by the twelfth bell. I went to check on my family, to see how they were weathering the storm. When I got to the cabin, I discovered that my wife had given birth. She needed fresh bedding, so I went to the storeroom and got a clean pallet for her. I intended to inform the steward today so that he can deduct it from my pay."

"Was she with your wife when you went to check on her?" The captain nodded at Elen.

"Elen left my wife momentarily to go find me. When she got to the deck and was turned away, she immediately started back to the cabin."

Jorgen was prepared for more questions, but for the time being, the captain seemed satisfied with what he had heard. Or maybe it was Fyke's translation, which to Jorgen seemed longer than his own replies. He hated all the lies that he and Elen were forced to tell, but he knew the truth would endanger their lives and the lives of the sailors who had come to their rescue. *The first mate was an evil man; he—and he alone—was responsible for his fate*, reasoned Jorgen.

Jorgen did his best to maintain the pretense of innocence. The relaxed slump of his shoulders, hands open and idle in his lap, a placid facial expression, all masked the turmoil that raged within him. It was challenging to maintain the appearance of indifference while the captain allowed the mates to have their say. They raised their voices, pointed, and shook their fists at him. Jorgen looked at Elen. She, too, remained composed throughout this fiery exchange, and her steady, reassuring gaze quelled Jorgen's nerves. He wished that Fyke would translate what they were saying, but that didn't happen.

The captain asked the mates a question. One of them started to answer but was drowned out by the other. An argument ensued. The captain looked from them to Jorgen and back to them. He put up a hand to silence them, spoke briefly to the two, and then dismissed them.

As they stormed past him, Jorgen returned their glowering looks with an expression of total disinterest.

The captain stood up. Fyke, Jorgen, and Elen got to their feet too. It seemed the meeting was over. The captain spoke to Jorgen, and Fyke translated. He congratulated Jorgen on the birth of his daughter and said he hoped that the mother and baby would endure the rest of the voyage in good health. He asked if the baby had been named.

"No, sir," Jorgen replied. "We haven't had the opportunity yet. We weren't expecting her so soon."

The captain and Fyke conversed briefly, then Fyke said to Jorgen, "The captain thanks you for your help during the storm. He assumes that's when you scraped your knuckles. He says you should take the day off to be with your family, and when you've named the baby, you should let him know so he can enter her name in the ship's log."

The captain took the teacup from Elen and escorted her to the door. He warned her to take care moving about the ship, especially during rough weather.

Jorgen's curiosity about what was said to the mates would have to wait another day as the captain requested that Fyke stay behind when he and Elen were finally escorted through the door. He hoped that Fyke's involvement in helping to cover up the first mate's disappearance was not apparent and would not jeopardize his good standing with the captain.

On the way back to their cabin, Jorgen looked at his hands and noticed, for the first time, that skin was missing from some of his knuckles.

"Jorgen," said Elen, "I'd like you to say nothing to Marta or Mary about what happened last night. As far as they know, I fell when I went to find you. I'll tell Marta when we are safely off the boat, but in the meantime, I don't want her to worry every time I leave the cabin."

"You know," said Jorgen, "we're both in danger from the mates. They have their suspicions and are clever enough to arrange an accident for one or both of us. We'll need to be cautious until we reach America."

"Believe me," said Elen. "I have no intention of stumbling into trouble again."

"Does Mary ever leave the cabin by herself?"

"Ja, she does. She's still wary of strangers, but her desire to be helpful has led her to volunteer to empty the chamber pot every morning. I think she feels that no one will bother her when she is armed with such fragrant ammunition."

"I'm glad that she is feeling brave enough to venture out on her own," said Jorgen, "but I feel it's not safe for her to be moving about the ship by herself. I usually stop by in the morning and could take over that chore."

"Nei, Jorgen, with all you have to do, we'll manage. I'll tell Mary to wait and go with Sophia when she takes out their slops."

"As long as she waits...she can be an impatient little thing."

"But she is obedient. If I tell her not to leave the cabin by herself, she won't."

★ ★ ★

The somber mood in the cabin brightened considerably when Elen and Jorgen entered. Both Marta and the baby were awake, and the sight that they made, even in the dim, drab cabin filled Jorgen with such unexpected joy that he felt light headed.

He sat on the edge of the berth, gathered them both in his arms, and inhaled their scents. Marta smelled of the lavender soap he had purchased for her in Liverpool. She had nearly swooned over its scent the first time they visited what would become their favorite shop on Waterloo Road, and he had bought it for her the week before they left Liverpool.

The scent of his newborn daughter was a mixture both foreign and familiar to Jorgen. It brought to mind the smell of fresh earth, a rich heady odor most pleasant to Jorgen who liked nothing better than to run his fingers through the soil, breathing in its earthy scent.

The baby turned her head and exhaled sweet milky breath through her pale, slightly puckered lips. He watched her eyes flutter open and a moment of bonding took place as father and daughter locked eyes. *This is as close to heaven,* Jorgen thought, *as I'll ever come.*

The quiet family moment was over too soon, and as questions and explanations filled the air, Marta placed the baby in Jorgen's arms.

He scrutinized her features and kissed the tip of her nose. "She looks a bit like Inger looked, and yet, different. Actually, I think she looks like you, Marta."

"She does resemble Marta as a baby, except she has a lot more hair, and it's darker, too," said Elen.

"That would be the Halvorson influence. Mor says we all looked like dark-haired gypsies at birth. I remember Inger's dark hair. When it fell out and the new stuff came in, she looked like a fuzzy baby chicken."

"I think that's mean, Jorgen. I'll bet your sister doesn't look like a chicken."

"Oh Mary," Marta said with a laugh. "Jorgen's just talking silly. Inger is as pretty as you are, and if our baby looks like her, I'll be a grateful momma."

"And," Marta said, still laughing, "this poor child needs a name. We can't keep calling her 'baby.'"

"Fyke asked me about that," said Jorgen. "He said that children born at sea are sometimes named after the ship or the captain. I don't think I want to name my daughter Newark, and I'm not fond of the captain, even though he did show concern about Elen's fall...And we need to tell the captain, once we've named her, so he can enter her name into the ship's log," Jorgen added.

The group fell silent, and then one by one they began suggesting names.

Jorgen looked down into the baby's face and then at his wife. "We could name her Marta," he offered, "after her beautiful mother. We all agree she does look like you."

"That's a sweet thought, Jorgen, but I'd really like her to have her own name."

"You could name her after the ocean, the Atlanta Ocean," suggested Mary.

"Atlantic," corrected Jorgen, "It's called the Atlantic Ocean, although, I must say, Atlanta sounds prettier."

"Atlanta," echoed Marta, "I like the way it sounds...Atlanta...thanks, Mary, that's a possibility."

"How about your mother's name," said Elen. "Marit is a lovely name."

"Mor would be pleased and honored that we thought of her," said Jorgen. "She told me, a long time ago, that her name, Marit, means pearl."

"Atlanta Marit, our own little ocean pearl," Marta said. "That is truly inspired, the perfect name for her."

"I like it," said Jorgen, "What do you think?" he looked first at Mary then at Elen. They both grinned and nodded in agreement.

Jorgen looked down on the sleeping baby. "Welcome to the family, Atlanta Marit." Then he looked at Mary. "You win the naming prize. You and Elen found the perfect name."

Mary wrapped herself in her own thin arms. Her joy

was so great she thought her heart could burst from her chest. She rocked back and forth, hugging herself and smiling so hard her face hurt. *They liked what I said,* she thought. *I named their baby...they like me.*

★ ★ ★

The trip had gone on for too long. They were already past the seven-week mark for a voyage that was supposed to take thirty-five days. Calm seas had been a good cure for the passengers seasickness but had delayed them almost a week. That was followed by a three-day long storm that drove the ship too far north. If Jorgen had been anxious before the baby was born, her birth only intensified the tension. Per's death was not the last; two more children and one adult had to be buried at sea as well. Several more children were very ill and Jorgen knew, with dwindling and spoiled food supplies, the situation was not going to improve. He feared it was just a question of time until Mary or one of the other children in the cabin came down with one of the many illnesses that infected so many of the passengers, and that would put little Atlanta at serious risk.

Elen and the German women kept the children isolated as best they could, but they couldn't keep them completely confined to the cabin. The children needed the fresh air and exercise that being on deck provided.

Jorgen worried constantly about his tiny daughter. She seemed so fragile and vulnerable. His job as Fyke's assistant took him to all parts of the ship and exposed him to passengers who were not well. He was not sure how sickness was spread, but remembered how his mother had kept her sick children quarantined. He decided to quarantine himself. Although he continued to visit the cabin, he kept his distance and refused to hold the baby.

Away from the cabin, Jorgen's other worry surfaced. He knew from Fyke's account of the captain's lecture to them that the mates had been warned not to harass or harm him or his family. Still, Jorgen knew that they were dangerous men who were capable of arranging accidents.

Also, he, Elen, and Mary had to come face-to-face with whichever mate was distributing the rations. Jorgen had insisted that Marta stay below with Atlanta. They would just have to make do without her ration for that week. Jorgen knew that they were nearing the end of the voyage, but they were also nearing the end of their food supplies. Making sure that his family ate enough nutritious food to keep their strength up and to stay healthy was Jorgen's third major concern. Sleep grew ever more elusive. Jorgen fell into bed each night, exhausted and awoke each morning barely refreshed.

★ ★ ★

On the morning of the fifty-ninth day, land was sighted, and by nightfall the Newark sailed into the Lower Bay, just off Staten Island, New York. The passengers were ecstatic but most were too weary, too ill, or too hungry to engage in celebration. They also were aware that their ordeal was not yet over. Because of the illnesses on board, the ship was placed in quarantine and all passengers needed to be cleared by health inspectors before going ashore.

After the anchor was dropped, the mates distributed the last of the food rations. Some in steerage, including Jorgen, received nothing. What water remained, half rations, was foul smelling and tasted bitter. Jorgen, sure they would all be ill if they had to stay on board for even one more day, found the wait maddening. Their food chest, initially so full that Jorgen had difficulty closing it, now contained just a few soft potatoes with long sprouts growing out of them, cheese that was edible after the mold was scraped from its surface, barely enough rice for a day or two, and a half dozen small dried fish. Elen and Jorgen took only enough food to quell their hunger pangs, but they insisted that Marta and Mary eat more normal portions.

The Newark had been the third ship to arrive in as many days, so it took three full days for it to clear quarantine. It sailed into New York Harbor mid-morning on the fourth day. Jorgen was convinced those were the longest three days of his life.

Disembarking was slow and ruled by utter confusion. The Newark was not able to pull up to the dock, so passengers and baggage were off loaded into small boats and ferried to shore. Jorgen and his family managed to stay together, but their trunks and chests did not arrive with them.

They walked down the dock to find a place where Marta could sit and rest with the baby while they waited for their baggage. In spite of fatigue and hunger, they were able to laugh at themselves as they staggered like drunks trying to walk again on firm ground. They had been on board a ship for sixty-two days.

"Jorgen, hold on to me, so I don't fall and drop Atlanta. My legs feel so wobbly."

After a few more steps, Marta was still so unsteady that she had to stop.

"I know you're afraid to hold Atlanta, but I think she's safer in your arms. I feel like I'm still on the ship."

"That will pass," Jorgen reassured her. "It takes some longer than others to get used to their land legs." He was both eager and reluctant to hold the baby but had no choice as Marta thrust the infant into his arms.

While they waited for their belongings to catch up with them, they were approached, as they had been in Liverpool, by runners and all manner of lowlife trying to sell them train tickets or talk them into renting cheap rooms in the city.

"Go! Go!" Mary shouted at them whenever they got too close. Emboldened by the family's presence behind her, she waved her hands and ran at the intruders.

"Will you be all right if I leave you here to wait for the baggage?" Jorgen asked after finding a bench for Marta and Elen. "I need to return to the customs office to speak with an interpreter."

"I think we'll be fine," said Elen. "Mary is quite effective at defending our territory."

Inside the custom's office, Jorgen was relieved to locate a Norwegian translator so quickly. He was nervous about leaving the women by themselves.

"Are you traveling alone?" the translator asked when he had read the address written on the slip of paper that Jorgen handed him. A badge on his coat read 'H. Peerson' and under his name 'Norwegian/Swedish.'

Jorgen described his traveling party and said that a friend in Norway had given him the address.

"When was your friend last in New York?"

It was now late afternoon. Although Jorgen was tired, hungry, and growing impatient with this man's prying, he answered curtly, "I'm not sure."

"I'm sorry to be asking so many questions," the interpreter said, "but this address is located near or perhaps in the heart of a violent neighborhood known as Five Points. Your friend may have had decent lodging there many years ago, but I would not recommend that area to anyone, especially a family with children. You would not be safe and the tenement housing is poor and overcrowded. And Five Points had a cholera epidemic just last year," the man added for emphasis.

Jorgen's shoulders slumped. What little energy he had suddenly drained away. Wearily, he took back the slip of paper, crumpled it and shoved it into his pocket.

"Can you recommend housing in an area that is safe and affordable? We only need something for a few days."

The interpreter was sympathetic to Jorgen's plight, but had to respond, "I'm sorry, we're not allowed to do that."

Jorgen thanked him and started out of the office.

Remembering something, he turned back. "Could you please give me directions to the city post office?"

With those directions in hand, Jorgen trudged back down the pier. It was time to consult Marta and Elen. It seemed their plans had changed. In fact, Jorgen fretted, they had no plan, and nowhere to stay in New York City.

PART THREE

Home

Twelve

Mid-October 1850

When their baggage finally arrived on the dock more than an hour later, Jorgen and the women were still in a quandary over where to go for the night.

"Go! Go!" Mary shouted. She rushed at an approaching figure flapping her hands as if she was shooing chickens.

Jorgen turned, expecting to see another pesky interloper. Instead, he saw the startled face of the interpreter.

"It's all right, Mary," said Jorgen, "He's not here to bother us. He's the interpreter I spoke to a while ago."

"Hei, I'm glad to see you're still here," the man said.

He had taken off his badge, but Jorgen remembered his name. "This is Mr. Peerson," he said to Mary. "And this is my wife and her mother."

Mr. Peerson greeted the two women and turned to Mary. "You're very good at that," he said smiling at her. He remembered standing on this very spot on his first day in America, and the relentless pursuit of strangers badgering him with deceptive offers of transportation and places to stay.

"I'm not allowed to recommend lodging when I'm working," apologized Mr. Peerson, "but I'm off work now and would like to help, if I can. I know a place where I think you can stay. It's not an inn or a boarding house, but it's clean and in a safe area."

Jorgen studied the man. Could he trust him? Was he just a runner too, out to make some money off an ignorant newcomer?

"There are five of us," said Jorgen, stalling for time.

"It is a large house," countered the interpreter.

"We don't need anything grand," said Jorgen, "We're trying to save our dalers to buy land for a homestead. Do you know what the rent would be for a few days?"

"I don't know that," Mr. Peerson admitted, "but I know the owner, she is the mother of a friend, a frugal woman struggling to make ends meet since her husband died. The last time I was at her home, she talked about wanting to take in boarders. She would be fair with you."

Jorgen couldn't believe their good luck. He suspected he was one question away from hearing the bad news, so he continued. " And she'll rent to strangers?"

The interpreter smiled. "If you'd like, I'll introduce you. I'm on my way home, and her house is not far from where I live on the lower east side of the city.

"She's a good cook, too," he added.

Jorgen looked at Marta, then at Elen.

"What do you think?" he asked both of them.

"I think..." Marta paused, gave Jorgen a wan smile and began again. "I hope... you've run out of questions." She liked the interpreter and sensed that he really did want to help them.

Once again, Jorgen was struck by how weary Marta looked. Fatigue and hunger had taken their toll on Elen, too. He knew they all needed a place to rest. Mr. Peerson didn't seem to be the kind of man to take advantage of others, so considering what their options were, he decided to trust him.

Jorgen nodded to the interpreter, who immediately whistled for a small carriage, which sat a short distance away.

"We'll let the ladies ride in here," he said, "You and I can follow with your baggage."

He opened the door and assisted Elen and Mary as they climbed in. He spoke in English to the driver, giving him an address.

Jorgen helped Marta into the carriage, and then handed Atlanta to her when she was settled. Marta's tired smile tugged at him. "This has been a difficult journey for you," he said, "I hope this will be a good place for you to rest up for a few days."

The interpreter had summoned a wagon and was

placing their baggage in it when Jorgen joined him.

"Takk," grunted Jorgen as he hoisted the last chest into to wagon.

Jorgen introduced himself when both men had climbed up next to the driver. The wagon pulled out and fell in behind the coach.

"My name is Halvor, but most people call me Hal," said the interpreter.

"My oldest brother's name is Halvor," said Jorgen.

"Then I'll wager your father, like mine, is Halvor as well," said Hal. His grin matched the broad brim of his hat. "My father was the second son. His brother Peer got the family name.

"Predictable, isn't it?" said Jorgen, and they both laughed.

"The house I'm taking you to is in a neighborhood called Corlear's Hook. As I said, it's on the Lower East Side. The Hook's not as nice as it used to be; most of the wealthier people have moved farther north in the city. There's an occasional theft, and a few women work the streets, if you know what I mean, but the majority of the Hook's people are good, hard working immigrants, like us. It's not a dangerous area, like Five Points, but your wife and her mother will want to stay off certain streets, especially at night."

Jorgen was distracted and found himself only half listening to Hal's information.

"I don't mean to sound rude or ungrateful for your assistance," he said, "but does the whole city smell like this? We couldn't wait to get away from the horrible odors of the ship, but this is not much better."

"It is bad," said Hal. "And some areas of the city stink worse than others. Sailors say you can smell New York City five miles from shore. The streets really are a mess, but you've no choice but to get used to it."

Jorgen looked at him dubiously. His choice would be to leave the city as soon as possible.

They rode for a while without talking. Jorgen was tired and felt queasy. He wasn't sure if his stomach was reacting to hunger—they hadn't eaten in hours—or to the stench that rose from the sludgy mixture of horse manure and rotting garbage that covered the road. He was concerned that Marta and the others might be feeling as poorly as he did. *This city is worse than Liverpool,* he thought glumly. *And that was worse than Bergen. I'm so sick of stinking cities.* Worry lines creased his forehead as he continued to brood. *This can't be good for Atlanta, for any of us.*

As one disgusting street led to the next and then to the next, Jorgen promised himself that he would, indeed, get the family out of this city as soon as possible. But there were things they needed to attend to before they could make their escape. He thought Atlanta and Marta should be seen by a doctor. Marta had refused the services of the ship's doctor for herself and her baby fearing he might do more harm than good. Elen and Jorgen had agreed. Their opinions of the doctor and the type of medicine he dispensed to the passengers became more cynical as the voyage progressed and additional bodies were buried at sea. Now that they were in a large city, and especially since they were traveling on to parts unknown, Jorgen wanted to be sure both his wife and baby daughter were healthy.

Jorgen mentally ticked off the other things that had to be done before they left New York City. Although he had exchanged a small amount of money before leaving the dock, he would have to exchange the rest of their dalers for American money. He needed to plan their trip to Kendall and purchase tickets for the Hudson River steamship. He wanted to find the post office to see if Andrew had sent a letter, and lastly, he felt an obligation to see if Mary's uncle was here in this city.

"My building used to look just like these," Hal said, breaking into Jorgen's preoccupation. He pointed to two nice-looking houses of brick and stone construction. They were surrounded on both sides by similar homes that had been converted to tenements; wooden additions had been built atop the original masonry houses. These added portions were wider and nearly touched the ones on either side. The tenement-look destroyed the beauty of the original houses and poorly done workmanship contributed to the general shabbiness of the neighborhood.

The odor coming from the streets wasn't as bad here, and Jorgen began to feel a bit better. Armed with his mental list of what he needed to do in the coming days, Jorgen plied Hal with questions, attempting to figure out the layout of the city and formulate a schedule for himself: Did Hal know a good doctor, preferably one that spoke Norwegian? Where was the nearest bank? Could Hal tell him how to get to the Hudson River? Did he have to make a reservation for the steamship?

"You are a thinker and a worrier," commented Hal, several questions later.

Jorgen merely nodded in reply. He did have a lot to think and worry about. He just needed to stay focused on his goal, the land he would buy, and the home he would build for Marta and Atlanta.

"This is where I live," said Hal. He pointed to a tenement building, next to a garment factory at the end of the street. "My room's not bad for a single man, but I hope to be able to move out of the city before too long."

Still following the coach, they rounded the corner just after the garment factory and turned onto a street lined with small businesses. Jorgen noticed a shoemaker's shop. His boots were in need of repair, something else for his list. They passed a tailor shop, a cigar maker, a tavern, and a cooper's shop. A dry goods shop was next to a grocery. The vegetables displayed on the outside stands made Jorgen's mouth water.

"Just another block," said Hal, "and we will be there."

"In that case," said Jorgen, "please ask the driver to stop for a minute." They were in front of a bakery and Jorgen thought some bread would tide the family over until they could see about an actual meal.

Several minutes later, they pulled up to low-rise house, identical to the two Hal had pointed out earlier. It was the only one left on the street that hadn't been converted to a tenement. The coach, having arrived a few minutes before, sat out front. Jorgen went to the window and handed a loaf of bread to Mary who accepted it and held it to her nose.

"Next to the limes, that's the best thing I've smelled in a long time," she said.

Elen broke off a piece of the bread. "Here, child," she said, handing it to Mary. She gave a piece to Jorgen, which he quickly devoured.

"Wish me luck," he said. "I hope this works out for us."

While Jorgen and Hal were inside the house talking to his friend's mother, the three women nibbled nervously on bits of bread.

"Where will we go if she doesn't want us?" Mary's question hung in the air because neither Marta nor Elen had an answer.

But when Jorgen returned to the carriage, the happy look on his face was all the answer any of them needed.

★ ★ ★

It was a relief to see a real doctor and hear him declare Atlanta as fit and healthy as any baby he'd examined. He thought, however, Marta looked peaked and prescribed a tonic. He also told her to eat more red meat after hearing that she'd been on a ship for the previous nine weeks.

"I think your wife would benefit from a few weeks rest before you continue on," the doctor said to Jorgen when he had finished his examination of Marta. "A woman suffering from exhaustion will not produce enough milk for her baby and is also more likely to become ill from other diseases."

The post office was not far from the doctor's office. On

the way there, Jorgen told Marta what the doctor had said about her health. She disagreed, saying all she needed was a few days rest. And I think we will all feel better once we leave this city behind us," she added.

A quick stop at the post office brought good news. Several brief letters from Andrew. Almost a year had passed since he had written the first; it was dated October 10, 1849 and told of his arrival in Quebec and subsequent travel down to Kendall, New York. He had found work on the Erie Canal and hoped that Jorgen and Marta would join him soon.

Andrew's second letter was written in response to the letter Jorgen had sent explaining the delays in their departure and the third letter acknowledged receipt of the letter Jorgen had sent from Liverpool.

In that letter, Andrew wrote that his savings were growing fat, and he had found a home in Kendall they could use until they made their final plans.

Jorgen felt a surge of optimism, things were falling into place. He felt confident that by this time next year, they would be settled on their own land. Buoyed by this hopeful thought, he convinced Marta that resting up in New York an extra week or two would not interfere with the total plan. Andrew had located a place in Kendall where they could stay through the winter. They would not proceed on from there until spring.

★ ★ ★

In Kendall, Andrew was in high spirits knowing that Jorgen was finally on his way. Although he had often threatened to move on and get permanently settled without Jorgen, he never actually considered doing it. It was his way of prodding his brother into action.

The small town of Kendall had not impressed him when he first arrived, but the friendliness of its citizens, many of them Norwegian born, more than made up for what the town lacked. Since moving there, he had worked on the excavation project to widen the Erie Canal. The pay had been more than enough to cover his living expenses.

The house he had found was available because the owner planned to be gone for a year or two. But the offer came with two conditions.

Andrew knew that Jorgen would agree to the first. They would be expected to make some repairs to the house—easy enough for two lads who had helped keep their father's estate in good order.

Although Andrew didn't think Jorgen would agree to the second stipulation, he didn't spend any time worrying about it. He suspected it would be weeks before Jorgen arrived and the problem, most likely, would be resolved by then. So, Andrew settled in.

True to his nature, and because it involved helping someone in need, Andrew gave little thought to the dangers inherent in the second condition. He did attempt to exercise some caution but was not as vigilant as he could have been. Then again, he never expected that trouble would come from someone he knew, someone from his own homeland.

★ ★ ★

"I'm feeling rested this morning and need an outing," Marta said to Jorgen several days after her visit to the doctor. "And Atlanta needs some proper clothes. She squirms so much she doesn't stay wrapped in her blankets."

"Well, if you think you're up to it," Jorgen said. "Would you like me to go with you?"

"I'll take Mary with me. She can help carry the bundles, and I think she would enjoy getting out, too. We won't go far. Why don't you stay home and get acquainted with your new daughter? You've been running around this city ever since we landed. You need a day off."

Marta was right; he had hardly been at the house. It was

such a big city; every errand seemed to take twice as long as he thought it would.

He sat down and held out his arms to receive the baby. Marta had just finished nursing her, but Atlanta still fussed.

"Hei, little one," Jorgen crooned as soon as the baby was placed in his hands. She gave him a solemn look and he bent to kiss her forehead. They studied one another for another minute then Jorgen held her to his shoulder. She nestled her face against his neck and was quiet.

"She knows her Pappa," said Marta. She walked behind Jorgen to see Atlanta's face. The baby's eyes were open, but as Marta's watched, Atlanta slowly closed them. Marta wasn't sure if it was her imagination, but it looked like the baby smiled.

"You're a miracle worker," said Elen. She sat across the room, her mending basket at her feet as she altered a dress of Marta's to fit Mary. "This is her fussy time; it usually takes longer than that to get her settled."

Jorgen suspected both women were humoring him. It seemed to him that most of the time Atlanta seemed contented, but he accepted their compliments nonetheless.

"You forget," he said. "I'm an old hand at this."

"That you are," said Elen. She winked at her Marta. "Go, now, enjoy your outing. Atlanta is in good hands."

Jorgen had to admit, it felt good sitting there with Atlanta's little body curled against his, her bony knees pressed into his chest, her downy hair tickling his cheek. Her steady, even breathing worked its magic on Jorgen. He let go of the tension and worry that had built up over the weeks. He was aware there would be obstacles to overcome, but as the warmth of that little body penetrated deep into his own chest, he felt restored and ready for the challenge.

One of the things that had weighed on Jorgen's mind the last few days was the question of Mary Bjorn. Since their arrival in New York City, no one had mentioned looking for her uncle. The issue, Jorgen sensed, had become complicated.

Mary was just a child. Naturally she would want to stay with a family that had shown her kindness when the only parent she had ever known had treated her so poorly.

Jorgen sensed that Mary filled the void left in Elen's life after her husband's tragic and senseless death. The two had bonded over the past weeks, and it saddened Jorgen to think that they might have to go their separate ways. He understood why each had kept silent on the subject of the uncle.

They could, of course, just move on and take Mary with them. Jorgen knew they could provide her with a good life. But then, his conscience spoke. How would he feel if it were Atlanta, orphaned and no real attempt was made to reunite her with family?

Jorgen kissed the top of Atlanta's head. That thought was unimaginable. *I will always be there for you,* he vowed.

"I'm going to speak to Hal about helping me locate Mary's uncle," he said to Elen.

"It's the right thing to do," she replied. She stopped sewing and looked at him. "Although I must say it makes me sad to think of losing her. As you may have discovered, I've grown quite fond of her."

"We all have," said Jorgen, "but as you say, it is the right thing to do."

"If you find him, I'd like to be with Mary when she goes to meet him," said Elen.

"I wouldn't have it any other way," said Jorgen. "I know how she depends on you."

★ ★ ★

Out on the street, Marta was glad that Mary was with her. The younger girl had been out with Elen on previous days and had learned a few of the city's ways. Following the younger girl's example, Marta pressed her handkerchief to her face when the street odor became unbearable. At the corner, Mary took a coin from her pocket and gave it to a boy about her age who was leaning against the nearest building. He picked up the large broom lying on the ground next to him and proceeded to sweep a path through the muck in the street. Mary took Marta's arm and together they followed close behind the boy, able to navigate the street crossing with barely a smudge on their shoes.

"Aunt Elen gave me some money" Mary said, in response to Marta's quizzical look.

"Well, thank you for taking such good care of me. What do you intend buying with the rest of the money that I hear jingling in your pocket?"

"She told me to look for a bonnet to wear with the dress she is fixing for me. Maybe you can help me find one."

"With pleasure, miss," said Marta. And with arms linked, they marched into the dry- goods store.

It was undoubtedly the most pleasure the two had enjoyed in a long time, and they returned to the house breathless with laughter and cheeks glowing with the excitement of their purchases.

They had found a bonnet for Mary, just the right shade of blue that not only complimented the dress, but it matched her eye color perfectly. She tried it on with the dress Elen had completed while they were out shopping, and the result was stunning.

The frightened little girl was no more. In a proper dress and bonnet, Mary was transformed into a most attractive young lady. The three adults were speechless for a moment. Marta finally broke the ice. "Mary, you picked out the right bonnet. It looks lovely on you."

Mary seemed embarrassed by all the attention. "Now it's your turn. Show them what you bought for Atlanta."

But as Jorgen, Elen, and Marta looked at the baby clothes, they couldn't help stealing glances at the new Mary.

★ ★ ★

That evening, Hal stopped by, and Jorgen enlisted his help in tracking down Mary's uncle. Hal suggested they check immigration records and other registries at city hall. Eventually, they got names and addresses of several men in the city with the surname Bjorn. That was all they had to go on as Mary said she didn't know her uncle's first name.

A few days into his search for the unknown Mr. Bjorn, Jorgen stood across the street from a run-down looking house. The front of it had been converted into a shop with a sign outside that advertised in bold letters, 'BLACKSMITH.' Something near the bottom of the sign had been painted over and it now read, 'Peder Bjorn, proprietor.'

A boy, not yet old enough to shave, tended a forge located a short distance to the right of the front door. Three small children sat playing in the dirt on the opposite side of the doorway.

Jorgen was about to cross the road when a man came out of the shop and spoke to the boy. Jorgen stared in astonishment. It was like Mary's father had come back from the dead.

"Uff da!" Jorgen said, the expression escaping just under his breath. "That has to be Mary's uncle."

Needing a moment to gather himself and figure what to do next, Jorgen turned away. He bent down, pretending to adjust his boot strap.

Almost immediately, a woman came flying out the door yelling and cursing at the man. As they stood in front of the shop arguing, two children engaged in a punching and shoving match tumbled out the doorway into the yard. The man cuffed one child on the head then the other. He threw up his hands and turning his fury on the woman, swore at her then stalked away. After a few seconds, Jorgen stood and followed him at a discrete distance. Two blocks later, the man disappeared into a place called Mick's Tavern.

On the long walk back, Jorgen pondered how to handle the situation. In the end, he decided to tell Mary exactly what he had witnessed. He would leave nothing out including the fact that he was sure the man was her uncle. The decision to visit Bjorn the Blacksmith would be entirely in her hands.

Mary listened to Jorgen's tale with a mixture of curiosity and dread. Her father never told her she had cousins. She thought she might like to meet them, but she was afraid she might be forced to stay with them.

After two nail-biting days, Mary said to Elen, "I want to stay with you, but I think I should go visit my relatives. I may never have the chance again. Will you come with me?"

The next morning Jorgen, Mary, and Elen approached the shop. The boy was at the forge, as before, but there was no sign of anyone else.

"I want you to remember what I told you," said Jorgen. "Don't be shocked by his resemblance to your Pappa. We'll go in and tell him what happened to your father, then it will be up to you to tell him who you are. Are we ready?" He looked at Elen, who nodded, and then to Mary.

She swallowed, took in a deep breath, and nodded. The three of them entered the blacksmith shop.

When Jorgen began to talk, the realization that he was not there for business soured the blacksmith's disposition. But the invective that poured from his mouth when he heard the news of his brother's death was shocking, even for one who had been exposed to the language of sailors and fishermen.

Jorgen interrupted. "Watch your tongue, there is a lady and children present."

The children, not counting Mary, numbered six or seven. They wandered about underfoot and were swatted like flies if they came within range of their father. They were dirty with runny noses, and to Jorgen's dismay, he noticed that one of the little girls looked strikingly like Mary. The boy who had been tending the forge had come inside and now stood an arms distance from Jorgen, staring at him.

"You were here the other day," he said to Jorgen. "You

stood across the road but I noticed you."

"Get back outside," the older man snarled at his son then returned his attention to Jorgen.

"He owed me the money I paid for him and his brat to get here. Who's going to pay what he owed me?"

Out of the corner of his eye, Jorgen saw Elen shift her weight, an effort to conceal Mary from her uncle's sight.

"I see you've brought the girl with you...looks like Vidar. I don't need another mouth to feed, but she could be useful to my wife."

"This is my niece," said Elen.

The blacksmith looked suspiciously from Elen to Jorgen.

"Let me see you, girl," he commanded. At the sound of his voice, Mary cowered even further behind Elen. He sounded eerily familiar to Mary, and she fought the urge to run out the door.

The blacksmith began to approach her, but Jorgen stepped between them.

Mary had made her decision. Jorgen had seen that look before and he knew she was terrified. He had to get her away from there before she fell apart.

"He was here," the son shouted from the doorway. "I saw him follow you down the street."

"Your son is right, I was here." Jorgen was glad to take the attention off Mary. "I have spent days looking for the right Bjorn so I could explain what happened to your brother.

"The captain put your niece in the care of a woman named Clark who was to see that the child made it safely back to Norway. The child told us she had an uncle in America. She thought he might be in New York City and since I was going to be in the city for a few days, I promised the captain I would try to locate you."

His mouth opened as he processed Jorgen's words, the blacksmith stared dumbly at Jorgen. Hoping to get out of the shop before the blacksmith came to his senses, Jorgen hastily added. "And now, if you will excuse us, I have delivered my message."

The three hurried out the door with Mary's uncle close on their heels. He followed them down the street. "I want my money!" he shouted after them. "That girl belongs to me! I'll have you arrested for kidnapping and theft."

Jorgen hailed the first carriage that came along and when they were out of sight of the blacksmith he released a long sigh.

"Will you get arrested?" Mary asked. Her voice was shaky; her hands were clasped tightly in her lap and she tried hard not to cry.

Jorgen took one of her small hands in his to try to comfort her. In spite of the cool temperature, beads of sweat had formed under the brim of her bonnet and trickled down her face. He took a handkerchief from his pocket and dabbed her wet face.

"No one is going to jail," he said quietly. "Your uncle does not know my name or where we're staying. People like him like to make a lot of noise. I'll send him the money we collected from your father's ticket and the cost of yours. That much is due to him and I think he will be satisfied."

"And we'll be out of this city in a few days," added Elen.

"I'm sorry you spent all that time looking for him," said Mary. "I don't think he's a nice person."

"I'm not sorry," said Jorgen. "We'd always wonder if adopting you into our family was the right thing to do. But now we know...it is...and you are."

"It is...and I am." She repeated. It took a few seconds to sink in, and then her face relaxed into a smile radiant with happiness.

Still holding Jorgen's hand, she grabbed one of Elen's with her free hand.

"My family," she said, with a sigh.

"Yes we are," agreed Jorgen and Elen in unison.

★ ★ ★

Departure day can't come fast enough, Jorgen mused. He was through with city life and anxious for them to be on their way. He didn't think Mary's uncle would track them down. Still, it would be good to put some distance between them.

The women had gone out for one last shopping trip. Now that Mary's future in the family was secure, Elen wanted to get her a warm coat and boots to replace those worn items in the girl's meager wardrobe.

This was Jorgen's first time alone with Atlanta. Marta had nursed her before she left, and soon after, the baby fell asleep on Jorgen's shoulder. He kissed the top of Atlanta's head and returned to his thoughts. He remembered how his father would sit, after middag, with an infant slumbering on his chest. Was it Inger or Ole? Jorgen couldn't recall. Most likely Inger, he decided.

After a while, he gingerly placed Atlanta on the cot he and Marta shared, and when she didn't stir, he retrieved his journal. He wanted to record Mary's entry to the family, and the celebration they had the night when they returned from the blacksmith. Mary had declared that day would become her birthday.

Elen solved the age problem with a quick look into Mary's mouth. "You have only one of your second molars, so today is your twelfth birthday," she told the girl.

Jorgen finished writing in the journal, and then wrote a quick letter to Andrew telling him when he could expect their arrival. He would mail it first thing in the morning and hoped the letter would arrive before they did.

Jorgen picked up the journal again and turned to a fresh page. He thought he'd make a sketch of what he'd like his future farm to look like. He had often pictured the scene over the past months, but his dream had always seemed so far away. Now, his reunion with Andrew was only days away. With mounting excitement, Jorgen drew in the farmhouse, barn, and fields. When he was finished, he looked it over and laughed out loud. The farm scene he had depicted looked exactly like the gard on which he had been raised.

Jorgen's abrupt laughter startled Atlanta; she awoke and began to cry.

"It's all right Attie, that was only your foolish pappa." He scooped her off the bed, soothing her. "Thoughts of home," he whispered, more to himself than to the baby.

Jorgen had heard Marta and Mary call her Attie, but this was the first time he had said it. It slipped out easily and somehow seemed to fit the tiny little being.

 He sat down and looked into her face as she stared up at him from the crook of his arm. "You're no bigger than Thumbikin," he told her.

"Ah, that's right," he said, "You don't know that story."

And so Jorgen proceeded to tell his infant daughter the story of the tiny boy, no bigger than his father's thumb.

Just as he neared the end of the tale, the part where Thumbikin is perched on a pat of butter in a bowl of porridge, the shoppers returned.

"Oh Jorgen," said Mary when she overheard him telling the story, "that has such an unhappy ending."

"Actually," Marta chimed in, "drowning in butter isn't half as bad as slipping and falling in a New York street. A woman fell, right in front of us and landed in the most disgusting muck. Honestly, Jorgen, I'll be glad to leave this filthy city behind us."

★ ★ ★

Later that day, Hal stopped in on his way home from work with distressing news. A man had come into his office looking for information about a tall Norwegian man traveling with a young girl.

"His description of you, Jorgen, was quite accurate. Because of your height and short haircut, you do stand out. People notice you. He didn't seem to know that you were married and have a baby traveling with you. He said that your travel companion is an old lady. Sorry, Mrs. Aksdal," Hal paused in his story and looked at Elen apologetically.

"That's all right, Hal," Elen said. She smiled at him to prove she was not offended. "The interpreter who stands next to me in the office recognized the description and remembered that I had talked to you," Hal continued.

The room was deadly quiet, all eyes were trained on Hal.

"The man was very rude, interrupting me while I was trying to help someone else. When I told him he would have to wait his turn, he became very angry. Yelled that he didn't have time to wait, that he was after a man who had stolen money from him and kidnapped his niece. He created such a disturbance that I had to deal with him immediately"

Mary gasped when she heard Hal say 'kidnapped' and buried her head in her hands. Elen sat beside her and patted her back.

"But you sent him the money," said Marta.

"Yes," said Jorgen. "Perhaps he hasn't received it, yet." He nodded to Hal to continue.

"I admitted to him that a man fitting that description had come to me asking directions to an address in Five Points. I asked him if he knew where Five Points is and he shouted, 'Everyone knows where that is.' He demanded to know the address. When I told him that I couldn't recall it, he swore at me and stormed out of the office.

"You're safe here," Hal continued. "Five Points is a large neighborhood. It will take him days to look for you there, if he even tries."

Thirteen

A Few Days Later

The family stood on the pier on the west side of Manhattan ready for the next leg of their journey. Hal had offered to see them aboard, and after he helped Jorgen load the baggage onto the boat, the two shook hands.

"You've been a good friend," said Jorgen. "If you should decide to go west, make sure you come to see us."

"He's a nice man," said Marta, after Hal left. "We were fortunate that you met him."

"He said we reminded him of his family," said Jorgen. He watched his friend enter a carriage, and as it disappeared around a corner, and commented, "I think Hal is homesick. I wouldn't be surprised if he went back home to Norway."

The boat left on time and all thoughts of New York City, the good memories, like Hal, and the bad ones, like Mary's horrible uncle and the dirty, disgusting streets of the crowded city were left behind.

The powerful steamship sped them up the glassy smooth Hudson River past small towns, forests, and gently rolling hillsides dotted with farms. Inhaling the sweet, pure, country air had the travelers almost giddy with relief. It was late October, harvest time, and men worked the fields that blanketed long stretches of land on both sides of the river. Jorgen viewed them with envy. The muscles in his arms and back, hardly used in recent months, twitched with the memory of toil and sweat.

Their route took them north to the small town of Troy where the Hudson connected to the Erie Canal. A canal boat waited for the passengers to transfer from the steamship and continue their journey, this time down the Erie Canal.

Marta, Atlanta, and Elen got settled in the cabin while Jorgen and Mary dealt with the task of stowing their belongings. The baggage area was inadequate and as more passengers boarded the small boat, arguments broke out over where bags could and could not be stored. Immigrants like Jorgen were harshly criticized by other passengers for the amount of baggage they carried with them. Ignoring the rude comments and complaints, Jorgen pretended to not understand what was said. An official with the canal line eventually came on board to settle matters and solved the problem by allowing some baggage to be stored inside the cabin.

With the exception of the storage area and a compact kitchen, a long narrow cabin occupied the remainder of the interior of the seventy-foot boat. The tiller was located outside the cabin, in the stern, and a small open deck with stairs to the roof was up front.

A table ran almost the length of the cabin with benches on either side. A row of windows above the benches afforded an abundance of light and gave passengers a good view of the passing landscape. Using a couple of their quilts to pad a section of bench, Marta and Elen settled in with Attie.

Jorgen and Mary sat with them for a while but were drawn to the roof deck when they heard the noisy groan made by the first lock gate as it opened. They hurried up the steps in time to watch as the lines connecting the horses to the boat were dropped and the horses plodded a short distance ahead. The boat floated into the lock, and when the gate creaked to a close behind it, sluices opened in the upstream gate. As soon as the water level in the lock equaled the level upstream, the front gates opened and the boat floated out. The horses were quickly retied and they continued down the towpath.

"This is so much nicer than being below," said Mary. She and Jorgen relaxed on a long low bench at the rear of the roof deck. She pointed to the boy who led the three horses. "He looks like he's my age," she said.

"Or younger," Jorgen added. The boy was forced to move quickly on his short legs to keep up with the horses, which Jorgen judged to be going about three miles an hour. That made it a leisurely stroll for the passengers who chose to walk along the ten-foot wide towpath. It ran along the right side of the canal for boats traveling west although it was the same towpath used for boats going east.

"Does he have to walk all day?" Mary wanted to know.

"Nei," Jorgen replied. "I heard someone say that there is a different boy and fresh horses every four hours, and if he gets tired before that time, he can ride one of the horses."

They weren't seated for long before someone up front cried out, "Low bridge." Mary watched in amusement as people around her dove this way and that to flatten themselves on the deck.

"Get down," Jorgen yelled from where he lay. He reached up and pulled her from her seat. He pushed her down just in time as the boat passed under a very low bridge.

"I didn't see that coming," Mary giggled nervously. "I was watching all the people. When they say low I guess they mean it." She knew that she had just had a very close call.

"Yes," Jorgen agreed as they got up and returned to their seats. "We'll have to be more careful or we'll lose our heads."

"Please don't tell Aunt Elen," Mary begged. She looked at Jorgen anxiously. "She probably wouldn't let me come back up here if she knew how close I came to getting killed."

"I think we both learned a lesson," Jorgen said. "I won't say anything if you promise to be more careful."

"I will, I promise I will," she said. "And if Aunt Elen or Marta comes up here, I will tell them what to do when someone yells, 'low bridge.'"

As it turned out, that was the lowest bridge they encountered that afternoon. It was so low, in fact, that the passengers who had been walking the towpath for exercise were able to step from the bridge right back onto the boat, mindful of course, not to step on those who had flattened themselves on the deck.

Although Jorgen and Mary found the next few locks just as fascinating as the first, their interest waned as the canal boat passed through twenty-seven locks in the first thirty miles. Both Jorgen and Mary were curious about the canal, so when they discovered that the helmsman was Norwegian, they plied him with questions.

He was happy to oblige them with answers and conversation, telling them he had begun working on the canal shortly after he arrived in America many years before.

"My first job was swamp work," he told them. "We had to drain acres and acres of marshland and the mosquitos were thick and thirsty. I got swamp fever and was ill for two months. After that I got sent to where they were blasting through rock. I had to stuff wool in my ears because of the noise, but I liked that job better than being in the swamp."

"It sounds too dangerous," said Mary. "Why didn't you do something else, like farming?"

"Well, in the first place," explained the helmsman, "I don't know anything about farming. I was raised in a small fishing village and am better at pulling fish from the sea than potatoes from the ground.

"Also, I was broke when I landed in New York City and needed to find a job. I heard that they were looking for workers on the Erie Canal, and that the pay was good, so I signed up."

As the helmsman spoke, he was mindful of a line boat going east that had dropped its tethers into the canal allowing the helmsman to steer his boat over the other boat's lines. With only one towpath running beside the canal, boats heading west had the right of way.

"Given the time of year, that boat is most likely loaded with wheat headed for processing in the city," said the helmsman. "This canal makes it so much easier and faster for farmers to take their goods to market than using the rutted, bumpy roads."

"The canal looks finished," said Jorgen, "yet my brother

wrote me that he's been working on it."

"You'll see men at work with their picks and shovels when we get a little farther along," said the helmsman. "They're enlarging the canal all the way to Buffalo. Where they've completed the work, like right here, the canal is seventy feet wide and seven feet deep. Originally, all three hundred sixty-three miles was only forty feet wide and four feet deep."

"Are we taking it to Buffalo?" asked Mary.

"Nei," Jorgen replied. "We're only going as far as Holley. That's where Andrew will pick us up and take us to Kendall."

As they passed through dozens of locks, Jorgen was surprised to learn the canal rose five hundred feet in elevation from east to west. He was also intrigued by the aqueducts, which allowed streams to cross the canal and carried the canal over ravines and rivers.

Compared to what others passengers had paid, Jorgen felt that he had negotiated a good price for this trip. He had paid thirty-two dollars for the four of them, and their fare included their meals and four berths.

At dinner that first day on the boat, Jorgen looked around the cabin and commented to Marta that he had serious doubts that sleeping arrangements were possible for this many passengers. "Where will they put all of us?" he wondered aloud.

His answer came when the dishes were cleared away and the sun began to set. The crew hung a large curtain that divided the front and back areas of the cabin and placed a sign that informed the passengers that the front portion was for women and young children. The benches in both areas were turned into lower berths. Two levels of canvas upper berths were hung from hooks in the ceiling. Jorgen was assigned to one of those. He had to admit the portable berths made the best use of available space, but after a few short moments in his, he felt like a puffin in a sparrow's nest. Then again, it was definitely better than sitting up all night, or sleeping on the floor, which the overflow passengers were forced to do.

The weather, which had been so pleasant on day one, turned cool and rainy on the second day. The towpath walkers and those who wished to sit on the outside deck were forced indoors. The monotony of the slow voyage and the now crowded confines of the small boat began to take their toll. Squabbles broke out among some of the travelers and on two occasions had to be settled by the captain.

From where they sat near the stern, Jorgen, Marta, and Elen watched these disturbances with indifference, glad that the troublemakers were not seated near them. Oblivious to the action and accompanied raised voices, Mary stood at a window at the front of the cabin with her nose practically touching the rain-streaked surface. Elen was surprised that Mary would choose to position herself in the midst of strangers. She got up to stretch her legs and went to stand next to her. Looking through the heavy downpour, Elen could just make out the horses on the towpath and the boy riding one of them.

"What if he falls?" said Mary. "No one will know."

"Is that why you're here? To watch him?" said Elen.

"No one is watching him. No one is looking out the window because there is nothing to see today," said Mary.

Elen looked around the cabin. The child was right. All eyes seemed to be focused on the commotion inside the cabin. She returned her gaze to the boy and watched for a few minutes. "He seems steady on the horse," she said.

"I know," said Mary, "but what if he does fall?"

Elen knew that it was pointless to argue. Mary was going to worry about the boy no matter what she said. Most likely, the boy was safe; he was not going to fall off the horse. But in a storm, thunder, lightening, nearly anything could spook a horse and the boy could get thrown. So Elen did not feel comfortable assuring Mary that nothing would happen.

"Perhaps the helmsman is watching," said Elen. "Would you like me to ask him?"

Mary nodded.

Elen went off to check with the helmsman, who assured her that he did, indeed, keep a watchful eye on the boy and the horses.

★ ★ ★

The weather improved on the fourth day, and the travelers' spirits rose with warmer temperatures and sunshine.

"Two more days," said Jorgen. They were crowded at a table eating their morning meal.

"I can't wait to meet your brother," said Mary. "Do you look like each other?"

"I don't think so," said Jorgen. "What do you think, Marta?"

"Definitely not," she replied, "although your voices sound almost the same. You're taller and your hair is darker, and probably a lot shorter now than Andrew's."

"Does he act like you?" Mary asked.

Jorgen laughed. "And just how do I act?"

"Oh, you, you know," she stammered.

"You mean like a big brother," Marta helped.

"Yes," Mary said. "You think about things and then decide what we should do."

"Well," said Jorgen, "I think Andrew sometimes decides first and thinks later, but things generally work out just as well for him."

★ ★ ★

Ironically, that was not the case on that particular day. Andrew's sense of justice and fairness had prompted him to confront an evil and help a fellow human. He was, at the very moment Jorgen spoke about him, paying a painful price.

"Where one of you goes, I know the other is not far away. I will find Jorgen and make him sorry that he didn't drown when I threw him overboard." Hauk delivered that statement, before throwing his first punch at Andrew, who was restrained from behind by one of Hauk's accomplices.

Andrew managed to break free, and he sprang at Hauk. He landed one hard blow into Hauk's face, which sent him sprawling to the ground. Andrew turned to face the other man who brandished a knife as he advanced on Andrew. Backing up to avoid being stabbed, Andrew stumbled over Hauk. Desperately flailing his arms, Andrew's attempt to maintain his balance brought his hand into the path of the flashing knife. Blood gushed from a cut that nearly severed three of Andrew's fingers. He fell and his head hit the road hard, momentarily stunning him. Someone kicked him in the ribs, and when he was able to focus, Hauk was standing over him with a pistol aimed at his head.

"I'm not going to kill you," Hauk said, "because I want you to tell your brother I'm coming after him, too." He lowered the gun, fired a shot into Andrew's thigh, and laughed wickedly when Andrew writhed in pain, his uninjured hand desperately clawing the dirt road. Hauk stomped on that hand, shattering bone, then kicked Andrew several more times. A final kick to the head and Andrew lapsed into unconsciousness.

★ ★ ★

On the morning of the fifth day, their last day aboard the canal boat, the weather changed as cold winds pressed down from Canada and overran the warm, summer-like autumn breezes from the south. The morning's foggy mist became a steady drizzle and by mid-day sheets of rain draped the boat and blotted out even the nearest objects from view.

They waited out the worst of the storm just one stop before Holley, and Jorgen was relieved when, at last, they were on their way again. Andrew was waiting for them.

But, as it turned out, Andrew wasn't waiting. They disembarked and stood under a shelter surrounded by crates, chests, and all their belongings and watched the canal boat depart and disappear into the moonless night. The rain, which had been light and intermittent, began again in earnest. The women, huddled together for warmth, were dry for the moment, but puddles of water spread toward the group and threatened to engulf their baggage.

Jorgen felt their only option was to rely on the kindness of strangers, so he set off intending to make their plight known at the nearest house. He hadn't gone far when he heard the approach of a horse and wagon. *At last*, he thought, *Andrew*.

The man in the wagon didn't see Jorgen until he had nearly run him down, but at the last moment, he reined in his horse. The wagon bumped to a stop. The horse snorted in Jorgen's face.

Jorgen looked up expecting to see Andrew, but instead looked into the startled eyes of a black man. When they both had regained their wits, Jorgen called out an apology and took a step back to allow the man to pass.

Upon hearing the Norwegian words, the man said, "Are you Jorgen? Andrew sent me to fetch you and your family."

"Ja, mitt navn er Jorgen." Jorgen didn't know what the man had said about Andrew, but understood that he was there to help them. He climbed up next to the black man and they returned to the shelter.

Underneath the oilskin, which had covered the back of the wagon, were several inches of dry straw for the women to settle in for the remainder of their journey. With the oilskin to protect them from the rain, they rode off into the wet chilly night. The black man pulled a small piece of oilskin from under their seat and gave it to Jorgen. Jorgen offered to share it with the man, but the offer was refused. The driver hunched his shoulders, stoically enduring the cold and wet, but Jorgen was grateful for the protection the oilskin provided.

Although time does not have the ability to speed up or slow down, there are times when its passage seems interminable. This was one of those times, and Jorgen couldn't help but wonder if they would ever reach their destination. Neither the women nor Mary uttered a word of complaint, yet Jorgen knew that riding in the back of a wagon was far from comfortable. Eventually, Atlanta began to fuss then settled down after Marta nursed her. Jorgen judged the time to be close to midnight, the baby's last feeding until early morning.

At some point, they pulled off the road and started down a narrow cart path. Jorgen wondered how the driver had known the path was there. It was so well hidden from the road that Jorgen doubted that he would ever be able to find it on his own. They bumped along the path for at least a mile until they came into a clearing and stopped before a small log house. A dim, but welcoming light glowed from one of two windows that faced the yard.

"Andrew." The driver said, pointing to the house.

Although the hour was late, Jorgen expected to see his brother bound out to greet them. Instead, the driver led the tired group into the house. They stood just inside the door, eyes blinking in the light cast by a lantern that hung in the window.

Marta was the first to notice the bed in the shadows along the far wall.

"Jorgen, I think Andrew has gone to bed."

Jorgen went to the bed and looked down on Andrew's sleeping form. He reached out, about to rouse his brother when the black man stopped him by placing a hand on Jorgen's outstretched arm. The man moved closer to the bed, took the top of the blanket that covered Andrew into his large, rough hands and gently folded it back.

Jorgen gasped at the sight of his brother's bandaged body. Both hands were wrapped in white with only the thumb of one hand visible. Blood stained a large bandage on Andrew's left thigh and there was a splint and more bandages on his left arm. When Jorgen placed a hand on his forehead, Andrew felt feverish. Jorgen knew that was not a good sign.

The man covered Andrew and then motioned Jorgen to follow him.

"Come," he said. He took the lantern from its hook and led the weary travelers back outside. They crossed the yard, and he guided them into a barn where he lit another lantern and hung it from a beam near a large pile of hay. He gathered up a pile of blankets and quilts that had been neatly stacked on a bench and handed them to Jorgen before leaving the barn. Jorgen heard him outside tending to the horses.

The anxiety Jorgen felt at seeing his injured brother was now compounded with dismay at the thought of the women and baby Atlanta having to sleep in a barn. *There are probably rats in here,* he thought, upset with himself for putting them all in this situation. He stood motionless, blankets in hand, wallowing in self-recrimination.

Elen started to arrange the straw. "We'll make this do for tonight," she said, "The straw is clean and smells fresh, we'll find something better in the morning."

She came to Jorgen and took the blankets from him, "It's about time we had some adventure in our lives." Her eyes twinkled and her lively step was not that of a woman who was exhausted after a long day's journey.

Jorgen's feeling of despondency lifted slightly. *Elen's right,* he thought, *there's nothing we can do about this tonight. At least we're out of the rain.* He began to help her prepare sleeping arrangements for the night. He poked and prodded the straw to make sure there were no unwanted residents. *We'll keep the lantern lit,* he thought, *that should keep any rats from coming near us.*

"We'll be fine for the night," said Marta. She handed

the baby to Mary while she removed her wet outer garments, and then sank down onto the bed of straw so that she could tend to Atlanta.

Their situation improved slightly when their host, presumably the owner of the house, returned with a platter of food, a late meal of bread and cheese and a jug of cold milk.

They sat huddled together for warmth in the piled straw and ate slowly, in spite of their hunger; chewing seemed almost too taxing. Mary's eyes closed and she would have toppled over had Jorgen not steadied her. Even Elen, who moments before had bustled about, felt the yoke of fatigue pressing down on her.

One by one, as their hunger was satisfied, they lay back into the straw and gave in to sleep, leaving Jorgen to finish a solitary repast. He washed down the last bits of bread and cheese with the final swallow of milk and fastidiously picked the crumbs off their blankets, placing them on the platter.

He rose, platter in one hand, jug in the other, and stole out of the barn. He had intended to leave those items just outside the barn door, but when he saw that the lantern was still lit in the house, he headed there, dumping the crumbs as he went.

Jorgen had no plan. He knew that the black man would not be able to communicate what had happened or, even more important, tell him if Andrew would survive his injuries. He only knew he wanted to be with his brother. He hoped Andrew would sense that he was there.

He looked through the small window and saw a black woman standing at the table. She appeared to be kneading dough. *When do these people sleep?* Jorgen thought. But peering deeper into the room, he saw that the man was most likely asleep. His head hung almost to his chest as he slumped in the chair next to Andrew's bed. Jorgen decided that intruding on this couple was no way to repay their kindness, so he set the platter and jug next to their door and returned to the barn.

He lay in the straw next to Marta waiting for sleep to overtake him. He resisted the urge, an almost desperate need he felt to draw her and the baby in close, afraid he would wake them. As if sensing his distress, Marta shifted in her sleep to nestle against him, and he lightly kissed the back of her head.

Marta's presence calmed him somewhat, but sleep would not come. Jorgen was vigilant; every sound put him on guard. Against what, he knew not. What had happened to Andrew? How had he ended up out here, in the middle of...? Jorgen didn't know where. He guessed that Kendall was still miles away.

Had the black couple bandaged Andrew's wounds? Did he have other injuries besides those wrapped in white? Should he go back to the house? What if Andrew didn't make it through the night?

Jorgen tussled with his questions, but in the end, had to hope that the man who appeared to be taking care of Andrew would have had Jorgen stay at the house if he thought Andrew was dying.

The shadowy form of a bat flew above him in the rafters, a horse nickered a soft, low whinny and shuffled its feet, the wind rattled the door, and someone coughed. Mary? Elen? Jorgen hoped they weren't catching cold, although that wouldn't surprise him after the rainy day they had all just endured.

Who were these people, the ones looking after Andrew—in fact, taking care of all of them? Did the black man own this barn? Jorgen knew enough about America to know that New York was not a slave state. *Perhaps,* Jorgen decided, *the man and his wife were cotters, like Olav and his family, paying to live and farm someone else's land.*

In all his years in Norway, Jorgen had little contact with black people. Few, if any, lived in the interior of Norway. There were some black families in Bergen, and black sailors did come into port. Jorgen had seen them coming and going on the streets down near the Bryggen Wharf. A few of the wealthier town residents employed black women to clean their homes and black men to drive their carriages. Those, Jorgen knew, were servants, not slaves. Slavery had been abolished in Denmark and Norway in 1803.

Jorgen knew of a black man in Bergen who was considered the best wheelwright in town. But he had never needed a wheelwright, so had not met the man. Nor had a black person ever entered the Aksdal's shop.

Onboard the Newark, Jorgen had been warned by the carpenter, Fyke, not to engage any of the black sailors in conversation. "The mates and white sailors treat anyone who is friendly with the blacks unkindly," he said. "You're best off treating them like they are not present." Jorgen found dealing with the mates difficult enough without incurring their wrath over befriending a black man. Anyway, he didn't think any of the Africans spoke Norwegian, so he had not spoken a word to any of them. He had, however, shown them respect, smiling at them when they chanced to meet, nodding his thanks when they were ordered to help him with a job. He recognized that the black sailors were treated unfairly, they got the most dangerous jobs and were constantly being flogged for some slight infraction of the rules or simply because one of the Mates was drunk and in an ugly mood. When he mentioned this to Fyke, the old man nearly had an apoplectic fit. "Listen to me!" His voice had been uncharacteristically raised. Jorgen couldn't be sure if the man was angry with him or spoke from fear, but his message was unequivocal. "Stay away from the Africans, your safety and that of your family depends on it."

Lying there, in a black man's barn under a black man's blanket, his hunger fed by a black man's food, Jorgen had cause to contemplate the irony of Fyke's words. He thought back to the ugly incident on board the Newark. He wasn't sure what the outcome would have been had the black men not come to his rescue. He was angry enough to strangle the first mate with his bare hands, but now wondered if he could have killed the man. If the black men hadn't come to his rescue, would he have lived to see America and to provide for his family's safety?

Jorgen felt shame that he had not shown his appreciation to the two men who had helped him. Instead, he had spent the remainder of the trip trying to avoid any contact with them.

Atlanta's whimpering brought him back to the present. He sat up, reached over his sleeping wife, and picked up the baby. He held her to his chest and when she snuggled into him, he lay back into the straw. They were both asleep in minutes.

★ ★ ★

When Marta shook him awake, Jorgen was embarrassed to find that he had slept through breakfast, but he had to admit he felt rested for the first time in days. Then he remembered Andrew. He rose quickly and started for the door.

Marta called to him, and he turned. She handed him some bread spread with preserves and a mug of coffee. "A man in a buggy and a rider on horseback came into the yard a few minutes ago," she said.

"I peeked out the door," said Mary, "I think one of the men is a doctor. He was carrying a doctor bag."

"Thanks," he said, stuffing the bread into his mouth. "You're a good spy." He took the tray of empty cups and the coffee pot out of Elen's hands and started for the house.

Much to Jorgen's surprise, Andrew was awake and talking to the two men, both of whom spoke Norwegian. Mary was correct in her assessment. The older of the two men introduced himself. He was a doctor and said the other man was the town sheriff. There was no sign of the black couple.

"Andrew!" Jorgen exclaimed when he saw that his

brother was awake. He crossed the floor in three giant strides, leaned over Andrew, and grasping his brother's shoulders gave them a gentle squeeze. They exchanged looks that communicated a host of feelings, and after a few seconds, both grinned, delighted in each other's company. " I wanted to pry your eyes open, last night, but Marta wouldn't let me." Jorgen quipped and backed away from the bed, making room for the doctor who commenced treating Andrew's wounds.

The sheriff introduced himself and started to fill Jorgen in on what he knew about Andrew's ordeal.

"A week ago," the sheriff said, "Artemis," he pointed to a closed door across the room, "Artemis came into my office and said that three men had tried to force him into a carriage. He said he thought they were slave hunters."

"But I thought New York was a free state," said Jorgen. "What are slave hunters doing in a free state?"

"New York is a free state for black people who have been freed," said the sheriff. "But many slaves run away from their owners in the slave states to seek refuge in the free states. Slave hunters come up here to find the runaways and collect a bounty when they return them to their owners."

"What an awful thing to do," said Jorgen.

"Yes, it is," said the sheriff, "but it's legal. The problem is, if they don't find the runaways they're looking for they don't make any money, so they sometimes kidnap blacks who are free. There is a ready market for black workers on farms and plantations down south, and some folks down there don't question whether a black man is slave or free. They'll buy them and keep them in chains to keep them from running away."

"And Artemis thought that was going to happen to him?" asked Jorgen.

"Yes," the sheriff replied. "Artemis was freed by his owner many years ago and has lived in these parts longer than most of the white settlers. He's a good man, a good neighbor, and people around here respect him. But sadly, attempts like this have been made before. Artemis has had more than one close call."

Jorgen glanced over to see how things were going with his brother. The doctor was working on Andrew's thigh. Jorgen heard him tell Andrew that the wound looked worse than it was, that the shot had not damaged the bone. Jorgen knew that was a good thing, and turned his attention back to the sheriff.

"Artemis reported to me that he had gotten off his horse to help men who he thought had a broken wagon wheel and was set upon by those same men he had tried to help. Fortunately for him, workers in a nearby field heard the ruckus and came to his rescue. The slave hunters jumped into their wagon and fled down the road.

"The day after Artemis came to me, he was on his way to a farm north of town to help with the harvest. He was being extra cautious because that was the direction the slave hunters had headed when they were chased away. About two miles from town, he spotted the three men in the road ahead, and they seemed to be in a fight with three other men. Artemis recognized the people in trouble. One was Andrew; the other two were runaways. Artemis took his rifle and fired once in the air. The fighting stopped just long enough for the runaways to break free, and they ran into the woods. Your brother looked briefly at Artemis but was then knocked to the ground.

"Artemis saw the flash from a gun before he heard the sound. It was fired at him, and so he fled to the woods. He turned when he reached the safety of the trees and fired a couple of shots at the man with the gun, but he was too far away. He saw that Andrew was back on his feet fighting off the other two assailants. The man with the gun got on a horse and started to come after Artemis. Artemis was forced to flee. He left to go get help."

"Jorgen," Andrew said, interrupting the sheriff's story. The doctor had finished tending to him and was packing up his bag. All three men looked at Andrew. The doctor's ministrations had caused him great discomfort and though he had been listening to the sheriff, Andrew had remained quiet while the lawman spoke. His voice was strained with the effort of talking through his pain. "Jorgen," he repeated. "One of the slave hunters was Hauk."

Fourteen

Early November 1850

"Do you own a gun?" The sheriff looked down on Jorgen from where he sat astride his horse. A rifle was strapped to his saddle and a pistol bulged from a holster on his hip.

Surprised by the question, Jorgen did not immediately reply. Up till now, guns had not played a significant role in his life. His grandfather had guns; he had served in the war before Jorgen was born. And in mid September, for as long as Jorgen could remember, Bestefar and the 'big ones' took the guns and went off into the mountains to hunt tripe. Jorgen and Andrew had participated in the hunt a few times, and though Jorgen was an accurate shot, he preferred fishing to bird hunting.

"No, I don't," Jorgen answered.

"I don't recommend taking the law into your own hands," said the sheriff, "but you should own a weapon for protection. I'll stay alert for any signs of that man, Hauk, in case he comes prowling around town again. I'd like to put him behind bars for what he did to your brother, but it's a big country with many places to hide.

"You're safe enough here with Artemis," the sheriff continued. "This place is difficult to find even if you know where you're going, but you've got to be prepared to take care of yourself and your family when you leave here."

Jorgen had assumed that he would buy a gun when he owned his own land. Chickens had to be protected from foxes, and sheep from wolves, but he had never even considered the possibility of needing a weapon to protect himself from another man.

He nodded, acknowledging what the man had said, and then watched the lawman turn his horse and walk him down the path. Whether on the ground, or especially astride his huge, nut-brown mount, the sheriff was an imposing figure. Most people would describe him as tall in stature but, in fact, he was much shorter than Jorgen. He exuded absolute confidence, and seemed to possess a toughness of spirit befitting his occupation. *He's not the kind of man who needs to think a thing to death,* Jorgen mused. Admittedly, he was in awe of the lawman's decisive mien.

Unaware that the doctor had come out of the house, Jorgen turned at the sound of his voice.

"I gave Andrew something for his pain; he'll probably sleep for a while. Would you like me to have a look at your baby while I'm here?" He nodded in the direction of the barn. Jorgen looked back over his shoulder and saw that the women were standing just outside the open barn door. Marta had Atlanta in her arms.

"I think my daughter is well, but I'm sure my wife and her mother would like to meet you," said Jorgen.

They started to walk to the barn.

"If you're going back to town, I would be grateful for a ride. I would like to buy a horse and wagon and a few other things," said Jorgen.

"You're welcome to ride with me, but that's your brother's horse and wagon," said the doctor, indicating the horse that Artemis now led toward them. He had attached the wagon, and Jorgen saw that all their baggage was still neatly stowed in it.

"Surprisingly, when your brother was attacked his horse and wagon were not stolen. Those two things could have been sold for as much as a slave...but then maybe its not so surprising," the doctor said, stroking his chin thoughtfully, "since your brother knew the identity of one of the men. Horse thieves are hanged or at least jailed. Sadly enough, I don't think I've ever heard of anyone being hanged for stealing humans—black humans, that is."

The doctor greeted the women and commented on

how fit they seemed in spite of their travels. "When I emigrated, almost everyone I traveled with arrived half-starved and many remained ill for weeks," he said.

"My wife and her mother had us well supplied with food, although had the trip lasted any longer than it did, we might not have fared so well."

"And we tried to stay away from sick people," ventured Mary.

"That probably saved your life," said the doctor, patting her on the head. "I can see you're not going to be one of my best customers."

"My niece is a strong, healthy girl," affirmed Elen. She placed a protective arm around the girl. The doctor probably knew everyone in the area and Elen wanted Mary's place in the family known, just in case Mary's uncle had ties to anyone in Kendall.

The doctor was an affable man whom Jorgen judged to be the age of his father. The light friendly exchange between him and the women afforded Jorgen a few moments to organize his thoughts.

Where do I begin? he thought. And then one of his grandfather's sayings came back to him. "A sip at a time empties the cask."

Jorgen took a breath prepared to take the first sip.

"Marta, Elen," he began, looking at each in turn. "I wouldn't ask you to sleep another night in a barn if I didn't think it necessary, but that is what I'm asking you to do. I'll explain why in a few minutes."

Mother and daughter looked at each other and then back at Jorgen. They nodded in agreement.

Jorgen turned to the doctor. He asked if he would speak to Artemis and ask his permission to use his barn for one more night. "Also, please tell him that I won't be needing the horse and wagon today, that I will be going to town with you and if he would make a list, I'd like to replace what he and his wife have used to feed us and Andrew."

The doctor left to deliver the messages to Artemis, and Jorgen motioned Marta and Elen to follow him. He led them a distance from where Mary sat with baby Atlanta in her lap. What he had to say might frighten the child. He would let Elen talk to Mary after he left. She knew, better than he, how much to tell the child.

"How is Andrew?" Marta and Elen asked, simultaneously.

"Andrew is in a lot of pain," Jorgen told them, "but he should, in time, completely recover from his injuries. His condition is not the reason we're staying an extra night. I am really very sorry that you will have to sleep in a barn, again, especially since there is a house that Andrew has been readying for us. But Andrew has told me something very troubling."

Jorgen paused, and Elen jumped to what she considered to be the worst possible conclusion, "It's Mary's uncle, isn't it?" she said. "He's come looking for her."

"Nei," said Jorgen, quietly.

"Jorgen, what is it?" said Marta. She was alarmed by his uneasiness. She placed a hand on his arm, but still he paused, looking beyond her into the woods. He had been struck with a terrible thought. Hauk could be in there, hidden behind any one of those trees, with a gun aimed at him right now. Jorgen looked at Marta and felt a surge of resolve; he would not let fear become his master.

"I have to go into town to buy a weapon. We may need to protect ourselves," Jorgen said with conviction. "Hauk is here in America. He's the one who injured Andrew."

Marta reached for Jorgen and clutched his arm. Her eyes widened and tears formed in the corners. "Oh no," she said, shaking her head in disbelief.

Elen's dazed look registered her shock at the news.

"The sheriff thinks that Hauk will stay away for a while because he knows Artemis and Andrew can identify him. No one around here has seen him since the attack on Andrew. But I think Hauk will return. He told Andrew that he would come back for me."

"Why does he hate you boys?" said Elen. She turned to Marta, "And why did he attack your father?"

Jorgen shook his head. There were no answers to her questions.

Marta tried to console her mother with a hug.

"You're safe here with Artemis" Jorgen assured them. "I won't be gone long."

★ ★ ★

As they left Artemis's homestead, Jorgen was careful to note exactly where to turn off the main road to get back to his house. *Wouldn't do to get lost and delay getting back,* he thought. He suspected Marta and her mother might be anxious until he returned.

"A horse, a weapon, and food," the doctor repeated after he had asked Jorgen what he needed from town. "Artemis asked if you could pick up salt and a sack of flour. He said that's all they needed."

Jorgen nodded in reply.

"There's a stable at the far edge of town with a harness shop next to it. You can usually find a good horse or two for sale there. And we will pass the general store on our way into town where you can make your other purchases."

The doctor asked about Hauk and let out a low whistle of surprise when Jorgen told him the details of Mr. Aksdal's death and his own near drowning. "I understand why you want a gun. He sounds like a dangerous man."

"He comes from a good family. His sister is married to my brother," said Jorgen. "I don't know what happened to turn him against our family, but he seems to hate us. I don't trust him. I think he's capable of anything, even harming women."

Jorgen heaved a big sigh. "It's such a big country," he said, "I can't believe that we've run into Hauk."

"Kendall could be the reason," the doctor said. "It began as a Norwegian settlement, and most Norwegian immigrants still think of it that way. Hauk may have come here thinking slave chasing would be easier in an area where people speak his language. In reality though, Kendall has changed. Many people now speak English and a lot of the Norwegians who originally settled here have moved on to other locations."

"That was our reason for coming here. We thought that we could stay among our own people for a while until we learn English and decide where we want to settle permanently. What happened to all the Sloopers? I thought they all came to Kendall."

"Ja," the doctor said, "they did. But they weren't here long before they began moving on. Some thought the land here was too marshy for farming. They complained that there were too many mosquitoes and too much fever. But there are still some of the original Norwegian settlers, and a few more have come and stayed, for one reason or another."

"Were you one of the Sloopers?"

"Nei, I did not come over on the Restoration. I brought my family here five years later, in 1830."

"You stayed," Jorgen said. "You must like America and Kendall. What about your wife, is she happy here?"

Because he was feeling guilty about bringing Marta and Elen here, to a life that, for now included sleeping in a barn, Jorgen hoped that the doctor's wife liked living in this country. If indeed that was the case, Jorgen would consider it a good sign.

"My wife died," the doctor replied.

Jorgen's spirits sank.

"She's buried here, which is the main reason I've stayed in Kendall. My daughter also lives here, but my sons have moved west. Three are in Illinois, one is in Wisconsin, and my youngest recently moved to Texas."

"I'm sorry for your loss," Jorgen said, and he truly was. He could not imagine life without Marta.

They rode in silence for a while, until the doctor picked up the thread of their previous conversation.

"That's another reason Hauk may have come to Kendall," he said. They had crested a hill and the doctor pointed to a large body of water that was now visible in the distance. "That's Lake Ontario, and Canada is on the other side. It's just a boat ride to freedom for runaway slaves who make their way to Kendall."

"Do many come here?" asked Jorgen.

"Yes," the doctor replied. "Especially at this time of the year. In late fall and winter, winds and the rough seas they create make it too difficult for small boats to travel across to Canada. The runaways know this; they would have been told by someone on the Underground Railroad that they need to reach Kendall before November. After that, escape to Canada is difficult and unsafe until spring. The longer they have to stay here, especially if they are stranded over winter, the more dangerous it becomes for the runaways and for those who harbor them."

Jorgen asked about the Underground Railroad and the doctor told him it was made up of homeowners and churches that sheltered runaway slaves and enabled them to get to Canada.

"And you are one of those?"

"Ja," the doctor nodded, "I do what I can to help the cause. They don't stay at my home because I live too far from the lake, but I treat them if they need a doctor. Your brother, though he was here just a short time, helped several runaways. The house that he is staying at has been a stop on the Underground for a long time."

This bit of information came as an unwelcome surprise. *What was Andrew thinking,* Jorgen wondered. He couldn't have his family stay at a house that was involved in such dangerous activity. For the second time since coming to America, Jorgen faced the possibility of having nowhere to stay.

Annoyed with Andrew, but anxious to get as much information as possible, Jorgen went back to questioning the doctor. "The black men who were with him when he was attacked, were they runaways?"

"They were only dressed as men to help with their escape," the doctor said. "They are Artemis and his wife's grown daughters."

Jorgen thought about that for a moment and said, "I guess that explains why Andrew ended up at Artemis's house."

"Yes," the doctor agreed. "He feels responsible for what happened to your brother. Artemis' girls stayed with him and his wife for a few days, but his house, also, is too far from the lake. No one is ever quite sure when the boat that takes runaways to Canada will arrive, and it doesn't stay moored for long. Runaways need to be close to the lake and ready to go at a moment's notice."

The doctor went on to tell Jorgen all that he knew about Artemis's daughters and Andrew's confrontation with Hauk.

"Did they make it to Canada?" inquired Jorgen.

"I assume they did. The man who Artemis went to for help when your brother was being attacked later found them hiding in his barn and he took them to the boat."

There were more houses and movement on the road as they drew closer to town. People recognized the doctor's buggy and waved from their gardens or from passing wagons. The doctor waved back and called to them all by name.

He pointed out the general store when they passed by it. "You can stop here after you get a horse. They sell everything else you need, including guns, although there is a gunsmith whose shop is located down this road." The doctor indicated a narrow dirt path that began a short distance from the general store and seemed to disappear into a dense copse. He reined in his horse, slowing it to a walk to avoid other wagons and a group of children who darted across the street.

"The stable is on the other side of town. Both it and the general store are owned by Norwegians, so you'll have no difficulty making your purchases. Like I said, Ernst usually has a couple of good horses for sale and probably sold your brother his horse and wagon. He is a rough-looking character, but he's honest and his prices are fair."

★ ★ ★

Jorgen had been right about the women waiting for his return. Marta and Mary came out of the barn as soon as they heard the horse enter the yard.

"What a sweet looking horse," Marta said as Jorge dismounted. She reached out and rubbed the white, diamond shaped area right above its nose. It was the only distinguishing feature on its dark brown body. The horse nodded as if in agreement with Marta's appraisal.

"I'm pleased you like her," said Jorgen. "I bought her for you... and for you," he added, grinning at Mary.

"Does she have a name?" Mary asked.

"Kendall," Jorgen replied, "Her name is Kendall, just like the town."

"I haven't ridden since I was a young girl," said Marta.

"I've never ridden a horse," said Mary "but I can't wait to learn."

"That's the spirit, Mary. We're all going to have to learn to do a lot of things we've never done before...or haven't done in a long time," Jorgen said, handing the reins to Marta. He walked around the horse and began to untie bundles.

Marta surveyed the quantity of goods Jorgen had tied to the saddle and raised her eyebrows when a rifle joined the pile on the ground.

"I thought you said you didn't like hunting," Mary said. She picked up the gun and aimed it into the woods.

"I don't," Jorgen said. "But sometimes it's necessary to do unpleasant things." He glanced at Marta and saw she was staring intently at him. "Here, let's trade," he said to Mary, taking the rifle from her and laying it on the ground. He held out a large sack. "You can take this up to the house. Careful now! Don't let it escape."

Mary took the bag and cautiously peeked inside, right into the beady eyes of a large, dead hen. "Ooh, chicken! I can't wait till middag!" And she set off, calling out "Aunt Elen!" as she ran to the house.

"Mor and Esther, Artemis's wife, have been baking up a storm," Marta said in response to Jorgen's puzzled look. "I sure hope flour is in one of those bags."

"Flour, salt, and a few other things not on the list," Jorgen replied.

"I wondered if you were serious about a weapon," Marta said, indicating the rifle with the toe of her boot.

Jorgen's demeanor changed abruptly. "I take threats from Hauk seriously," he said. A minute before he was chatting playfully with Mary, his manner light, his eyes crinkly at the corners. His face now looked hard, his chin jutted defiantly. He picked up the rifle and took the reins from Marta. He led the horse to the barn, the new rifle tucked under his arm. Later, he would tell Marta about the pistol in his saddlebag.

★ ★ ★

While the women prepared dinner, Jorgen huddled with Andrew. Their conversation continued for several minutes at a level barely above a whisper. Marta glanced up from where she sat by the fireplace shelling peas and saw that their heads were almost touching. From where she sat, she couldn't see Jorgen's face, it was turned away from her, but his back was tense, ramrod straight as he leaned forward in the chair. *He's angry,* she thought.

Marta couldn't help but stare at Andrew. His expression was grave as he listened to Jorgen. She hoped he wasn't in pain. As she watched, Andrew whispered something to Jorgen and rested a bandaged hand on Jorgen's knee. Jorgen sighed. His back relaxed into the chair.

The two were silent for a time. Then Jorgen stood and went to the water bucket. He emptied what was there into the water pitcher on the table. He picked up a pea pod from the pile in front of Marta and examined it. Peas had been a new food for him when he moved to Bergen, and he liked them. He held up the pod so Andrew could see it and said, "We'll have to grow some of these," then left to go refill the bucket.

When he returned, Jorgen poured cups of water for himself and Andrew and went to sit beside him again. Their conversation was now loud enough for Marta to hear what they were saying. They discussed, revised, and at times, argued about the next steps to be taken in their plans, when to leave Kendall and where they should purchase their land. Andrew still favored Illinois while Jorgen thought Wisconsin held the better possibilities. That decision, they finally agreed, could wait until they could investigate the availability and cost of good farmland in both places.

Marta enjoyed listening to them, to the animated give and take of their opinions. She remembered how exasperated Jorgen used to get at Andrew, but it seemed that time and experience had tightened the bond that had always existed between them.

She thought back to when they were all in school and remembered how she had, at first, been captivated by Andrew's carefree, happy-go-lucky manner. He was friendly to everyone and laughter usually boiled up around him.

Jorgen was quieter. Although he participated in all the same things as Andrew, Jorgen was content to stay in the background and to let his brother steal the show. Almost a year younger than Marta, Jorgen eventually caught up to her in schoolwork, and from then on, sat beside her in class. That was when she got to know him. She realized that what she had dismissed as moodiness was actually thoughtfulness. Something said in class would lodge in his brain and he would think on it for hours. He might mention it at lunch or get a far away look in his eyes in the middle of a game, and she would know that his mind was working out something he had heard.

But mostly what she liked about Jorgen was that he listened to her. From the beginning, he seemed to enjoy talking to her more than any other person at school, and valued her opinion. That made her feel very special because she thought he was the smartest boy she had ever met.

Seeing the brothers reunited, Marta was happy for them. Although Andrew's injuries now added to the burden that Jorgen shouldered, it was obvious to anyone who saw them together that Jorgen's spirit was nourished by his brother's presence. Besides, Andrew would recover soon enough. Marta allowed her mind to wander into the future. She pictured Andrew's house across the road from theirs, Andrew's wife and children coming for Sunday dinners.

Marta finished shelling the peas. She poured some water over them, set the pot on the stove, and then turned to Mary.

"Would you like me to take Attie?"

Mary sat on the floor. Her legs were crossed and the baby was propped in her lap. She had been amusing Attie with songs she made up. The baby's dark blue eyes focused on Mary's lips and as she worked her own little lips, imitating Mary, she made soft cooing sounds.

"I'm teaching her to sing," said Mary. "Do you need to feed her?"

"Not yet," replied Marta. "You can play with her a while longer. I think she likes her singing lessons."

Marta joined Elen at the table. They watched Esther make something she called, 'corn bread.' All afternoon the women had filled the kitchen with laughter as they attempted to pronounce the names of various food items and kitchen utensils in each other's language.

Esther had also made cranberry sauce, which Elen and Marta thought quite similar to what they made from lingonberries in Norway.

"I don't think cranberries grow in Norway," said Marta.

"I had cranberries when I was in Christiania," Andrew offered when he heard the two talking about the tart red berry. "They must grow somewhere near there."

"Ja," Elen said, "I saw them in the market in Bergen, but they were very expensive."

"Maybe we can grow them on your farm," said Mary. Esther had given her a taste of the sauce after it had cooled, which Mary had obviously enjoyed. "I can't wait to spread some on the lefse for dessert." Elen had made the thin, sweet pancakes while Esther watched and nodded her approval after sampling one.

★ ★ ★

When dinner was over and all that remained of the hen was a bony carcass meticulously picked clean, the women cleared away the dishes and cleaned up while Jorgen went to the barn with Artemis to help with animals. Later, when they returned to the house, Jorgen had his fiddle with him.

"I was hoping you had brought that thing," said Andrew. "I've missed hearing all those sad songs from home."

"They're not all sad," said Mary. She had never been exposed to the light banter siblings often engage in, and her loyalty to Jorgen compelled her to defend him. "Jorgen knows some happy ones too."

"And when I'm finished," said Jorgen, "we'll have Andrew tell us a happy story, if he knows one."

★ ★ ★

Jorgen smoothly bowed the last note on his grandfather's Hardanger. The dulcet sound hung in the air as he lowered the fiddle and placed it in the case at his feet. "Your turn," he said to Andrew. "Mary would like her story now."

"We all would like a story," Marta said, "but perhaps Andrew's not feeling up to telling one just yet."

Andrew had dozed off during the music, but the prospect of telling a tale appeared to perk him up.

"It should be a short one," said Marta, "Artemis and Ester will not understand it and we don't want to take advantage of their hospitality."

"Well then, I guess I better get started." Andrew inched himself back in the bed until he sat somewhat propped up against the wall, facing the others who looked at him with expectant smiles.

"A farmer owned three goats," he began. "He kept them penned up when they weren't working, but the farmer worked them hard. Their job was to keep the fields well trimmed of tough weeds and prickly thistles. The farmer also had meadows of tender green grass and sweet clover, but these were reserved for the sheep and cows that grazed idly and napped when the sun was strong. The goats yearned for life on the meadow, a life that was forbidden to them. It was so tantalizingly close, just over a short wooden bridge that spanned a cool stream that lay beyond their pen." Andrew closed his eyes and sighed, for effect, as if picturing a heavenly meadow.

He opened his eyes and acted surprised that the group was looking at him.

Mary giggled.

"Get on with it," said Jorgen. He couldn't help laughing with the others.

"Each day, when the goats returned to their enclosure, they watched the sun set over the meadow and the sheep and cows who were privileged to roam there. The goats' lives of captivity stretched endlessly before them and their eyes glazed over with longing.

"One evening, as they stood staring over the bridge, the smallest goat bumped the gate and it popped open. The startled little goat crept past it and walked tentatively to the bridge. The other two watched in trepidation as they had heard that horrible things happened to goats that strayed from their place in the world. But all seemed to go well for the little goat as he tap-tapped slowly onto the bridge...until he reached the middle. At that point a hideous troll leaped from the water and landed in the path of the frightened goat. In a voice that sounded strangely like the farmer's, the troll condemned the goat for venturing where he didn't belong and threatened to eat him. 'Please,' implored the goat, 'I am small and weak. My friend is much larger than I and would make a better meal.'"

Andrew slumped into the bed propping himself up on an elbow. He was starting to tire, but he continued the story. "The troll thought about this piece of news and decided that the goat did look a bit scrawny so he jumped back into the stream and the small goat proceeded to the meadow where he began to nibble the juicy grass.

"When the second goat saw his young companion on the other side of the bridge, he pushed his way through the gate and stepped onto the bridge. Just like the first goat, when he got to the middle, the troll leaped over the side and into his path. For the second time, the greedy troll was told that a much larger, more appetizing goat was available and so the second goat was free to pass on his way.

"Now, the largest goat, the one with sharp, pointy

horns felt emboldened. If his two smaller friends could get past the troll, surely he could as well. He banged through the gate and charged to the bridge where he clomped to the middle. As expected, the troll leaped in front of the large goat and threatened to eat him. The goat pointed his horns at the troll and shook them in warning. When the foolish troll ignored the threat and prepared to pounce, the goat lowered his head and butted the troll into the hereafter, whereupon the third goat joined his friends in the meadow."

By the end of the story, Andrew's voice had become little more than a whisper and, despite his struggle to keep his eyes open, they now drifted shut.

Jorgen thought about the old familiar tale and wondered how many times would they have to face the troll before they reached their grassy meadow.

★ ★ ★

Later, snuggled in the hay, a thick quilt tucked around them and the baby, Jorgen told Marta all that he had learned from the doctor on the ride to town, and the details of Andrew's whispered conversation earlier in the evening.

"When Andrew agreed to rent the house," Jorgen began, "the owner requested payment in the form of repairs to the house. He said he knew someone who would help Andrew until I got here. That man, Artemis, showed up every day and when the house was restored to good order, Artemis stopped coming.

"About two weeks ago, Artemis surprised Andrew with a late night visit. He was not alone. The owner of the livery stable, a Norwegian named Ernst, was with him and he did the talking. He explained to Andrew that they had two runaway slaves hidden outside in the wagon, who needed a place to stay for a few days.

"The plan was," Jorgen continued, "that the two slaves would stay in the root cellar until the boat came that would take them to Canada. It was Andrew's responsibility to escort the slaves secretly to the boat.

"Andrew agreed to help, and the two slaves, young women dressed in men's work clothes, were taken to the root cellar. Artemis had a hamper full of food for them. The man from the livery stable told Andrew all he needed to do, besides getting them to the boat, was to place a jug of water, every evening, outside the entrance to the root cellar."

"The doctor told me today that the two women had escaped from their owner when he took them to a slave market to be sold. They traveled all the way from Kentucky, on foot, and were helped and hidden along the way by members of the Underground Railroad."

"What's that?" Marta whispered.

"Near as I can tell, it's just people who don't like slavery and want to help runaways by feeding and sheltering them, and sometimes taking them to the next town. The risk is very great. Both Andrew and the doctor told me that helping runaways is against the law."

"If the sheriff knows that Andrew was helping runaways escape, will he arrest him?"

"Nei. I don't think the sheriff agrees with that law. Like most people here in Kendall, the sheriff does not believe in slavery. He is aware that people in Kendall are helping runaways, knows exactly who they are, the doctor told me, but he pretends not to know."

"Why aren't Artemis' children free?" Marta asked. "Like he and his wife."

She had been silent for several minutes and Jorgen had assumed she had fallen asleep.

"The man who owned Artemis and his wife sold their children, all six of them. The children were all quite young at the time. Artemis' four sons went to unknown buyers, and he does not know their whereabouts. His two daughters were slightly older, in their teens, and they continued to have some contact with their parents. They were sold to an estate not far from where Artemis and his wife lived. When Artemis' owner eventually died, his will freed Artemis and his wife. It wasn't safe for them to stay in Kentucky, so they came to New York."

"He probably freed them because he felt guilty about selling their children," Marta hissed.

Jorgen drew her body up against his own and kissed the back of her neck. "I'm sorry that I've upset you. Maybe we should save this for another time," he suggested.

"Nei, finish telling me what Andrew had to say. Were Artemis' girls with Andrew when Hauk attacked him?"

"Ja," said Jorgen. "When word got around town that slave hunters were in the area and that they had tried to kidnap Artemis, it was decided that his daughters were in grave danger and needed to leave town immediately. Andrew was supposed to take them to the dock where someone there would hide them until the boat showed up. He tried to stay in the cover of the forest, but as luck would have it, the one open stretch they had to cross brought them into contact with Hauk and his men."

Attie awoke and began to fuss. Marta unbuttoned her chemise and put the baby to her breast.

"Go on," Marta whispered when Attie quieted and began to nurse. "What else did Andrew tell you? I get the feeling that you've left something out."

"Well," Jorgen began, then paused.

"Jorgen?"

"The house that Andrew found for us is a stop on that Underground Railroad."

Jorgen felt her body stiffen and heard her startled intake of breath. "I'm sorry," he said, "I should have waited until morning to tell you. Now neither of us will be able to sleep."

When she didn't say anything, he added, "We don't have to take the house, Marta, we can look for something else tomorrow."

"If it were just us... just you and me" she whispered, wearily.

"If it were just us," he said, "we might not have stopped here in Kendall. But with a baby, your mother, Mary, and now my injured brother…we have others to consider and are trapped here for the time being. Somehow we've become ensnared in this country's slavery problem and on top of that, we have a disturbed person determined to cause me bodily harm."

Marta had no reply. After several minutes passed, he heard her sigh. Many minutes later, he realized that she had fallen asleep.

He marveled that she could do that. That she could take in troubling news and still fall asleep.

"Jorgen, the middle of the night is for sleep, not problem solving." Marta scolded on more than one occasion when he complained about concerns that kept him awake.

Knowing that things always look worse when seen through the eyes of predawn worry, Jorgen set his mind to recalling a peaceful memory. He thought about working alongside his father and grandfather in the wood shop and could almost hear the rasping sound of their planes on wood. He fell asleep trying to make out Bestefar's shadowy image, his face blurred by the passage of time.

★ ★ ★

Jorgen, Andrew, Marta, and Elen spent the next morning discussing the situation concerning the house. Andrew told the women what he had said to Jorgen the day before; he had made no commitments to anyone about their involvement with the Underground Railroad. The only promise he had made to the owner was that they would see to the upkeep of the house and do the necessary repairs.

"I only agreed to help Artemis because I thought his daughters would be gone before you all got here. Artemis and the others here in Kendall know that we will not be participants in the cause."

"Well, we are sympathetic," said Elen. "Perhaps there's some other way we could be helpful."

"The church in Kendall is active," said Andrew. "You can ask Pastor Haugen after Sunday service."

"And if Hauk comes back?" said Marta.

"I don't think Hauk would be foolish enough to return to Kendall so soon after what he did to me," said Andrew. "He knows the sheriff will be looking for him. Eventually he'll be back, but I think he'll wait a while, and hopefully, we'll be gone by then."

Jorgen agreed. He, too, hoped they would be safe for the time being.

That afternoon Artemis showed them the way to the house. It was situated on a well-traveled lane, not far off the main road to town and less than five miles from where Artemis lived. It was easy to see why Andrew had chosen it. The construction was stone and wood, and Jorgen noted the fresh tiles on the roof, one of Andrew and Artemis's recent repairs. Inside, the house was clean and smelled pleasantly of pine due to several new floor planks. A fireplace, reminiscent of the one in Jorgen's home in Norway, dominated a large, sparsely furnished room, which was both kitchen and general living area. Two rocking chairs stood on either side of the fireplace, a long table flanked by benches was placed squarely in the middle of the room, and in the corner, near a small window there was a spinning wheel.

Marta walked over and gave the wheel a turn. "It's in working order" she said. "I remember when we lived on the farm, Mor. You spent most evenings spinning yarn. We moved to Bergen before I got very good at it. Why didn't we take the spinning wheel when we left?'

"I think I was ready for a different life," said Elen. "And with all the new machines for making yarn and cloth, I decided it didn't make sense to do it by hand when you could go into a shop and buy it ready made."

"Ja, but you always complained that store bought wasn't as good as yours." Marta turned to survey the room. Besides the front door, through which they had entered, there were three more doors leading off the main room. Jorgen came to stand beside her but seemed lost in his own thoughts.

She led the way and he followed, their footsteps echoing as they crossed and recrossed the room to see the rest of the house. The doors on either side of the great room led to two bedrooms. The third door, opposite the front door, opened into a storage room with a back door to the garden and root cellar behind the house.

The two bedrooms were large; each contained a bed, a bureau, and handsome floor-to-ceiling wardrobes.

Jorgen ran his hand down the door of one of the wardrobes. "This is nice work," he commented. "I wonder if it was made here in Kendall." He had seen a wood and cabinet shop in town.

After sleeping in a barn for two nights, Marta thought the house looked like a little bit of heaven. "I can see why Andrew chose this," she said. "Why would anyone want to leave this beautiful home?"

Jorgen saw excitement and anticipation in her flushed face, but before he could reply, her question was answered by a familiar voice.

"They'll be back in a year, or so," the sheriff said from the open doorway.

Jorgen turned to face him as he continued, "I was on my way to Artemis's to see how you were all getting on when I saw your wagon pull off the road and come down here. The Burtons are happy to know someone will be living here for a while. Doesn't suit a house to stand empty. Are you moving in today?"

"We are," Jorgen replied. "It looks like it will suit us perfectly, although I don't like the history that comes with it. If it were just my brother and I, I wouldn't be worried."

"Completely understandable," the sheriff said, nodding. "I presume you're referring to the Underground Railroad and the rumors that this house is part of that effort."

"As much as I do not favor slavery," said Jorgen, "I can't participate in something that will draw the likes of Hauk to my home."

"And that is the other reason for my visit. I received word this morning that slave traders were arrested in Brockport."

"That's not far from here. We passed it on the canal," said Jorgen.

"It is close by,'' the sheriff continued. "so I inquired about their identities and learned that one is our man Hauk. He was arrested for robbing and beating a man almost to death, and will most likely spend some time in jail."

"Well that's the best news you could give us," Marta said, "I think we will all sleep better knowing that he is locked up."

When the sheriff had said goodbye and walked out the door, Marta turned to Jorgen and noted his look of relief. Gone was the tightness around his eyes, the lines across his brow. The Jorgen of her youth was back once again, with his beautiful smile and blue eyes as bright as a summer sky.

★ ★ ★

Andrew hobbled into the house several days later with support from Artemis and Jorgen, one at each elbow. His leg wound was healing, but the bullet must have nicked the bone; it was still too painful to put his full weight on the leg.

"Look," he said raising his right hand, "I can feed myself." The bandage and stitches had been removed earlier that day, and though there remained a nasty scar, Andrew wiggled his fingers to show that they all still worked.

"How is your other hand?" Mary asked. "When does all that come off?"

Andrew lowered himself into one of the rockers by the fire. His broken left hand was still bandaged.

"It's going to take a couple more weeks, but it's coming along fine. Told the doctor I'd be back to milking cows in no time."

"But Andrew," said Mary, "We don't have any cows."

"No cows? Jorgen did you forget to bring the cows?" said Andrew.

Mary started to giggle. She was catching on to Andrew. "Well, we had some when we started out," she said, "but they didn't swim fast enough."

"I hope that answers your question," Jorgen said, laughing along with the others.

"It does, I'll just have to find something else to sink my hands into."

To that end, when the bandage and splint came off, Andrew announced that he would take over the bread making for the family. Though the others laughed at the idea of eating bread that Andrew baked, Elen saw its wisdom and practicality and tutored him through the process. In return, she asked him to teach her to use the rifle. Eventually the shooting lessons grew to include Marta and Mary.

Freed from her bread-baking chore, Elen spent even more time at the spinning wheel. She had ridden to town one afternoon, shortly after they had moved in, and bought two sacks of wool. The spinning wheel was never idle after that as she, Marta, and Mary took turns spinning out skeins of wool. They sold some of the yarn and purchased more raw wool, but kept some yarn for their own use. Just in time for the really cold weather, they were all soon clad in new socks, caps, and sweaters.

With his brother at the house to look after the women, Jorgen took a carpentry job in town. He had to admit he was grateful to his father for insisting that his sons learn how to use basic tools. Even Andrew, who hated the workshop, knew how to put pieces of wood together to fashion a table or chair...not that he would ever willingly do it. Jorgen smiled to himself at the thought of Andrew baking bread. What would his father say to that?

As the weeks passed and Andrew grew stronger, Jorgen saw restlessness set in. One night, he surprised his brother with several traps that he purchased at the general store on his way home from work.

"Are you hinting that I need to do more than bake bread to earn my keep?" Andrew asked. His face had lit up when he saw what was in the large bundle that Jorgen had given him.

"I'm not hinting at anything," Jorgen said with a laugh. "I'll tell you to your face. Get out of the house...we're all tired of you moping about all day."

"What about the bread?" said Elen. "I think Andrew has a talent for baking."

Mary stifled a giggle. Andrew's efforts produced loaves that were edible, but more often than not, contained lumps and were terribly misshapen. But she knew how happy Elen had been to relinquish that duty, if only for a few weeks.

"Don't worry about that." Andrew raised his hands in front of him and slowly flexed his stiff fingers a few times. "You're safe until I have a cow to milk."

The days passed quickly. There was always so much to do. The holidays came and went in a blur of activity. A letter from Norway arrived in mid January. News from home pricked Jorgen's conscience. It had been a long time since he had written the family. A few nights after receiving the letter, Jorgen sat at the table with his pen, paper and pot of ink.

Dear Familie,

Our situation improves every day. You asked if Andrew had recovered from his injuries, and he has. You will be surprised to hear who attacked him. Fortunately, the man responsible has been caught and is in jail. It was Hauk. Andrew says that Hauk is full of hatred for our family. We think that he has gone mad; there seems to be no other explanation for his actions.

Andrew's injuries have healed sufficiently to allow him to take up trapping again. Now everyone in the family, except for baby Attie, is contributing to our farm fund, and it grows daily. We have the use of a spinning wheel and it is idle only when Marta, Elen, and Mary are asleep. The general store sells the yarn for us and complains that there is never enough. It sells out faster than the milled yarn even though we charge more for ours.

Pappa will be happy to hear that I have not lost my woodworking skills. Besides making a bed for Andrew and a cot for Atlanta, I have a job in town working for a cabinet maker. I must say that I am grateful that Pappa and Bestefar were such good teachers.

I wish you could all see Attie. She is a happy little thing and reminds me so much of Inger when she was a baby. She has captured even Andrew's heart and I have to smile every time he picks her up and talks to her. Marta fears that he will spoil her, but Elen says that you can't give a baby too much attention.

Mary continues to be a big help to Marta and we are all thankful that she is with us. She has a sweet manner and is so good with Attie.

We tried to make our first American Jul as festive as possible so that we wouldn't be sad about being away from home. Marta, Elen, and Mary prepared for the holiday with a thorough housecleaning. When it was as clean as a pauper's kettle, we gathered pine boughs for all the doorways and decorated them with pinecones and strings of berries. Our neighbors, a German family, brought a whole tree inside their house. They decorated it with small trinkets and put candles on it, which they lit on Jul. Marta and I decided that is a tradition we would like to start when we have our own home. The general store in Kendall orders a barrel of lutefisk every December from somewhere in New York City, so our

Jul feast most likely looked like yours: a platter of lutefisk, boiled potatoes with cream sauce, turnips, and other vegetables. There was also a large pile of lefse, which Mary made with a little help from Elen, and a dish of cranberry sauce. After middag was over, I got out the Hardanger, and we sang and danced until bedtime.

Now that the new year has begun, the weather here has turned cold. It is colder even than home and there is deep snow everywhere. We had a mild fall and so this has taken us all by surprise. The house we are using is well built, our supply of firewood is plentiful, and so we manage to stay warm. Fortunately, we are not far from a well-traveled road so I am able to get to town and to work most days.

We are all trying to learn English. Our little church is filled every Sunday with Norwegian immigrants and is the only place where we all still speak Norwegian. Marta insists that we speak English at home, although I hear Elen talking to Attie in Norwegian. Many people here refuse to learn any English at all, and there is even a newspaper in town printed in Norwegian, but we think it is important to learn the language of our new country.

Taking care of a baby has been new to all of us except Elen. She has taught us a lot. My job is to settle Attie down in the evening so that she will sleep. I sit by the fire and rock her, like Pappa used to do with Inger.

Andrew has taught the women how to use a rifle and a pistol, and has learned to bake bread. Mary is learning to ride a horse and to set traps. I learned how to bandage a wound and hope I will never need that skill again.

Before I left home, Mrs. Larson gave me the name of her nephew. She wasn't sure where he had settled. Tell her that I found him right here in Kendall. He owns a small farm and he manages the dry goods store in town.

I'm sorry it has been so long since my last letter. We think fondly of home and all of you and hope that you are well.

Your loving son and brother,
Jorgen

It had taken him half the night to write his letter, the longest one he had ever written. In the morning, on his way to work, he mailed it at the postal station in the general store. He knew he'd probably feel tired later in the day as a result of his short night's sleep, but for now, thoughts of home and family made him happy and gave him energy. He could picture them sitting around the table while his mother read his letter and was pleased with himself for the effort he had put into it.

★ ★ ★

Sunday service was over. Marta and Jorgen joined their fellow worshippers in the narthex for the social hour while they waited for Sunday school to end. Mary looked forward to these classes; it was the first school of any kind she had ever attended. The weather was unusually cold for late February and heavy dark clouds held the promise of a large snowfall.

Elen had not come. She had offered to stay home with Attie, who was getting over a cold. Andrew also was absent. Although he usually attended services with them, he had taken note of the impending storm and had decided he should pull his traps before they became buried in deep snow.

Marta felt at home seated among the women. Most of her fellow worshippers at this Lutheran Church had come from Norway. Listening to the group, one would have thought they were back in the homeland. Normally, Marta conversed with the women, but on this morning the men's conversation had piqued her interest. They were talking about a young couple who had left Kendall in the fall for a settlement in Illinois.

"Where in Illinois?" Jorgen asked, and was told it was a fairly large settlement on the Fox River, southwest of

Chicago.

More questions followed and knowing that Illinois was one of the places that Jorgen and Andrew talked about, Marta was curious to hear what the others had to say.

Finally, a gentleman who Marta had not seen before, spoke up. "Many of you know that I recently returned from Illinois. I think the area does hold promise, the land is good, but the prairie is very difficult to clear. The summers are too hot for me and swarms of flies and mosquitos make a misery out of outside work."

The man slowly shook his head. "I'm not going back there. Whole settlements are moving on to places in Iowa and Texas, but I think they're not much better. I wouldn't want to farm in either place, one is hotter than the next."

"Where will you go?" someone in the group asked. "You didn't like it here, either. You're going to run out of states, if you keep on." The men all laughed at the stranger. These were the immigrants who had tired of the journey. Kendall was not the Promised Land, but they had all found a reason to stay when so many before them, like the stranger, had moved on.

"Laugh if you will," the man continued, "but I've found what I've been looking for. I've only come back to convince my cousin," he stopped talking and placed an arm around the shoulders of the general store owner, "to join me in building a homestead."

"Where is your land?" Jorgen asked. But because of noisy conversation that erupted when the man finished speaking Jorgen's question went unheard and unanswered.

Jorgen leaned in to talk to the owner of the general store. Marta couldn't hear their conversation; it, too, was lost in the buzz of so many other conversations.

Also lost in the fellowship and friendly exchanges was an awareness of how the weather outside had worsened considerably. Had it been warmer, the steady drumbeat of rain on the roof and windows of the church would have alerted everyone to the severity of the storm. But the silent onslaught of snow had passed unnoticed by those sheltered inside.

★ ★ ★

Meanwhile, Andrew hurried to pull all his traps painfully aware of the ferocity of the wind and snow that pelted his face. Not one to give up or give in to adversity, Andrew persisted in his task, which took him further and further from home, and shelter.

"C'mon Kendall, not much further, then we can head back to our dinners." Andrew leaned forward in the saddle, talking to the small, dark brown horse that Jorgen had purchased, urging her on. He brushed the snow from her mane as she continued to trudge through the snow. Visibility was so poor that Andrew didn't see the doe until she darted in front of Kendall. Nor did he see the large buck that charged from the forest and plowed into the horse. Andrew was thrown by the force of the collision, and his body slammed into a tree. Kendall's leg was broken. She staggered a short distance and went down. The buck fell next to Andrew, its neck broken.

★ ★ ★

Jorgen, Marta and Mary were relieved to reach the warmth of the house. The three stood inside the door, stamping snow off their boots and brushing it off their clothing and eyelashes. When the storm had settled in and gusty winds whistled around the corners of the house, Elen had built up a large fire in the fireplace.

"It's good to be home," Marta said. "And it was a relief not to have Attie with us. I'm so thankful that you suggested staying home with her today."

"We should have paid more attention to this weather and left sooner," said Jorgen. "It's nasty out there. Is Andrew back yet?"

"Not unless he's in the barn," said Elen.

Jorgen stayed only a few minutes to warm up then left to take the horse and wagon to the barn. He knew that Andrew could stay out in the barn for hours if the traps had been successful, but it was so cold today that he didn't think Andrew would stay away from the fireplace for long.

Andrew was not there when Jorgen reached the barn. "The snow must have slowed him down, too," he thought. It had, after all, taken twice as long as usual to get home from church. He unhitched the horse, placed it in a stall, rubbed it dry and covered it with a blanket. The barn offered meager protection, at best. He filled a bucket with feed and gave it to his horse and filled another for Andrew's. He placed the second bucket and a blanket in another stall knowing that Andrew would be freezing by the time he got home and would appreciate this slight help from Jorgen.

An hour later, when the family was ready to sit down for middag, and Andrew still hadn't returned. Jorgen—in fact the whole family—was concerned.

"It's not like him to miss middag," Marta said. She stood by the window and anxiously looked out at the snow that seemed to be blowing from every direction and had formed a deep drift that curved around the side of the house.

"Especially when we're having chicken," said Elen. "He saw me preparing it before he left this morning and said it was his favorite dish and that he'd be thinking about dinner all day."

Mary laughed. "Yesterday when I went to the barn to tell him that middag was ready, he told me that he was no longer eating middag, and would I please call him when dinner was ready." She caught herself mid-laugh and her expression abruptly changed to one of fear. "Jorgen, I think something's happened to Andrew. We need to look for him."

344

"I was thinking the same thing," said Jorgen, "but you're staying here."

"I think you should take her with you," Elen said.

Jorgen raised his eyebrows at her suggestion. He wondered if Elen realized the severity of the weather.

"She has gone with Andrew many times, and knows where he places his traps. She knows better than you do where to look... and I know that you will keep her safe," she added.

Jorgen knew Elen was right; he had no idea where Andrew had gone. He nodded to Mary and told her to put on the warmest clothing she had. They would ride together to a neighboring farm and ask to borrow their sleigh. He hoped that from there, Mary would be able to find the way to where Andrew set his traps.

Minutes later they were astride Venn, the horse Andrew had purchased and named after the horse back home. He was bigger than Kendall and easily carried the two riders. He was also faster and despite the blowing snow, quickly covered the distance to their neighbor's house. His reward was a rubdown by the neighbor's son because the kind neighbor insisted they use his horse, which, he said, was used to pulling the sleigh.

They set off with the neighbor driving and Mary giving directions. After offering profuse thanks, Jorgen fell silent. The effort it had taken to get them to their destination had consumed his thoughts and now, relieved of that duty, panic poured in to fill the void. *Collecting his traps never takes long...he should have been back by the time we returned from church. Mary and I should have gone out then.* One accusatory thought after another sprang into his mind until thinking became unbearable.

"Are we close, Mary? How much farther?"

"We've already passed some of the places where I know he had traps." Her next words were lost, pierced by a high-pitched shriek. It sounded like an animal in extreme agony.

The neighbor reined in his horse until he could determine where the horrific sound was coming from. They approached the scene of the accident and Kendall's pathetic whinnies of pain drew their attention to her. The noise she made when she attempted to stand sent shivers through Jorgen's body, but he forced himself to look away from the horse to look for Andrew. The sleigh stopped a short distance from the struggling horse and both Jorgen and his neighbor bounded out at the same time.

"Stay here." Jorgen heard the other man say to Mary as he headed for the horse.

Jorgen stumbled off in another direction, toward an ominous looking lump in the snow. As he drew near to it, he was relieved to see that it was the body of a dead buck partially covered in snow. He was about to turn away when he made a shocking discovery. Andrew's crumpled body lay on the other side of the deer.

Later, Jorgen would say that he had no memory of the gun shot that ended Kendall's life or Mary's scream when she saw the poor animal put down. He did, however, remember every detail of those first awful seconds when he found Andrew's dead body.

Fifteen

March 1851

Andrew had been part of the Kendall community less than a year, and yet the people all expressed the same sentiment when they paid their respects to Jorgen.

"He was like my son," said one, "like my brother" said another. "He was a friend, always willing to offer a helping hand." The tributes were all sincere and gratifying in their own way, but Jorgen remained inconsolable.

For a time, he was riven with guilt. He thought if he had just gone to look for Andrew sooner, he could have saved his life.

Hearing Jorgen say that, the doctor disagreed. He contended that when Andrew was thrown headfirst into the tree, the blow had killed him instantly. "After he hit that tree, no one could have saved him," the doctor told Jorgen. "I hope it comforts you to know he did not linger in pain or freeze to death."

No one, however, could dispute one immutable fact. The refrain, *"if I hadn't bought those traps"* played relentlessly in Jorgen's mind. Any thought of Andrew—any mention of his name summoned into Jorgen's consciousness those six words.

That Andrew would never see their goal in America accomplished, would never marry or have children...these things Jorgen mourned for his brother. That he would never again enjoy the companionship of a brother who added so much to his own life, this Jorgen mourned for himself. He did find comfort in the pastor's words spoken at the funeral: "A life lived with love and compassion for others is a full life, no matters how few the years."

After trying several times to put the tragic news in a letter home, Jorgen finally asked Marta to help him. But, even she could not she get beyond the first words without dissolving into tears.

"I'm sorry, Jorgen," she wept, "I keep thinking of your family reading this and....I can't find the words."

"I know," he said. He knelt on the floor next to where she sat and put his arms around her. They clung to each other for several minutes.

"It's the same for me. I'm grateful to you for trying," he whispered.

Later that day, Jorgen turned to Elen for help. Although she had endured the deaths of several loved ones, those hadn't prepared her for the passing of one so young and vibrant as Andrew. Despite her sadness, she turned her thoughts to Andrew's parents and family and hoped her words would soften the anguish this letter would bring to them.

She wrote from the heart, expressing not only her sympathy for the loss of a loving son and brother, but she put into words things that parents long to hear about their child. She wrote about what a happy person Andrew had been, about his patience in spite of the injuries he had suffered weeks before, and how he brought joy and laughter to those whose lives had touched his.

"He was considerate and respectful of me and always spoke lovingly about his family especially of you, his parents. I wish you could have seen him with our grandchild; he would have made a good father. He was the big brother that Mary never had. He spent hours teaching her how to shoot, trap, and ride a horse."

Her letter was everything that Jorgen wished he had been able to write, and he said that in a postscript, promising to write soon. Marta, too, apologized to the family for her brief condolences, and also promised to write more later. Jorgen was about to seal the letter when Mary asked if he would help her write something.

"Andrew was kind and brave and I loved him. He made

us laugh. From Mary." By the time she finished her contribution, perspiration had formed on her upper lip. Watching her labor over this task, painstakingly forming each letter, Jorgen was touched.

★ ★ ★

Andrew was buried six weeks after his body was found. Artemis insisted that he be the one to dig the grave when the ground finally thawed enough to allow him to put a shovel to the task.

The weeks between his death and burial saw little change in daily life. Jorgen returned to work less than a week after that fateful Sunday, but his focus was no longer on making money. He just needed to keep busy. The women had their own work, and as the weeks passed, they began to wonder if Kendall would be their final home.

"If this is to be Andrew's final resting place, I wonder if Jorgen will want to remain close by," Marta said one day after Jorgen had left for work.

Elen paused her spinning to consider this. She knew Jorgen often went to visit his brother the first weeks when his casket was in the basement of the church, then at the cemetery after he was buried. Elen looked at Marta, but had no reply before returning to her task.

They had already dismissed the idea that he would want to return to Norway, and they tried to remain neutral about staying in Kendall. The farmland along the Erie Canal had looked promising, but Marta and Elen doubted that Jorgen would be able to afford any land that was for sale there, especially after sending Andrew's share of the money back home. Land was far more expensive here than land farther west. Although there was plenty of cheap marshland in the area, draining it would be costly.

When Jorgen was with the family, talk was kept to the here and now. No mention was made of moving on or purchasing land. Occasionally, Andrew's name would be mentioned and after some uncomfortable moments, conversation would be replaced with a sad silence.

Marta and Elen were in agreement; they would give Jorgen all the time he needed to grieve, to sort out his plans, and to adjust those plans—to life without Andrew. They knew he would have to reach some decision before the end of the summer because the owners had recently informed them that they would be returning then to reclaim their home.

Jorgen knew he was struggling. In his darker moods he actually did consider the idea of moving back to Bergen. Nights were difficult. He tried to lie still, knowing his tossing and turning disturbed Marta's sleep. However, thoughts of home kept him awake far into the night; he thought of Theo's wise counsel and the comfort he would feel surrounded by his family. Perhaps his father was right, thought Jorgen. Maybe he should have stayed in Bergen and continued running Mr. Aksdal's shop. What was he doing in this town of strangers?

But at those times, when his mood seemed darkest, one of the 'strangers,' perhaps the doctor, would stop by. "I was in the area and thought I'd see how that beautiful baby of yours is doing." Or someone would knock on the door with a fresh baked pie, or some meat from a newly butchered hog. Jorgen's spirits would rise and hope would flicker and propel him into the next day and the day after that, until dark thoughts would return to weigh him down once more.

In the late afternoons, coming home from work, he would ride past the small park in town and see children playing on the seesaw. He could not catch the words to the rhyme they chanted as they rode up and down, but their laughter, echoing in the air, both cheered and depressed him.

★ ★ ★

One morning, several weeks after Andrew's burial, a man entered the wood shop where Jorgen worked. He recognized the man, remembering that he was the one at church who tried to convince his cousin to move west with him. Jorgen had seen him a few times since, working at his cousin's general store.

"I'm sorry, the owner will not be in today," said Jorgen. "Is there something I can do for you?"

The man smiled briefly and looked around the shop in a disinterested way, then cleared his throat. Jorgen waited patiently. He had experienced this awkwardness toward him often in previous days. He knew that grief surrounded him like a moat that others weren't sure how to cross.

"I'm very sorry about your brother," the man began.

Jorgen nodded. "It was good of you to come by to say that."

"Well, I truly am sorry, but that is only part of my reason for wanting to talk to you. My name is Karl Pierson." He took a couple of steps towards Jorgen and extended his hand.

"Jorgen Halvorson," Jorgen said shaking the man's hand. "I remember you from church several weeks ago." In fact Jorgen remembered every detail of that day. "Your conversation interested me."

"Yes, I recall that it did. You asked questions about Illinois versus Wisconsin and talked about your desire to purchase land and set up your own homestead...I'm hoping that your plans have not changed due to the unfortunate death of your brother."

There was another self-conscious pause before Karl continued. "I had hoped to convince my cousin to move out there with me, but he has decided to stay here in Kendall. He has established his store here, and his wife has family nearby. He has no wish to start over. I don't think land ownership is in his blood. But I sensed from what you said at the church, that it is in yours. I am in need of a homesteading partner and wonder if you would be interested in discussing it with me."

Jorgen studied Karl as he spoke. He was forthright,

healthy looking, and appeared to be no stranger to hard work. His calloused hand had been firm in its handshake. The fact that Jorgen knew this man's cousin and considered him to be a person of good character was also in Mr. Pierson's favor.

"I'm sorry," Karl said, when Jorgen didn't immediately respond. "I hope I haven't offended you. I'm not presuming to take your brother's place. I only thought that if you were hesitant to continue your journey by yourself, you might consider a partnership. It would also be a tremendous help to me as I'm not a wealthy man and can't afford to establish a homestead on my own."

"Your offer is generous," said Jorgen, "but unexpected. I wasn't offended. It's just something I've never had to consider. I've always had my brother and assumed we would always be there for each other. Since he died…well, I don't think I've even considered the possibility of another partner. In all honesty, I haven't given any thought about how to proceed with our…with my plans."

Karl was silent. He liked this younger man and could feel the burden of his sorrow. He had said he had no intention of taking his brother's place, but wasn't that exactly what he was proposing?

"Tell me about the land." Jorgen spoke so softly that had it not been for the expectant look on his face, Karl would have doubted he had spoken at all.

"I've bought land in central Wisconsin, outside a town called Oshkosh." Once Karl got started his enthusiasm escalated and the words poured out. "It is beautiful land, fertile land, you would not be disappointed. There are no mountains, but the forests stretch for miles. Logging has become a huge industry and there are plenty of sawmills in the area. With this land we could do both that and farming. Or we could have a herd of cows. Oshkosh is on a large lake, Lake Winnebago, and the climate is similar to many places in Norway. A number of our countrymen have already settled there."

Karl stopped when he saw Jorgen's smile. "Guess I've rambled on long enough," he said a bit sheepishly. "I'll give you time to think about my offer and come back in a few days. I've been helping out at my cousin's store and am staying with him and his family. You can find me there if you want to talk to me before then."

★ ★ ★

"The ground is warming up," Marta stated at dinner that night. "Mor and I thought we could plant some vegetables. Maybe you could stop at the general store and pick up some seeds."

How selfish I've been, thought Jorgen. *I have thought only of myself. Marta and Elen have no idea what to make of their future.*

"I'm sorry," he said, addressing all of them. "We should have been facing the future together; I should have discussed it with you right after Andrew died."

Marta placed her hand on Jorgen's arm. "There's no need to be sorry," she said. "We wanted you to have time to grieve for Andrew. I knew you'd talk when the time was right for you. We only thought that if we'd be staying here for a while longer, we should think about planting a garden."

Jorgen laughed at the coincidence and proceeded to tell them about Karl Pierson's offer. "So you see," he concluded, "on the day you were making plans in case we stayed, I was offered a plan so that we could leave."

After the dishes were cleared away, they sat at the table and talked about what they hoped would be their final move. In the end, it was decided that they would ask Mr. Pierson to the house so that Marta, Elen, and Mary could get to know him.

"He seems like a good person, but this will only work if we are all in total agreement," said Jorgen. "If we form a partnership, we will be traveling with him and will most likely live together until we get our houses built. Our futures will be joined for a long time to come, so I want you all to be sure before I say yes to his offer."

"Even me?" said Mary, who was surprised but pleased to be part of this grown up discussion.

"Most especially you," said Jorgen, giving her nose a playful tweak.

★ ★ ★

Karl's cousin paid Jorgen a surprise visit at work the next morning. There was no formal greeting. Instead, he got right to the point.

"Karl told me about his offer and before you accept it, there is something I think you ought to know. My cousin is a good man but he has radical ideas. He is an active abolitionist and has seen the inside of many jails for assisting runaway slaves. I hate slavery too, but the law says that captured runaways must be returned to their Southern masters. I know you're a family man, and I wouldn't want my cousin's disregard for the law to threaten your family's safety. I felt I should warn you."

He ended his speech as abruptly as he had begun, turned, and quickly walked away before Jorgen could say a word.

★ ★ ★

Two nights later, Karl Pierson sat at the Halvorson kitchen table smiling amiably as the women peppered him with questions.

Jorgen's first impression of Karl had been favorable. His intensity and passion for the land he owned in Wisconsin was infectious. He had conducted himself well that day at the church when some of the others had chided him; he remained confident and polite in spite of critical comments that had been directed at him.

Jorgen studied the man as he answered Marta and Elen's questions. He was a patient listener. He gave the women as much time as they needed to list their concerns and in turn, answered those concerns with respect and understanding.

He was a short man, shorter even than Andrew, and thin, but wiry. At the general store, Jorgen had seen Karl lift hundred pound sacks of flour like they were pillows. If they went into a partnership on the land, they would be neighbors, quite possibly for the rest of their lives. They would be dependent on each other's strengths until both farms were established and would rely on each other as neighbors for years to come.

Another thing in Karl's favor was that he had helped build houses in Illinois, experience that Jorgen did not have.

"How much land are you willing to sell?" Marta asked.

"My parcel of land is three hundred twenty acres," Karl said. "I have offered Jorgen half. Our homesteads would each have one hundred sixty acres."

"Do you have a house there?" asked Mary.

"There are no buildings on the land, but we would build your house first."

"I've seen the land," he went on, excitedly looking from Mary to Marta and Elen. "Some is cleared and ready for planting, much of it could be excellent grazing land if we decide to add livestock, and there is good timberland as well."

Turning to Jorgen, Karl said. "We would need a barn and outbuildings, but we can talk about those later.

"I know cotton is grown in America," said Mary. "I saw some on a ship in Liverpool. Is that what we'll plant? I'd like to see how cotton grows."

"I would too," said Karl. "I've never seen a cotton plant either. But the weather is not warm enough in Wisconsin to grow cotton."

Mary looked disappointed. She brightened, however, when Karl asked her if she liked apples.

"Apples and berries, most vegetables, and many different kinds of grain, lots of things can be grown in Wisconsin," he told her.

"How do you get there? Will it take a long time?" Mary asked.

Jorgen was again made aware of how much Mary had changed from the frightened, withdrawn child they first met on the Lykke Til.

"The long way is to go by land. You would travel many miles south through the state of New York, then through parts of Pennsylvania, Ohio, Indiana, and Illinois before you reached Wisconsin. The roads are terrible. In many places there are only rough Indian trails. It would be a difficult journey and would take us weeks. The shorter, faster way is to take the canal to Buffalo and then a steamship across the lakes to Wisconsin."

Marta and Mary groaned simultaneously at the mention of travel on the canal. That part of their trip had been less than pleasant the previous fall.

Jorgen smiled at the two, knowing full well their feelings; he shared them as well. It had been so cold at night, and the little boat had been so uncomfortably crowded that sleep had been next to impossible. Jorgen related their experience to Mr. Pierson, who nodded sympathetically.

"From Troy to Holley is a long, tedious canal trip," he agreed, "but be glad you weren't going east... that's so much worse. I don't know if you noticed, but boats going west, the way you came, have the right of way going through the locks. It took me more than two weeks last year when I had to go back to Troy. But the good news," he continued with a broad smile that was definitely contagious, "the good news is that we're not going east. We only have get to Buffalo, and that's less than a two-day trip."

"And the trip across the Great Lakes is made by

steamer?" said Marta sounding unsure of that fact.

"Yes," said Karl. "And those steamers are similar to the Hudson River steamship you took out of New York City. They are reasonably comfortable."

When Karl left later that evening, Jorgen walked him out to his horse. "There is one thing that concerns me," he said, "and that is your involvement with the abolitionists. I agree with what you are doing and would assist in the effort if I didn't have a family to worry about."

"We will be too busy establishing our homesteads for me to continue my work with the Underground Railroad. You have my word, Jorgen, I will never bring trouble to your door." Karl extended his hand, and the two men shook to seal Karl's promise.

★ ★ ★

It took only one more late night session to work out the details with Karl Pierson, for in the end, the family decided to throw their lot in with him. "There are more reasons to join with him than there are to go it alone," said Marta, "and I think he is someone we can all live with."

Elen said she trusted his judgment regarding the land. "He seems to have traveled extensively in Illinois and Wisconsin looking for good land at the best price."

Jorgen continued to work in Kendall, eager to have the extra money now that the promise of buying his own land was near. Karl was so sure that Jorgen would like the land that he told Jorgen not to pay him until he could see what he was buying. That finalized the deal for everyone.

The family began their final preparations. They sold the baby's cot, the bed Jorgen had made for Andrew, and the wagon that Andrew had purchased. They would continue their travel with what could be fit into their assortment of trunks and chests.

"We won't have to tote large quantities of food. Plenty

is available along the way at a reasonable cost." Karl assured the women. "A small hamper with some essentials is all we'll need to see us through."

Elen looked sideways at him. He was treading on her territory. Did he really know what a family's needs were? She fretted about it but eventually took his advice seeing as the many things they had accumulated in Kendall could now be packed in the food chest.

The clothing trunks, which had been large enough when they left Bergen, were now crammed and overflowing due to Mary's and Attie's clothing. Mary's suitcase only just made it to Kendall before it had fallen to pieces.

When they closed the last trunk Marta said, "I don't think we have room for even one more handkerchief."

★ ★ ★

Jorgen rode out to Artemis's house three days before leaving to ask him to drive them to Holley to catch the canal boat.

"I wish we could take the horse with us," Jorgen said. "But since we can't, I'd like you to have him. You and your wife were our first friends here, and I know that Andrew would want you to have his horse."

Communication between the two men was a mixture of Norwegian, English, and gestures, but from the first time they met, bridging the language gap had been no obstacle to their friendship.

The family attended church service the day before their departure and was surprised by how difficult it was to say goodbye to the people of Kendall. As sad as it was to say farewell to their neighbors, parting with Andrew, later that day, was heartbreaking. Jorgen stood at the foot of the grave and for a fleeting moment had the insane idea that he should dig up his brother and rebury him in Wisconsin.

"How do you stand it?" he murmured to Elen who stood

next to him. "Knowing there's no one there to visit him?" Jorgen was referring to her late husband.

"The dead don't need visitors. What they need are thoughts and prayers." she whispered back. They stood silently for another minute before she continued. "He will be with you, his memory will be alive whenever you think about him and speak his name. That way, even Attie will remember him."

★ ★ ★

Artemis's wagon clattered into the yard the morning of their departure. He had picked up Karl on the way, and the two men yelled out cheery greetings as the wagon came to a stop near the crates and chests that Jorgen had piled outside the front door.

Marta sat on one of the chests, holding Attie so that she could look out into the yard. She had been fussy all morning and Marta thought being outdoors would provide a diversion for the baby. She worried that Attie might be coming down with something, but the child's disposition brightened and she babbled with excitement as the horse and wagon drew near.

"We've all been so busy, I guess you just wanted someone to pay a little attention to you." Relieved that the child seemed well after all, Marta kissed the top of Attie's head and waved to the men.

Jorgen came around the side of the house leading Venn. "The wagon will be crowded. I thought you might like to ride him to the dock," Jorgen said, handing the reins to Karl. "Then, he's all yours," he said to Artemis.

Jorgen sensed that Artemis had mixed feelings about accepting the horse. It was a beautiful animal, stronger and healthier looking than the old swaybacked mare that was attached to the wagon.

"You don't need to worry," said Jorgen. "I told the sheriff and several others in town that I intended to give the horse to you."

Artemis smiled, his gratitude obvious. "I'll take good care of him, and if you return, he will be yours again."

The two shook hands, then the men began to pack the baggage into the wagon.

Elen came out of the house and stood next to her daughter. "Mary doesn't want to leave," she said.

"Poor thing," Marta replied. "I think this is the first real home she's known and she's made some friends here. We talked about it yesterday, and I tried to reassure her that our next house will be just as nice and she'll make new friends in Wisconsin. Let's give her a few more minutes. I think she'll be all right."

When the last crate was placed in the wagon, a stony-faced Mary came out and climbed into the back of the wagon. "May I take Attie?" she said, reaching out to take the baby. Mary's eyes were fastened on the house until it disappeared when the wagon rounded a curve. Then, she hugged Attie to her chest and stifled a sob.

★ ★ ★

The Great Lakes steamer out of Buffalo was just as Karl had described, roomier and newer than the steamer they had taken out of New York City.

"It's a relief to be off that canal," said Marta.

It was a statement of fact made to no one in particular, and the others nodded or merely grunted in agreement. They stood at the rail watching the city of Buffalo recede in the distance as the boat glided effortlessly through the waters of Lake Erie. "Is it always this calm?" she asked, turning to Karl.

"Hardly," he replied. "When storms occur, especially in late fall, these lakes can be treacherous. Spring and summer are much safer for travel.

"She's finally asleep," Jorgen whispered over the limp,

little, body cradled in his arms.

The last miles on the canal had dragged on and on and were noisier than usual. Attie had not napped at all that day and had grown fussier by the hour. It was, therefore, a relief to all of them that she had finally given in to slumber. Evening was coming on and they would all be glad for a quiet dinner and a good night's rest.

Jorgen and Karl had been forced to sit up the previous night. All cots in the men's section of the canal boat had been taken by passengers who had boarded the boat on stops before Holley. The women and Mary had taken turns sharing the one available cot in the women's section. Attie slept fitfully, waking each time the women changed places.

The sun hadn't even risen when they were all awakened, earlier that day, by the trill of whistles, followed by the irritating screech of lock gates as they slowly swung open. A sixty-foot difference in elevation necessitated a series of five locks to raise or lower boats passing through. Unlike previous locks they had passed through, these were wide enough to accommodate boats going in opposite directions. As the boats bumped into one another and into the pier, workers from opposing boats shouted instructions and traded insults with one another all of which added to the noise and commotion. This kept everyone, including Attie, from further sleep and resulted in headaches and short tempers among the passengers.

When the last lock had been cleared, Jorgen suggested that they all go topside. Marta worried that it might be too dangerous for the baby, but Jorgen insisted that she would be safe with him. "We could all use some fresh air, including her, and it might help her to fall asleep," That was the argument that won Marta over. She was weary of Attie's fussiness, and despite the fact that they had all taken turns trying to soothe the baby, her fretfulness played most heavily on Marta.

Jorgen's idea didn't work out as he had planned. No

sooner had they situated themselves on the deck than the boat entered a section of the canal called the Deep Cut. The boat traveled between walls, in some places more than twenty feet high that had been cut out of solid rock. They were all amazed to learn that the workers had used little more than pickaxes to accomplish this feat. People crowded on deck to see this engineering marvel that continued for two miles. Attie fidgeted and squirmed in Jorgen's arms to watch the comings and goings of all the sightseers. Their chatter and laughter proved too stimulating to the child to make napping possible.

★ ★ ★

Jorgen's last entry had been made just before Jul, the winter holiday. It seemed so long ago. His grief was still too fresh to read that happy account, so he skipped over those pages to the first blank page. This was the perfect time to get caught up in his journal. The others were all napping or relaxing, and they weren't due to reach their port for several hours.

He started with the most recent events, writing a few lines about the Great Lakes part of the journey. "The lakes," he noted, "are surrounded by dense forests and remind me of home. Our travel on them has been uneventful, but we will be glad to be on land again."

He wrote about meeting Karl Pierson and the land agreement they had struck.

Then, he heaved a sigh. *The next part will not be easy,* he thought as he began to write about Andrew's death. He described the circumstances of the accident and then related his recent dreams about his brother.

"Many nights I dream about Andrew. It is usually the same dream. He and I are in Pappa's barn arguing about when we should leave Norway.

"'We have to go now,' I tell him in the dream.

"'Nei,' he responds, 'It's too soon; I'm not ready.'"

"I walk to the door, 'I'm leaving,' I call over my shoulder. I turn when I reach the door to face him. I start to say, 'Come with me.' That's when I realize that he's an old man, older even than Bestefar, and I know that he will never come with me."

Jorgen closed his journal. He was surprised to discover a sense of peace; he felt freer than he had in months. He gathered up his writing materials. They would be arriving in Sheboygan shortly and he was eager to join the others at the rail.

★ ★ ★

"We're there," Mary crowed. "Our trip is over."

"Well, almost," said Karl. "We still have three days of travel left."

"But we're in Wisconsin," Mary continued, her optimism unchecked, "the long part is over."

"It has been a long journey," agreed Elen. "It seems a lifetime ago since we left Norway." She reached for Mary, drew her close, and said, "I am so happy that you are with us."

Jorgen wrapped his arms around Marta and Attie. "I can't wait to build you a home," he said, kissing each of them before releasing them.

Karl observed his happy travel companions. "I think I need a wife," he said. He put on a sad face then brightened when a thought popped into his head. "Mrs. Aksdal, do you have another daughter?"

Elen laughed. "I can't help you, Mr. Pierson, but Jorgen has sisters."

"Hmm," Karl said. He looked at Jorgen expectantly until they all laughed.

A ship's horn sounded nearby, and the group turned to watch the activity that was beginning to surround their steamer.

Although smaller than other harbors they had sailed into, Sheboygan, Wisconsin was, nonetheless, a busy place with barks, brigs, and large two-and three-masted schooners all competing for position to approach or leave the port.

Once on shore, Karl told a wagon driver where to deliver their baggage and the group set out on foot for the short walk to where they would spend the night.

Because of their experience with thieves and other unsavory characters in the larger ports, Mary worried that their baggage might not be safe. She said as much to Jorgen, and he assured her that Karl knew the people in Wisconsin and said they could be trusted.

Satisfied, Mary relaxed and looked around at the bustling, small town.

"That doesn't look like English, and I know it is not Norwegian," Mary pointed to signs on a store. Her ability to read both languages had advanced quickly under Elen and Marta's tutelage.

"It's German," said Karl. "Not many of our people have settled in this town, it's mostly Germans and some Dutch."

Karl led the way to a large, dazzlingly white frame house where a pleasant looking German woman greeted them at the door. Jorgen had insisted on carrying Attie, and he trailed behind the others. He couldn't help but notice the looks of approval that passed between Marta and Elen as they surveyed the house. He was pleased for them; they deserved a night of comfort. Although it proved more comfortable than the canal boats, the overheated and noisy steamer was not conducive to sleep.

Jorgen and Karl left the women sipping tea on the large porch that wrapped around two sides of the house. Steam rose from two pies recently placed on the window ledge directly behind where Marta sat, and the aroma of fresh bread assailed Jorgen's nostrils as he and Karl waved from the stairs. One short trip to the stagecoach office and then he hoped to spend some time in the empty chair next to Marta.

They returned an hour later to join the women. The pies had disappeared off the ledge, but a faint reminder of baked bread still wafted in the air.

"We had a choice," said Jorgen. "There is room for us both tomorrow and the day after. Karl wondered if you would like to rest up here an extra day. He says the next two days' journey is tiresome."

"I'd like to keep going," Marta said. "Attie is healthy and all I need is one good night's sleep. We're so close to seeing our land. I just want to get there."

"I think we should take advantage of this good weather and I'm anxious to plant a garden," added Elen.

"And build our house," said Mary.

Karl shook his head. He smiled as he addressed the women. "I knew this was a hardy group when I asked you to join me. I underestimated, however, your energy and determination."

"I don't know about that," Marta said, "But we are ready to put down roots."

Jorgen pulled a voucher out of his pocket dated for the next day and waved it at Karl.

"What did I tell you," he said. He knew the truth of what Karl had just come to realize. Over the many months they had traveled together, his wife, her mother, and the orphaned child had impressed him time and again with their ability to adapt to any situation. He never had reason to question their resilience and understood their impatience, now, to reach the end of the journey.

Sixteen

June 1851

It took a while to secure all the baggage on top of the stagecoach and the driver grumbled in German throughout the whole process. One of the chests fell to the ground before it was secured and a large crack appeared down one side. Fortunately, the chest didn't split open. Jorgen hoped it would remain intact until they reached their final destination.

Three male passengers were already in the coach when Marta climbed aboard and Jorgen handed Attie to her. Two of the men looked at the baby and quickly offered to ride up front with the driver. The third man had a window seat on the forward facing bench. He sighed loudly and with a great show of irritation, he moved his leather valise from the seat next to him onto his lap to make room for Elen. Jorgen suggested that Marta ride facing forward, so she moved, with Attie, and sat next to her mother. Mary sat facing the stranger. Karl was next to her, and Jorgen sat across from Marta.

The stranger sat with his eyes closed, opening them only to glare at anyone who dared say anything. In the silence that followed, Attie fell asleep. Before long, the stranger nodded off and began to snore. The sound was most peculiar. Mary looked across at Marta and Elen and let out a small giggle.

"Shh," Marta warned with a grin. She cocked her head toward the stranger and made a face as the snoring grew louder.

Mary put her hand to her mouth to stifle another giggle but couldn't control the snort that resulted from her efforts. That, of course, caused her giggle even more. Karl was soon laughing silently, his body shaking with the effort to keep quiet. Jorgen elbowed him in the ribs, but he, too, was fighting back laughter, as were Elen and Marta.

The harder Mary tried, the worse it got until she could no longer contain her mirth. Laughter burst from her like the sudden crow of a rooster at dawn. That woke up Attie, who upon seeing Mary's hilarity, began to clap her hands and squeal with shared glee.

The commotion woke the stranger, who demanded to know what it was all about. The Norwegians, pretending to not understand English, ignored the man, and once their laughter was spent, began talking to one another in their own language.

"Why is this ride not as bumpy as a wagon?" Marta wanted to know. Her attention had been focused on Attie when she climbed aboard, and she had not noticed the leather straps that supported the body of the coach.

Karl explained how the straps acted as braces and kept the coach from lurching when the wheels hit holes or bumps in the road.

"The padded benches help, too," said Elen.

"How far are we going?" asked Mary.

"We're going twenty miles to Greenbush today," said Jorgen, "and tomorrow we'll continue on to Fond du Lac, that's another twenty miles. The day after that, we'll take a short steamer trip to Oshkosh."

"Why can't we go straight through to Fond du Lac today?" said Marta. "Forty miles doesn't seem that far."

"Especially since we've got four horses pulling this thing," added Mary.

"It's the road," said Karl. "Construction has begun on a new plank road, but not much has been completed yet. This rutted, dirt road becomes little more than a trail the farther we go. But you're right about the horses, Mary. On a good road, a stagecoach can travel sixty miles in one day."

"And just like the horses on the canal, stagecoach horses are usually changed several times a day," added Jorgen.

When his repeated glares during the others'

conversation brought no results, the stranger reached into one of the deep pockets of his frock coat and produced a cigar, which he promptly stuck in his mouth.

"Nei," said Jorgen pointing to the women and baby Attie. "No smoke, please."

The stranger glowered at Jorgen and lit the cigar. He puffed on it a couple of times, drew in a mouthful of smoke, and blew it in Jorgen's direction.

"No smoking," said Karl, waving the smoke away from his face.

The man smirked at Karl and continued puffing on the cigar.

Nothing more was said, the man continued to smoke and conditions inside the coach, even though the windows were down as far as they would go, grew more and more offensive.

The wagon slowed, then suddenly came to a complete stop. The driver's face, now florid with anger, appeared at the stranger's window. He pulled open the door and when he spied the cigar, ordered the man out.

"You know the rules, Kohler, they haven't changed since the last time you rode with me. I've a mind to put you off and make you walk."

The two men scowled at each other, silently daring the other to take action. The man threw the cigar to the ground and smashed it with the toe of his boot. "It's a damn stupid rule," he said in defiance.

"And that's against the rules, too. There'll be no cussing on my coach. You're riding up top with me so you don't give these folks any more trouble."

Kohler's replacement eyed Attie with suspicion, but as the baby's behavior continued to be above reproach, the man relaxed and was, in the end, an amiable companion.

"I think we're there," said Mary when the wagon came to stop.

The driver's face again appeared at Mary's window. He

wasn't smiling, but neither did he seem to be angry. This time she noticed his dark brown eyes; they were the exact shade of the velvet trim on Aunt Elen's Sunday bonnet.

"I'll need the help of all you men," he said. "There's a wagon with a broken wheel blocking the road."

Marta, Elen, and Mary waited while the men took stock of the situation, and when they understood that they would be detained for some time, Marta and Elen decided a short walk into the woods was called for. They walked back down the road a short distance and when they started for the trees Mary refused to follow them.

"Come, child," said Elen. "At the pace we're going, it may be hours before we stop again."

Mary shook her head. "There's Indians in there." Indeed, she was sure she had seen some hidden in the trees a mile or so back.

"Nonsense!" said Elen. "Even if they're here, they wouldn't bother with us."

Mary refused to budge.

"Well, then will you hold Attie while I take care of business?" Marta returned to the road and handed the baby to Mary.

"Don't go far," Mary pleaded, "I don't like being here by myself." She turned her attention to Attie, not daring to look into the woods. She was sure if she did, she would see an Indian behind every tree. She was grateful for Marta's quick return and again repeated her claim that she had seen Indians just a short distance before they had been forced to stop.

The women returned to the coach and waited while several minutes stretched into more than an hour. The wagon could not have found a worse place for a breakdown. The wheel had collapsed while navigating a sharp bend in the tree-lined road, and the wagon had tipped, spilling its contents. A pile of coal straddled the width of the narrow road. The coal was headed for the blacksmith shop in

Greenbush, which the driver said was two miles down the road.

There was nothing to be done to fix the wheel, and it took the combined effort of all the men to right the wagon, maneuver it out of the way, and deal with the mound of coal.

Finally, the stage was on its way. The wagon's owner rode his horse to Greenbush, arriving there shortly after the stage. He would have to purchase a new wheel and return the next day to fix his wagon.

The village of Greenbush was a fast growing community. Originally, it was just a staging area for coaches heading to Fond du Lac and points farther west, but it now boasted several other shops besides the wagon shop. It had a sawmill, a small schoolhouse, and Wades Inn, the centerpiece of the town. It was a handsome looking, three-story building less than two years old and the largest structure in the village.

What mattered to the travelers, though, were the comfortable beds and the accommodating nature of the Wades. "Beer never tasted better," declared Jorgen that night at dinner.

The next day started out sunny, but by mid-afternoon the weather had stopped cooperating with travel plans. Intermittent showers, which at first were a nuisance but tolerable, escalated into a steady, soaking rain, and finally into a blinding downpour. There was nowhere to shelter along the road, so the stage driver urged the horses forward through mud many inches deep. To stop would prove disastrous; the stagecoach would mire in the thick muck. The driver and riders up front huddled under protective pieces of canvas attempting to stay dry.

The windows had to be closed to keep out the blowing rain, and the interior of the coach became hot and stuffy. Attie was beside herself. Two days of confinement her movements restricted were more than the active baby could tolerate. She wriggled and kicked and cried and made life miserable for all. Marta finally gave up trying to amuse her and just let her cry. After a very long hour, she eventually cried herself to sleep.

The stagecoach arrived in Fond du Lac in the early evening and Karl proceeded to a small inn. Rooms were available, however, the stagecoach passengers were too late for dinner. Elen rummaged in one of the food hampers and discovered enough bread and cheese for each to have a small snack. "It's better than going to bed hungry," Karl said as he chewed thoughtfully on a tough piece of crust.

The rain continued all the next day, making travel impossible. They were able to continue their stay at the inn, and actually welcomed the opportunity to rest and dry out their damp clothing and the quilts that had gotten wet when rain leaked through the cracked chest.

Karl walked outside several times to frown at clouds that seemed to hold endless amounts of water.

"I suspect he's anxious to see his land again," commented Jorgen when he looked out and saw Karl standing once more in the rain.

After a good night's sleep, Attie was a bundle of energy. Marta put her down on the floor and the little one delighted in the freedom to move about on her own. She scooted around on hands and knees and grinned impishly when she managed to pull herself up and stand on wobbly legs.

"What a big girl you are" Jorgen said, snatching her up and swooping her into the air. She giggled and laughed, showing off her eight small teeth and the dimple in her right cheek. It was one of those moments that Jorgen would remember, years later.

The mood around the dinner table that night was relaxed. Like a mother who gives birth and soon forgets the pain associated with the blessed event, the promise the next day held for each of them, the start of their new lives, was already working to dim the memories of the hardships and sorrows of the long journey. Their optimistic conversation bounced from topic to topic as they talked about Oshkosh, the crops they planned to grow, establishing a homestead, their future. Even Karl managed to put aside his worry and imagined with the others the big house, fat cows, lush gardens, and bountiful fields that now seemed within reach.

Mary was quiet while this conversation took place. Her life experience left her bereft of ideas that enable one to speculate on the future. She seemed lost.

"Jorgen," she said, at last, "Would you please read some of your letters to us? You haven't done that in a long time."

"Yes," said Karl, "Mary's told me about the letters you get from home. I'm not good at writing letters, nor is anyone in my family, so I don't get any. I'd love to hear yours."

Jorgen was hesitant, but one glance at Mary and Karl's expectant faces and he couldn't refuse their request.

He dug the letters out of one of the chests and handed them to Marta, saying, "Would you mind? You're a much better reader than I am."

Most of the letters had been written by Mor and Karine, and as Marta read them, it was as if his mother and sister were right there talking to all of them. What also struck him, now, was the humor in Karine's writing. How had he missed that? Was Marta adding things that hadn't been there before?

Marta paused to laugh with everyone after reading Karine's description of a picnic she'd attended with a beau. It had been a disaster, but was funny in the telling.

"Your sister sounds good-humored," said Karl. "I hope she doesn't see that fellow again."

"Maybe you should write to her and tell her," said Jorgen, who was still laughing, "although my sister is quite sensible and tends to think for herself."

"Maybe I will," said Karl, "do you think she'd write back to me?"

He looked so serious that Jorgen stopped laughing and

gave Karl a straight answer. "You won't know till you try," he said.

★ ★ ★

It stopped raining some time during the night, and when Jorgen awoke towards morning, Marta was already sitting up in bed, nursing Attie.

"Good morning, early birds, you're both up before the sun."

"Good morning, my love," Marta said, and she leaned over to place a kiss on his lips. "It looks as though we might get an early start today. Mor and Mary have already gone down to breakfast, and Karl must be outside. I heard his voice through the open window minutes ago."

The rooster behind the inn was just beginning to crow when the eager party left the inn for the short trip by wagon to the Fond du Lac harbor. They planned to take the steamer, Manchester, to Oshkosh. Karl wasn't sure how long it would take. "Depends on how many stops we make along the way, but we should reach Oshkosh no later than midday."

They found seats on the steamer, but no one could sit for long. The prospect of their long journey's end made them all restless and impatient to reach the final destination. Jorgen, Marta, Elen, and Mary took turns at the rail, scanning the horizon for their first glimpse of Oshkosh.

Normally a calm individual, with each passing mile, Karl's anxiety grew. Was the property he owned really as good as he remembered? In his desire to have a partner, had he exaggerated its beauty and possibilities? What would he do if Jorgen found the land unacceptable for some reason that he had not taken into account?

His confidence continued to waver the closer they got to Oshkosh. The boat traveled close enough to shore that Karl noticed the recent rains had left the land between Sheboygan and Fond du Lac saturated. They passed vast areas of flooded marshland and rain-swollen rivers and creeks.

Yesterday's deluge could only have made things worse, Karl fretted. He knew a stream crossed his property. It came out of the forest on the northwest portion of his land and ran southeast where it emptied into a river about one mile south of his property. He had viewed the land and the stream in the fall, the dry season. How much had the small trickle of water increased with all the recent rain? Was the rest of his land on high ground? Karl wasn't sure. He wanted to share his fear with the others, but what was the point?

Karl took a deep breath, exhaled slowly. *There's no point in worrying,* he told himself, *they'd all find out soon enough.* For now, he allowed himself to be buoyed by the optimism and excitement of his travel companions.

Looking out over the sparkling waters of Lake Winnebago, Marta and Mary speculated about the town that would be their new home.

"Why don't we ask Karl?" Marta said.

"Ask Karl what?" he responded when he heard his name mentioned.

"We were just wondering about Oshkosh,"said Mary. "Did you see many children when you were there? And a school?"

"And stores and a church?" added Marta.

"I've only been there the one time, when I went to see the land I bought. I stayed in the town for the few days it took to make the sale official. It is small, about the size of Kendall. But as Kendall loses people to settlements in Illinois and other places out west, Oshkosh is growing. I saw men working on several new buildings."

"A school?" Mary asked again. "Did you see a school?"

"I did not," Karl admitted. "But I wasn't looking for one. The town is large enough that I'm sure there is a school. Maybe even more than one school.

"As for churches and stores, I was there over a weekend and did attend Sunday service at a Lutheran church. I think I saw some other steeples in the area. You'll see for yourself when we arrive, there is every kind of shop that Kendall has—and more. I don't think any of you will be disappointed in what Oshkosh has to offer."

Satisfied that she would be able to attend school, Mary turned her attention to another fear that friends in Kendall had instilled in her.

"I hear that there are lots of Indians in Wisconsin," she began, cautiously. "I'm sure I saw some in the trees two days ago."

"You saw Indians in Kendall when they came into town to trade their pelts at the general store," Marta said, "I imagine they are no different in Wisconsin."

"There are a few in town," said Karl, "They go about their business like anyone else, but most have moved farther north to the reservations that the government has set aside for their use."

"My friend Anders told me that the Indians in Wisconsin are not the same as the ones in New York. He said that they are wild and dangerous," Mary said.

"This boy, Anders, is he the same Anders as my cousin's son?"

"Yes," Marta replied. "I believe he is."

"I think my cousin's imagination is the wild thing," said Karl. "He's never been to Wisconsin, yet he fills the minds of his children with all sorts of stories that are not true."

"Mary," Karl leaned down so that he was eye level with the girl. "You have my word on this. The Indians in Wisconsin are friendly. You must forget what Anders told you about them. Sometimes people are fearful of those who live differently than they do. The Winnebago Indians were and are friends to the settlers. Unfortunately for them, their reward for friendship with their white neighbors was the disease they caught from us. Nearly one-fourth of their tribe was wiped out by smallpox about fifteen years ago."

"Like all the people who got sick and died when we

came across the ocean," Mary added.

"Something like that," said Karl.

Jorgen approached the three at the rail. He was holding Attie who was starting to fuss. "I think she's hungry," he said, and handed her to Marta when she reached out for the child.

Marta and Mary left the two men at the rail. They stood there in silence, inches apart, each absorbed in speculation about the other.

Karl has been helpful on the journey from Kendall, Jorgen reflected, *but a good travel companion is not the same as a good homestead partner. He's likable, seems to have no annoying habits, unlike Andrew, but how will he perform as a partner? Is he reliable? Does he really want to be a homesteader or is he merely caught up in the idea? He's traveled a fair amount; will he be content now to stay in one place?*

Jorgen shaded his eyes and looked out across the water. His thoughts had turned to memories of Andrew.

Although Karl was feeling apprehensive about his land, he had no reservations about Jorgen. In his travels, he had seen his share of homestead failures. He was not averse to hard work nor did he give up easily when confronted with difficulties. He was constantly taking Jorgen's measure, and his initial impression of this earnest young man had not changed. He was worthy of Karl's trust; they would have a successful partnership.

A private person, Karl had shared little with Jorgen about his stint, eight years earlier, with a group of fellow Norwegians in Illinois. Although only seventeen at the time, he had done a man's share of the work, pulling his weight against men who were slackers and drifted away at the first sign of hard times. He labored ten hours a day, but fourteen hour days were not unheard of in the rush to build houses, stores, a school, and two churches, the first having burnt to the ground. And all that had been accomplished in less than three years' time. Although he hated the climate and the mosquitoes, he had been determined to make Illinois his home until the love of his life died from pneumonia at the age of eighteen, three months shy of their wedding date.

★ ★ ★

"Seventeen!" Wedged between Karl and Jorgen, who held Attie on his lap, on the front bench of a buckboard, Mary counted each child she saw, her voice rising in pitch with each addition.

"That's wonderful," said Elen, pausing in her own tally. She sat with Marta on the rear bench, both eagerly taking stock of the number and variety of shops they passed as Karl drove down Ferry Street, the main street in Oshkosh.

Since arriving at the port, the group had moved at a feverish pace, so great was their desire to reach "the land." In less than two hours time, they had rented a horse and wagon, deposited their baggage at the Winnebago Inn, and had eaten a quick dinner.

 Both the men had been so preoccupied during the meal that neither remembered what he had just eaten.

Karl had been good at concealing worries that had niggled him for days. He had mastered the art of allowing himself only a short time to dwell on things he could do nothing about, before putting them out of his mind. *We'll soon find out,* he thought, and encouraged the horse to pick up the pace.

Jorgen's confidence in Karl's original description of his land had been complete. He had taken him at his word and had not thought twice about it since. That is, until they steamed into Oshkosh. *This is it,* he thought. *This will be our town.* Unexpectedly, a terrible thought came to mind. *What if I don't like the land?*

Unlike Karl, who had pointed out a silversmith shop the women had missed and was now engaged in helping Mary count children, Jorgen was unable to set aside bothersome thoughts. He sat mute as a stone, untouched by the enthusiasm that swirled around him, until Karl reined in the horse and the buckboard came to a stop.

It was good that Karl hadn't wasted too much time worrying about his land. Although they passed many areas under water, which added to Jorgen's concern, Karl's land was high and dry.

The land being high had another advantage: the view was spectacular. It was possible to see for miles in three directions. The forest on the north side of the land was thick and extensive; one couldn't see beyond it.

Karl drove them around the perimeter of his land, and then suggested they walk along the right side of the stream towards the forest and the high point of the property. That, Karl said, would be their parcel.

"That's very generous," said Jorgen. "I think you are offering me the better half." He could barely conceal his excitement for what he considered to be a perfect farm-site.

"Better perhaps for farming, but I'm more interested in raising cows. I think the other parcel is more suited for that. I'll stay here and talk to the horse," Karl said. His nonchalance was not faked. After seeing the land again, he was more confident than ever in its value, but he wanted to give Jorgen and his family a private opportunity to discuss the purchase of their half of the land.

The group walked in silence for several acres, each waiting for someone, besides Attie, to say something. Her contented babbling had begun the moment Jorgen had hoisted her to his shoulders. When they reached the top of a small hill, Elen stopped and looked expectantly at Jorgen. He knew that if he spoke first, she and Marta would agree to whatever he said. So he waited.

"I think it's a good piece of land," said Elen. Her broad smile was Jorgen's answer.

Mary nodded her head in agreement. "It's so big," she said. The sweeping gesture she made with her arm took in the enormity of the landscape. Then she did something quite unexpected for the usually solemn girl. In a display of exuberance, she ran down the hill, yelling something as she went. To Jorgen, it sounded like, " home, home, this is home." She collapsed at the bottom and lay there with outstretched arms, looking up into the sky.

"And you, Marta, what do you think?" Jorgen held his breath. He had already fallen in love with the land and hoped she had, too.

"Oh Jorgen," she wrapped her arms around him, "Look at this view! We'll be able to see the sun rise and set, right here, every day for the rest of our lives."

Karl saw the hug and interpreting it as a positive sign, ran all the way to where the others stood.

"Good news?" he said.

"Yes, good news," Jorgen said. He lifted Attie from his shoulders and handed her to Marta.

"You won't regret this," said Karl, and the two men shook hands on what they referred to thereafter as the best deal of their lives.

★ ★ ★

Jorgen was a planner and Karl was someone who could get things done. Together, they made an effective team. By the end of that summer, the family was able to move into the small cabin the men had built and out of the tent which the women had insisted upon living in. Jorgen had wanted them to stay at a boarding house in Oshkosh, but Marta and Elen said they couldn't help build the house if they were living in town. He lost the argument and in the end, was amazed at how much work Marta and Elen were capable of doing.

Karl had struck a deal at the sawmill for the framework, studs, rafters, and beams in exchange for logs from their forest. Karl also found two young men, eager for work, to help cut the logs and build the house. With four men working on it, the house went up quickly.

Jorgen checked with other farmers in the area and discovered that winter wheat could be planted during the month of September. So, while Karl dealt with the sawmill deal, Jorgen worked at clearing the land and saw to the purchase of seed and the equipment he would need to plant it.

The women had taken charge of putting in a vegetable garden. This became Mary's favorite chore. She had never seen a proper garden, and she marveled at each day's growth. Weeds didn't stand a chance with her nimble fingers plucking them away from the tender seedlings. Although they had gotten a late start, the women hoped to have fresh beans, peas, and squash by fall. They also planted some greens, including lettuce and spinach. They were familiar with these but had not grown them before.

Unfortunately, it was too late in the year to plant cabbage and potatoes, staples they were familiar with, having depended upon them in Norway. These would have to wait until the following year.

The woman who worked at the general store suggested they try planting pumpkin seeds. "They take about four months to grow," she said, "and should be ready just before the first frost." Although Marta and Elen were unfamiliar with this vegetable, they were willing to try something new. The woman assured them that they were delicious. "You can even bake pumpkin in a pie," she informed them.

"How strange," Elen said when they left the store.

"Sounds terrible," Mary added with a giggle.

"Well, we will see who will be daring enough to try it," said Marta.

"If you bake it, Jorgen will try it. He says you're the best cook ever."

"Thanks, Mary. Jorgen is kind to praise my cooking."

"Well, it's true," said Elen. "You are a good cook. You're actually a much better cook than I am, or ever was, for that matter. I don't think your father ever bragged about my cooking."

"Perhaps not," Marta agreed. "But I heard him say many times that you were better at running his business than he was."

"Well, I guess it just shows that we're all good at something," said Mary. "I'm good at minding babies."

"You certainly are!" Marta agreed emphatically. "But your arms must be getting tired; you've carried her around all morning. Here," she said, reaching out to take Attie. "Let me carry her for a while."

Mary loved to spend time with Attie. She sang to her when she was fussy, held her hand as she learned to walk, and chased after her when she mastered that skill. She took Attie into the garden and told her the names of all the vegetables. Attie's first word was peas. Her second was mamma. Mary was sure it was the baby's attempt to say her name. Whether that was true or not, for a short time, Attie called everyone mamma, including Jorgen.

★ ★ ★

By now, they were all becoming fluent in English. Jorgen and Marta were determined that their children would grow up speaking the language of the country they had adopted. Elen supported that idea. She thought all their countrymen back in Kendall were shortsighted. She wanted to fit into this new country. She didn't want Mary teased at school because she couldn't speak English. Most evenings, even though they were tired from their daily labors, they quizzed each other on English vocabulary. Any visit to town was an occasion to buy the latest edition of the Oshkosh Democrat, which they read and reread until they got their hands on the next edition of the newspaper. Karl had been in America a year longer and had picked up a bit more of the language. Yet, he too, joined in on the lessons, saying he didn't want to fall behind the others.

That first summer the days tended to fly by. Finish one chore, start the next. Go to bed, bone weary, get up the next day and do it all again. The only complaint was lack of time. They all felt they could use two or three more hours every day.

They were building a life, rushing to get as much done before the first winter set in. Once the house became habitable, they went to work on enclosures for the farm equipment and the animals they had acquired; a chicken coop for the twelve hens and two roosters, and a shed for the three horses, a mule, and two cows. Later in the fall, they planned to dig a root cellar and fence in areas for a corral and pigpen. Pigs, they had all decided, would be the next animal purchase.

In spite of the fatigue brought on by daily physical labor, there were nights when sleep didn't come easily to Jorgen. Those were the nights when images of Andrew haunted his thoughts. He would get up the next morning, unrefreshed, morose, engulfed in a sadness he didn't understand and couldn't explain. When these moods came over him, the only respite he found was in hard physical labor. It was as if grief seeped out of his body like sweat. Sometimes, when he finished a job he found himself thinking...*There, Andrew, how does that look?* Or, searching for a solution to a problem...*What should I do, Andrew?*

Gradually, as the days of summer wound down, the images faded. He found that he could rely on Karl's experience and turned to him more and more for advice. But in mid September, when they planted their first wheat crop, Andrew was again heavy on Jorgen's mind. When the last seeds were sown, Jorgen stood at the edge of the field. He bent down and scooped up a handful of the rich soil. He stood, and as the dirt filtered through his hand, he thought of his brother. "We did it, Andrew," he said, under his breath, "We finally did it." Caught up in the moment, he raised his head and shouted across the field. "Andrew! We did it!"

Seventeen

1856
(5 years later)

"They're here! They're here!" Attie yelled from her perch atop the front porch railing.

No one within earshot paid any attention to the child's enthusiastic announcement. She had deceived them too many times in the preceding days when she had mistaken dust blowing in the road for a wagon or thought she had seen what her eager, but impatient eyes wanted to see. Her mother did, however, call out to her, "Attie, if you're standing on the railing, please get down. You know what your father said."

She did remember and knew she was being naughty, but how else could she see what was causing that cloud of dust in the distance? She had climbed up carefully and tried her best to stand still so as not to loosen the rail her father had fixed earlier that week. "Next time you break it, you fix it," he had said with a wink. She knew he didn't mean that, but still, his look had said 'do not break it again.' She had stayed away from the railing for three whole days, and now that they had finally arrived, she told herself she wouldn't need to climb on it ever again.

"But, Mamma, they really are here," Attie protested. She landed with a thud on the porch then scampered down the steps.

A few minutes later, when Marta heard a wagon pull into the yard, she quickly brushed the flour from her hands. "Come Lise," she said to the two-year-old who was busy shaping small bits of dough to bake alongside the bread her mother had just readied for the oven. "Let's go greet your aunt and uncle."

Anticipation had gripped the household for days, so it was no surprise that they all converged in the yard as the wagon lurched to a stop. Elen and Mary emerged from behind the house where they had been weeding the garden, and Jorgen came at a trot across the yard. The hens clucked noisily as they scuttled out of his way. He had been working on repairs to the chicken coop; an attempt to thwart a scraggly looking fox that prowled the premises nightly and took advantage of any opening large enough for its skinny body to pass through.

Karl arrived on horseback, right behind the wagon. He had been checking the wheat fields for signs of leaf rust and locust damage when the wagon passed on the road that ran alongside the field. He caught enough of a glimpse of one of the passengers to recognize him. *He looks so much like Andrew,* Karl marveled, and he spurred his horse to catch up with the wagon.

Karl had as much reason to be excited as the others. He had been exchanging letters with the other passenger in the wagon for almost four years, and he finally convinced her to visit. He had proposed to her several months ago, and although she hadn't said yes, she also hadn't turned down his offer. He knew this was a trial period for both of them, but he was convinced that, in the end, they would get married. Karl was an optimist. He liked Jorgen, and remembered Andrew as a good-natured, likable fellow. *Could their sister be any different?* His correspondence to her had been cordial, at first, but a friendship had blossomed and her letters had become the highlight of his life.

There was much waving and shouted greetings, but when the travelers were finally on the ground, emotions took charge and a stunned silence enveloped the group. Exhaustion was etched on the faces of the newcomers and their bodies sagged with the relief of reaching their final destination. Jorgen's huge grin belied the fact that a lump had formed in his throat. The sight of his brother and sister brought back the tug of home, but even more than that, was the need to convince himself that he was not staring into the eyes of his dead brother. He shook his head in disbelief that they were really standing beside him. Marta's thoughts were similar to Jorgen's and she too was speechless. Lise had taken refuge behind her mother and even Attie, not given to shyness, was suddenly quiet. She had been on the lookout for her aunt and uncle for days and now that they had finally arrived, she scrutinized them, looking repeatedly from one to the other. There was something very familiar about their faces, but their clothing looked strange.

Mary was the first one to say anything. As soon as the young man looked in her direction, she blurted what the others would not say, "You look exactly like Andrew."

"Yes," Elen said, anxious to get this first meeting off to a positive start, "Such a good looking family, your resemblance to one another is striking." There would be plenty of time to talk about Andrew later, this time, now, was about beginnings, and it belonged to Niels and Karine.

She and Marta reached out to Karine at the same time for a three-way hug while Jorgen stood face to face with Niels, his hands on his brother's shoulders. Then, everyone began talking at the same time.

"I can't believe my little brother has caught up to me," Jorgen said. He gave his brother's shoulders a playful shake.

"Actually, Jorgen, your little brother is now your big brother," said Karl, laughing. After dismounting, he had come up to them and extended his hand to Niels. Jorgen made the introduction over the delighted, and growing louder by the second, exclamations of the three women.

"You haven't changed!"

"We're so glad you're finally here!"

"Your hair is so much longer!"

"Motherhood becomes you!"

"You must be hungry!"

Karine then noticed Mary and the two little girls staring and took a step back to see them better.

Mary was holding Lise. She had picked up the

youngster when Lise had become agitated with the commotion that ensued when the strangers alighted the wagon. Suddenly all the grownups were hugging each other, and everyone was talking at the same time. Mary was happy to have something to hold on to. She was feeling nervous about this meeting, wondering if Jorgen's sister would like her or treat her as an outsider.

Attie stood by Mary's side, silently watching the animated greetings, fascinated by her father's behavior. He was always quick to smile at her and sometimes laughed when she said or did something he thought was funny, but she had never seen him act this excited or heard such hearty laughter. She felt sad, and the more he laughed, the worse she felt. She stared at him so intently that she was unaware that someone had come and was crouched down next to her until she heard a quiet voice say, "You must be Attie."

Before Attie could tear her eyes from her father, he looked her way and stopped, mid-sentence to exclaim loudly, "Karine, I see you've discovered our children," he paused, then added, "the family treasure." His eyes met Attie's and his broad smile seemed to grow even larger than before. Attie's sadness vanished with her father's words, and she turned to look into the face of the pretty lady, to meet her Aunt Karine.

"I'm Attie. I'm glad you came 'cause I got a new bed."

"And I'm your Aunt Karine. I'm glad I came and I'm happy to hear you got a new bed."

Karine stood and extended her hand. "You must be Mary," she said, addressing the tall young woman. "Jorgen has written about you often, I'm so pleased that we finally get to meet."

Mary took Karine's hand in hers while she adjusted Lise to her hip. In spite of her jittery nerves, she managed to say, "Pleased to meet you." Then thought to add, "Jorgen reads all the letters that you and the rest of the family send. I feel like I know everyone in his family."

"It's your family, too," said Karine. "We all think of you as part of the family."

Mary blushed. She felt like she had passed some sort of test and was really and truly a part of this wonderful family. For a brief moment, she buried her face in Lise's curls to hide the huge grin of relief and happiness, then spoke to the little girl. "Can you say hello to Aunt Karine?"

Lise looked briefly at Karine, then looked down at the ground and shook her head.

"She just needs to get to know you," said Mary putting the child down so that she could run to her mother.

Marta scooped up the little one. "I think it's time we went inside. I've got bread that needs to go into the oven, and the baby should be waking up soon.

Attie reached for Karine's hand. "I'll show you where you're sleeping. It used to be my room but now it's yours, and then you can see my new bed."

★ ★ ★

As they walked to the house, Marta looked it over like she was seeing it for the first time. Changes had happened so gradually over the years that she had taken them for granted. Their simple log house had grown to twice its original size. The great room with its spacious loft was the only part left unchanged. The one small side room, where Karl had stayed before his house was built, had been rebuilt twice as large and was now Elen's domain. That had been the first major change. Jorgen had gone to great lengths to make the room as comfortable as possible and to give her a quiet spot to retreat to when family life became overwhelming. He appreciated the fact that her financial help had greatly assisted in the establishment of this homestead. She generously had turned over all her money when Jorgen sent Andrew's savings home to his parents. Although she didn't seek refuge very often, Elen was grateful for the comfortable chair in front of her own fireplace and a door she could close behind her.

The second and larger addition was finished after Lise was born. It consisted of two rooms. A short hallway opened on the left into the kitchen. It had been built over the root cellar. Although there was still a cellar door outside, a trap door in the corner of the kitchen opened to stairs, which also lead down to it. This feature, along with a pipe that brought running water into the kitchen, had made Marta almost giddy with joy.

The second room was Marta and Jorgen's bedroom. This new room had a spacious alcove, which proved large enough for two small cots. Lise and three-month-old John now shared that space.

"My room is up there," Attie said, pointing to the loft as she led Karine into the house. "And yours is too." There were two rooms in the loft. Karine would be in the one that had belonged to Marta and Jorgen. Mary and Attie shared the other one.

Attie ran to the ladder, "C'mon," she said, "I'll show you my new bed."

"Let's give Aunt Karine a chance to rest," said Marta. "She's had a long trip."

Karine stood in the middle of the great room and looked around her. "This is lovely," she said, "It reminds me of home."

"The fireplace is not is big as the one Bestefar built, but I did have his in mind when we constructed ours," said Jorgen

"As soon as I get rid of this bread mess, I'll get us all a snack," said Marta. "Please, sit down and tell us about your journey."

"We'll be back for that snack in a little while," said Jorgen. "I thought I would give Niels a short tour while it's still light out. "

He took a couple of biscuits off the table and handed them to Niels, "In case you're hungry," he said, then Karl and the two brothers left. Marta could hear them talking crops before their feet hit the front walk.

"It will be light out for several more hours," Marta laughed. "Jorgen couldn't wait another second."

Elen took the bread that Marta had been working on and put it in the oven while Marta cleaned up the bits of dough and flour that stuck to the table.

An infant's cry caused Marta to straighten up from the table and look in the direction from which the sound came as if she were looking through the great room wall.

"I'll get him," said Mary.

"I swear, " said Marta, when Mary had left the room, "I don't know what I would do without that girl."

"Me, too," said Attie.

"Well then," said Karine, patting Attie on the head as she spoke, "you're both very lucky that she's here."

Marta finished washing her hands just as Mary came back with the baby. Mary nuzzled the infant's head and spoke in a soothing manner that had quieted his cries. She handed him to Marta, and said, "I think he needs you, I'll take care of the snack."

"May I hold him for a moment?" said Karine. "It's been a long time since I've been around one so small...Oh isn't he precious!" she exclaimed when Marta placed him in her arms.

John remained precious for just ten seconds, then he let out a yelp followed by angry sounding cries.

" He's hungry," Marta laughed. "It's not you."

Mary poured coffee and put some butter out for the biscuits. When Attie had finished her snack, she ran out the door to join the men. She had little patience for adult conversation unless it involved her. Lise had gotten down from the table and had climbed into Jorgen's large overstuffed chair. With thumb in mouth, she had fallen asleep.

A quiet moment and a big question hung in the air. Three pairs of eyes latched simultaneously on Karine.

Her face turned red. She was in her late twenties and

couldn't remember the last time she had blushed. She laughed self-consciously.

"Oh, we are being rude," said Elen, apologizing for the three of them.

Marta started to titter, followed by Mary and soon all four of them were giggling like schoolgirls.

"I know you've just met him," said Marta, "but what was your first impression?"

Karine thought for a moment. "Well, he seems as nice as he sounded in his letters, but he sounded taller when he wrote."

There was a pause while the three absorbed this tidbit, then more laughter.

★ ★ ★

When Jorgen, Niels, and Karl finished touring the farm, they stopped in front of the baggage that had been left in the front yard. Jorgen recognized two of the three chests. One was the chest he had made for Karine's birthday years before. The other was the chest that he, Marta, and Elen had carefully packed a few days before they left Bergen. He let out a low whistle when he recognized it.

He picked up one end of the chest, and Niels picked up the other, explaining as he did that Theo had met them at the dock with it in tow. "He gave me some dalers so I could pay porters to carry it for us and told me to be sure it was handled gently. He said you would know what was in it."

"I sure do," Jorgen said, "and I think it will make someone very happy."

They put it in the middle of the great room and Jorgen called Elen over. He didn't have to say anything, she recognized the chest immediately. Her hands flew to her cheeks. "Well look at that," she said. "I never expected to see it again."

"What is it, grandmother? What's in there?" said Attie

"What did she say?" said Karine.

"I'm sorry, Aunt Karine, Mamma said I should use Norwegian when I talk in front of you but I forgot and talked in English. I asked Bestemor to tell me what is in there," Attie said in her best Norwegian.

"What a clever girl you are. I didn't know that you could speak English."

"We all can," said Attie. "We only speak Norwegian when we go to church and when Pappa reads the letters that he get from his Norwegian family."

"It's your family too, silly," said Mary. "It's all your aunts and uncles in Norway and your Bestefar and Bestamor."

"I know some German words, too. I have a friend who talks in German." Attie added, ignoring Mary's comment.

"Well, that'll be enough bragging," said Marta. "Let's see if your Pappa can get these straps off so we can see what's inside."

Elen's hands trembled as she lifted the items carefully out of the chest, unwrapped them, and placed them gently on the table. She commented on a platter she had inherited from her mother and another dish someone had given her for a wedding present.

So many items with so many stories. Jorgen had never seen this sentimental side of Elen. He felt ashamed. He had walked away from the chest that day at the dock and had never thought of it again. *Leave it to Theo,* he thought, *bless him and his thoughtfulness.*

Elen was finally down to the bottom of the chest. When she unwrapped the last thing, she gasped and clutched it to her chest.

"What is it, Mor?" said Marta.

"I forgot this was in there. I thought I lost it somewhere on our trip." Tears welled in her eyes. "Look, Marta!" she said. "It's that nice picture of Johann."

Marta remembered the picture and the circumstances

surrounding it. Her poor father had started on the downward spiral of senility and a photographer in town had taken advantage of him. When her father brought home the picture in its fancy frame, he was so excited to present it to Marta's mother. Marta had been aghast when she had seen the price on the paper wrapper; it had been outrageously expensive. She was angry and wanted to give that photographer a piece of her mind, but Elen had waved her off. Instead, she graciously accepted the picture telling her husband that it was the nicest present she had ever received. And now, all these years later, Marta had to agree.

"Who is that?" said Attie, pointing to the picture.

"That was my Pappa," said Marta. "Johann Aksdal. Baby John is named after him."

★ ★ ★

The family, still adjusting to one newcomer, baby John, was now faced with weaving two more people into the fabric of their lives. This was easier for some, but presented some challenges for all.

For Jorgen, the days following his brother and sister's arrival were bittersweet. He found looking into their faces both balm and bane. Their presence resurrected a host of happy memories, and yet reminded him of all that was now lost to him. His disposition was unpredictable. One day he would appear energized and in good spirits, the next, he was withdrawn and gloomy. Niels recognized this pattern. It was the same way Jorgen had acted, years before, when Andrew had left home. It pained Niels to think that his presence may have triggered Jorgen's distress.

Recalling how music seem to cheer the family in times of stress, like the time he and Jorgen had played when their younger brothers were so sick, Niels unpacked his fiddle one evening and began to tune it.

"Have you learned to play that thing yet?" asked

Jorgen.

Niels playfully tapped Attie on the head with his bow. She sat at his feet staring up into his face with doting eyes. He raised the fiddle to his chin and performed a lively tune, one that had been new to him when he heard played on the steamship.

Attie clapped her hands and shouted out, "Oh, Susanna, don't you cry for me," each time Niels got to that part of the song. Those were the only words in the song she knew, so she made up the rest of the words and sang them with equal confidence.

Jorgen also knew the song. He joined in after retrieving his Hardanger from the top of his wardrobe.

"You're good," said Jorgen when the song was over.

"And you're rusty," laughed Niels. "Let's see if we can fix that." By the time the two put their fiddles away for the night, Jorgen's bow once again controlled the strings of his Hardanger.

"That's the fiddler I remember," said Niels. "Tomorrow night?" he asked.

"We'll see," laughed Jorgen.

"That means no" said Attie, turning to face Niels.

"It meant no when my Pappa used to say it, too" said Niels, exchanging mischievous grins with his niece.

"I think it means it is time for bed," Marta said as she scooped up Lise and carried her off to the bedroom.

The music continued, if not nightly, at least frequently enough to serve as an antidote to Jorgen's darker moods.

★ ★ ★

As for the children, once they were used to Karine, she became just one more caretaker. She was someone to help them get dressed, or bathe, someone to fix them a snack or read them a story, someone to settle their squabbles and soothe their scrapes and hurt feelings.

Attie was quite taken with her uncle. She followed him around chatting nonstop while he did chores, and he had the patience to listen. He even encouraged her with questions and laughed at her silly humor. When he was done working, he would carry her back to the house on his shoulders.

"She'll be off to school in a few weeks," said Jorgen one evening after Attie had gone to bed. "Then you'll have some peace and quiet."

"I don't mind," said Niels. "She reminds me of Ole. He used to follow me around and had about as much to say."

"Strange," said Jorgen, "how some in the family like to talk a lot and some don't." Niels simply nodded in agreement.

★ ★ ★

Not a family member by birth yet very much a part of this one, Mary fell into the less talkative group. There was a time, in her early teens, when she had asked a multitude of questions. Deprived, not only of an education, but also of anyone who would engage her intelligent and inquisitive mind, she had had much to learn. Elen and Marta's patient tutoring, along with five years of formal schooling had made a world of difference for the girl. Now, as a young woman, she had the confidence to be herself: serene, contemplative, and quiet. She discovered that she learned more when she listened to others than when she talked. She was an observer.

She now watched with fascination as a little drama played out between Marta and Karine. To her way of thinking, they were both right and both wrong. *It's so easy to get along with people,* she thought, *all you have to do is watch them. They'll tell you what you need to know.*

Mary idolized Elen and Marta. She thought of them as her mother and sister. Watching Marta nurse her babies always caused her to imagine her own mother loving her like that.

She was pleased that Karine seemed to like her and

considered her part of the family, but she secretly worried that she would lose Attie's affection to this newcomer.

She also had conflicted feelings for Niels. He, too, was popular at the moment with Attie. But, Mary had to acknowledge, she was attracted to him, as well.

★ ★ ★

It was ironic that Elen was the one person in the family with a room to retreat to, for she was the one who needed it the least. Nothing seemed to faze her. Yet, she was quick to offer her room to one of the others when they became stressed. She kept a bag of knitting on a table next to her small fireplace and a slim book of poetry was strategically placed on the arm of the chair where she encouraged others to go and sit for a while.

Elen looked at Niels and saw Andrew. She made a special effort to see through that similarity and to find the individual inside that familiar face. It was difficult for her; she thought it must be a nightmare for Jorgen. Her thoughts returned to Norway and those idyllic days surrounding the wedding when everything was yet unknown. She thought about Jorgen's mother and wondered how one coped with the notion of not seeing a child ever again. *How do you stand it when it's two children, or three, or four?*

Respecting Karine's privacy, she didn't question her about her relationship with Karl, but as the weeks passed, found that she had become the younger woman's confidante. Karine shared her feelings about Karl, her homesickness, and her hopes about her future as the two labored over the washtub and hung clothes out to dry. More and more, as the years had passed, Elen had taken over the laundry while Marta did most of the cooking. Elen was grateful for Karine's help; she enjoyed the companionship and two more hands cut her work in half.

★ ★ ★

Marta, on the other hand, was not pleased to share her kitchen with another woman. She was used to doing things her way. This wasn't a problem when Mary helped; Mary always followed Marta's directions. But Karine, older than Marta by two years, knew her way around a kitchen and never needed to ask how, she just did. Though there was nothing wrong with the way she accomplished things, her ways just differed from Marta's. At times, this annoyed Marta and then she would become irritated with herself for being annoyed.

As her mother, it wasn't difficult for Elen to spot Marta's ill moods. At these times she would gently suggest that Marta might like to spend some quiet time in her mother's room. Other than that, Elen never commented on her daughter's inflexibility, her need for total control, or Karine's insensitivity to the problem. She figured it was something the two would eventually work out between themselves.

Jorgen listened sympathetically to Marta's complaints when they were alone, but he, too, wisely stayed out of the fray.

What eventually brought Marta and Karine closer together was their affinity for knitting. Marta was actually better than Karine but was willing to teach her a particular stitch, when asked. Mary often joined them, and when all was quiet in the evening, the clicking of their needles in the great room accompanied the drone of the men's voices from the porch.

★ ★ ★

The fact that Niels had little privacy, his bed was in one corner of the great room, never fazed him. Karl had offered to put him up at his house, but for the time being, Niels was happy to be reunited with Jorgen. And since he tended to burn the candle at both ends, being the last to bed and the first up was normal for him.

Karine and Niels had spent their entire lives as part of a large family. Adjusting to others was something they just naturally did. What they found most difficult about this huge life change was the new language. It hadn't occurred to either of them that they would have to learn English. In trying to do so, they were frustrated trying to keep up with the others who were so far ahead of them. Marta tried to put it in perspective for them. "By the time baby John is speaking English, you will be too. Remember, the rest of us have been working on it for six years."

★ ★ ★

Going into town each Saturday was an organized affair. The family and Karl who by now was considered family—sat around the large table in the great room on Friday nights. Pencil in hand, Jorgen listed the shops where they needed to stop, and next to it, the person's name who would visit that particular store. This was a lively exercise, especially when there were five or six places on the list. Everyone had their favorites, so there was lots of give and take. Niels and Karine, new to the process, weren't sure which place to pick, so they asked Attie. She had two categories: interesting and boring.

"At least it's a place to start," said Niels the night before his first trip to town. So, on Attie's advice, he chose the harness maker. Karl's horse had a broken harness that he said wouldn't take long to fix.

The next morning, everyone piled into the wagon and when they got to town, they all went to their assigned shops. They would meet back at the wagon when they were finished.

Attie led the way to the harness shop and once inside, told the man, in English, what needed to be done. Niels handed him the harness, then discovered why the shop interested Attie. The owner's house was attached to it, and he had several children. Attie knew them all by name and they were soon engaged in some sort of make-believe game.

Niels walked around the shop for a while, and then went to stand outside the front door. A man on horseback came down the street, and when he saw Neils, he stopped.

"Hei," said Niels.

The man continued to sit and stare even after Niels went back into the store.

Attie was waiting for him, harness in hand. "Do you know that man?" she asked as she peered out the window of the shop.

When Niels said that he did not, she wanted to know why he was looking at them. Before Niels could answer, the man reeled his horse around and took off up the street at a full gallop. Niels shrugged, turned to the shopkeeper and paid for the repairs. Attie ran back to say goodbye to her friends, the incident with the man on the horse forgotten by both.

★ ★ ★

In the weeks that followed his brother and sister's arrival, Jorgen was puzzled by several strange occurrences. In the first instance, the corral gate was left open and the horses wandered off. It was annoying and a careless mistake that no one took responsibility for. That wasn't like the family.

Another time, the clothesline broke. Freshly laundered clothing landed in a heap in the dirt. "That was a new line," muttered Elen as she rewashed the dirty items. Karl fixed the line for her and reported to Jorgen that the line had been cut.

"Do you think a bird could do that?" Karl speculated.

Elen was always having to chase birds off the clothesline.

Jorgen said he doubted it, but was too preoccupied inspecting the hen house to give a clothesline much thought.

"I don't understand it," he said. "Two hens are gone and there is no way a fox got in here. I've gone over every inch and there is no opening."

Up at the house, the bell was being vigorously shook. "Sounds like Attie," Karl laughed. And with two mysteries left unsolved, the men went to lunch.

Days later, work gloves went missing from the shed. Niels said he had used them and knew exactly where he left them. When he returned, later, they were not there. Niels brought up the missing gloves at dinner that night.

"Do you think a troll followed us from Norway?" he joked.

"I don't know about trolls," said Mary, "but I did see a stranger on the road today, just past Karl's house. He made me nervous."

"I wish I had known that," said Jorgen. "I would have ridden after him. Which way was he going?"

"You were out in the west fields," she reminded him, then added, "He might have been headed for town."

Jorgen didn't pursue the subject. He would check in at the sheriff's office when they went to town on Saturday to see if others in the area had reported unusual incidents. No point in asking about strangers as there seemed to be a continual stream of people coming to settle in central Wisconsin or passing through on their way further north or to the Minnesota Territory.

That night, Elen's scream awakened the entire household. Niels and Jorgen arrived at Elen's door at the same time. Marta paused in the great room to light a lamp and was a few steps behind them when they entered the room. Elen stood near the window, pointing her finger into the black night.

"Someone opened the window," she said in a shaky voice. "My scream scared him off."

Jorgen snatched the lamp from Marta and dashed from the room. Niels was close behind as they both tore from the house.

Marta crossed to the window, closed it, and pulled the curtains shut. She lit the lamp in her mother's room and helped her into her dressing gown, then they went to the great room. Karine had lit another lamp in there and she, Mary, and Attie sat huddled together. Attie's eyes were wide with fright.

Marta sat down and took Attie onto her lap. "Everything will be all right," she said, more calmly than she felt."Pappa and Uncle Niels will make sure that no one is out there."

"Maybe it was the man who gave me the stone. I put it in my pocket." Attie said. She began to cry. "Maybe he came back to get it," she added between sobs.

Marta was stunned. Before she could react, Attie jumped off her lap and ran to the ladder.

"Attie, wait."

Attie scampered up and out of sight.

"Attie," Marta called to her again.

The child returned just as quickly as she had left.

"I forgot," she said, still sobbing. "He told me to give it to Pappa, but I forgot." She opened her fist to show Marta the stone.

The edges had been worn smooth, faint traces of carving were barely visible, but Marta recognized the object.

A startled "Oh!" escaped before she could squelch it. *Stay calm,* she told herself. *Don't frighten Attie.*

"I'll take that and give it to Pappa," She said, taking the button from the still weeping child. "It doesn't matter that you forgot. I forget things lots of times." She handed the button to Elen and lifted Attie back onto her lap. She smoothed her daughter's hair and kissed the top of her head.

Marta looked up when she felt her mother's eyes on her. Elen also recognized the button. It was a match for the one she kept in her top bureau drawer. Marta's stomach was turning over and over. She could only imagine what her mother was feeling.

Mary disappeared into the kitchen and returned with a mug of warm milk for Attie.

"Takk," Marta said lapsing into their native language.

★ ★ ★

By the time Niels returned, Attie had finished her milk and was asleep, snuggled against Marta's chest. Marta put her finger to her lips before he could say anything, then motioned for him to carry the sleeping child up to her bed.

When he returned, he told the women that Jorgen decided to ride down the road as far as Karl's.

"We checked all around the house: the yard, the corral, and all the out buildings. Nothing." Niels shrugged. "Whoever was here has gone. Jorgen told me to come back and tell you all to go back to bed. I'll wait up for him," he added.

That just wasn't going to happen. Elen placed the button on the table and when she went to her room to retrieve its mate, Marta told Niels how it had been given to Attie. Sensing a long night, Mary went to the kitchen to prepare a pot of coffee.

Jorgen was surprised to see everyone still up when he returned. His eyes widened then narrowed as he took in the two buttons lying side by side on the table. When he had heard the story and knew that his beloved Attie had been within arm's reach of Hauk, the man responsible for so much physical harm to the family, Jorgen could hardly conceal his fury. *What kind of man uses a small child as a weapon against another?* he thought.

They stayed up, drawing on each other's nurturing presence. Eventually, weariness won over fear and anger and the household succumbed to a few hours of fitful sleep.

★ ★ ★

Attie, the only one who enjoyed a good night's rest, arrived at breakfast looking fresh-faced but very serious.

"Did you chase that man away?" she asked, coming to a halt before Jorgen.

"Yes, we did, big girl, and today I'm going to town to tell the sheriff to find him and put him in jail."

"Why does he have to go to jail?" she wanted to know. "Is it because he gave me that stone?"

"No, Attie. It is because he frightened your grandmother."

Attie turned to face Elen and nodded her head in sympathy. "He has mean eyes," she offered. Then went to sit in her chair.

Attempting to ease Attie's mind and lighten the tone of the conversation, Niels said, "I don't know how anyone could look at your sweet face with mean eyes. See," he continued, "I'm looking at you and my eyes are happy."

"He didn't have mean eyes when he looked at me," Attie said. Her voice had taken on the patient tone she used when explaining something to Lise. "He had mean eyes when he looked at you."

All at the table were startled by this new piece of information and Niels, the most surprised of all, was aware that many sets of eyes were now focused on him.

His eyebrows came together as he tried to remember meeting someone, recently.

"That time when we took Mr. Pierson's harness to get it fixed," she said helpfully.

"That was the same man you saw here, yesterday?"

Attie nodded, then picked up her spoon and began eating her porridge.

The adults looked at each other in silent agreement. Because of Attie, the conversation was over for now. But later, Niels told Jorgen about the strange incident in town. "He scowled at me for the longest time," Niels said. "I thought he had me confused with someone and when he realized his mistake, he turned and rode out of town. I didn't give it another thought."

"I wish I had been the one to run into him," said Jorgen. "I wonder how long he's been in town and why he is here."

"Do you suppose he thought I was Andrew?"

"I don't know,"said Jorgen, "but he'd better not show up here again."

★ ★ ★

Jorgen rode into Oshkosh the next day and was dismayed to learn that the sheriff was not in town. He was an older man who had the reputation of a skilled keeper of the peace. His wife and Elen had organized the church picnic the last two years, and as a result, the two families had become friends.

The young deputy listened politely to Jorgen's story, asking questions and writing down Hauk's name and a few details as Jorgen spoke.

"There are so many new families coming here to homestead and young men who want to work in the mills or the mines. I used to know everyone in Oshkosh, but I can't say that anymore."

As he spoke, the deputy walked over and began leafing through the pages of a large book that sat on the sheriff's battered desk.

"Here it is," the deputy said, pointing to a name in the book. "Hauk Lande," he read out loud. "Sheriff enters the name of everyone who comes in with a complaint."

"And what was Hauk's complaint?" Jorgen asked. "Do you remember what he said?"

"I must have left the office right after he came in, I don't have any remembrance of what the man had to say."

"Does the sheriff write in the book what the complaint is?" asked Jorgen.

"He doesn't like to write much so his notes don't

always make sense to me, but it looks like he didn't agree with the man anyway. Here, take a look, I don't think the sheriff would mind, the two of you being friends and all."

The deputy turned the book so Jorgen could see and indicated an entry midway down the page. After the date, it read:

Hauk Lande accuses Jorgen Halvorson U RR.

"Underground Railroad," Jorgen muttered to himself. He wasn't surprised to learn that Hauk was still doing the devil's work, hunting slaves.

Jorgen took a few moments to work out the date in the ledger, and was not surprised to find that it had been a Saturday. Hauk had seen Niels that day at the harness shop and had probably gone straight to the sheriff.

"One last question," said Jorgen. "Have you seen Hauk in town, since then?"

"No, but if he's a single fellow, most of the rooming houses and the taverns they prefer are down near the saw mill."

Jorgen started for the door.

"You're not thinking of going after him, are you?"

Jorgen turned, gave a slight wave, but didn't answer.

"Sheriff will be back soon. I think it's best if you let him handle this. This man, Hauk, sounds like he could be dangerous."

Jorgen nodded, knowing the harm that Hauk had already caused. He turned, walked to the door, and giving a slight wave over his shoulder, he left the office.

★ ★ ★

Jorgen was unwilling to go home without confronting Hauk. He went to the sawmill and his inquiry as to Hauk's whereabouts was met with frowns and anger from the three men who worked there. One of the men told him that if he was a friend of Hauk's, he wasn't welcome anymore on the premises.

"He's not a friend. He has threatened my family" said Jorgen, "which is why I need to find him."

"I gave him a job," said the owner of the sawmill, "but he caused so much trouble with his drinking and fighting that I finally had to chase him off."

The tavern owner glowered at the mention of Hauk's name. "He picked fights with my customers. I hope he doesn't come back."

The blacksmith also had nothing good to say about Hauk, but at least he knew where to find him, or at least where he had last seen him.

"He keeps his horse at the saddler's and sometime helps out with odd jobs."

Jorgen had no plan, considered no consequences. He only knew he had to find Hauk, keep him away from his house, stop him from threatening his family. His focus was narrow...find Hauk.

The saddler's shop was housed in the front part of a large barn that rented out horses and wagons. A bell over the door tinkled when Jorgen entered, and he waited briefly for a response. When that didn't happen, he walked to the back of the shop and through the open doorway into the barn, calling out to the owner as he went. If he wasn't up front, Jorgen knew to look for him in the back as he was most likely tending to the horses. Although there was the possibility of running into Hauk, Jorgen hoped he would come upon the saddler first.

Some light filtered through gaps in the siding, but it was difficult to see, as most of the shutters in the horse stalls were closed to keep out the heat. Jorgen repeated his call halfway through the barn and almost collided with someone who darted out of a stall. It was Hauk. The two men stood, just inches apart, glaring at each other. Hauk didn't seem surprised to see him.

"I see you found me, just like I found you." His words

were slurred and he grinned maliciously at Jorgen.

Hauk smelled so badly that Jorgen was forced to take a step back. His clothing reeked of sweat and dried urine, but his breath, powered by the stench of cheap whiskey, was even more offensive. It was the stink given off by someone whose life is one long drunk.

Jorgen was jolted by the unpleasant memory of when he was taken captive and was chained to men who smelled like this. He forced himself back to the here and now and answered Hauk.

"Yes, Hauk, it looks like we found each other. But I am here to tell you that you are not welcome on my property. Stay off my land and stay away from my family."

Jorgen started for the rear door of the barn. Hoping to find the owner, he called the man's name.

"Your family!" Hauk's voice roared behind him. "I'm sick of your family."

Jorgen continued to walk away. The sooner he found the saddler, the better.

"Stop!" Hauk bellowed. "I'm talking to you. And don't think someone is going to save you this time, because there's no one here but us."

Jorgen was less than ten paces from the door when Hauk caught up with him.

"You'd better stop, Jorgen," said Hauk. Jorgen heard the unmistakable sound of a gun being cocked.

He stopped. Hauk walked around to face him. He aimed a pistol at Jorgen's chest. Hauk was agitated, and the hand with the gun trembled as he yelled. "Your family! You ruined it all!"

Fearful that the gun might go off accidentally, Jorgen sought to calm Hauk down.

"I'm listening, Hauk."

His comment had the opposite effect. It seemed to stoke Hauk's temper.

"Don't tell me!" he shouted, "You people always think

you're in charge." He waved the gun at Jorgen, "But look who's in charge now."

Jorgen did not respond. He hoped that Hauk's rant would eventually spend itself and he'd settle down or that the saddler would return.

"It's all Theo's fault, and yours too." He waved the gun in Jorgen's face. "Why was he put in charge? It is the Lunde's business, my family's business. My brothers and I should be running it.

"My brothers," he sneered. "My brothers are useless. All they're good for is taking orders from Theo. Theo marries my sister and he gets to run things. She was a traitor to my family and someday I'm going back to show them all who's in charge."

Spittle flew from his mouth and landed on Jorgen's face. Fearing that a raised hand might appear aggressive, he resisted the urge to wipe it away. *Don't make a move that might provoke him,* Jorgen thought.

Sounds from occupied stalls, horses moving and swatting flies with long tails, a snort, a soft, low whinny; each noise seemed to startle Hauk. He would pause nervously, look around, then continue his tirade.

"And I didn't try to drown you I just grabbed your feet to scare you, and you lost your balance. You fell overboard on your own and I got blamed. You ruined my life."

Jorgen knew this wasn't the truth. Hauk had forcefully pitched him overboard, but Jorgen held his tongue.

"You didn't drown, did you? Too bad, because then you wouldn't have stolen my girl."

The light from the door fell on Jorgen's face and Hauk noticed his puzzled look.

"You know what you did. Because of you, my father made me leave my home and my job. I was hardly gone when you married Gudrun. I could have come home again, I could have married her, but you took her away from me."

"Hauk," Jorgen began tentatively, "I married Marta,

Marta Aksdal."

"Lies, all lies," Hauk shrieked. "I saw Gudrun when I was out at your house... And what about the runaway slaves you're keeping out there. I suppose you're going to tell me that's not true either?"

Hauk didn't give Jorgen time to answer, he just continued to rant. "Well, I was out looking around your place and I think I know where you're hiding them. You have a cellar that goes under the house. That's where they are and that's why you keep that door locked."

"If you think that is true" Jorgen began cautiously, "why don't we ride out there together? We'll stop to pick up the sheriff on the way, and he can arrest me when you show him where the fugitives are staying."

"I don't need the sheriff. I'll get the slaves back right after I kill you for stealing them, just like I killed your brother." Hauk was no longer shouting. He sounded cocky and boastful.

"You didn't kill him." Jorgen said, again attempting to reason with Hauk. "Andrew survived your attack on him. You haven't killed anyone yet, and I don't think you want to start now."

"He's dead, I know he's dead, and he wasn't the first. I've killed plenty of people, and after I kill you, I'll get rid of your other brother. And someday I'll go back home and destroy Theo, and that weasel Halvor, and any other brothers you have."

Shocked by Hauk's admission of murder and at his crazed obsession with him and his brothers, Jorgen's began to fear for his life. *He's mad,* he thought, *I need to do something...*

"And then I'm going to take Gudrun and set fire to your house."

"It's her home, too," said Jorgen. "She's not going to like you if you burn it down." Jorgen knew he was treading on dangerous ground, but he needed to keep Hauk talking until he could think of something.

"It's not her home...it's yours. Her home is with me." Hauk raved on. "Gudrun and I made plans. She loves me...not you."

Hauk's anger was escalating, again. He was yelling. His speech came in short choppy sentences punctuated by shallow, rapid breaths. His unblinking eyes bore menacingly into Jorgen and spittle dripped off his chin.

A noise outside distracted Hauk, Jorgen, seizing the opportunity, took a quick step forward and veered slightly to one side hoping to avoid a direct hit from the gun. Hauk's reflexes were not as quick; he fired but a fraction of a second too late. Although the bullet tore through Jorgen's upper arm, he had already launched himself, shoulder first, into Hauk's alcohol ravaged body. The force of the impact sent Hauk sprawling and another shot rang out when his gun hand hit the ground. It whistled past Jorgen as he threw himself atop Hauk, pinning him down. Jorgen easily subdued the smaller, less fit man, and he wrestled the gun out of his hand. When he heard his name, he looked up and into the faces of the sheriff, his deputy, and the saddler. The sheriff's gun was trained on Hauk.

★ ★ ★

After dinner, his arm bandaged and nestled in a sling, Jorgen sat on his front porch. Marta sat next to him. The others, Elen, Mary, Niels, Karl, and Karine had gathered and were making a big effort to direct the conversation away from the day's incident. The conversation swirled around Jorgen who was too steeped in his own thoughts to be distracted. He knew, in time, the painful wound would heal and fade from memory, but the hate in Hauk's eyes and the terror of that morning's encounter would not be so easily forgotten. He wondered about the state of Hauk's mind. Was it just alcoholic blather or had Hauk lost his grip on sanity when he accused him of marrying Gudrun? Jorgen recalled the time he met Gudrun, shortly after arriving in Bergen. She and Marta looked nothing alike.

The sheriff and his wife stopped by, just before sunset. They joined the group on the porch to watch the beautiful show of sky colors. At the horizon, bright orange turned to rosy pink, then streaks of red spread from the west and mingled with purple and blue clouds overhead.

"It's a marvel, isn't it?" gushed the sheriff's wife. "And you've the perfect spot to view it."

"Yes," Marta agreed, "It's a sight we never grow tired of watching because it seems no two evening skies are ever alike."

Marta took the children indoors for their bedtime. When Elen offered to make coffee, the other women followed her inside.

When the men were alone, the sheriff spoke up. "I wanted to come tonight to tell you that Hauk will be out of your lives forever. He's wanted for murder in two states and will most likely be hanged for his crimes."

Jorgen winced. He thought of the Lande family and the pain Hauk had already caused them. Jorgen would put this news in a letter to Theo. His brother would know best how to tell his wife and her family.

"That's too bad," the sheriff continued, pointing to Jorgen's arm. "It's not like you to be so impulsive. If you had thought it through, if you had gone home after talking to my deputy, you could have avoided that injury. When I returned to my office this morning, I was told about your visit. The saddler was there filling out a complaint. I'm surprised you didn't see him; your paths must have crossed. He tried to get Hauk to leave his barn, but Hauk wouldn't go. He threatened to kill the saddler and his entire family. It was a good thing we went out to arrest him when we did. Although, it appeared you had the situation under control. But, as I started to say, you should have thought it through...you should have waited for me."

Jorgen considered for a moment what the sheriff just said. "Yes," he began, a slight smile washing across his face. "I guess I didn't think it through."

Eighteen

1871
(15 years later)

Jorgen squatted and scooped up a handful of soil. He stood and let the dry earth sift through his fingers, his eyes wandering the cornfield where parched, stunted plants stood in tawny rows. The drought was taking its toll, and he knew that yields would not be as good as they had been for the oats and wheat he harvested in late August. Back then they had welcomed the sunny, pleasant weather, but in the past six weeks, little rain had fallen and the situation was becoming more urgent by the day. He was glad they had not devoted much land to corn this year, though he and Karl had talked about doubling the corn acreage for the coming year. But that was last spring's conversation, when rainfall had not been an issue.

Even more than the corn crop, Jorgen was concerned about the autumn pastureland. If the dry spell lasted much longer, those fields would also suffer. Although this year's hay crop had been excellent, with a diminished supply of silage corn, the dairy herd would be even more dependent on good pasturage.

Jorgen pulled an ear from a stalk and peeled back some of the husk. "What do you think, John?" he said, handing him the ear of corn, "Harvest it tomorrow?"

The eyes of the fifteen-year-old boy, a look-alike, younger version of Jorgen, had taken in the field as he turned in a circle scrutinizing the land all the way to the horizon. He took the corn, glanced at it, and nodded absently to his father's question.

"I smell smoke," John said. There was concern in his voice, "Must be a fire nearby."

Jorgen sniffed the air. He didn't smell smoke, yet a haze

partially obscured the bright sunlight. He was surprised he hadn't noticed it earlier, but then his mind had been focused on the crops. Jorgen turned, sniffing the air as he went until he caught a whiff of the telltale odor.

"I think you're right, John," he said.

Father and son looked at each other. No words were said as they tacitly understood what the other was thinking. The damage that a drought could inflict on crops was survivable but a fire could wipe out a homestead; animals, crops, the forest, and all buildings; the entire livelihood that Jorgen and his family had worked so hard to establish. And both father and son knew that in the preceding weeks that had been the unfortunate fate of some farmers in the drought stricken Midwest.

"We'd better be heading back," said Jorgen, forcing aside their concerns of drought and fire. "We've got a big day ahead of us and your mamma will be anxious to get going."

John's long, lanky legs matched Jorgen's stride, and as they covered the distance back to the house, the two made plans for the harvest that would take place the next day.

Over the past few days, Marta was anxious, just as Jorgen predicted, but not for the reason he thought. She had hidden her anxiety in a flurry of activity. There had been much to do to prepare for today's big celebration, and without Attie to help with the baking, Marta had managed to stay very busy. But now, everything was done and she sat at the kitchen table, sipping coffee. She didn't think of herself as sentimental, and normally didn't fret about things, yet here she was, preoccupied with thoughts of her children. Where had the time gone? Her babies were growing up and lately, when she looked into the future, she experienced bouts of melancholy.

Elen came through the kitchen door with an armload of flowers. The twins followed closely behind her, each with his own bunch of blossoms. The three gardeners brought their bounty to the table where several large jugs of water were waiting.

"Boys." When she had their attention, Marta pointed to the trail of flowers that led to the door and most likely, all the way to the garden,

The twins scampered to pick them up, turning the task into a race to see who could get the most.

"Thank you, you were a big help," Elen said when they dropped the strays into the pile on the table. "Now you'd better run along and get cleaned up for church." She fastened a big smile on her grandsons, who grinned in return and ran from the room.

"Wash your hands!" Marta called after them. She would have added, "and faces, too," but she knew that was too much to ask of impetuous eight-year-old boys.

"They really are helpful to me in the garden," said Elen as she and Marta began sorting through stems of lavender asters, black-eyed susans, and some late blooming daisies, arranging them in the water jars.

"And you do wonders with flowers and little boys," said Marta. "Those two love the attention you give them and the flowers must as well. These are beautiful! They will look lovely on the tables outside."

Three long tables constructed of sawhorses laid with planks and benches for each had been hastily assembled in the past week and sat between two pine trees in the front yard. Marta wasn't sure how many of their friends and neighbors would come for the celebration, but there was room for thirty-six at the tables. If more came, she could accommodate them with quilts spread on the ground to sit on.

As for food, Marta and Elen had made platters of fruit and cheese, baked ham, smoked fish, and roasted chicken. Those were down in the root cellar along with cold salads that Karine had made and Karl had delivered the day before. Although Attie was the best pie baker, in her absence, Marta had made four apple pies, and a neighbor had offered to bring a cake.

The baptisms of two new family members were today's special occasion, four-month-old infants born a week apart. The older one, a girl, was the fourth child of Karine and Karl. They had married six months after Karine arrived from Norway, and this child evened the count; they now had two boys and two girls.

Mary and Niels were the parents of the other baby; he was their first. Their marriage had taken place shortly after Niels returned from fighting in the Civil War. This had been Mary's third pregnancy, the other two sadly terminated in a miscarriage and a stillborn child. Although the baptisms would be the focus of that Sunday morning, the joy that everyone felt for Mary and Niels was the true inspiration for the huge celebration that would follow the church service.

"I was so busy last night getting the children's clothes ready for today, I didn't get a chance to ask you how your visit went with Mary. You didn't stay very long."

"I know," Elen replied. "I went to see if she needed help with the bread, but she already had the last two loaves in the oven. After she fed the baby, I rocked him for a while then put him down for the night. I told her to go to bed. Poor thing was exhausted. I stayed just long enough to take the bread out of the oven, then came home."

"I noticed you brought some of the loaves back with you," said Marta. "They smell delicious."

"I brought the ones that had cooled. Niels said they'd bring the rest today."

Everything was ready. Marta's efficiency as a homemaker and her cooking skills had left nothing to chance. Morning had dawned gloriously sunny; it was going to be a wonderful day... except for the fact that Attie and William would not be present.

Twenty-year-old Attie had taken her younger brother to Peshtigo, about one hundred miles north of Oshkosh. They had been gone only five days and would be back mid-week, but it seemed a long time to Marta. She knew she had to get used to her children's absences; they weren't babies any more. William would be home for several more months, but Attie was going to return to Peshtigo in a few weeks to begin a new teaching job. For her, the purpose of this short trip was to find lodging and to get the schoolhouse cleaned and ready for the students. William would help her with this.

Thirteen-year-old William would soon begin his last year of school. He found bookwork tedious, preferring instead to work with his hands. Woodworking came naturally to him.

"How could it not," said Elen, years before when the boy had constructed a chair for her to sit on in her garden. "He takes after his father and both grandfathers."

"And my grandfather, too." Jorgen had added.

Marta and Jorgen recognized William's talent, but they also wanted their children to finish school. With that in mind, they struck a bargain with William. If he would devote himself to his studies for one more year, they would allow him to apprentice as a carpenter. That was the other reason for the trip. William was going to visit the mill in Peshtigo in hopes of procuring an apprenticeship for when he finished school the following spring. Marta was not looking forward to that eventuality; William seemed too young to leave home. But, that wouldn't happen for months, and she took comfort in knowing that her two children would be in the same town and could even live together.

"Marta'" said Elen as she picked up two of the flower jugs, "if your face froze, right now, it wouldn't be a happy sight." She headed out the door before Marta could respond.

Marta smiled. She hadn't heard her mother say that in years. She picked up two of the arrangements and followed her mother outside. "I don't like having the children away," she said.

"I guessed as much," said Elen. "And I do sympathize. I miss them, too."

"They're not going that far. I'll get used to it, in time...I hope." added Marta.

The sound of a wagon approaching caused both women to turn and wave at Karl and Karine.

"Goodness, is it that time already?" said Marta.

Karl pulled his wagon into the yard and the women went over to peek at the baby in her Christening gown and to greet the children sitting in the back. "How nice you all look!" said Marta. "Lise, is that the dress you made?"

Her seventeen-year-old daughter blushed when she felt everyone's eyes on her.

"Yes, mama," she answered.

"Well, it turned out lovely."

"And it fits you perfectly," Elen added.

"That's exactly what I said this morning, when she put it on," said Karine.

The girl blushed even more. "Thank you," she murmured.

Lise had gone to stay with Karine to help with the children when the baby was born. But since the two houses were close by, Marta saw her almost daily.

Mary and Niels also lived just a short walk down the road. He farmed one hundred acres that adjoined Jorgen's land. Jorgen and Karl helped him purchase it after the war, and Niels was slowly paying them back. The whole group functioned as one large family living in three houses and there was always much visiting back and forth.

Marta started to apologize for not being ready to go. "Jorgen went out to check on the fields..."

"There's Uncle Jorgen," one of Karine's children interrupted, pointing to the barn. Jorgen was closing the large doors and John was hitching two horses to the wagon.

Having heard Karl's wagon come into the yard, the twins, Steffan and Peder, charged from the house like runaway colts, pale manes fluttering in the air, shirttails streaming behind them.

"I'll run in and get our bonnets. Will you please try to

get their shirts buttoned and tucked in?" Marta said to her mother, even though she knew it was futile. They'd be untucked again before the family left the farmyard.

Within minutes, Niels and Mary arrived with their baby. Niels jumped down from their wagon and sprinted to the house with the remaining loaves of bread. By the time he returned, Marta had her family assembled in their wagon, and the high-spirited caravan set off for the church.

About two miles from home they came upon a field, blackened and still smoldering. Here and there, wisps of smoke curled skyward and its bitter odor clung to the air.

"Damn fool," Jorgen muttered, ignoring the man who waved from the far end of the field.

"He ought to know better than to burn stubble in the middle of a drought, " said Marta.

"And so near to his own house," added John who eavesdropped from the back of the wagon.

"Perhaps that's why he did it," Jorgen said grudgingly. "He probably figures that a burnt out field next to his house will protect it from a wildfire."

"Well that's selfish reason to put everyone else at risk," said Marta. "We're fortunate that he wasn't the cause of a wildfire."

★ ★ ★

Smoke in the air was also the topic of conversation in Peshtigo that same Sunday morning. While Attie had been alarmed by the smoky atmosphere when they had arrived two days earlier, most of the townsfolk had gone about their business and seemed unconcerned. She had even asked some of them if they were worried and was told that although the smoke had been drifting in and out of town for days, the fires burning in multiple locations were all a safe distance away. So Attie had tried to put it out of her mind.

The previous day, Saturday, had been productive for

both Attie and William. He had spent the morning touring the huge sawmill and woodworking factory. The handsomely carved jewel box he had brought with him had impressed the shop manager.

"You made this?" The man had sounded incredulous.

"Yes sir, I did." William assured the manager.

The shop manager then offered to let William start an apprenticeship that very day.

"I told him I needed to finish school first," William told Attie when he met up with her later in the afternoon, and she said, "That's what I'd tell you to do if you were my son."

The two were in the classroom where Attie would start her new teaching job at the end of the month. She had spent her morning sorting through books, taking stock of what was there, and jotting notes for future lessons. William had joined her after his interview, and as he swept the floor and washed desks, his spirits were high. He was more animated than Attie had ever seen him.

"He shook my hand, like I was a grown up." William said, demonstrating a handshake like it was something new to Attie.

She laughed with affection at her younger brother and he carried on. "He told me his offer was good whenever I get here. How do you like that?" William had shaken his head in disbelief. His acceptance by the shop manager seemed too good to be true.

"Good for you, Will. I know how much this means to you, and I have to say, I'm pleased that you'll be here next year to keep me company."

"You know Attie? The Peshtigo Company's wooden ware factory is the biggest in the country. You wouldn't believe all the stuff they make there. I'll bet it's even the biggest in the world."

"Well, it sure looks large from the outside," said Attie. "You'll have to give me a tour, when you start working there."

By late afternoon, Attie determined that all was done that could be, for now. She had wanted to wash the classroom windows but decided it was pointless with there being so much smoke in the air. That would have to wait until she returned.

"I think we can leave tomorrow," she said to William. "We've finished here in half the time I thought it would take." They would go back the way they came: the steamer to Green Bay and then the coach back to Oshkosh. "I hope the steamer runs on Sundays...I didn't think to check the schedule because I thought we'd be here at least until Monday."

About the time the christening was taking place, Attie and William walked down to the dock to inquire about the steamship. More people than usual were out on the streets and all people could talk about was the smoke. It seemed everyone had finally taken notice and were now showing concern. One man was digging a hole in his front yard while his wife placed things of value on the ground next to him, presumably for burial and safe keeping in case of fire.

When they arrived at the dock, the news wasn't good. There would be no steamer that afternoon. The one due the day before had passed the town by because of the dense smoke in the harbor. "If it remains this smoky," the harbor master explained, "the one tomorrow might not stop, either."

By the time they got back to the boarding house, Attie had a severe headache, and both she and William were rubbing their smoke irritated eyes. Attie went up to their room. She hoped if she closed her eyes for a while, the headache would go away.

★ ★ ★

Back in Oshkosh, the women at church dabbed their eyes as they watched the two babies being christened. They knew how desperately Mary had wanted to be a mother, and their tears were joyous ones for her. For their part, the babies behaved stoically and didn't cry out when the water cascaded over their tiny heads. Although startled by the cool water, Ina's big blue eyes merely grew larger while her cousin, Niels Andrew, blinked twice and then smiled.

At the party later, Mary reveled in the attention she and baby Niels received. With her husband, Niels, at her side and the baby in her lap Mary felt life's fullness. The once shy little girl had grown into an outgoing, confident woman admired and respected by her neighbors for her thoughtfulness and midwifery skill. As it turned out, Attie's birth was the first of many births which Mary would attend, first as Elen's assistant and later by herself. Now, she had her own family, a large extended family, and many good friends. She thanked God daily for choosing Jorgen's cabin door as the place where she would trip and drop the pots. She shuddered when she remembered the incident...what would have happened if Jorgen had not intervened on her behalf? If Aunt Elen had not taken pity on her and then loved her like her own daughter? Indeed, Aunt Elen had become her mother, and with her permission, Mary would teach Niels Andrew to call her grandmother.

The passing years have a way of smoothing the bumps in memories; all but forgotten was Jorgen's initial reluctance to include Mary on the voyage to America. Niels, however, suffering no such reluctance, had fallen in love with the orphan girl in Jorgen's letters home in much the same way that Karl had become interested in Karine through the letters she had penned to Jorgen.

Mary looked up at Niels and smiled. He stood by her side with one hand resting lightly on her shoulder as he talked crops with a neighbor. She remembered how his arrival, years before, had thrown her into a state of confusion. He was so like Jorgen in some ways and an exact copy of Andrew in others, especially in his looks, that she hadn't been sure who this person called Niels really was. And when she began to have feelings for him, she just wasn't sure...did she love him or who he reminded her of? She knew her father never really loved her for who she was. She never had an identity with him and was afraid of doing the same thing to Niels. It wasn't until after he left to fight in the Civil War, when she began writing to him, that her confusion lifted. As she read his letters to her, she pictured Niels, heard his voice and remembered the way he always looked at her, and she knew she loved him as much as he loved her. She told him so in a letter and accepted his next proposal. "That was the reason I survived," Niels admitted whenever he talked about 'those wretched war years.'

Marta and Elen approached Mary and Niels. Marta was holding baby Ina, and Elen held out her arms to receive baby Niels.

"Let me take him while you two get some food," said Elen.

Niels had finished his conversation with the neighbor and had plucked his son off Mary's lap moments before. "I was just about to suggest to Mary that she go eat," he said. "But you look eager to hold him," Niels said as he place his son in Elen's outstretched arms, "so perhaps I'll join her. "

A quilt in the shade of a maple tree was the perfect place for Marta and Elen to sit and relax with the babies. The tree, blazing a brilliant yellow in the afternoon sun, was beginning to lose its leaves. One drifted down, and picking it up by the stem, Marta twirled it between her thumb and forefinger to amuse the babies. Ina studied the spinning leaf and when Niels chuckled, she looked at him and smiled.

"You've always been so good at amusing the little ones," said Elen.

"It's easy when they're small, like this." Marta replied. "It's when they get bigger that I seem to lose patience. I guess I expect too much of them once they learn to walk and talk."

Jorgen arrived with a plate of food and offered it to the women.

"We'll eat later," Marta said, moving to make room for

him.

Jorgen sat at the edge of the quilt. "Looks like most everyone's here," he said. "Guess it was too fine a day to pass up a picnic."

"Everyone but Attie and William," said Marta. "I do wish they had chosen a better time to go. It's a shame to miss a party."

"Yes, it is, but I suppose we have to get used to the fact that they are growing up," Jorgen said just as the twins chased past.

"Steffan! Peder! Slow down, boys!" he called after them, "before you run into someone."

The twins slowed for a brief moment, then took off round the corner of the house.

"Now where were we?" he said laughing.

"You were saying something about the children growing up," said Elen and she shook her head, laughing at the retreating figures. "I assume you didn't mean them."

"I hear what you're saying," said Marta. She appeared to be addressing little Ina as she spoke. "But I doubt if a mother is ever ready to see her children leave home."

★ ★ ★

Little was said as the ten boarders ate their dinner that evening. On the two previous nights, conversation had been quite spirited. Six of the boarders were working on the new rail line and their banter and stories had proved entertaining. But on this day, when they had gone out to the work site, they had confronted a small fire that seemed to spring up out of nowhere. Fortunately, their work team was able to extinguish it, but rumors of larger blazes advancing on the town had everyone's nerves on edge. Attie's headache had not improved, and when dinner was over, she told William that she was going to retire for the night.

The six railroad workers finished their dessert and

coffee then relocated to the tavern across the road. Following their departure, William sat at the table for a long while chatting with the elderly couple who had the room upstairs next to one that he and Attie were sharing. The window was open and the curtains that had ruffled in the smoky breeze all evening suddenly became still.

"That's a hopeful sign," said the old woman. "With no wind, maybe the fires will die down."

The clock in the parlor struck eight moments later, and the couple excused themselves to their room.

Not the least bit tired, William went to sit on the porch. The sounds of laughter, music, and loud singing echoed from the tavern and kept him company. A stiff wind blew for a short while, then the air went still again. Thunder rolled in the distance. More wind, stronger than before, felt warm on William's face. He sneezed several times. The smoke was heavier, and when the wind suddenly died again, small bits of ash floated in the air.

A dog raced past the house and down the road as if the devil was on its tail. William left the porch and went into the road. There was no sign of the dog, but from that vantage point, the sky was visible and it glowed red. A rumbling noise that he attributed to thunder gave him hope that maybe it would rain. But unlike thunder, the noise didn't subside. Instead, it appeared to grow in intensity. He walked a short distance down the road to where it curved and joined the main street. He was surprised to see so many folks hurrying towards town. "What's going on?" he asked a woman who rushed past him. The man behind her yelled at William. "Get to the river, fire's coming!"

William turned and ran for the house. "Get up, Attie!" he commanded, when he reached their room. "Fire!" When he saw that she was getting out of bed, he ran back into the hallway and pounded on the door of the old couple. "Fire!" he yelled. The man opened the door and William told him that they needed to get to the river. "The sky is red and there are ashes in the air," Hysteria crept into his voice. He didn't know how much time they had. He yelled at the old man. "We need to go, now!"

The owner of the boarding house charged up the stairs and when he saw William demanded to know why he was making so much noise.

"The fire is coming into town...get your wife...get out!" William shouted. The man turned and fled down the stairs.

Hearing the panic in her brother's voice, Attie moved quickly. She slipped into her shoes, put her coat over her nightdress, and rushed out into the hallway. She pushed past the man in the doorway and addressed the woman in the dark room.

"Get up, we'll help you get to the river, but we've got to go now." Attie and William helped the man and his wife into their shoes and coats. The woman protested about going outside in her bedclothes, but Attie took her by the arm and hustled her down the stairs and out the house. William and the old man followed right behind them.

Thick, choking smoke enveloped them as soon as they stepped out the front door. Grasping the gravity of the situation, the old woman grew quiet and quickened her step. She pulled a handkerchief from her pocket and held it over her nose and mouth. Attie reached down and grabbing the hem of her coat, brought it up to her face to cover her mouth and nose. William and the old man did the same with their coats.

When they got to the street, William told Attie to keep going, that he would catch up with them. Then he dashed into the tavern. The noise inside was too loud to shout over, so William just yelled to the two men nearest the door. The look on his face should have been enough to alert them to danger. "Fire!" he warned. "Tell everyone to get out now!" William rushed out hoping the men would take him seriously, but was too frightened to stay any longer to convince them.

Attie had made good progress even with the old couple

in tow, and they were just two blocks from the river when William caught up with them. The roar that he had earlier mistaken for thunder was now deafening as the firestorm bore down on Peshtigo. The road was chaos, choked with a frenzied mob of people and animals desperate to get to safety. Everyone was coughing, suffocating on the acrid smoke that blanketed the town and blotted out the few sources of light. Families, separated in the crowd, called out for one another but couldn't be heard. Children, dragged from their beds, sleepy and disoriented, clung to their mothers skirts and stumbled along on short little legs, trying to keep up with parents who carried babies and toddlers. A horse reared, broke away from its owner and ran off, trampling people in its path.

Fire was now visible. It shot high into the air and broke over the tops of trees at the edge of town. One by one, houses erupted in flames. A collective cry of alarm escaped parched throats and those not already in the river became frantic to reach it. The bridge that divided the east side of town from the west side was jammed with confused citizens moving in both directions trying to determine which way led to safety.

William, Attie, and the old couple reached the river and plunged into its cold, wet protection. They clung to each other, shivering in waist-deep water, and watched in horror as tongues of flame shot out from the inferno overtaking some unfortunate souls on their way to the river, while others, just feet away, were spared. Whole families perished in an instant.

The wind was howling and hot. With tornadic force, it ripped the roofs off burning houses and scattered fiery debris in all directions. The houses next to the river became engulfed in flames, and all those in the river had to move to deeper water to escape the heat and burning wreckage that rained down on them.

Attie and William clung to the old couple as the four attempted to escape the intense heat. The couple came to a halt when the water was chest high.

"We can't swim," the old man said. His speech was remarkably calm considering the terror and futility of the situation. "You go on without us."

"William and I are strong swimmers," said Attie. "He'll help you climb onto my back," she told the old woman, "and he will take your husband."

Attie and William made their way further into the river stopping as soon as the air was a bit cooler and easier to breathe. A short distance away the bridge caught fire and collapsed. Those who had taken shelter on it were trapped. Some fell; others jumped into the river and were injured. Many drowned. Those who had sought shelter under it were crushed.

The river proved to be no match for the fiery onslaught, as flames began to shoot out across it. William and Attie became separated when a ball of fire rolled across the water toward them, igniting everything in its path. They had been holding hands to steady themselves in the deep water, but separated when forced to submerge to avoid the fireball. William felt the old man let go of him. Feeling the heat of fire on his back, William struggled to stay underwater until he could no longer hold his breath. He surfaced, gasping for air, a safe distance from the flames. He made a frenzied search for the old man, diving repeatedly, but could not find him. He thought he saw Attie's head bobbing in the water, but with so much wreckage in the river, he wasn't sure. As he attempted to make his way back to Attie, an ear-splitting explosion ripped through the air. William looked to shore and saw that the wooden ware factory had exploded. Chunks of wood, large and small, the bits and pieces of all the useful items that the mill manufactured, were instantly transformed into shrapnel that shot through the air with deadly force and crashed into the river all around him. Something smacked him in the head. Momentarily stunned, he sunk under water, and when he resurfaced he could no longer see Attie.

Nothing mattered now, but finding his sister. He swam

to where he thought he had last seen her and dove down, over and over again, each time trying to go deeper than the last. His search was hampered by floating debris and others, like himself, who struggled to stay afloat. Cows, horses, dogs, and many smaller animals had also taken to the river and swam in a confused state, not knowing which way to go. William paused to catch his breath and a small creature latched on to his hair and attempted to climb onto his head. He flicked it off, hoping it wasn't a rat; he detested rats. But fear of losing his sister superseded his rat phobia, and he resumed diving in the infested water. Over and over he dove until his body could take no more. A large piece of wood floated within arm's reach. William hoisted himself so that he lay partly on it and passed out.

The flames raged on that Sunday night, consuming the town of Peshtigo. There were more than twelve hundred casualties. Jorgen and Marta's ocean pearl, Atlanta Marit, was one of many who drowned in the river, attempting to escape the flames.

★ ★ ★

Jorgen was pleased with the way the corn harvest had gone. Several men from neighboring farms had helped, and by Tuesday night, corn sheaves stood drying in the empty field. When called upon by these neighbors in the coming weeks, Jorgen and his sons would return the favor. The yield, as near as he could figure, would probably be eighteen to twenty bushels an acre as opposed to more than thirty bushels in past years. The drought's effect, though significant, was not as bad as he had feared it would be.

Jorgen was relaxing on the porch that evening when Karl's wagon pulled into the yard. He had gone into town to pick up some new equipment he needed for cheese making. The dairy side of their farm, which Karl ran, had done so well that they had expanded into cheese production. Twenty years of hard work, favorable weather conditions, and a collaborative partnership had produced a successful farm operation. Though neither man could be considered wealthy, their combined farms had produced enough profit to allow them to expand and to purchase additional acreage. Karl employed two farmhands year round while Jorgen's extra help tended to be seasonal.

"Just stopping by to see if you heard the news," Karl called from his wagon before it came to a stop. "Big fire in Chicago...the whole city was destroyed."

Jorgen's look of surprise prompted Karl to join him on the porch and tell all he'd heard in town.

"It must be as dry down there as it is here. The fire started Sunday night and burned all day yesterday. The fire department couldn't keep up with it," Karl reported.

The two men sat quietly for a few minutes.

"It's hard to believe that a city that large could be totally destroyed," said Jorgen. "What about the people?"

"For now, all they can do is estimate the loss of life," said Karl. "They say as many as two to three hundred."

"How tragic!" said Jorgen.

"What is tragic?" inquired Marta. Coming out onto the porch she had overheard Jorgen. "Oh, hello Karl," she added when she saw him sitting on the other side of her husband. "I thought I heard a wagon come into the yard. How is Karine? I hope the party on Sunday wasn't too much for her."

"I think she's fine, perhaps a bit tired, but the party was wonderful and I know she enjoyed it. It was generous of you and your mother to have everyone here, and we both thank you for it."

"You're welcome," said Marta. "Now, tell me what's so tragic."

"I'll let Jorgen tell you," said Karl. "I've been gone for several hours and really must get home."

★ ★ ★

Thursday morning Marta was up early. Knowing that Attie and William were returning that afternoon, she was back to her cheerful self, humming a tune Jorgen had played at the party. As she prepared breakfast, she thought about what she'd fix for a welcome home dinner. She finally settled on chicken and dumplings. That was everyone's favorite.

The coach, having left Green Bay on Wednesday, was due in the early afternoon. John was going to town to pick up his brother and sister.

During breakfast, Elen said, "Jorgen, why don't you and Marta get Attie and William? Other than church, I don't think the two of you have gone anywhere in days. You were even too busy on Saturday for the trip to town. I'm sure John can handle whatever you were planning to do, or he can help the twins and me in the garden"

John smiled at his grandmother in appreciation. He disliked the long boring drive to town.

Jorgen thought for a moment then looked at his wife. When she nodded her approval Jorgen turned to his son. "John, if you don't mind, your mother and I will go to town. I'll need your help for an hour or two this morning, but after we leave, you can work with your grandmother."

It was a solution that pleased everyone, especially Steffan and Peder. Spending a whole afternoon with their oldest brother didn't happen often.

★ ★ ★

Jorgen and Marta got to Oshkosh about an hour before the coach was due to arrive and they stopped at the sheriff's office to visit with their old friend. Although retired now, his wife had passed away, so he spent most afternoons in his old office, visiting with his multitude of friends who still affectionately called him sheriff.

"We missed you at the party on Sunday," said Marta after initial greetings had been exchanged, "but I know family has to come first. How's your brother's leg?"

"It hasn't healed yet, but I did convince him to come stay with me until it's better. What brings you two to town on a Thursday? It's about time you took a day off, Jorgen."

"More like a half day off," Jorgen replied. "Two of the children are coming in on the coach from Green Bay. It should be here in an hour or so."

"Old habits are hard to break. I'm still the nosy sheriff so I have to ask, what were two of your children doing in Green Bay that they couldn't do here in Oshkosh?"

Marta and Jorgen's laughter accompanied the sheriff's jovial chuckle. Marta answered him. "Actually, Green Bay was their half way point. They took the steamer from there to Peshtigo last week.

The smile disappeared from the sheriff's face. "Haven't you heard?" he said, his voice barely above a whisper, "About the fire?"

"Yes, we heard about Chicago," said Jorgen. "dreadful news...so many casualties." Jorgen was used to the sheriff's habit of changing subjects, sometimes mid sentence.

But Marta had seen the quick change in their friend's demeanor and found it unnerving. His face had lost its color and his hands had started to shake. She suddenly had a sick feeling in her stomach.

A long moment passed before the sheriff spoke again. "There was also a fire in Peshtigo."

Marta thought she was going to be sick. She dropped her handbag and ran out the door. Jorgen hurried after her and caught up with her when she stopped and leaned her head against the corner of the building. He was there in time to catch her when she fainted.

Marta and Jorgen sat beside the sheriff as he drove their wagon to meet the coach. Jorgen had one arm around his wife; her two hands were tightly clasped in his. Little was said. Earlier, Jorgen had carried Marta back to the sheriff's office, and while she recuperated from her fainting episode,

Jorgen had read the telegraph message the office had received, the day before, concerning the fire in Peshtigo. Fatalities numbered in the hundreds, but there had been survivors. Jorgen clung to that hope.

Mercifully, they didn't have to wait long for the coach to arrive. It clattered up to the inn and jerked to a stop when the horses reached the hitching post.

"Don't be alarmed if they're not on this one," the sheriff said. "They may have had difficulty getting out of Peshtigo. And in that event could have missed this coach."

They climbed out of the wagon and as they approached the coach, the doors on both sides were thrown open. Jorgen's heart thudded in his chest as he watched a man get off and turn to help a woman. On the other side a tall man stepped down followed by a shorter figure. The poor thing was dressed in clothes far too large for his small frame. His hat came down over his ears and eyebrows.

Marta tore her hand loose from Jorgen's grasp and began to run. "William!" she shouted. She reached the boy and wrapped him in her arms. Jorgen came up behind them and placed a hand on the boy's back. He removed the ridiculous looking hat and was shocked by the boy's hair. What little was left was singed; angry red burns covered his scalp. William stood stiffly in his mother arms and didn't say a word. Jorgen blinked back tears and very gently replaced the hat.

The other passengers had gotten out and stepped around the tender homecoming. Jorgen took two steps to the coach door and peered inside. It was empty.

Marta looked at Jorgen and he shook his head. William saw the gesture and began to weep. "I'm sorry," he said between sobs. "I'm sorry...I tried to save her...I couldn't find her..."

Their son's anguish tore at Jorgen and Marta. Instinctively, they set aside their own pain and grief, the awfulness of Attie's death, to help William cope with his ordeal.

Marta led the boy back to the wagon, attempting to comfort him, willing herself not to fall apart. Jorgen was following behind them when the tall man stopped him.

"I'm sorry for your loss," he said, "but I want to tell you about your son. He is a brave boy. I've been with him since Monday afternoon and this is the first time I've seen him cry. When I came upon him, he was making a coffin out of pieces of wood he had fished out of the river. He told me it was for his sister. He had located her body that morning, floating in the river, and had brought it ashore. When he finished the coffin, I helped him place her inside. We marked the grave, and your son and I prayed for her. Before he left, he talked to her, told her he would be back to get her and bring her home.

"Thank you for telling me this and for your kindness to my son. You must have also paid his fare. I'd like to repay you."

"I did sir, and I need no repayment. The scene I entered on Monday was devastating. I was grateful to be of assistance to someone and, as I said, he is a fine boy. His actions touched me deeply."

"Thank you," said Jorgen making eye contact with the man. Nothing could express the depth of his gratitude to this stranger. His reached out to shake his hand and saw tears in the man's eyes. It was then that he felt the tears on his own cheeks.

★ ★ ★

The next few days passed in a blur of sadness and grief. The close-knit family was in shock and not a day passed without someone in tears. Marta and Jorgen consoled the children as best they could during the day, and at night clung to each other and wept.

As the days became weeks, Marta found no respite from

her grief. Every item in the house seemed to be associated with a memory of Attie. Mornings found her reluctant to leave the refuge of bed, of Jorgen's arms, with the knowledge that he and he alone understood her loss. They talked late into the night until sleep would overtake Jorgen, but Marta found no such relief. She couldn't close her eyes for fear that Attie's face would disappear forever. Despite her grief, she thought she was coping well with the children and with all the duties the house and farm demanded of her. But her eyes betrayed her. Dark circles bore testimony to her lack of sleep. Her lethargy was evident in every move she made, taking her twice as long to do a simple task. Worst of all was the absence of joy she once derived from her role in the family.

Jorgen felt Attie's death just as keenly as Marta, but Karl and Niels conspired to keep him so busy during the day that he didn't have time to dwell on it. Karl remembered how hard work had been Jorgen's salvation after Andrew's death. It also helped that Attie had spent most of her days at home with Marta, Elen, and Mary; Jorgen's work was not tinged with memories of his daughter.

Lise came home to stay, and she took over some of her mother's chores. Jorgen urged Marta to stay in bed a while longer each morning to get more rest, and when the twins and William started the fall session of school, the household was quieter. Marta gradually began to retake an interest in life. She finally acknowledged to herself that Attie, who was always so full of life, would not want anyone to dwell on her death.

★ ★ ★

Jorgen and Marta had experienced the deaths of beloved family members. They knew the hurt in their hearts would eventually ease, and if they were patient with their grief, in time, they would come to accept the death of their oldest child. But until they brought her body home for burial, and they were both adamant that it should be done, it was difficult for them to move forward. William would have to go with Jorgen, and he was the reason the trip had been delayed.

"He's not ready to face that," Marta argued. "He's still having nightmares."

"He will probably have those for a long time to come," said Jorgen. "I'm more worried about the fact that he doesn't speak to anyone, he's closed himself off from...from..."

"From everything," Marta finished for him. "even food. He used to eat as much as John, now he merely picks at his plate."

Jorgen and Marta weren't sure how to help their child. He had survived the worst fire in history, witnessing countless horrific deaths, including that of his sister. It was no wonder that he had frequent nightmares, calling out for Attie in his dreams and, during the day, withdrawing from others at home and at school. He was absentminded about his chores, had no appetite, and seemed to prefer solitude. He never mentioned his trip to Peshtigo, or the fire, or Attie. In fact, he didn't talk at all. The burns on his head healed without scars, and Marta was optimistic that his hair would grow back, but could his spirit be healed?

★ ★ ★

After more than six weeks had passed, and their now gaunt son still wasn't communicating, Jorgen and Marta approached him.

"William," Jorgen said, addressing the boy in a quiet voice, "Shall we go get Attie and bring her home?"

William nodded. He looked up at his parents with a glimmer of light in his eyes. "Yes, Pappa," he said, "We should go."

Jorgen figured the trip would take a minimum of eight days. He consulted with Karl, Niels, and John, and they decided that, with the harvest completed, John would be able to handle things with the help of one hired man.

Marta was conflicted. As much as she wanted Attie buried at home, her concern for William's health and the thought of Jorgen and William going away made her anxious. "I don't think I could go on living if anything happened to them," she confided to her mother.

"Nonsense!" said Elen. "You would go on living. Life is God's gift to you. He alone knows when it must be returned."

Marta was silenced by the rebuke.

"I'm sorry," said Elen, "that wasn't helpful. Forgive me, I know this is difficult for you." She placed a hand on Marta's shoulder. "I'm anxious for them, too. You know you have my support, and Mary's, and the others'. We'll see you through this. We'll keep busy...we have candles to make and a pile of wool waiting to be spun. We'll make the time go fast. I promise."

★ ★ ★

On the third day of their journey, they reached the outskirts of the fire-ravaged area. Jorgen was aghast at the total devastation that stretched on, mile after mile. The forest had ceased to exist, and in its absence there was quiet, an eery quiet. The breeze did not whoosh through pine trees; no birds sang; no branches cracked under the feet of fleeing deer, for there were no pines, or birds, or deer. No animals foraged in the black rubble. Charred stumps and leafless, blackened stalks, mere shadows of once stately trees jutted into the sky. Jorgen would have rather seen nothing at all than these obscene reminders of what used to be. Recent rain had dampened the area, clearing the air of soot and smoke, but a pungent odor arose when winds brushed over the burnt landscape.

The farther they went into this backdrop of horror, the more Jorgen feared the sight of it might be too much for

William. Indeed, William was reacting to the decimated landscape. When each turn in the road brought more destruction into view, when William imagined the millions of tall, healthy trees that had been consumed, he began to realize how fortunate he had been to survive the ordeal. From all that death, William began to get a sense of his own life. Little by little, on that third day, William began to tell his father all that had happened.

Jorgen was only too willing to share the burden of his son's experience. He cringed when William described how everything, trees, buildings and people had burst into flames. He felt immense pride when he heard how his children had assisted the old couple and wept with his son as William related what happened in the river.

"I tried, Pappa. I wanted to save her. Why did it have to happen to her?"

"I know you tried, and Mamma does too. Sometimes, William, things are beyond our understanding, and hard as we try, we can't fix what's happening. Sometimes William, hard as it is, the only choice we have is to stand it, to just live through it."

For a full day, they traveled through the charred landscape. The next day, Jorgen sensed they were getting close. William had stopped talking and just pointed when he wanted his father to turn. When the road brought them near the river, William yelled, "Stop!" and jumped to the ground before the wheels on the wagon had stopped turning. He ran a short distance to where a small mound had been cleared of debris. Jorgen took the shovels out of the wagon and joined him.

Attie was buried the day that Jorgen and William returned home. Niels and Karl had dug her grave on the small hill next to where Mary's stillborn baby was buried. The spot was easy to see from the front porch. Even a small child could see it, if she were to stand on the porch rail.

Postscript

The journey that Jorgen and Marta undertook to make a home proved far more successful than a young Norwegian boy could have dreamed. The farm grew large and prospered. Over many years, generations of Halvorsons were buried on that hill, including one person who never lived there. The year after Attie was laid to rest, Jorgen undertook a trip to Kendall, New York, and Andrew made his final journey home.

Author's Note

Well into my sixth decade I decided to end the procrastination that had kept me from writing a novel, something I had intended to do my entire life. I supposed the main reason for putting it off was that I couldn't come up with a story to tell. Immigration had been in the news for several weeks when an idea occurred to me. I remembered a family tale my mother told about one of my ancestors whose family immigrated to America. It was really my father's story but he wasn't the storyteller in my family. My mother only knew two facts: first, a distant relative was born aboard the ship on her family's journey across the Atlantic, and second, she perished years later in the great Peshtigo fire.

I found some of the immigration stories on TV upsetting. They reflected disdain, a certain lack of respect some people exhibited toward immigrants. They seem to fear their otherness. Truth is, we are all descendants of immigrants unless we have the good fortune to be born native American. Immigration has touched my family in personal ways. My sister emigrated from Chicago to England many years ago and my daughter-in-law immigrated to America from Panama. Their decisions and those of other immigrants are not made lightly, they take courage and can be heartbreaking.

My sister is convinced that Mary Bergstrom, our grandmother, was given the middle name Atlanta, and that she was named after the child referred to in my story. No one is alive who can dispute or confirm this. Since Bergstrom is a Norwegian surname, I thought it made sense to begin *Journey Home* in Norway.

The large Norwegian family and the bonds that exist between them mirrors my own experience of growing up in a large family. I named one of the boys Edvard, in memory of my brother, Ed, but the characters and story are products of my imagination.

CPSIA information can be obtained
at www.ICGtesting.com
Printed in the USA
BVOW06s2151060218
507442BV00001B/11/P